DREAM CATCHER

DREAM CATCHER

IRIS GOWER

Thorndike Press • **Chivers Press**
Thorndike, Maine USA **Bath, England**

This Large Print edition is published by Thorndike Press, USA and by Chivers Press, England.

Published in 1999 in the U.S. by arrangement with Transworld Publishers, Inc.

Published in 1999 in the U.K. by arrangement with Transworld Publishers, Ltd.

U.S. Hardcover   0-7862-1952-1 (Romance Series Edition)
U.K. Hardcover   0-7540-1298-0 (Windsor Large Print)
U.K. Softcover   0-7540-2223-4 (Paragon Large Print)

The text of this Large Print edition is unabridged.
Other aspects of the book may vary from the original edition.

Set in 16 pt. Plantin by Al Chase.

Printed in the United States on permanent paper.

British Library Cataloguing in Publication Data available

Library of Congress Cataloging in Publication Data
Gower, Iris.
  Dream catcher / Iris Gower.
    p.   cm.
  ISBN 0-7862-1952-1 (lg. print : hc : alk. paper)
  1. Large type books. I. Title.
  [PR6057.O845D73 1999]
  823'.914—dc21   99-10056

To Dr Lorainne Cook,
whose love of history exceeds
even my own and whose
expertise has proved invaluable.

To the girls, Hilary, June and Babs.

CHAPTER

ONE

The rain had ceased and a pale sun elbowed aside the clouds. The brighter light enhanced the green of the folding Welsh hills, slanting in through the stained-glass windows of the tiny church of St Mary and falling like a benediction on the couple standing before the altar.

Llinos Savage looked up at the man at her side, Joe, tall and splendid, his long dark hair tied back from his face. His skin gleamed red-gold now, the sunlight skimming the fine contours of his jaw and highlighting the sharpness of his cheekbones. He looked so foreign, so wonderful, and she loved him so much it hurt. How she had longed to be his wife. How she had waited in a fever of impatience to possess and be possessed by the man she loved. But now, after many weary months of waiting, she was going to become Joe's bride.

The vicar smiled down at them as if they were old friends, and so they were. Martin, appearing strange now in the accoutrements of his calling, had dined at Pottery House on many occasions, sharing with the couple a glass of port or a mug of beer. He began now to speak in the resonant tones of a man used to projecting his voice into the vaults of old churches and Llinos felt tears burn her eyes. It was as though the words of the marriage ceremony were new and fresh, invented specially for her on this wonderful day.

Joe's hand touched hers and she clung to it, curling her fingers into his. He smiled down at her and his eyes were full of the dreams and promises he had shared with her so many times. His voice was strong and rang through the church, echoing high into the rafters. A fine, cultured voice, a voice at variance with his appearance.

He slipped the ring onto her finger, a simple ring of silver chased with the designs of his culture: the buffalo, the twisting curve that indicated the great river that wound through the plains of America and the tiny sun and moon that promised happiness and fruitfulness. He lifted her veil and kissed her tenderly and her heart soared with happiness.

The music from the ancient organ swelled majestically through the church; a paean of triumph as the couple walked down the aisle towards the sun-splashed porch. Llinos was aware of faces turned towards her. Joe's sisters, Charlotte and Letitia, who had travelled miles from the marches of Wales to be with their brother on his special day, smiled their blessing along with the familiar, loved faces from Llinos's childhood, her neighbours and friends. Her dear, best-loved friend Eynon Morton-Edwards inclined his head, his unhappiness clear to read as he looked at the girl he had loved for so long, the girl he had irrevocably lost.

Old Celia from the end house of Pottery Row, midwife, nurse and layer-out of the dead, smiled toothlessly as the couple passed. And there was one face dearer than the rest: that of Llinos's father. He was sitting in his chair, sick and weak, just well enough now to attend the marriage of his only child. But his recovery was an illusion, the colour in his cheeks not brought there by health but by fever. Llinos pushed the thought aside; this was her day, hers and Joe's. It was one she would remember until the day she died.

'We are really married.' She looked up in wonder at her husband standing a foot or more taller than she and for a moment was frightened. Would the reality live up to the dream she had harboured for so long? The dream of belonging to Joe? She belonged to him in spirit, in soul, in the depths of her being, but would their physical love enhance or destroy the harmony that had grown between them?

'Don't be afraid.' Joe had the uncanny knack of knowing her thoughts almost before she did. 'We are meant to be with each other — it's our destiny, you know that as well as I do.'

He leaned closer. 'In any case, I can't wait to taste the delicious fruit so long denied to me.' He was laughing at her now, the old Joe, her friend and soon to be her lover.

She shuddered in anticipation. How many times had she longed to forget everything? To forget that her father was sick, to forget the ring, the marriage service, and give in to her desire to make love to Joe? But now she was happy that they had waited until her father could witness this day.

At the door of the church she turned and watched the approach of her father. It had been Joe's idea to make a chair with wheels so that Lloyd could have at least a small degree of independence. As the sickness progressed and Lloyd Savage became increasingly fragile, a more comfortable chair had been made, padded with plump cushions and a rest for Lloyd's head.

'You look lovely, Llinos.' Lloyd held his hand towards her. 'Kiss your father. Show me that I still have a place in your life.'

She hugged him carefully, fearful of breaking the brittle-thin bones. 'You will always have a place in my life, Father,' she whispered, and he looked up at her with the over-large eyes of the mortally sick.

'Even when I'm dead and gone?' he asked.

Llinos swallowed the lump in her throat and smiled. 'Especially then.' She forced herself to speak briskly. 'Then the angels will have to put up with your nagging.'

He pinched her cheek. 'That's my brave girl.' He turned to look over his shoulder at the thin young man standing behind him, large hands, potter's hands, resting on the cushioned chair back.

'Come on, Watt, let's get back home before the weather turns nasty again.'

Llinos touched Watt Bevan's arm. 'Look after him for me and mind he doesn't have you at his beck and call for the rest of the day. If you're lucky, you might even have a chance to check the ovens.'

The pottery workers had all been given a day off in honour of the marriage, but the large, bottle-necked kilns needed to be kept at a steady temperature or the pots inside would be ruined.

'Damn the pottery.' Lloyd spoke thinly.

'You work too hard, Llinos, and worry too much. The business will be there long after my day, yours too, my girl.'

Llinos watched as her father was wheeled away. He did not turn; his head was back, resting against the chair as though he had no strength to hold himself erect. Llinos stifled a sigh and slipped her arm through Joe's.

'We'd better climb into the carriage or we'll be late for our own wedding feast,' she said, attempting to force a note of lightness into her voice.

The wedding breakfast was to be held in the great room at the Morton-Edwards residence. Eynon had insisted on it. As the carriages entered through the open gates of the lush park the doors were flung wide and the entire staff stood to attention on the steps. Maids in crisp white and serviceable black and butlers and footmen in livery lined the entrance hall and, at the head of the line, Maura Dundee, Eynon's housekeeper, watched the proceedings with an expert eye, ensuring that nothing went wrong on this important occasion.

Joe led Llinos inside. The smell of roasted wild boar and mint and honey permeated the air.

'I'm very hungry,' Joe whispered in her

ear, 'but perhaps not for the food.'

'Behave!' Llinos reproved him, but suddenly her worries about her father were forgotten. Her heart seemed to dance and her eyes brightened with mischief. 'Just because you are my husband doesn't mean you can boss me around, you know.' She looked up at him. 'I might yet refuse to have you in my bed.' She arched her brows at him. 'I will see how I feel, later.'

He slipped his hand around her waist. 'I will make sure that later you will feel very happy indeed.' He pinched her cheek. 'If I'm in the mood, that is.'

'You always have the last word!' Llinos said in mock anger. 'I feel like stamping my foot at you.'

'Not quarrelling already?' Eynon was at their side. 'I knew marriage was not a good idea. I told you what a vixen she could be, didn't I, Joe? I did warn you.'

'Hush!' Llinos said. 'You men always stick together.'

'Where's Lloyd?' Eynon looked around him, his eyes searching the crowd. He was a handsome man, Llinos thought, with his fair hair and his pale eyes. If Joe had not come into her life she would probably have married Eynon.

'He asked Watt to take him home. He's

13

very tired,' Llinos said. 'I think his own fireside is the place for him to be.'

Eynon touched her hand. 'Try not to worry. Lloyd wouldn't want to spoil this day for you.'

'I know.' Llinos swallowed hard. 'But he will be all right, won't he?' She looked questioningly at Joe.

'Of course he will. I've told Watt to give him his medicine as soon as possible,' he said gently. 'Your father will sleep for a few hours yet.'

'Come along,' Eynon said. 'No mournful faces, I will not allow it. A feast is waiting to celebrate this long-overdue marriage.'

The great table was polished to perfection; crystal and crisp linen napkins gleamed in the light from the candelabra and guests were already seated, awaiting the arrival of the bride and groom.

'I feel like a lamb going to the slaughter,' Joe said and Llinos began to smile. She pushed him forward, speaking quietly behind his back. 'You've got it wrong there, my lad. It is always the bride who is the sacrificial lamb.'

The celebrations seemed to stretch endlessly towards evening. Voices rose and fell, wine was drunk by the barrelful and food brought continuously to the table only to disappear as rapidly as it had appeared. At last, when fresh candles were brought, Llinos looked at Joe. 'I think it's time to go home.'

He rose to his feet and in his fine, cultured voice, began to speak. 'Eynon, our good friend, thank you for your hospitality, which has been great indeed. And to our neighbours and guests, my wife and I,' he paused and smiled, 'offer our gratitude. We shall treasure your gifts as mementoes of this, the happiest day of our lives — so far!' To a burst of applause and laughter, Joe took his bride's hand and led her from the hall.

In the house at Pottery Row Lloyd was asleep, as Joe had predicted. Llinos looked down at her father for a long moment and then left the room. The bridal chamber was waiting, decked with flowers and washed with rose water. Dried lavender hung over the bed, a sign of health and fertility. Joe was in the dressing room and the maid who had followed Llinos upstairs began to undress her mistress quickly, as though eager for the consummation of this beautiful couple, who were so much in love that joy radiated from them.

Llinos felt the coolness of her nightgown as it slipped over her shoulders and fell to her feet. The maid turned back the bed, waiting for Llinos to slip between the sheets.

'Thank you, Meggie,' Llinos said. 'I can manage now.'

When the door closed Llinos crossed the room and turned the key in the lock. This was the night she was to become a wife and she wanted it to be free of interruption. It must be perfect, a night she would cherish for the rest of her life.

Joe came into the room and stood for a long moment looking at her. He was naked and his broad shoulders and lean belly gleamed in the candlelight. He came to her and undid the fastenings of her gown, slipping it from her shoulders and allowing the soft cotton to fall to the floor. They stood there, naked, and Llinos knew it was the right way to be. There would be no false shame, they would be as natural as the birds of the skies and the animals of the fields.

'You are so beautiful.' His voice was thick with emotion. He took her in his arms and she felt him warm against her. She felt the power of him as she ran her fingers along his back and tentatively touched the roundness of his buttocks.

He bent his head to kiss her mouth and she drew in a ragged breath. Desire flared through her, desire that no longer need be

16

denied. She was his wife.

He led her towards the bed and together they lay, side by side, exploring, touching, learning about each other. Love grew like a fireball inside her, searing her skin as his fingers traced her breasts. She felt him kiss her neck, moving between her breasts to the flat of her belly. She moaned softly, wanting him so that it was almost a pain. She wound her arms around him, drawing him even closer to her. He touched her innermost secrets as he caressed her and then, when she felt she could stand it no more, he came to her.

There was little pain; Joe was a skilled lover. He took her tenderly, kissing her mouth, her hair, her eyelids. She began to move with him, crying now in her pleasure. It was as though the roaring winds and the rolling waves were possessing her, lifting her from the earthly world into a place where she had never been before. The joy, the sensation, went on as though it would never cease. She lost herself in the delight of it; her mind no longer functioned, she was all feelings and emotions.

When it was over she lay beside her husband and kissed the silk of his shoulder. 'I never knew it could be like this, Joe,' she said.

He turned to her and tangled his fingers in her hair. 'The night is only just beginning, my wife, my Firebird.' As he uttered his pet name for her, he drew her close. She felt his arousal and marvelled at the strength of this man who was hers for now and for always.

She closed her eyes and let the fire of their love draw her into the wonderful red-gold flames of passion.

CHAPTER

TWO

The rain had stopped, but the wind continued to howl, twisting the swaying branches of the pine trees into grotesque shapes, shedding leaves, iced with rain, which settled, needle sharp, on the grass. Across the sands, the sea ran in pewter bursts towards the shore as though trying to escape from the cold clutches of the wind.

As she glanced up at Joe, loving him even more than she had on the day of their wedding, Llinos smiled. She was Mrs Mainwaring now, a fulfilled woman, a happy woman. The only cloud on her horizon was her father's increasing pain and weakness.

Against all the odds, Lloyd had lingered on for the long weary months of winter, tired of living but unable to die. He was a wasted, unhappy man. No-one who knew him as the robust pottery owner he once was would recognize the gaunt, pain-ridden figure who was too weak to rise from his bed.

She forced the thoughts from her mind. She was determined that nothing would spoil the day, the one day, she had managed to snatch alone with Joe.

'You're a handsome devil. Has anyone ever told you that?' She paused, touching his cheek, brushing back the long dark hair which clung wetly to his strong face. Even now, in the cold of a November day, his skin glowed golden in the dim light. 'I don't know what I would do without you, Joe. I would be lost, I couldn't survive if we were ever parted.'

He kissed her mouth and she clung to him for a moment, in spite of a group of ladies tutting in disapproval. 'We'd better get home,' she said softly. 'The coach is waiting and, in any case, we're shocking the old ladies over there!'

Joe held open the door and Llinos climbed aboard the coach and seated herself on the creaking leather seat. She shivered, feeling the cold as her damp clothes settled around her. Joe sat beside her and took her hands in his, rubbing them. 'Here,' he said, 'put on your gloves, you should have had them on all the time, you silly little girl.' Joe was smiling indulgently as he settled back in his seat. The carriage jerked into motion and Llinos rested her head against his shoulder.

'It has been good to get out of the house,'

Llinos said. 'It's given both of us a break. You get the sharp end of Father's tongue, I know, but he relies on you so much now and he is fond of you.'

'I've known Lloyd for a long time. I understand the pain he's in and make allowances.'

She felt love for him overwhelm her. Joe was so good, so caring. How lucky she was to have found a man like him. Of course, her father did not share her views on her marriage, and that still had the power to hurt.

'My father knows you care and he's grateful,' she said, as though answering her own thoughts. 'It's just that he . . .' Her voice trailed away.

'He would have preferred me to be all white instead of half American Indian,' Joe said wryly. 'He can't forget I was once his batman, his Indian guide. He relied on me when we were fighting Napoleon, respected me. Now?' He hesitated. 'You know something? Lloyd has never once used my birth name.'

Llinos's smile was a little askew. 'Well, you must admit that Wah-he-joe-tass-e-neen is not the easiest name to say!' She pushed at Joe's arm. 'Even I have difficulty with it.'

'Ah, now that's more like my Llinos — the

laughter in your eyes, the flash of spirit, that's what I've been missing.'

'I'm sorry, Joe. I've been a misery lately and I know it.'

Joe pinched her cheek. 'I suppose I have to put up with a nagging wife the way most husbands do!'

'What cheek!' She sounded indignant but she knew he was teasing her. Life had not been easy lately, not for either of them. She nestled into Joe's shoulder, her hand in his, and breathed in the coldness of the day, knowing that the chill would make her father's pain so much worse. The cold got into his bones, made him ache. Suddenly she wanted to weep for the old Lloyd, the strong, healthy father of her childhood.

As the carriage bumped along the lane towards the town, Llinos stared through the window at the lowering clouds and wished she shared Joe's firm belief in an afterlife. It would be so comforting to know that her father would one day be at peace in a better place, removed from the coldness and sorrow that his life now often was.

The glistening rooftops of the pottery came into view just as the rain had begun to fall again. In a moment she was transported back to the flooding in what seemed, now, another lifetime.

The banks of the River Tawe had been breached, the buildings of the potteries, nestling cheek by jowl, overwhelmed with the greedy waters of the river. People had died that day. She had almost died.

She glanced at Joe from under her lashes; he had been the one to save her. He had known, as he always did, how much she needed him. In profile, his features were well defined, his jawline strong. The light touched his high cheekbones and he looked for a moment like a man carved out of warm, red stone.

He felt her gaze and looked down at her, his eyebrows lifting. 'Do I pass muster, then?'

'Well, just about.' She smiled. 'I have no intention of praising you, of feeding your vanity. You must know how handsome you are; you must see it every time you look into a mirror.'

The carriage jerked to a halt. Joe opened the door and, without waiting for the groom to lower the steps, leapt lightly down into the road. He held up his hands and Llinos felt them encircle her waist and then Joe was lifting her onto the pavement.

She stared up at the walls of the Savage Pottery and nestling beside it the edifice, grand and stately, of the Tawe Pottery, still the most successful pottery in the area. It remained so in spite of the fact that much had changed over the years. Most of the residents of Pottery Row who had not died on the night of the terrible flood had moved away, although Celia who lived in the end house was still there. She was very old now, gnarled and bent but as spirited as ever.

The gate to the pottery yard opened. 'Thanks, Watt,' Llinos said warmly. Watt had been employed at the Savage Pottery as a child, when his job had been to collect shards of broken pottery, and to carry the debris of the working day to the bin. But now he was a young man, tall for his age and with a maturity about him that touched Llinos's heart.

'Your dad's been asking for you,' he said quietly. His rough accent had vanished; his closeness with the Savage family, living as he did in Pottery House, had seen to that. 'He's not feeling too good.'

Llinos felt guilt hang like a millstone around her neck. She had taken a drive with her husband, needing to be free of the aura of sickness that pervaded the room where her father lay all day, every day, too weak now to even sit in his chair.

'I'll go to him.' She entered the house, aware that Joe was beside her, tall, strong,

24

invincible; but even he, with all his skills, could not take away the shadow of death that hung over the house.

Lloyd was propped up against his pillows, with Meggie holding a cup to his lips. He lifted his head and tried to smile when he saw his daughter, but his flesh was sunken and his cheekbones stood proud against the yellowed skin.

'Been anywhere nice?' His voice was weak, faded, as though there was not enough strength in him to give weight to his words.

'Yes, I've been for a lovely ride with Joe.' Llinos untied the strings of her bonnet, giving herself time to swallow the tears that were blurring her vision. 'We stopped the carriage and stepped out along the promenade for a breath of fresh air.'

She tidied the sheets around him, wanting to help him, pity for him gnawing at her stomach. The tall, strong father figure she had known as a child had vanished for ever. Now all that was left was a sickly old man who wanted to die.

He waved her away. 'You too, Meggie,' he said. 'I've had enough of that foul tea, it's been stewing in the pot for too long.' His voice was sharp; she knew he did not want pity, he resented it in the way that sick people resent the healthy.

Ignoring his ill humour, she sat down beside him. 'The medicine the doctor gave you, is it doing any good?' She tried to speak cheerfully as though her father had nothing more than a slight cold, but she knew he was losing his grip, even on his mind. Slowly, the pain of his legs, damaged in the war with Napoleon, was creeping through him, paralysing his reason as well as his body. Meggie hovered in the door, uncertain whether she should leave or not.

'Not a bit of good.' Lloyd made an attempt to smile. 'The stuff he gives me tastes like poison. He thinks it will kill me off but they can't get rid of an old soldier that easily.'

His words were an attempt at bravado; he was weary of lying in bed looking at the four walls of his room. He had been an active man, a soldier, and he sometimes wished he had been killed outright by a shot from an enemy musket. Llinos wanted to cry for the strong father she had once known.

Joe entered the room. He had taken off his coat and rolled up the sleeves of his white shirt. He was carrying a heavy silver tray; on it steamed a jug of water. In a pot beside the water was a mixture which only Joe knew the essence of.

Lloyd's face lightened. 'Ah, Joe, your medicine is better than all that of the good doctor. Don't know anything, these fellows. I don't know what doctors are coming to, they don't care what they give you. Jones wants me to die out of it and stop being a nuisance to him.'

Joe nodded to Llinos. 'Go and change out of those damp clothes,' he spoke gently. 'We don't need you here, this is man's work.'

She rose to her feet. 'I know when I'm not wanted.' She left the room, taking the maid with her.

'Go on, Meggie, I'm sure you've plenty to do.' Once in the warmth and comfort of the drawing room she breathed more easily. She knew she was a coward, knew she should stay and help Joe to nurse her father. But he would feel better soon. Once Joe had finished coating the ulcerated wounds on Lloyd's legs with the paste he had made the pain would ease. It was not a cure, but then nothing would cure Lloyd, nothing.

The house had grown dark and the maids were already lighting the lamps. The smell of tallow permeated the air and the candles threw shadows that danced in the dark corners of the rooms. Llinos looked up and smiled as Meggie entered the room with a glass of hot cordial.

'There's a good girl, I'll leave this here for a moment and go and change out of these damp clothes.' She paused. 'Otherwise my husband will be displeased with me.' She caught a strange look in the maid's face before she left the room. Meggie did not make any secret of the fact that she did not like Joe, but, then, how could a girl like her understand that the man inside the foreign exterior was kind and good and honest? She hurried upstairs and quickly cast aside her damp clothes. She opened the drawer and took out a fresh nightgown, smiling at her own actions. There were not many ladies in her position who dressed themselves without the help of a maid. Perhaps Llinos was regarded as strange in her habits by the servants, but in the difficult days when her father was at war Llinos had known what hardship was. She had learned very well how to fend for herself without the luxury of someone to wait on her.

Even now she was rich, even with her husband's fortune added to the excellent level of profit made from the pottery, with the house refurbished and with a good, if small, staff of servants, she did not see the necessity of being waited on hand and foot.

She pulled on a warm robe and tied back

her long hair. It might be supper time, time when most families dressed for the evening meal, but Llinos was not happy to conform to the mores invented by others. So she hurried down the stairs and pushed open the door to the drawing room. The warmth of it folded around her and she stood for a moment before the window staring outside into the garden. All was darkness, the shadows made deeper by the shimmering light thrown up by the fires of the bottle kilns.

Beyond the walls of the Savage Pottery stood the elegant house belonging to her dear friend, Eynon, warm-hearted, generous. He was the man her father believed she should have married. It would have been an eminently sensible match, joining the two potteries together. But it was not to be. In Joe, Llinos had found the only man she could ever love.

The door opened and Meggie bustled into the room, her round face cheerfully rosy, her plump hands carrying a tray with a plate of hot muffins on it.

'Here, miss, you look frozen, you'll need something to keep you going until supper is laid. Shall I shut the curtains and build up the fire? You'll feel more cheerful then.'

Llinos nodded and sank into a chair,

taking the glass from the maid. 'Thank you, Meggie, I appreciate your thoughtfulness.'

The girl hummed brightly as she went about her business. She was deft in spite of her plumpness and soon the fire blazed up the chimney, scattering sweet-smelling sparks of applewood into the room.

'Your dad's not looking too good, is he, miss?' Meggie brushed her cheek leaving a dab of smoke dust across her chin. 'You know what I think?' she continued. 'I think he wants to die out of it.'

Llinos winced at the maid's bluntness but she nodded, accepting the truth of the words. Meggie continued remorselessly. 'When you think of it, a dog or a horse would be put out of its misery but a man, a good man like Captain Savage, got to suffer.'

Llinos sipped the cordial, warming her hands around the base of the glass, and swallowed hard, afraid she might cry. She took a deep breath, trying to remove the constriction of tears from her throat.

'There, all done.' Meggie had risen and was brushing the dust from her fingers. 'That's unless I can get you something else, miss?'

Llinos nodded. 'Yes, you can bring in some cold food on a tray for my husband.

Don't bother to set up supper in the dining room.'

'Very good, miss, I'll tell Cook.'

When she was alone the silence settled around her; dark, like a cloak that covered her head and face. She tried to see pictures in the fire, tried to think bright thoughts, but instead came an unwanted vision of her father moaning in pain as Joe administered to him. All the happiness of the hour she had spent with Joe seemed to have dissipated, drifting away like an ethereal spirit. She smiled suddenly; she was as bad as Joe. Spirits indeed, what next?

She rose and wandered to the table where the book she had been reading earlier still lay, took it up and flicked through the pages trying to find her place. But she could not concentrate. The book was about an intrepid explorer who had walked across the continent of Africa and survived unscathed. It was unreal, far removed from her own small world. She could admire the explorer with one corner of her mind and yet she could not help wondering how his wife and children had fared while he was away finding new worlds.

Putting down the book, she returned to her chair and sighed heavily, knowing she could not rest. She knelt before the fire, tucking her bare feet under her robe. She felt the heat of the flames on her face and closed her eyes.

'Hey! Not asleep already, surely?' He had entered the room silently as he always did, leaving the door open behind him. Without turning, eyes still closed, she spoke to him.

'Come here and give your wife a kiss.' She felt him kneel beside her and then he took her in his arms. He knew instinctively that she needed to be comforted.

'Your father is much more comfortable now,' he said. 'And remember, Llinos, nature will take its course however much we fret.'

She looked up at him then. 'I know, but it's so hard to watch him suffer.'

Joe frowned. She faced him, her hands on his cheeks. 'What is it?'

'Let's talk about it in the morning, when the nightmares no longer ride,' he said.

Llinos shook her head. 'No, tell me now, what's wrong?'

'He wants me to help him die.' The words fell like shards of ice and suddenly the room was cold in spite of the blazing fire.

'Oh, Joe!'

He regarded her steadily. 'He says I could do it if I wanted to because I have the means.'

Meggie entered the room, a loaded tray balancing precariously on her arm. 'Supper, miss.' She stared in suspicion at Joe. She had obviously heard what he had been saying.

'Thank you, Meggie. Put the tray down there on the table.'

'Anything else, miss?' Llinos noticed quite suddenly that the maid never deferred to Joe. She did not even look at him. When she spoke, Llinos was aware of the almost hostile tone of her voice.

'No, thank you, and please knock before you enter a room, do you understand?'

Meggie looked down at her feet. 'Yes, miss, sorry, miss.'

'And it's Mrs,' Llinos said. 'Mrs Mainwaring, please remember that.'

Meggie hurried from the room, her face flushed, tears trembling on her lashes.

'That was uncharacteristically harsh of you, Llinos,' Joe said mildly, knowing, in the strange way he had, what had prompted her flash of anger. 'The girl doesn't know what to make of me. People gossip about us, still, you must know that. A respectable lady married to a half-breed, what can you expect? In any case, Meggie had her hands full; she would have been hard put to knock on the door and carry the tray.'

'I think she heard what you said about my father,' Llinos said. 'You have to be careful, Joe, you mustn't say things like that, not when people might misunderstand.'

She looked down at the tray of food, a selection of cold sliced turkey, some minted lamb chops and crusty, buttered bread, and as she stared at the muffins, the butter cooling, she knew she could not eat a thing. She filled a plate and brought it to her husband.

'Would you like a glass of wine, Joe?' she asked. He shook his head and she saw him pick a little at the meat. She knew then that he was upset too. She sat at his feet and without looking at him asked him the question that had been trembling on her lips.

'Joe, you wouldn't . . . do what Father wanted, would you?'

He did not pretend to misunderstand. 'Never.' The words brought a sigh of relief from Llinos but she remained silent, waiting for him to go on.

'It is not in the Indian philosophy to kill.' He paused and put down his plate. He had hardly touched his meal. 'In my homeland, among my tribe, a man knows when he is dying. He will go out into the plains or the mountains and wait for the gentle hand of death to touch him.'

'But what if he is a man like my father who is too sick to walk?'

'His relatives will take him wherever he wishes to go. He will be set down in the shade of a rock or a tree, food and drink will be left for him. After that he will be left alone.'

Llinos sighed. There was no way she could implement the Indian way of life, not here in Swansea. Her smile was involuntary as she looked up at Joe.

'I know,' he said. 'It would be impossible in Swansea. What is an act of kindness would be understood as an act of cruelty.'

Llinos found herself giggling. 'To say the least of it! Can you imagine anyone being left in the hills of Wales in weather like this?'

He ruffled her hair. 'Come along, Llinos, let's get an early night. It's high time we were going to bed, don't you think?' He rested his hand for a moment on her shoulder and she understood him completely.

She pretended a coyness she did not feel. 'You want your husbandly rights, is that it?' Her eyes were lowered and he caught her chin and tipped her face up so that she could not avoid looking at him.

'I want to make love to the most beautiful woman in the world,' he said.

She clung to him, hesitating. 'Should I look in on Father?'

'He will be asleep. Don't worry, Llinos. Lloyd is as comfortable as I can make him.'

Together they climbed the stairs, and through the high landing window Llinos could see that the sky had cleared, the stars were abundant, bright. It was going to be a frosty night.

As her husband took her in his arms, she felt his strength, the silkiness of his skin, felt the warmth of his naked body against hers, and she wanted him with a ferocity that never seemed to diminish.

She gasped in pleasure as he came to her, joining them as one. She was lifted on waves of love and delight, her mind, her sense of reason, deserting her. She was all nerve endings; filled with sensations.

Would their loving always be this way? Would their passion ever fade? She touched the silk of his skin with her fingertips, felt along the bones of his spine to the hollow in his back. She arched towards him, wanting the joy to go on and never cease. At last, in a delicious agony of release, she cried out his name.

Afterwards, as the moonlight slanted across the room silvering his hair and highlighting the contours of his face, she kissed her husband, knowing that nothing would ever change between them. Their love was as deep and as lasting as the ocean that divided his land from hers.

The morning sky was leaden with the continued threat of snow as Llinos crossed the yard towards the painting shop. The familiar sounds and smells wrapped around her. She breathed deeply, knowing she loved this world of potting.

'Mr Bevan, may I have a word with you?' she said. Watt came to her side at once and smiled down at her.

'Yes, Mrs Mainwaring, what can I do for you?' He was respectful, formal in the presence of the other workers. He followed her to the end of the room where it was comparatively quiet and waited for her to speak.

'How are the stocks of clay and stone? Have we enough to last until spring?' she asked, knowing the answer but allowing Watt the privilege of his position as overseer.

'Production has increased rapidly over the winter months, as you know. Stocks are getting a little low, Llinos. I think it's time I took a trip to Cornwall to order some more clay and stone.'

'In an emergency we could bring in some clay from Penllergaer, of course,' Llinos said. 'But you're right, Watt, I think you should go to Treherne's quarry and have them deliver enough clay and stone to last us throughout the summer months.'

He nodded. 'Providing the weather is all right, I'll leave first thing in the morning, shall I?'

'I think so. I'll have payment ready for you and, Watt, take care. I don't want you to be robbed on the way.'

As she walked towards the door, Llinos breathed in the atmosphere of the paint shed with a sensation of satisfaction. In the bedroom she might be the passionate, flighty wife Joe loved, but here, in the pottery, she was every inch a successful businesswoman and she loved it.

CHAPTER

THREE

It was wet at the bottom of the quarry and very cold. The rain drizzled mercilessly, running down the sides of the quarry in small waterfalls, bringing with it silt and stone. It was John Pendennis's first day at Treherne Stone, his first experience of working the china stone as a labourer. He was eighteen years of age, a man doing a man's job, and yet he felt no pride.

'Come on, mister, or we'll never earn a penny piece.'

John smiled at the boy: a pale, weedy lad, his rags already saturated, his thin arms holding the borer with difficulty as he pushed the bit against the wall of rock.

'You're right enough, Richie.' John raised his hammer, hesitating for a moment; one false move and he would break the child's arm. He swung, the hammer connected and the boy shuddered.

'How long have you been working down here?' John asked, lowering the hammer to the ground.

'How long have I been working down here?' The boy paused. 'About two years, I s'pose. I don't rightly know.'

John looked at his red, chafed hands with pity. 'Do you like working in a quarry?'

'Do I like working in a quarry?' The boy had the habit of repeating everything John said. 'No, I don't. I bloody well hates it.'

'What do you think of the boss?'

'What do I think of the boss? I don't think nothing of 'im, don't see 'im much, only from a distance. Why, what do you think of 'im?'

'I hate the bastard,' John said bitterly. 'Treherne should try working under the same conditions he forces children like you to work.'

'I ain't forced, sir. I works to earn money like everyone else. Besides, I'm a man grown, can't you see that? I can read and write an' all. My grandfather was a preacher and showed me how to figure and everything. It broke his heart when my father didn't take after him for learning and such.'

He beamed, suddenly a handsome young boy. 'But then I took after him and, afore Grandad died, he wanted me to go to school and learn to be a gent.'

John looked at the boy, his thin shoulders and bony arms, his chin without even a trace of beard, and smiled.

'Of course you are a man, more of a man

than many of those in charge of this place will ever be.' He put down the hammer. 'But surely you have dreams, Richie. Don't you want to do anything better with your life than this?' He waved his hand round the deep quarry.

The boy shook his head. 'I don' have dreams. Nightmares, more like. It's akin to being in a grave, working here. Buried afore we've even died, we are.'

'Well, what we don't like we must change,' John said with a sudden sense of resolve. 'We're getting out of here. We can both do better than this.'

Richie looked at him in surprise. 'You might be able to walk out just when you please but I can't.' He squared his shoulders. 'I got to work 'cos I gets my father a pound a month and he needs it to live.' He peered up at John. 'What about your father, sir, will he kill you for leaving work 'fore the shift is done?'

'I doubt it.' John thought of his father, a bankrupt, sitting at home in disgrace, not even trying to rebuild his life. 'But what I do know is I made a mistake coming to work here. It's not for me, nor for you, Richie. I'm going to find us something better.'

'We'll have to ask my father,' Richie spoke nervously, pointing to where a bent old man was working. In the dim light of the clouded day he looked worn and miserable; his wispy hair was matted, his shoulders hunched as he began to cough.

'I'm taking your son out of here,' John called, dispensing with the preliminaries. 'It's no work for a young boy, six hours in this hellhole breathing in foul air and then the long, hard climb to the surface.'

'He can't go,' the man said. 'I needs the money.' He looked hopelessly at John. 'Do you think I want him down here any more than you do? He has no mother. What else is there for him, tell me that.'

'I'll find him something, believe me,' John said. He urged Richie towards the ladder. 'Get climbing, we're leaving.'

'I can't,' Richie hung back. 'If my father says I can't go, I can't.'

'Let me take him, for pity's sake,' John appealed to the man. 'I'll find him something more suitable, you have my word on it.' The men stared at each other in the fading, leaden light.

'How old are you?' John said abruptly. His question took the other man by surprise.

'You've no right to ask me anything but I'll tell you anyway.' He rubbed his sleeve across his wet brow. 'I'm thirty-seven years come pay day.'

'And you look sixty,' John said bluntly. 'Is that what you want for your son?'

The man looked down at Richie for a long moment in silence. 'Aye, young man's right. Go with him, Richard, and go with my blessing.'

John pushed Richie towards the ladder and the boy began to climb. Behind him, John watched the skinny shanks with an overwhelming feeling of pity. Anger replaced the feeling as John mused on the misfortune that had befallen his family.

It was Treherne who had thrust the final blade that had ruined the Pendennis business. The families of Treherne and Pendennis had long been enemies, the bitter feud begun many years ago when a Treherne had ruined a lady from the Pendennis family. John had been brought up to think of anyone bearing the Treherne name as a potential enemy. And so it had been proved.

Wilbur Treherne had gulled John's father, tricking him into a merger of the quarry and the china clay pits owned by the Pendennis family. Treherne had undercut John's father on quotes for china stone and china clay to all the major potteries and most of them had fallen for it.

The Savage Pottery in Swansea was one

exception. The owners had always enjoyed good relations with the Pendennis family. John had known his father to supply small quantities of clay and stone when the pottery was in financial difficulties, and the family had remained faithful as had the larger Tawe Pottery. It was the owners of the South Wales potteries, out of all the potteries including those from Derby and Worcester, who had shown loyalty until the day the Pendennis clay business finally failed.

John climbed steadily, impatient to get to the surface. He had been a fool ever to agree to come to work in the quarry but Treherne had twisted the knife very effectively, allowing John and his father to remain at Pembroke House on the condition that John worked for him as a labourer. Treherne had gloated as John signed in for work, watching while the son of his great enemy descended the ladder to the quarry face. His revenge, he clearly felt, was complete and the pride of his enemy dragged into the dust.

Well, John Pendennis would not knuckle under the pressure. He would find a way to rebuild the family fortunes. Of one thing he was certain: he would not work at Treherne Stone for one more minute.

Once on the pitted surface of the quarry Richie stood still, his small chest heaving, dragging in the dust-choked air. John swung himself onto the top, clear of the ladder, and looked around him. A stranger, clearly a customer, was talking to Treherne and one of the managers was standing near by nodding with the sort of servility that Treherne enjoyed. As if drawn by John's gaze Wilbur Treherne turned. His normally red face became redder and in a moment he was striding across the ground.

'What do you think you are up to?' he said loudly. 'You're supposed to be underground with the rest of the common labourers.' He stared at Richie, his mouth twisted into a sneer. 'And don't even think about back-chatting me or you'll feel the weight of my hand across your mouth.'

He turned to look at the stranger. 'You see the sort of riff-raff I have to deal with, Mr Bevan? Scum of the earth, so they are.'

'Shut your noise, Treherne!' John said loudly and several of the overseers moved closer, anxious to hear the heresy from a man whose family was ruined. 'If you open your mouth any wider, you'll find my fist in it.'

Treherne moved forward a pace and then stopped, warned by the gleam in John's eye.

'How dare you talk to me like that!' he blustered. 'Get out of here before I have you thrown out, you scum!' He was beside himself with rage. 'And tell that arrogant father of yours to pack up and be out of my property before I arrive with the bailiffs.'

As John strode past Treherne he saw the man lash out at Richie, catching the boy across his thin face. John paused, measured his distance and then deliberately threw a punch that connected neatly with the point of Treherne's jaw. The man fell to the ground, arms and legs spread-eagled in the mud whitened by china-stone dust.

John looked at the overseers and they stepped back as one man, not willing to confront him. 'Come on, Richie,' John said. 'Let's find a place where the air is fresh and clean, shall we?'

'You will get into trouble for hitting Mr Treherne,' Richie said anxiously. 'He is a bad man to cross, you knows that.'

'He has already done his worst,' John said easily. 'Come on, I think there's some fine cheese in the house and a loaf or two of bread. We shall eat and then we shall plan what we are to do next.'

Pembroke House was hidden from the lane behind a hedge of mature trees. Richie gasped in wonder as he saw the mellow stone building, glowing in the light from the sun, the many windows appearing as if they were lit from within.

'You got servants, sir?' Richie was suddenly in awe of John, realizing that he came from a very different station in life from himself.

'Not any longer,' he said. 'And don't be fooled. This all belongs to Treherne now; he's stolen it by trickery and by foul deeds from my father who is a weak man.'

Inside the hallway John and Richie left grey footprints across the polished floor. The house was silent and the kitchens to the rear of the building were empty. The fireplace was full of dead ash; grey cinders had rolled onto the hearth. The servants had departed some weeks ago and already the place smelled of staleness and neglect.

John took the bread from the slatted box hanging from the ceiling. Alongside it was a cheese wrapped in cloth. 'This will do us, Richie. It will me, anyway, I'm starving.'

The two ate in silence, sitting at the kitchen table that was bleached from much scrubbing.

'Do you live here on your own, then, sir?' Richie asked, his mouth full of food. John smiled at him.

'Close your mouth while you eat, Richie,'

he suggested, 'and don't speak until you have finished chewing. No, I don't live here alone. My father is in the house somewhere, probably in his bed.'

Richie ate in silence, head down. He was easily rebuffed and John made a mental note to treat the boy more gently in future.

'I think there's a few leaves of tea left in the tin. Would you like a drink, Richie?'

'Tea, I never tasted tea, I don't know if I like it.'

'Well, there's one way to find out.' It took only minutes for John to light the fire. The dry sticks flared up, igniting the coal. 'Fill the kettle,' John said. 'Not too full, mind.'

The brew was weak but hot and fragrant and Richie tasted it tentatively before deciding that he liked it. 'Much better than the beer Dad fetches from old Mrs Foster's place. They say she brews it in an old bathtub and still does her wash in it afterwards.' He smiled, showing a glimmer of humour. 'Tastes like she peed in it.'

John rose from the table. 'I'll take some tea to my father and see how he is at the same time.' He felt no pity for his father, only scorn that a Pendennis had allowed a Treherne to fool him so easily. He climbed the stairs, feeling the warmth of the house where he had been born folding around him.

Hatred burned in his gut. Curse Wilbur Treherne and all his family for taking away the house John loved and should have inherited. Where he should have brought a bride and where he might have reared fine sons. All that was nothing but a dream now.

His father was lying in a darkened room, the air stale, the curtains still closed. John approached the bed and placed the tea on the table, covered now in dust.

'Father!' he said. 'Why don't you get up? Nothing can be gained by lying in bed all day.'

His father did not reply. John lit the lamp and took a deep breath as he looked down at the man in the bed. His face was pale, his mouth dragged to one side, his breathing shallow. It was clear that he was a very sick man. It seemed that Treherne had broken his will to live as well as ruined him financially.

John realized he should send for someone, perhaps the old nurse who lived in the village. 'Witch', some called her, but Cassie would know what to do and would be good enough to wait for payment or take it in kind.

John was on the landing when the front door opened with a crash. On the threshold stood a group of men wielding clubs. One even brandished a pitchfork.

'What's going on here?' John hurried downstairs, anger churning in his gut.

'You've got to get out of here, man.' A burly man stepped forward. 'I'm Mr Treherne's bailiff and he says you get out now, tonight.'

'I can't do that. My father is sick,' John said. 'In any case, proper notice should be given.'

The bailiff looked at John, his lips in a wry smile. 'I think enough notice was given when you took it into your head to attack Mr Treherne. Now, you can go peaceably or you can be thrown out.'

'My father needs a doctor.' John felt desperate, impotent. He knew that nothing would move the man standing before him and he was right.

'Take him to the workhouse, then.'

Richie came in from the kitchen, his eyes wide in a white face. 'What's the matter, Mr Pendennis?' he said, his voice trembling.

'I'm being evicted, Richie.' John looked at the bailiff. 'At least help me to get my father some help.'

'That's not part of my duties. My job is to see you cleared out of this house tonight, so get on with it.' He turned to the men with him. 'Up the stairs and bring Mr Pendennis down. He can't stay here, sick or not.'

'You can't be so inhuman!' John protested. He longed to strike out, to hit anyone and everyone, but it was no use. The men were ascending the stairs with purposeful tread and, after a few moments, they carried John's father down into the hall.

'Can't you even allow us a blanket to cover him?' John asked, looking at his father who was grey and trembling, his bony legs protruding from the flapping nightshirt.

'Not one of my duties.' The bailiff was implacable. 'Come on, out, the lot of you. I got other work to do. And no trying to get back in. There will be men stationed here all night.'

John followed as his father was carried towards the road, tears thick in his throat. He felt the urge to kill rise within him. Treherne might think he had beaten John but he would pay heavily for what he had done this night. John stood in the cold wind supporting his father who, unable to speak, was crying weak tears.

'What shall we do, Mr Pendennis?' Richie's voice was filled with fear. John lifted his head and stared at the night sky. An iron resolve was born within him at that moment. He would succeed beyond his wildest dreams, he would one day be rich and powerful and Wilbur Treherne would have to guard his back or he might find a knife in it.

'We'll find lodgings for tonight,' he said at last. 'I have a few shillings left. Tomorrow we leave Cornwall and head across the Bristol Channel towards the coast of Wales.'

Early, before first light, John roused Richie from his makeshift bed on the floor of the humble room he had rented.

'Come on. We're getting out of here,' he whispered.

'What about your father?' Richie glanced at the silent man in the bed and shivered.

'My father died in the night.' John was pulling on his boots. 'I have very little money as it is. Let the parish bury him.'

'But he will have a pauper's grave,' Richie said, buttoning his ragged coat. ' 'Tis a shame, that.'

'I can't do anything about it,' John said. 'In any case, one hole in the ground is the same as any other. Come on, let's go before anyone spots us.'

The road was rimmed with frost as John strode out towards the coaching inn. Richie panted behind him, the air rasping in his lungs. If he had harboured any doubts about taking the boy with him, they vanished now in the light of the day.

He looked into the pouch containing his meagre supply of money, wondering if he would have enough to take two of them to Wales. Against his thigh swung the concealed bag that held the last of the family treasures, among them the gold watch his father had given him. John felt a lump in his throat. For all his brave, even callous words to Richie, it hurt him to think of his father being put in unconsecrated ground. But what else could he do?

Later, as he sat on the coach, glad of the shelter from the sting of the wind, he looked across to the other seat and saw the face of the stranger who had witnessed his attack on Treherne.

'Morning,' the man said. 'Travelling my way, are you?'

'I am that.' John looked at the stranger defiantly. 'I know you think me a barbarian, but Treherne asked for all he got and more.'

'I don't doubt it.' He leaned forward, holding out his hand. 'Watt Bevan, overseer at the Savage Pottery.' He smiled. 'I never much liked Treherne myself.'

John looked down at Richie and sighed. 'Well, Mr Overseer, I wonder if you might find work for two honest labourers at the Savage Pottery?'

'You never know,' Watt said. 'I will put in a word with the owners for you, if that's any use.'

'It's a start,' John replied. 'A very good start.' He settled back in the seat and closed his eyes. He had not slept the night before but had sat with his father until the last breath left the old man's body. Suddenly, despite his eighteen years, John Pendennis felt like weeping.

CHAPTER

FOUR

The paint shed was alive with voices and sunlight. The sharp smells of lead, oil and drying clay permeated the long building. Watt stood in the doorway with John Pendennis and looked along the line of workers.

'So, do you think you can fit in round here?' Watt asked. 'I know you'll be working mainly in the office but it's just as well to familiarize yourself with all aspects of the job.'

'I'm sure I'll adapt,' John said. 'Anything must be better than the Treherne stone quarry.'

Watt's eyes were drawn towards Lily, one of the finest painters in the pottery. She was still very young but like him she had come to the pottery from the workhouse as a child.

She smiled when she saw him watching her and then quickly turned away. Her silky hair was tied back and pushed beneath a cap. She was beautiful; he wanted to touch her soft skin and kiss the full pouting lips that were pursed now as she concentrated on the tall pot she was painting. He had fancied Lily for some time but she was a shy little creature and the last thing he wanted to do was frighten her off.

'Llinos — Mrs Mainwaring — wants you to be happy here,' Watt said, turning his eyes away from Lily with an effort. 'She knows that your family business stood by her when she needed help and she's grateful.'

John nodded without comment. He was a man who would not easily become a friend and Watt knew it. Perhaps it was just as well; he did not want any competition from the handsome Cornishman where Lily was concerned.

He showed John the various operations required to decorate the pottery, skimming through the tour as quickly as possible. Then he led John outside to the yard where the new apprentices, Richie among them, were spending their first few days clearing away the bits of wasted clay.

'He seems happy enough,' John said. 'Let's hope he can learn a better way of life here than he did back home.'

Watt was pleased when the tour of duty was over and John safely installed once more in the elegant office building. He returned to the painting shed, walked the length of the room, carefully inspecting a jug here, a bowl there, before pausing beside Lily.

'That's nice.' Watt knew as soon as he spoke that his words were inadequate. The sweep of stout rushes, executed in fawns and greens, stood proudly against the still river water and were so lifelike in appearance that he felt he could touch them.

Lily looked up at him from beneath her lashes and his gut contracted as he saw the blush spreading up her throat and into her cheeks.

He wanted to lean closer to her but he was too awkward, so he moved away instead. He must mention Lily's talent to Llinos, he decided. She was a gifted decorator and it was time someone noticed that.

'Hey there, Watt, feel like a roll in the hay this weekend?' He knew the voice, recognized the banter.

'I might take you up on that, Pearl, then what would your husband say?' He was learning to overcome his shyness with the women. Since he had been made inspector of the paint work, he had been teased unmercifully and was at last learning how to deal with it.

'Oh, him.' There was a world of scorn in Pearl's voice. 'My Joshua sleeps, drinks and farts; it's all he's good for.'

There was a roar of laughter from some of the other women. 'Go on, Pearl, you haven't got three kids for nothing, have you? Josh has fathered three big strong boys, so what you got to complain about?'

'All right, girls,' Watt said, grateful that he was tall for his age and that his voice was as strong and deep as any man's. 'Let's stop the larking and get back to painting, is it?'

Pearl persisted. 'Not going to take me up on my offer then? I could teach you some tricks that might come in useful when you get married. Sow your wild oats now, boy *bach*, before you jump the broomstick with a nagging wife!' She laughed uproariously. 'Anyway, if you are not willing, what about that handsome Englishman you just fetched here, is he ready for a laugh and a tumble, do you think?'

Watt deftly changed the subject. 'Well, Pearl, your work's improving, just look at those Indian feathers, they are very good indeed.'

Pearl smiled widely. 'You'll have to do better than that, my lado, if you are to please the ladies.'

Watt ignored her remark. 'You are a talented artist, Pearl, but you talk so much that you are falling behind with your work.' He tweaked at her cap. 'I can see that your mouth moves faster than your hands.'

The roar of laughter followed Watt as he

continued on his way, inspecting the work, noting the progress the painters were making. Soon he found himself standing once again beside the bench where Lily was working. She kept her eyes averted and he very much wanted her to look up at him. He could see a strand of silky hair escaping from under her cap, curling into the hollow in the nape of her neck. He wanted to touch it badly.

'You want to watch yourself, Watt,' Mrs Smedley said sourly. 'You can see your thoughts writ plainly on your face.'

He turned away in embarrassment. 'Right, ladies,' he said a little too loudly, 'it's time to finish work for the day. Go on, get on home, all of you.'

He took off his paint-smudged apron and without a backward glance walked out into the chill evening air. He crossed the yard and entered Pottery House through the back door. The smell of beeswax mingled with roasting meat drifted along the passageway. He paused and breathed deeply. This had been his home since Llinos had taken him in from the outhouse which he had shared with the other men and given him a bedroom of his own.

Llinos had been good to him; she had treated him more like a brother than an employee brought from the workhouse to clean the floors of the pottery sheds. He had learned to read and write as well as anyone from the gentry. He wore good clothes: crisp white shirts and tight-fitting breeches. His tall boots were of the finest leather, but inside he was still Watt Bevan, an orphan, uncertain, knowing that his good fortune depended not upon himself but on the good will of Llinos, her husband and her sick old father. What he really wanted was to own a business of his own.

Watt made his way upstairs to his room and closed the door behind him. Here the silence wrapped itself around him. He looked at himself in the mirror over the mantle. He was fair, very young, beardless. What could he offer a girl like Lily? His good fortune could vanish like mists before the sun. In any case, he was far too young to think of settling down. And yet his loins ached, his urges strong; he needed a woman badly. He smiled to himself, perhaps he should have taken Pearl up on her offer.

He thought of her bare arms, sleeves rolled above her elbows. Her breasts were the full, heavy breasts of a mature woman. He smiled as he imagined himself kissing her lips; yet he could not deny it, he was aroused.

He had never experienced the joy of lying with a woman. Some of the other men employed at the pottery frequented the streets of Swansea looking for quick release with one of the many whores to be found touting their trade. But Watt was neither fish nor fowl; not one of the workers nor yet one of the higher orders. In any case he would not have the courage to take a prostitute; a stranger who would expose him to ridicule if he failed in his task.

Later, after supper, he sat and talked for a time with Llinos and Joe. They were kind, they tried to include him in their lives, but he knew by their glances, by the small touches, that they longed to be alone. It was shortly after ten when he rose.

'If you will excuse me, I think I'll take a walk before I go to bed.' He paused near the door as Llinos spoke. 'You said there was something you wanted to tell me, Watt, have you forgotten?' she smiled at him. 'Not in love, are you?'

'I might be,' he said, pleased that he was learning, albeit slowly, to conceal his feelings. 'It's Lily,' he said. 'I've noticed how very talented she is at painting. Her work is exceptional, Llinos.'

Llinos turned to her husband and rested her hand on his arm. 'Well, Joe, isn't this an opportune moment to bring out your new patterns?' She turned to Watt. 'Could you delay your walk for a while?'

'Of course.' He returned to his seat. 'What new patterns are these?'

Joe rose and took a sheaf of papers from his pocket. 'They are very rough drawings,' he said, handing them to Watt. 'But I think it might be time to introduce some new designs.'

Watt looked at the designs; he was no mean artist himself, and though the drawings were rough, he could see the power of them. The central decoration was a bird: not an eagle, nor a dove, nor any bird Watt had ever seen. Perhaps a peacock was the nearest he could get to it.

'It's a firebird,' Joe said, knowing as always what others were thinking. 'It's a bird from myth and legend, an imaginary bird. What do you think?'

'It's most impressive,' Watt said and meant it. The full flush of feathers cascaded from a crested head and neck. Watt could see them painted in jewel colours, perhaps predominantly red and gold. He voiced his thoughts and Llinos nodded.

'It shall be a trade mark,' she said. 'Let Eynon's painters experiment with designs stolen from China, with filled-in transfers and unoriginal flower groups. The Savage Pottery will be known for something far more exotic.'

Watt looked up at Llinos. 'And do you think Lily could try out some of these?' he asked.

'As she comes so highly recommended, I don't see why not.' Llinos smiled at him. 'I always knew that girl had talent from the moment she began work here. She's always been eager to learn, that's usually a good sign.'

Watt nodded. 'Shall I take these with me?' He held up the papers. 'I could show them to Lily in the morning, give her a chance to do some drawings of her own before she begins to paint on the pots.'

It was Joe who replied. 'Take them and let a real artist work on them.' He rested his hand on his wife's shoulder and, in that moment, Watt envied them their closeness. It must be fine to have another being care so much. Would he ever be fortunate enough to find someone like that?

It was cold outside but the night was clear. Stars hung low, crystal bright against the velvet of the sky. As Watt walked he could feel the chill of the road even through his good leather boots. When he breathed, the coldness felt like shards of ice in his chest. He walked towards the river bank and stood looking down into the water. It was fast running but calm.

Unbidden came the memory of the flooding. Watt could feel it now, the pain of the water closing over his head. He had panicked for a moment but then he had seen Captain Savage, helpless in the swollen river, his injured legs unable to work to keep him afloat. Watt held onto him, keeping his head clear of the water until help came. Later, in gratitude, the captain had settled a generous sum of money on Watt, money that he could draw on when he was twenty-one. He grimaced, that was still a few years away and what would happen when the captain died? Would the promise of money die with him or would Llinos see that he received it? He was not sure of the legalities of the matter but he supposed he was fortunate: his employment was secure, he would work at the Savage Pottery as long as Llinos drew breath. He knew this but a restlessness had gripped him ever since John Pendennis had come to work at the pottery.

He stared up at the sky, at the distant stars, and thought about his friend Binnie Dundee. Both orphans, they had been more like brothers with Binnie looking out for Watt, taking his part if anyone picked on him. He missed Binnie. He would have liked to ask his advice, to discuss the future with him. But Binnie was far away across the sea in the huge land they called America.

Watt kicked at a fallen branch and watched it slip silently into the river causing the smallest of ripples. That was him: small, insignificant, and would marriage, even to a girl like Lily, make his life any better?

Marriage had not suited Binnie. He had lived with his sweetheart Maura, given her a child and eventually married her and then, with the bed still warm from the wedding nuptials, Binnie had run away leaving Maura desolated and bereft.

On an impulse Watt began to walk towards the town. Some of the taverns in Wind Street would be open still to accommodate any late-night travellers who might step off the coach. As he passed by small, huddled houses, he saw the lighted windows and his loneliness increased. Was he destined to be a lone wolf, to live without love, without a family of his own? Would he always be Watt, the boy from the workhouse who no-one wanted? He recognized the self-pity but somehow his feeling of isolation persisted.

The Swansea Inn was filled with pipe

smoke and the smell of ale. Over near the fire, two old men sat on the wooden settle and Watt recognized one of them. Old Ben he had always been called at the pottery, old Ben the kiln man. His gnarled hands, deeply veined, rested on the worn, shining crook of a stick. Ben had long since ceased to work at the pottery. He was too old now to carry coal to fuel the fires.

'Evening, Ben.' Watt approached and sat on the opposite side of the fire. Ben peered at him, his watery eyes narrowed.

'It's me, Watt, don't you recognize me?'

'*Duw*, a man it is now, not a boy *bach* any more. How are you, Watt, married with a family, is it?'

'No,' Watt said flatly. 'Still on my own.'

'No, man, not on your own. Living with Llinos and her father, aren't you? So how can you be alone?'

'Aye, well, good as Llinos is, it's not like having kin of your own. Anyway, have a mug of something with me, Ben.'

'Aye, that's a good idea. My friend Bertie here is thirsty too, aren't you, Bert?'

'All right,' Watt said, 'Bertie is welcome to have a drink on me, too.' His brief look at the man took in a long stringy beard and close-set eyes that were somehow familiar. He shook away the thought, it was not important, and waved his hand. After a moment the landlord came over rubbing his hands along his apron.

'Three mugs of ale, is it?' He glanced at Watt's good clothes. 'Or is a measure of porter more to your liking, sir?'

'Ale will be just right,' Watt said. He settled back against the wooden chair and stared into the fire. Ben leaned forward.

'How are the folks up in Pottery Row? Celia-end-house still plodding along with her potions and such?'

Watt had not given the occupants of the row a great deal of thought but as far as he knew, Celia was all right. 'Same as usual,' he said, non-commitally.

Ben leaned a little nearer and Watt could see how sparse the old man's beard had become. 'Llinos with child yet?'

'Not that I know of,' Watt said, instinctively retreating; what went on in the private life of his employer, however caring she might be, was none of his business.

' 'Bout time she had a little one now, isn't it? How long has she been wed to the Indian fellow?'

'I suppose it's not very long, really. Anyway, Ben, how are you keeping? Enjoying staying in bed of a morning instead of carrying coal for the fires?' He had changed the subject adroitly and Ben smiled.

'It's not too bad. Living with my poor dead sister's daughter, I am, see? She loses her patience with me sometimes.'

Watt stared around him restlessly; he would have been better off having an early night, sitting in his room reading or thinking about Lily. How wonderful it would be to hold her, to touch her soft throat, to kiss her breasts. He had never seen a woman's breasts, not naked, not properly. He had once walked into the painting shed and found one of the younger women giving her child suck and the quick glimpse he had of the pink, damp nipple had fired his urges in a way that had shocked him. He had remonstrated with the girl but she looked up at him with large eyes and told him such a sorry tale of her husband falling sick and herself needing to work in spite of having the baby that he had said no more about it.

'Heard a strange tale about Binnie Dundee the other day,' Ben said and Watt sat up straighter.

'Oh, what was that?'

'Well, my niece's friend's husband went out to America and worked there for a time. Good pickings out there, lots of people with nice houses and the like and the weather sunny all the year, so they say.' He was given to rambling but Watt listened, trying to be patient.

'Anyway, he said that Binnie Dundee was married to one of them rich ladies out there in America. Can't be right though, can it? I mean he's married to that pretty little Irish girl, isn't he?'

'Yes, of course he is.' Ben must have got his story wrong somehow. America was an enormous country, the chances of anyone meeting Binnie there were remote.

'Where was this?' Watt asked and Ben looked up at him, frowning.

'Where was what?'

'Where did this man see Binnie?' Watt tried not to let his impatience show. 'Which part of America, I mean.'

Ben waved his hand. 'I dunno, somewhere called Troy I think it was but I'm not too sure about that, my memory isn't what it was.'

It clearly was not, Watt mused. Troy was a place in a story he had read about the Greeks, it was nowhere near America. He finished his ale and put some coins on the table.

'I'd better get back, I've got an early start in the morning,' he said.

'Well, give my love to all them up at the row, Jim Cooper and his wife, all of them.'

Ben smiled toothlessly. 'Tell them I miss 'em all.'

Poor Ben, his mind was going; Jim Cooper had died the night of the flood. The old man no longer knew dreams from reality. 'I'll do that, Ben.' Watt rested his hand for a moment on the other man's shoulder noting the jutting bones beneath Ben's jacket with a feeling of pity. He had worked hard all his life to end his days living with a niece who found him nothing more than a nuisance. Surely life had more than that to offer?

'Night, Bertie,' he said. The man did not reply, he simply touched his greasy cap, his piggy eyes averted. As Watt walked home through the darkness of the streets, he suddenly felt a sense of depression rest on him. He was young and strong, and yet he was in a rut, no doubt about it. He wanted more, lots more, but somehow he did not quite know how to achieve it.

'Watt!' The voice was low and he looked around, wondering where it was coming from. 'Up here.'

She was framed in the candlelight from her bedroom: Lily, the girl who had aroused the urges, the feelings of restlessness in him. Without pausing to think, he was climbing up the rough stone exterior of the house, clinging to the creepers until he was on a level with Lily's lovely face.

He longed to kiss her. Her silky hair touched his cheek and he almost lost his grip on the window-sill.

'Don't let anyone see you or I'll be thrown out of here,' Lily said anxiously. 'My land-lady is very strict about men callers.'

He was glad to hear that, it meant that Lily was safe from predators. 'Give me a quick kiss goodnight then, Lily.' He was amazed at his own daring. She leaned over the sill and for a brief heady moment, her lips touched his, and then she retreated inside, closing the window and pulling the curtains.

Watt lowered himself back into the road and stood for a moment looking up at the moon, wanting to bay at it like a hound. A huge wave of exultation swept through him, he had kissed her, he had actually kissed Lily and she had allowed it.

His head was held high as he returned along Pottery Row towards the gates of the pottery. He felt ten feet tall, his heart swelled within his chest and he laughed out loud. He was buoyant, the world before him, his oyster. He could do anything he wanted to. He was a man.

Bert Cimla smiled to himself as he drank

down his ale: it was a good thing young Watt did not remember him from his time at the pottery. Ah, those were the days; days when he had lived like a king. It was when Captain Savage was missing believed killed that Bert had moved in to marry Gwen Savage, charming her with his good looks and sweet tongue. She had been a silly bitch and that daughter of hers no better, but he had, for a brief time, enjoyed the good life. He had led a lazy existence with Gwen fawning over him.

Gwen had adored him, thinking herself lucky to get another man at her age. She had been no good between the sheets though he had made the most of it, taking possession of her whenever he felt like it and enjoying the way she gave in to any demand he might make. He would have liked to bed the girl, Llinos, with her small breasts and soft, young skin. But she had been too hoity-toity to return his enthusiasm and, when Gwen had died, Bert had been forced to flee from Swansea. Still, he was back now and if he could do Llinos Savage and that Indian husband of hers a mischief he would not hesitate. In the meantime he would sit by the fire and enjoy his drink and ponder on the time when he would have his revenge.

'Well, Eynon, how is the porcelain selling?' Llinos sat in the drawing room of Eynon's house and regarded her friend steadily. He had become a stronger person since the death of his father. It was as though the flood which had extinguished the life of Phillip Morton-Edwards had released something in Eynon: a new strength of purpose, the desire to do well in the world of china.

'The latest botanical designs have found favour with the London dealers,' he said easily. 'Though we still have a great number of breakages, over all the Tawe Pottery is doing very well. But then you know that, don't you, shrewd little businesswoman that you are.'

She put her head on one side in an uncharacteristically flirtatious gesture. 'I keep myself well informed, especially where my dearest, oldest friend is concerned. Tell me, have you met a lady-love yet?'

He leaned forward and took her hand in his. 'You are my lady-love, always were, always will be.'

'Seriously, Eynon, you must find a wife, settle down.'

'Why must I?'

'I don't like to think of you alone, that's why.'

He sighed. 'I am content to be as I am. You know I'm doing some china decorating of my own, now, don't you?'

'Of course, you always were a fine artist.'

'Ah, well, that's a matter of opinion.' He fell silent for a moment. His face in repose reflected a mood of sadness.

'What is it, Eynon, what's wrong?' Llinos grasped his hands more tightly. 'You aren't sick, are you?'

He shook his head. 'I'm fine but I'm afraid Mr Wright is sick. It's clear he will never work again.' He frowned. 'It's his lungs, I think the china dust has something to do with it, the poor man can hardly breathe.'

'But why should you think it's the china? Many of us have worked in the potteries and if what you say is correct we should all be sick.'

'Nothing is as simple as that, Llinos,' he said gently. 'Mr Wright is an old man, he might have a weaker constitution than most folk, there's no telling.'

'In any case you are going to shoulder the responsibility and pay for his keep for the rest of his life, is that it?'

Eynon nodded. 'You would do the same, you know you would.'

'I suppose so. Ah, here's the tea.' She

looked up at the maid. 'Thank you, Maura, put the tray down there.'

The girl did not obey, her eyes downcast, and Llinos knew she was not forgiven for her association with Binnie Dundee. It was as though Maura somehow blamed her for all the wrongs life had dealt her: the loss of her husband and even the tragic death of her child. In any event, Maura had never warmed to Llinos.

'I'll have to be getting home shortly,' Llinos said, aware that Maura was still awaiting instruction from Eynon, the tray balanced in her hands. On no account was she going to take orders from Llinos. Ah well, a few more minutes with Eynon and Llinos would return home, make sure Father was comfortable for the night.

'Please put down the tray, Maura, and thank you.' He turned towards Llinos. 'How is your father?' It was as if Eynon had picked up on her thoughts and she smiled.

'You are as bad as Joe, reading my mind like that. He's all right, there's no change in his condition, really.'

'Poor Lloyd, I'm so glad I passed my shares in the Savage Pottery back to him when I did.'

'That was a most generous gesture, Eynon, typical of your kindness.'

'Well, I only came into the pottery to help out, you know that. I don't need shares in your business, I have money enough of my own, more than enough.'

'Still, it was good of you and I know my father appreciated it.' She sighed and waited for Maura to leave the room before speaking again.

'My father is talking of dying,' she swallowed hard. 'He asked Joe to help him. Oh, Eynon, I'm so miserable about it all.'

Eynon nodded slowly. 'I'm so sorry, Llinos, but I think I can understand how Lloyd feels. He has suffered ever since he came back from the war. In spite of that, he has led a dignified life and he wishes his death to come easily and quickly. Who can blame him?'

'But it's asking too much of Joe, he can't do it.' She looked pleadingly at Eynon, begging him to understand but he shook his head.

'Why not? He has the knowledge and the means to ease your father out of his suffering. I can't believe that to be a bad thing.'

Llinos bit her lip, trying to hold back the tears; the trouble was, she half-agreed with Eynon. It wasn't fair that her father should be dragging through his last days in pain, unable to perform the simplest tasks for himself. And yet she wasn't willing for Joe to be the one to administer a fatal dose of medicine. She took a deep breath.

'Well, let's change the subject. I'm sorry, Eynon, I shouldn't be burdening you with all this.'

Eynon rose to his feet. 'Look, let me come up to the house with you. I'll go in and see Lloyd, talk to him. Perhaps in some way I can be of help.'

She was grateful. 'Will you come up tomorrow instead? He will be asleep by now. Tomorrow you might be able to take his mind off his suffering for a while,' she said huskily.

Unable to bear her pain, she rose, crossed to the window and stood looking out. The evening was dark with rain clouds covering the moon. She shivered, wishing for the spring, for the promise of fine days and sunshine, and perhaps for her father a release. But how could she think that, how could she wish him dead? She rubbed her eyes; she was confused, she was allowing the dullness of winter to dull her own mind. One thing she had determined on: while her father lived and breathed he would have the best care she could give him.

Eynon stood beside her and stared out into the night. 'Why not let Joe do it, Llinos?

It would be so much kinder.'

Llinos shook her head, too disturbed to speak. She couldn't ask it of him; it would be against his principles. But she could do it, a small voice inside her said, she could ask Joe how to prepare the medication and just administer an over-large dose.

When she returned home Joe was sitting in a chair bathed in firelight. His skin appeared red-gold, his hair had a sheen of blue-black. She smiled as he looked up at her.

'Eynon is still in love with you, you know that, don't you, Llinos?'

'Nonsense! We are old friends, that's all.'

'Come here.'

She knelt on the rug before him and rested her head on his knee. She could feel his hand gently caressing her neck and she closed her eyes as a wave of happiness washed over her. She was so fortunate, so blessed to have a husband like Joe. He leaned towards her and whispered in her ear.

'I want to take you to bed, Llinos.'

She rose in one swift movement. 'You don't have to ask twice.' She held out her hand, he took it and together they left the room.

CHAPTER

FIVE

The last weeks of winter had been bitter but now it was as though spring had suddenly burst forth. Daffodils cast splashes like sunlight on grassy verges and the birds were flying in pairs, calling sweetly on the warmer air. And Lloyd Savage still lingered against his will in a world that held only pain.

'Joe, get on with it, will you?' Lloyd heard the irritation in his voice and regretted it, knowing that without Joe's kindness he would be far worse off. The medication and the balm with which Joe covered the open ulcers on Lloyd's legs provided relief which the doctor's medicine did not.

Lloyd watched Joe's hands; strong, lean, brown-gold in the spring sunshine. He was a fine man, a man of many talents. He was wealthy in his own right and yet Lloyd could still find it within himself to wish Llinos had married someone more suitable.

Joe looked at him. The blue eyes were piercing, it was as if he knew exactly what Lloyd was thinking. Lloyd shook his head as if to clear it.

'Do you believe in an afterlife, Joe?'

Joe moved to the table and began to wash his hands in the basin. He took up a cloth and returned to the bedside before replying. 'You know I do.'

'Even with all the education your father provided you still believe in heathen ways?' Lloyd felt the urge to ruffle the other man's dignity.

'Are Christians heathens then?' Joe smiled. 'They believe as I do that there is a great source of light and power out there, that humans are spiritual beings and need to spend time in contemplation.'

'Do you have to be so sanctimonious?' Lloyd demanded. 'So damn superior all the time. Why have I no grandsons?' His abrupt change of tack should have discomfited Joe but the man merely smiled.

'The children will come. When the time is right, there will be grandchildren, have no fear about that.'

'But I will not live to see them.' Lloyd felt tears burn his eyes. His tone became conciliatory, pleading. 'Joe, I need to die, why can't you help me?'

'You know why.' Joe moved towards the window. 'I shall have some hot cordial sent to you. You can take the draught I prepared for you, then you will feel better.' He twitched the curtain aside and the sunlight slanted over the bed, pale but with the promise of sunnier weather to come.

'Soon, you will be able to sit outside. You can watch the flowers grow, see the buds come to life, listen to the birds sing. Life is sweet, don't wish it away before it's time.'

When Joe had gone, Lloyd leaned back against the pillows. His legs were easier now, that was good stuff Joe had applied even though it was green and evil-smelling.

When Meggie came in with his drink he took it gratefully, knowing that soon his spirits would rise, the pain would ebb to a dull ache. These times were almost happy, until the pain began to bite again. But the times of respite were becoming shorter, the pain more fierce.

Llinos came into the room, her dark hair hanging like a cloud around her shoulders. Her skin glowed, her eyes were bright. He had to admit that, being in love suited her.

'Why are you going around the place like a hoyden?' he demanded. 'Why haven't you tied up your hair like any other decent woman?'

'Oh hush, Father, stop being an old grouch, I'm not going anywhere so why should I dress up?'

He studied her figure, slim as ever beneath the high-waisted gown. Her breasts were pearly, fuller than they used to be but now she was a married woman, a fulfilled woman and he suddenly felt old and useless.

'I wish I was young again,' he said. 'I remember when I was first in love with your mother. Gwen was so beautiful she clear took my breath away. Why did she marry that man? Bert Cimla was a scoundrel by all accounts. Why are women so wrong in their choice of men and why did my wife lose faith in me?' He twitched the bedclothes in irritation. 'She should have known I would come home to her. I always did.'

Llinos shivered, her memories of Bert Cimla were all bad. 'Father, we had news of your death, remember?' She adjusted the blankets and Lloyd shook his head.

'She didn't wait long to find someone else, though, did she? I loved her so much. I wouldn't have gone to war but I believed it was my duty as a gentleman to fight that damned Napoleon.'

He heard his daughter sigh. Had he said all this before? His memory was not as sharp as it had been.

'Don't curse, Father!' She smiled and touched his cheek. 'Gentlemen do not give voice to oaths in the presence of ladies.'

He caught her hands. 'I do appreciate it you know.' He took a deep breath. 'I know you and Joe are well matched and I could not ask for a better son-in-law.'

She sat on the chair beside the bed still holding his hand. 'But?'

'But why didn't you marry Eynon Morton-Edwards? Then the two potteries would have become one. Your fortunes would be merged, your knowledge, your skills. The Savage Pottery would have been the finest in the whole of Britain.'

'It would not have been the Savage Pottery then, Father,' she said mildly. 'I'm sure Eynon would have wanted to keep the name of the Tawe Pottery, the way it had always been. In any case, I don't love Eynon. You know that.'

He thought about it and nodded. 'I expect you are right. Read to me, Llinos.'

'What shall I read, Father? Some poetry, perhaps?'

'No, read me something from the Bible. Find something comforting.'

He watched her move to the bookshelf and take down the worn leather Bible. She returned to her seat and balanced the Bible on her knee. He heard the rustle of pages as she searched and closed his eyes, feeling the hot sun through the window as though it was high summer.

'This is from the Epistle of James,

Father.' Llinos began to read. ' "Blessed is the man who endureth temptation, for when he is tried, he shall receive the crown of life, which the Lord hath promised to them that love him." '

Lloyd was beginning to drift into sleep, it was soothing listening to his daughter's voice. And the words she read seemed appropriate, he had endured the temptation to die for so very long. Wasn't he due now for his 'crown of life'? Was Joe merely comforting him when he encouraged him to wait for the spring buds, the sunshine, the promise of a few good weeks? Probably. More words drifted towards him but they were becoming distant, meaningless.

'Let every man be quick to hear, slow to speak, slow to wrath.'

Lloyd sighed and abandoned himself to the sweet, soft darkness.

Llinos woke abruptly. The warm sun and the soft breathing of her father had lulled her into sleep. She still held the Bible on her knee; how long she had been sitting there like that she had no idea. She became aware of Joe standing beside the bed, of the sheets drawn up over her father's face. She looked up at her husband and he nodded.

'Lloyd is dead.'

There were no tears to shed. She had wept enough when her father was alive. Llinos felt carved from rock; she did not want to think or feel, just to sit and stare at the white sheet which concealed the man who once was her father. A loving father who had lifted her high into the air, swinging the child towards the heavens, his eyes alight with love. The father who had laughed and played and then had gone away to war.

She took a deep breath. There were things to be done, she could not leave it all to Joe.

'We'll call the women in to see to my father,' she said. She handed Joe the Bible and moved slowly to the window, pulling the curtains across, closing out the sunshine.

'It must be Celia, Father would have wanted her.' Her voice sounded strange even to her own ears.

Joe held her close, smoothing back her hair. 'It was his time, he was ready. Come away now.' He led her into the sitting room and rang the bell. Meggie came at once, looked at Llinos, saw her distress and put her hand to her mouth.

'Send for Celia, Meggie,' Llinos said. 'My father is dead.'

'Oh my Lord!' Meggie began to wail, she

gripped her apron and twisted it between her fingers. 'He's dead, Captain Savage is dead!' She stared up at Joe, horror in her eyes. 'You have killed him with all that heathen muck! I hope you're satisfied!'

She flung open the door and rushed outside and Llinos could hear her screaming like a demented creature.

Llinos was sitting in a chair, her head in her hands, when Celia came into the room. The old woman rested her gnarled hand on Llinos's shoulder and made clucking noises.

'There, there, Llinos, it's for the best. You wouldn't want to see your father suffering any longer, would you?' She looked up at Joe and he nodded, leading the way to Lloyd's room. Slowly Llinos followed.

Celia stood beside the bed looking down at Lloyd Savage: owner of the pottery, rich, influential. Llinos heard her mumbling. 'All the money in the world won't help him now.'

After a moment, she glanced and waved Joe away. 'Leave me, this is my business. I will do whatever is necessary.' She paused. 'Oh, and you'd better shut that Meggie up, the girl is crying bloody murder to anyone who'll listen.'

Llinos allowed Joe to take her back to the drawing room. He knelt beside her and drew her head against his shoulder. Her tears came at last, shuddering through her small frame.

'Tears are healing, my love,' Joe said. 'The pain, the sorrow, the shock of death must be washed away before acceptance can begin.'

She heard him but she did not believe his words. Her pain and sorrow would never go away. There were still nights when she dreamed of her mother's death. Nights when she could not sleep for the injustice inflicted on her mother by Bert Cimla. The memory of her mother's last days would always haunt her. And now her father was gone from her too.

Joe held her for a long time and, at last, she sat away from him and dabbed at her eyes with a foolish piece of lace.

'I was reading to him, Joe. He was breathing so peacefully, he just closed his eyes and fell asleep. I let him die alone. How could I? When you woke me I looked at him and he was dead.' Tears welled again and rolled down her cheeks. Joe wiped them away with gentle fingers.

'You were with him, in the room with him. Your spirits were joined at the end, I'm sure about that. He didn't leave this world alone, believe me.'

'You always know just what to say, don't you?'

'Not always.'

Llinos looked up sharply, there was a commotion outside in the roadway; the sound of raised voices, ominous, threatening. Joe rose and moved to the door. A crowd had gathered: people of the row, men and women workers from the pottery. Watt elbowed his way through the people and entered the hallway.

'Is it true, Joe, is the captain dead?'

'It's true. Get rid of these people, Watt, their gossip and noise will upset Llinos and she's upset enough as it is.'

'There's the physician,' Watt said. 'He wants to see Mr Savage, shall I let him in?' Watt took charge, ordering the crowd to make way for Dr Jones.

Joe shook his head but stepped aside. 'It is too late for a physician, I've done what needed to be done.'

The doctor ignored him as he entered the house. Joe pointed the way to the room where Lloyd lay. Llinos heard Watt talking calmly to the people, telling them to return home or to their work.

Dr Jones looked at Joe oddly and suddenly Llinos was afraid. He walked away and the sound of a door closing abruptly echoed through the hall. The gesture was an indication of how little the doctor thought of her husband. Llinos saw Joe shrug and she knew what he must be thinking. Lloyd Savage was dead, there was nothing anyone could do about it.

'You can't stop people talking, Watt.' Lily was looking up at him. As she looked down at her hands, her slim neck bent forward, Watt felt his stomach contract with warmth and love and, if he admitted to it, with lust. They were sitting outside on the river bank. Lily's shawl had slipped from her shoulders revealing a pale area of flesh.

'But it's so daft!' he said, trying to concentrate on the conversation. 'Why should Joe want Lloyd dead?'

Lily shrugged. 'I don't know, perhaps he got fed up of looking after him. Perhaps he wanted the captain's money.'

'Joe has money enough of his own,' Watt said. 'He has lands and property just outside Monmouth. In any case, Joe could not hurt a fly.'

'Maybe, maybe not,' Lily said. She rose to her feet. 'I'd better get off home, my landlady is very strict about time. If I am not there when she serves supper I shall have to go without.' She smiled and he wanted to kiss the soft moist mouth turned up towards him. He almost leaned forward but Lily, as if sensing his intention, moved quickly away.

'I am a good girl, Watt,' she said in a low voice. 'I hope you realize that.'

'I do!' He fell into step beside her. 'I have the deepest respect for you. I wouldn't do anything to hurt or offend you.' He paused. 'Is it all right for me to walk you home?'

She smiled shyly. 'I suppose so.'

Watt felt ten feet tall as he walked towards the Strand with Lily at his side. One day, when they knew each other better, he would ask her to be his wife. She was beautiful, talented and good. He would love her for ever.

The boarding house was a tall, dour building but Lily's room was quite large and faced the street. It was on the first floor and the window jutted outwards, letting in light and air. Lily did not ask him inside.

'I'll see you tomorrow in work,' he said, hesitating on the landing. He felt awkward, not knowing how to take his leave of her, not wanting the closeness between them to end.

It was Lily who resolved the problem. She reached up on tiptoe and kissed his cheek. Then, with a flurry of skirts, she had gone, closing the door firmly against him.

Too restless to return home, Watt walked into Wind Street and stopped at the Swansea Inn. There some of the workers from the pottery usually gathered, men weary from the day's labour, seeking ease in a glass of ale and congenial company.

'Hey there, Watt, come and have a drink with me.' John Pendennis was sitting with a crowd of young men; he seemed to have made himself very much part of the community in the short time he had been in Swansea.

As Watt hesitated, old Ben the kiln man raised his hand in greeting. 'Watt, come here, I want to talk to you.'

Watt shrugged in John's direction and the man smiled good-naturedly. He was not one to be slighted easily, but then he had come from good stock; a rich and privileged background. John Pendennis might have fallen on hard times but he had the confidence that comes with breeding.

Watt made his way towards Ben and smiled down at the old man. Often they had shared a loaf when the going at the pottery had been hard.

'Hello there, Ben, you're looking well. How's the bone ache these days?'

Ben nodded to the wooden seat beside

him. 'Not so bad, not now the cold weather has relented a bit.' Ben looked at him closely. 'Old master is dead, then. Murdered, they say, by the Indian.'

Watt waved to the landlord, indicating he fetch two mugs of ale, giving himself time to think.

'That's nonsense,' he said at last. 'Captain Savage has been sick since the war, you know that, Ben.'

'Aye, but the doctor been up there to look at the corpse took some bottles away with him, looking for poison, so they say.'

Watt took the drinks from the landlord and drank deeply of the beer. If folks kept on gossiping what had begun as a burst of hysteria from one of the maids would become a fact in the minds of the townspeople.

'The captain will be laid to rest in the churchyard the day after tomorrow, then folks will forget all this rubbish.'

'Well, perhaps not,' Ben said. 'Seems Dr Jones has gone to some of the landowners. It might well be that the yeomanry will have something to say about all this. A constable could be brought in to sort things out.'

Watt felt a tingle of alarm begin to raise the hairs on his scalp. 'Who told you that, Ben?'

'The doctor's footman was in here earlier this evening, says the doc don't like the heathen giving a man of Captain Savage's standing foreign muck instead of proper potions.'

Watt drunk his ale in one gulp, threw some coins on the table and rose to his feet. He could not stay and listen to such talk. To pay attention to gossip was to give it substance.

'See you, Ben, look after yourself and don't believe too much in idle gossip.'

Watt strode out into the street and stared up at the sky. It had grown darker now, the clouds were gathering over the rooftops. He must get back to the pottery, talk to Llinos. What he would say he did not know, but somehow he must warn her that Joe might be in danger.

With one last look at the lighted windows behind him Watt set off towards Pottery Row and home.

Llinos stared along the dining table and in the mist from her unshed tears the candles in the silver holders shimmered and danced as if they had a life of their own.

'Joe,' she said at last, 'I know that this is a sad time for us, a time of mourning, but it's a time of hope for the future, too.'

He looked at her and put down the

damask napkin. His smile was warm and full of love.

'You are having our child.'

She shook her head in exasperation. 'Is there anything you don't know?'

He rose and came to her and kissed the back of her neck. 'I know my wife, my Firebird, very well indeed.'

'It seems you do.' She turned into his arms and felt his mouth on hers. She loved him so much and now she would give him the finest gift any woman could give her husband, a child. It was hard to believe, she, Llinos Mainwaring, was going to have a baby, Joe's baby. So absorbed was she in her moment of joy that she failed to notice the troubled look in Joe's eyes.

'If we have a boy, can we call him Joseph?' she asked.

'It would be a fine compromise. I suppose Wah-he-joe-tass-e-neen would be rather a mouthful for a small baby.' He spoke in a low voice, attempting a lightness of spirit which he did not feel.

She leaned forward in her chair. 'He will be brave and handsome like you, he will go to a good school to be educated and he will grow up with every advantage.'

'Except that his father is a half Indian.' For once Joe appeared uncertain and

Llinos was touched.

'He will be proud,' she said fiercely. 'We will take him to see the hills and plains and rivers of America. He will meet your mother's people and he will love them as I do.'

She sighed and looked down at her hands. 'But his birth is some months away. For now we are going to have to talk about the funeral.' She paused. 'I wish I'd told my father about the baby.'

'Don't worry, my love, as regards the funeral, I have attended to everything.'

She nodded gratefully. Joe was so kind, so thoughtful, she might have known he would spare her the distress of ordering a coffin, arranging transportation to the churchyard. She knew she could trust him to do everything with suitable dignity.

She sighed heavily, twisting her napkin and dropping it onto the table. 'I think I'll go to bed early, Joe, I feel a little tired.'

'You have eaten very little,' he said. 'But perhaps sleep will do you more good than food right now. I'll be with you shortly.'

As Llinos crossed the hall, she paused for a moment outside the room where her father lay. She pushed the door open and saw, in the shimmer of candlelight, the still form of Lloyd Savage: soldier, landowner, successful merchant. He was at peace. The lines of pain had eased from his face and his hair, freshly washed by Celia, still sparkled with droplets of water. He had been a handsome man once, no wonder her mother had fallen in love with him.

In the flickering light he seemed to be smiling, to be giving her his blessing. She leaned forward and the strong waft of rose water drifted from the bed. She glanced into the corner and shuddered as she saw the coffin, standing upright, waiting for her father to occupy it. From the house he would be carried to the cemetery looking over the hill and the sea. He would lie at peace. She placed her hand on her still flat stomach. Her son would carry the blood of Lloyd Savage. She would ask Joe if the name Savage could be given to the child.

'You will not be forgotten, Father, I promise you.'

She knelt and bent her head in prayer, saying the psalms she had learned as a child. The familiarity of the words comforted her. At last she rose and left the room, closing the door quietly behind her as if, even now, a sudden noise might disturb her father.

Upstairs, in the bedroom she shared with Joe, she began to undress. Meggie entered the room and bobbed a curtsy. Her eyes were downcast and red from crying.

'I'm sorry to disturb you, Mrs Mainwaring, but there's some people at the door. They're asking for Mr Mainwaring so I thought I'd best fetch you.'

'People, at this time of night? What people?' Llinos was frightened. What was going on?

'Well, there's the constable and some of the landowners. They say they have come to fetch your father's corpse, God rest his soul.' She made the sign of the cross. 'The constable said something about "death by poisoning".'

Llinos felt a coldness spread through her veins. Quickly she pulled a cloak over her shift and hurried from the room. In the hallway she could hear voices, loud and angry, and then, with a sigh of relief, she heard Joe's voice, calm as always.

'What is it, what's happened?' she demanded, standing on the stairs and looking down at the men. 'What do you mean by coming into my house at night like thieves?'

The constable moved forward. Llinos recognized him at once: he was the owner of one of the manufactories that stood on the river bank.

'Mr Jefferson, please explain what all this is about.' She appealed to him directly and descended the last of the stairs to stand at Joe's side.

'I'm sorry, Llinos — Mrs Mainwaring — the doctor is not satisfied that your father's death was a natural one.'

'How absurd!' Llinos said holding her cloak more closely around her. 'You all know he has been sick for a very long time.'

'That's true enough.' The constable looked around as if for support. It was Dr Jones who spoke.

'There have been accusations made, Llinos, please understand that they need to be looked into.'

'You are surely not giving credence to the silly stories about poison being administered to my father, are you, Doctor?'

He sighed heavily. 'Llinos, I'm sorry to tell you this but one of the potions I took away with me contained a substance that could, in excess, cause death.'

Joe raised his hand. 'And, Doctor, in moderation, the same substance eases pain, is that not the case?'

'Well, yes but we need to . . . to look at the body most closely to ascertain the amount of the substance in the organs. You do understand, don't you, Llinos?'

'No!' she said. 'I can not let you cut my father's body to pieces on a foolish superstition. I won't give my permission.'

The constable looked at her regretfully. 'I am afraid it is out of your control and mine. The order comes directly from Judge Cornwall.'

It was a nightmare. Llinos watched, her mouth dry, as her father was placed in the coffin and carried out of the front door and into the row. Doors were opened and lights from many candles spilled onto the cobbles as the coffin was lifted into the carriage. The rattle of wheels resounded in Llinos's head as Joe took her arm and led her back indoors, closing the door firmly behind them.

In the hallway he took her in his arms and held her close. She pressed her face against his broadness, knowing in her heart that he was in danger.

'Everything is going to be all right,' he said, his mouth against her hair. But, for once, the tone of confidence in his voice was absent.

CHAPTER

SIX

The morning light brought with it a sense of relief. Surely, with the rising of the sun, the events of the previous night would prove to be a bad dream. Llinos sat up in bed as Meggie drew the curtains open and it was then that she realized Joe was not beside her.

'Where is Mr Mainwaring?' Llinos knew her tone was sharp but her heart was beating fast and her mouth was dry with fear.

'He went out early, miss.'

'Did he say where he was going?'

'No, miss. Shall I bring you some tea, miss?'

Llinos was already slipping from under the blankets. 'No, thank you, Meggie, I shall come downstairs presently.'

She made a hasty toilet and for once wished she had asked the maid to lay out her clothes. She selected a darkly coloured dress at random and drew it over her shoulders. It was unsuitably thin for the time of year but it would have to do. Downstairs the house was held in a brooding silence, even the usual clatter of activity from the kitchen was hushed. But then, whatever else had happened, this was a house in mourning and the servants would respect that.

'I've taken the liberty of putting up a tray of tea and some toast for you, miss,' Meggie said.

'I couldn't eat a thing but a strong cup of tea will be nice.'

Meggie stood, head bowed, almost wringing her hands in agitation.

'I've got to talk to you, miss, this is all my fault.' She began to cry and Llinos led her into the dining room.

'Sit down, Meggie,' Llinos said. The girl looked up through reddened eyes. 'When I knew the captain was dead, I got a little mad. I ran into the street, I told everyone what I'd overheard Mr Mainwaring saying, you know about the captain wanting to die out of it and asking for help.'

'I see.' Llinos sighed heavily. She did see, someone had taken as gospel truth the hysteria of a maid and the appearance of the yeomanry on the doorstep was the result.

'I'm so sorry, miss, I didn't think, I was that upset.'

'It's all right, Meggie.' Llinos spoke woodenly, her thoughts flying beyond the confining walls of the house, trying to reach Joe wherever he was. 'Don't cry, everything is going to be all right.' She took a deep breath to try to steady her breathing.

'Listen, Meggie, when Mr Mainwaring left this morning, did he say where he was going?'

'No. I don't know. I couldn't look at him, miss, not after last night, not after them men took the captain away all because I blabbed.'

'Think, Meggie, please try to think. This is very important.'

Meggie squeezed her eyes together as if closing her eyelids would enable her to think more clearly. It seemed to work. The maid opened her eyes and looked at Llinos with a glow of triumph in them.

'I've remembered! He was going to see the judge. He was going to see Judge Cornwall, that's the name he said.'

'Good girl! Fetch my cloak, Meggie, and have the carriage brought around. I'll go to see Judge Cornwall myself.'

Meggie moved to do her bidding with alacrity, happy to do all she could to make amends. At the door she turned. 'Please, miss, while you're waiting, try to drink some tea. I think it will make you feel better.'

Llinos stared through the window, impatient to be outside in the lightness of the day. Everything had happened so quickly: her father's death, the baby and then this . . .

this ridiculous situation, the foolish accusations levelled at Joe on nothing more than the suspicion of a servant girl.

Prejudice was at the bottom of all this. The suspicion voiced against Joe was the deep-seated, ignorant suspicion of anything foreign. Anger flared through her. How dare they treat Joe as if he were a criminal?

Her defiance faded and she clasped her hands together. The suspicion that poison had killed her father could turn into certainty. No-one in Swansea understood the ways of the American Indians or their methods of healing. If the doctor and his lot thought they had a case against Joe, it would lead to Joe being imprisoned waiting a trial and that didn't bear thinking about.

She tried to imagine him in one of the small, dark rooms of the castle, surrounded by thieves and murderers, and shuddered. Joe was meant to be free, like the birds of the sky, a spirit flying above the rivers and mountains. He would die in prison. It could not happen, it must not happen.

She pulled her cloak around her shoulders with little care for her appearance. Now all her thoughts were with Joe.

She shivered, wondering what he was doing, what he was saying in his own defence. She felt tears burn against her lashes;

weak tears, tears that would do no-one any good. She brushed them away impatiently and, pulling back her hair, tied it loosely with a ribbon. As she hugged her cloak around her, suddenly she felt small, insignificant. How could she pit her weak strength against the might of the men of Swansea who wielded such influence and power? She tried to think clearly. Should she see a lawyer? Perhaps she needed advice right now, someone to point her in the right direction. To lead her to the people who knew the law.

She did not remember walking out through the front door. She felt the freshness of the breeze on her cheeks and the sting of tears was there, bringing her to her senses.

'What on earth is all this nonsense in the *Cambrian*?' Eynon folded the paper over and stared at the article headed, 'American-Indian suspected of murder.'

He looked up at the pink-faced man in clerical garb seated across the table from him. 'Have you seen this, Martin?'

'No, I haven't had a chance to read the paper. Anyway, what's important enough to distract me from my enjoyment of these devilled kidneys and hot bacon? I ask you!'

'It's Joe Mainwaring, they think he killed his father-in-law. It's absurd!'

'Ah, the husband of the beautiful Llinos is in trouble. I see you are still hopelessly in love with her, then?'

'Martin, I asked you to visit in the hope your company would prove a distraction. The last thing I intended was that you focus my mind on what I may not have.' Eynon threw the paper down on the table. 'In any case, whatever I feel for Llinos, I certainly don't want to see her husband falsely accused of anything as dreadful as murder.'

Father Martin bit into a round of toast, savouring the salty butter that melted on his tongue. He chewed in silence for a moment, his pale blue eyes staring out of the window as if trying to seek guidance in the light clouds.

'Are you sure the accusation is false?' he said at last.

'Look, I know Joe, he's a good man. He cared for Lloyd these past months as if he were a baby. No-one could do better for him than Joe did.'

'And he didn't believe in the mercy of a release from pain helped by his potions? Can you be sure about that?'

'I am sure.' Eynon spoke emphatically.

'I see. Well in that case, dear friend, go

and put in a word for the man. You are one of the richest men in Swansea so your word should carry more than a little weight.'

'You are right of course. You are always right. Why I befriend you at all, I don't know. After all, what are you? A poor servant of God and one who seems destined to be shuffled from one diocese to another.' Eynon was smiling.

'I could take offense, you know.' Martin dabbed his lips with a spotless napkin. 'But as you provide such good food and shelter I will not, at least not on this occasion.'

'Very wise.' Eynon pushed back his chair. 'Will you excuse me, Martin? I shall take your advice for once and go into town and find out what this nonsense is really all about.'

'Excuse you? I'm coming with you, dear friend. Would I allow you to walk into the lion's den without a man of God at your side?'

'You mean you fancy a look at the pretty cockle maidens selling their wares in the market, I suppose.'

'That too.' Martin heaved a great sigh of satisfaction and patted his rounded belly. 'That was a feast for a king, it will last me until luncheon — maybe.'

'And maybe not.' Eynon led the way out

of the dining room. 'Carriage or horseback?' he asked glancing over his shoulder.

'Oh the carriage, definitely. You couldn't expect a man to ride after such a feast could you?'

'Come along then, you sluggard, the carriage it is.'

It was an unexpectedly sunny morning. Towards the horizon the sea glinted as though lit with a thousand candles. The sandy bay, curving like an arm towards the headland of Mumbles, appeared almost white, ruffled into small scallops by the feet of many fishermen.

Eynon leaned back against the cracked leather of the seat and stared musingly through the window of the carriage. Llinos must be beside herself with fear, she had never been parted from Joe since the day they had married.

The closely built streets of the town were quiet, the dominating presence of the castle casting shadows into the Strand. Perhaps even now Joe was languishing behind the grey stone walls, imprisoned by those who trusted nothing that was unfamiliar. But no, events would not move that swiftly. Formalities would have to be observed, the presiding judge consulted. A meeting of the influential men of the town, including himself, would be arranged, and he had been given no notice of such a meeting taking place.

'Where shall we begin?' Martin said and placed a plump hand over his mouth to stifle a loud belch.

'I expect it would be wise to find out if Judge Cornwall is in town,' Eynon said. 'He usually lodges at the Castle Hotel with the frighteningly efficient Mrs Singleton.'

His driver, already primed, drew the carriage in at the entrance of the hotel and Eynon gestured for Martin to precede him.

'You first, dear friend,' Martin said apologetically. 'I fear I ate too much breakfast and at any moment now there will be something of a high and maybe noisy wind filling your carriage.'

Eynon shook his head and stepped out onto the roadway. His friend was incorrigible. He was also a rebel, holding some unorthodox views about the God he served. It was no wonder he was moved from church to church with some haste.

The judge, it transpired, was indeed in Swansea, having been summoned by the leading industrialists of the town. At this very moment, his clerk informed Eynon, the judge was in chambers and must not be disturbed.

'It seems you have been forestalled,' Martin whispered. 'I think this matter might well be a serious one.'

Eynon had no doubt that it was serious. The judge had been sent for, that was indication enough that matters had progressed beyond mere accusations and suspicions. The piece in the *Cambrian* had mentioned that Lloyd's body had been taken to the mortuary and was being examined for traces of poison. That the situation was serious was self-evident.

'We'd better take the carriage and get round to the chambers, try to see the judge there. At least we can find out what's going on,' Eynon said.

It took only a few minutes to travel the short distance from the Castle Hotel to the chamber buildings near the docks. Eynon led the way inside and stared above the head of the clerk at the desk.

'I wish to speak with Judge Cornwall,' he said in clipped tones. The man looked him up and down before politely asking him to take a seat. Eynon sat beside Martin and fumed with impatience. He wasn't used to being stalled by a mere clerk. After half an hour or so had passed with no sign of the judge appearing, Eynon rose and spoke to the man standing behind the desk.

'Is the judge free yet?'

The man looked up at him, his eyes narrowed. 'Judge Cornwall is still in consultation with several elders of the town, sir.'

'Damnation! Why did you not tell me this right away?'

'I am sorry, sir, I know nothing about the matter. I'm only trying to do my duty.'

Eynon returned to where Martin was sitting. 'Come on,' he said, 'I don't know what is going on but I intend to find out.' The clerk protested as Eynon strode along the corridor opening doors and peering through windows trying to locate the room where the meeting was being held. Once, he glanced through a high, outer window and the shadow of the castle fell over him like a warning of something ill-fated about to happen. He straightened his shoulders: nothing was going to happen to Llinos or to Joe, not if Eynon Morton-Edwards had any say in the matter . . .

'In the name of all that is holy what is happening?' Pearl's voice rang out raucously in the cool spring air and Watt shook his head.

'I wish I knew, Pearl, I wish I knew.'

She stood before him, her arms akimbo, hands resting on the shelf of her hips. Watt rubbed at his hair. 'I don't know any more than you do, Pearl. I'm sorry.'

'Well, did he kill the captain or didn't he? You must have some idea, an intelligent man like you.'

'I wasn't there when the captain's body was removed from the house, Pearl. I can only speculate the same as the rest of you.'

'Huh! A fine help you are. Well let's "speculate" then. Everyone thinks Mr Mainwaring put Mr Savage out of his misery and why not, I say?'

'Because it's against the law and, in any case, Joe wouldn't do it.'

'How do you know?' Pearl's jaw jutted forward. 'He's a nice enough fella but he's not one of us, is he?'

'He's half-white, half-American Indian, as well you know. That doesn't make him a killer.'

Pearl shook her head and sighed heavily. 'You are a young man, Watt, you don't understand pain and suffering and please God you never will.' She began to move away from him. Watt stopped her.

'Wait.' He caught her arm. 'I know Joe, it is not his way to harm or kill anything. I think it's against his religion or something.'

'He went to war, didn't he? Carried the captain halfway across them foreign lands from what I hear tell. If he loves Captain

Savage that much, wouldn't he put him out of his misery?'

'I understand how you feel, Pearl, but if we go about saying any such thing Joe will be in deep trouble.'

Pearl took a pipe out of the folds of her skirt. 'I'm not daft! I wouldn't "go about" saying anything to do with this pottery or the folks in it. Credit me with more sense, Watt.'

'Look, you're entitled to your opinion, Pearl, and you're a woman who knows when to keep her own counsel but I can't speak for everybody in the paint shed.'

Pearl nodded. 'I understand, Watt, and from now on I'll keep my mouth shut on the subject.'

Watt was deep in thought as he moved around the shed ostensibly checking the pottery that was being decorated. He was worried; the captain was dead but unable to rest. His body had been taken away to the mortuary and this morning at breakfast there had been no sign of Joe or Llinos. He wished he knew what was going on. Had Joe been taken before the magistrates? If he was being accused of murder Joe could be in serious trouble.

He walked outside into the sunshine and stared up at the sky. It was blue with scarcely a trace of cloud, a sky more suited to summer than early April.

'Watt!' He heard his name and turned. John Pendennis stood in the door of the office building, his forehead furrowed.

'What's going on around here?' John stepped out into the sunshine, his hair shining, his skin fresh with a healthy colour. He was a good-looking man all right, Watt thought a little resentfully.

'Don't ask me!' he said. 'I'm the last one to know what's happening.' He strode towards the gate, his hands thrust into his pockets. He needed to do something, but what could he do?

He felt a light touch on his arm and turned to see Lily staring up at him. Her smallness, the delicacy of her hands, touched a chord inside him. Still, he was in charge of the painting shed and she was taking time off from her work.

'Yes, Lily, what is it?'

She appeared confused. 'Well, nothing, I just wanted to see if you were all right.' She swallowed hard. 'I'm sorry, I can see I've overstepped the mark.' She turned away and he caught her arm, feeling the thinness of it beneath the cloth of her gown.

'Lily, wait.' He looked down at her. 'I'm not all right. I'm worried and sick at heart. I don't know what's going to happen to us all. I think that Llinos will go mad if anything happens to Joe.'

'No, Mrs Mainwaring is a strong lady,' Lily was trying to reassure him. 'She ran this place on her own when her mother died and her little more than a girl.'

'I know, but things are different now.' He led her a little away from the open door of the shed. 'She's not well.'

'Poor Mrs Mainwaring.'

'Look, Lily, don't talk to anyone about this. I've given the same advice to Pearl.'

She lay a hand for a moment against her small breasts. 'On my honour, no-one will hear anything from my lips.'

'Hey, Lily, what's going on here?' Pearl's voice rang stridently through the air. 'Chasing after Watt is not a very maidenly thing to do, is it? What would your mam say?'

The rich colour rose to Lily's cheeks. 'My mam's dead as you well know. In any case, I wasn't chasing . . .' her words died away. Watt intervened.

'Lily needed to talk to me. About work.' Watt's voice was hard. 'I know you are senior hand in the painting shed, Pearl, but I'll ask you not to try to usurp my authority.'

A smile broadened Pearl's face. Far from

being offended by Watt's tone, she seemed to derive some sort of satisfaction from it. 'Ah, little love birds, is it? I thought as much. Well why don't you let on that you're walking out together, save everyone,' she paused, '*speculating* about the two of you.'

Watt froze but only for a moment. A smile began at the corners of his mouth and spread to his eyes.

'You're jumping the gun as usual, Pearl, but it's a fine idea. What about it, Lily, will you allow me to come calling on you?' His glance took in a smiling Pearl. 'I assure you my intentions are strictly honourable.'

Lily looked down at her feet. Her face was scarlet and she was breathing rapidly. It was Pearl who broke the silence.

'Well, then, Lil, are you going to put the man out of his misery? Me too come to that!'

Lily took a deep breath and looked up for a moment into Watt's face. 'I would be honoured to have you as my gentleman caller.' Her voice was little more than a whisper.

Watt felt exultant. Lily had accepted him. He knew what he must do now: his place was here, keeping the pottery running. 'Right now, Pearl, shall we get back to work?' Watt's voice trembled, he was having great difficulty controlling the elation that was soaring through his blood. He ushered the women indoors, hoping that Pearl's sharp eyes had not detected the obvious signs of his arousal. Lily's demure shyness had excited him almost beyond endurance. He longed to sweep her into his arms, to kiss her rosy mouth, to touch the tiny globes of her breasts. He stopped his thoughts from travelling any further. He had work to do and it could well be that, for now and for some time to come, he would be in charge not just of the painting shed but of the whole of the Savage Pottery.

The office where Judge Cornwall sat was becoming more than a little crowded. The judge himself — a tall, ageing man with thick white hair and a moustache to match — was leaning back in his chair, trying to make sense of the case that had been placed before him. He shuffled his papers and then stared at the sea of faces watching him, waiting for his words of wisdom.

Llinos Mainwaring was seated across the desk, her eyes huge in her pale face. Beside her, standing with one hand on her shoulder, was her husband, his foreignness emphasized by the golden complexion and the fiercely dark hair that hung to his shoulders.

Judge Cornwall's glance moved to the constable. Beside him the doctor stood with several of the elite of the town's men of industry and, finally, the judge looked towards Morton-Edwards: influential and rich enough to buy the best defence in the legal world if he so chose.

It was a dilemma all right. The accused had come before the judge of his own free will; happy, it seemed, to answer any charge laid against him. He had been swiftly followed by his wife; a sweet-faced girl, articulate and intelligent but a mere woman when all was said and done. How much credence could be placed on the word of a woman in love?

The silence in the room lengthened. They were all waiting for him to make some decision. He coughed and shuffled his papers once more.

'So,' he turned to look directly at the constable, a man he knew well socially, a man of standing, a Christian gentleman, 'you say that a great deal of poison had been administered to Captain Savage, poison enough to bring about his demise?'

It was Dr Jones who replied.

'That is the case, Judge Cornwall. The poison in small doses would alleviate pain but large doses such as were administered to the captain would most certainly accumulate in the organs and cause death.'

'But, Judge, my father was a dying man, he was in terrible pain.' Llinos looked up at the doctor. 'Nothing else but Joe's medicines brought my father any relief.'

'The point is,' the constable said heavily, 'was the medicine administered in order to ease suffering or to bring about the untimely death of the captain? The latter seems to be the more likely, in my opinion.'

Judge Cornwall knew what he had to do. Even though his gut reaction was that the Indian was innocent, there was no way he could defend him against the formidable band of men who were his accusers. These men practically owned the whole of Swansea, one was even a member of parliament. He looked apologetically at Eynon Morton-Edwards, the man would have to do his worst. At this moment, he was on his own.

'This is my judgement,' he said heavily. 'The accused should be detained within the castle walls until someone can shed more light on the matter.' There, he thought, that was a fair compromise. Let Morton-Edwards call in some high-court lawyer from London to argue the case. All Judge Cornwall wanted was to wash his hands of the whole affair. Rather like Pontius Pilate, said a small voice inside his head. He rose from his chair and left the room, he was longing for a smoke of his pipe and a little relaxation. He was unaware that behind him, in the room he had left so abruptly, he had also left a woman, white-faced, racked with pains that signalled the end of her hopes and dreams.

SEVEN

The room was small, about twelve feet square by Joe's reckoning. It was also dark, the slit windows affording little light. There was nowhere to sit except the floor where layers of human excrement lay in various stages of decay. Quite clearly the place was never cleaned, not even sluiced down with water. It was a place that stank of despair.

From the moment Joe had been led into the room he had been aware of a dozen pairs of eyes watching him. He knew his good clothes were temptations to those whose coverings were mere rags. He also knew that his stature and his obvious physical strength were a deterrent to anyone planning an act of violence.

He moved from the doorway and walked around the small confines of his prison, noting the condition of some of his fellow inmates. One man lay moaning in pain, the sores on his body exacerbated by the friction of his involuntary movements against the dirty ground.

Joe removed his coat and rolled it beneath the emaciated figure so that the cloth afforded a little ease to the sick man. He felt someone at his shoulder and turned to see an old man staring up at him.

'My dear sir,' the voice was cultured, strangely at variance with the tattered appearance of the man, 'your act of generosity is in vain. As soon as you sleep, the coat will be stolen, offered to the jailer as a bribe for food.' He glanced down sadly. 'In any event, I fear the poor soul is about to depart the body of this wretched fellow. Why not take back your coat?'

Joe shook his head, moved to a corner where the ground appeared a little cleaner, and sat down, his legs crossed before him. The old man rested against the wall, his bony hand scratching at his tangled hair.

'Vermin,' he explained. 'The place is full of fleas and lice, not to mention cockroaches, but you get used to it. What are you in for? Debt, is it?'

Joe shook his head. 'Murder,' he said briefly. If he expected the man to recoil, he was mistaken.

'And are you guilty?'

'No, I am not.'

'Ah, I thought not.' He smiled thinly. 'No-one is in this place but in your case I believe you're speaking the truth.'

'And you, what have you done?' Joe asked.

'I am a debtor, alas.' The old man smiled, revealing gaps between his teeth. 'Samuel Marks, at your service.' He made a mocking half-bow. 'A Jew and not another one in the place. So you see, my friend, you and I are foreigners together.'

He seated himself with difficulty beside Joe, his thin knees protruding from the holes in his breeches. 'Have you family and friends, Mr . . . ?'

'I answer to Joe and yes, I have a wife. As to friends, I am not sure.' His eyes searched the older man's face. 'Unlike you, I look foreign; my skin, my hair, all speak of my mixed blood. Such an appearance does not auger well for a man accused of any crime, let alone murder.'

'And yet you speak like a gentleman,' Samuel Marks said easily.

'As do you.' Joe smiled. 'I don't think there is any law that says a half-American Indian and a Jew cannot be gentlemen.'

'I would say you have a point there, sir.' Samuel Marks eased his thin bones into another position, trying vainly to find some comfort on the hard, cold floor of the castle cell.

'I would like to put something to you,' Samuel said, hunching over his knees, his thin hands clasped together as though in prayer. Joe looked at him with a wry smile.

'You mean we can do deals in this fortress?' He gestured around him and Samuel nodded.

'We can make a mutually beneficial pact,' he said. 'I stay awake while you sleep and you stay awake while I sleep. That way we can protect each other.'

Joe nodded, knowing that he did not need protecting. He was used to sleeping with one eye open, used to feeling the enemy around him.

'How do you know you can trust me?'

Samuel smiled wryly. 'I used to think I was a good judge of character but even the most intuitive of us sometimes fail to sense danger.' He paused, regarding Joe steadily. 'But in your case, I'm going to go with my gut instinct.'

Joe acknowledged the man's words with a nod of his head. 'Someone close has betrayed you, then?'

'My son.' Samuel looked down at his lined hands. 'My own son. He cheated me, ran off with the proceeds of my business.' There was a hint of tears in his voice. 'He's illegitimate and he's never forgiven me for it. What brought you here, sir?' He looked directly at Joe.

'The ignorance and prejudice of a silly

girl,' Joe answered.

'Ah, women, the source of all man's woes.' Samuel sighed. 'My great sin was falling in love with a Gentile girl. I would have married her but she ran away from me, hid her condition. Then it was too late, she died in childbirth. Still, I brought up my son as best I could even though he is not a Jew; the children follow the mother's line, you see. Anyway, I'm rattling on like an old washerwoman here and you worse off than me by far. I am old, you are a young, lusty man; in here you will feel frustration burn you like hell fires.'

Joe did not reply. He leaned back against the dank stone and closed his eyes, seeing behind his lids a picture of Llinos, her dark hair flying, her arms held out to him. The pain of being separated from her would not be merely physical, it would go much deeper than that. He winced as he remembered his last sight of Llinos clutching her stomach, her eyes wide with fear.

He heard her voice then, as if she were in the miserable room with him. She was telling him to be brave, to be patient, she would set him free. He felt a breath against his cheek, the softness of her arms encircle him. She was here with him, her spirit joining with his, her love a shining sword that could sever any bonds. He felt the wind lift his hair, saw the softness of the contours of the hills. He watched the waves of the sea run into the shore; gently invading the golden sand, turning it almost amber.

'You need to sleep,' Samuel said quietly. 'I will watch and wait. You will be safe with me.'

Joe doubted it, though he was grateful for the man's kindness. He would rest and then he would reassess the events of the past weeks. That done, he could clear his mind of the debris of the past. Concentrate on getting out of here and starting his life anew.

The days passed in a slow succession of nightmare images. Fights broke out frequently; the men were hungry and thirsty and would kill for a slice of bread. Joe did not interfere. His own food, sent in by Llinos, he shared with Marks. No-one attempted to take it away from him. The set of his jaw and the light in his eye kept the others at bay.

'Joe.' Samuel Marks was sitting cross-legged, eating some stale crusts that he had saved from the previous day. 'I have a proposition to put to you.'

'Another one?' Joe smiled.

'You will be out of here soon, you have money, influence, you will be released soon and when you are . . .' Samuel paused. 'I want you to get me out of here.' He took a deep breath waiting for Joe to reply.

Joe looked at the old man for a long moment and nodded. It was an easy promise to make; he had talked through the dark hours of the night with the old man, he liked and trusted him. 'I will see to it.'

'I don't do my faith justice but I hate the shame of being thought a debtor. I will repay you, you know that.' A rat scurried to take the last crust from his hand and nibbled delicately at the bread, brazenly staring at Joe as though daring him to snatch away his prize. Joe smiled, even rats had to eat.

He allowed his mind to travel beyond the walls of the stinking prison to his homeland in America, to the vast plains and the soft breezes that caressed the hills. Soon, he would be free and then he would not forget the old man sleeping trustingly beside him.

London was a sprawling place with a winding river that cut through the land like a knife. Street vendors called their wares in a language which Eynon barely recognized as English.

He left the offices of William Grantley, eminent lawyer and advocate, and stepped into the street. Tonight he would rest in the comfortable accommodation he had found for himself on the outskirts of the town. To-morrow, Grantley, who had agreed to take up the task of defending Joe against the charge of murder, would travel with him to Wales.

Eynon looked around him, at the thick mist low over the buildings; the cluster of houses with smoking chimneys; the brightly lit tavern windows; the crowds thronging along the pavements. London, he decided, was a strange place. It was huge compared to Swansea and yet with a spirit of liveliness and gaiety about it that warmed the blood. He longed to be part of it.

He thought of his room in the inn, the emptiness, the silence, and decided to explore the unfamiliar streets rather than spend the evening alone. He turned into Gloucester Place. It was very different to the street of that name back home in Swansea. The roadway was more elegantly cobbled; wide steps led up to large, grand town houses with windows reflecting many lights. And yet Eynon sensed that those sturdy doors protected the inhabitants from any intrusion. It would not be here, in these respectable streets, that he would find con-viviality and companionship. He was wrong.

A carriage drew up alongside him and the lawyer he had spoken with only a short time ago opened the window and stared out at him. 'Going anywhere special?'

'Mr Grantley! I didn't expect to see you again so soon,' Eynon said cheerfully. 'I was just taking the air before returning to my lodgings.'

'My dear fellow, I can't leave you to explore London alone, allow me to offer you hospitality. Now that we have met up by some happy chance, won't you please accompany me to dinner with a little friend of mine?'

He smiled. 'A fine lady is Elizabeth, full of fun and ready for anything. They say she was once the King's mistress but of course that might simply be conjecture.' He winked meaningfully.

'It's very kind of you but I really couldn't impose.'

'Not at all, my dear fellow! My little lady friend loves nothing better than to meet new, young blood.' Grantley pushed open the door of the carriage. 'Come along, I won't take any refusal. I really think you should see a little bit of life before you return to your quiet abode in Wales.'

Eynon nodded and climbed aboard, sinking into the leather seat with a feeling that he was being coerced into something.

'That's the way,' Grantley said. 'I'm sure you will extend the same hospitality to me when I come to your fair town.'

The carriage jerked into movement, the whip cracking against the backs of the horses. Eynon relaxed, he might as well enjoy his evening, anything was better than sitting in his room alone.

Within a few minutes the carriage drew to a halt outside one of the tall, town houses with pillared porticoes. Eynon climbed onto the pavement and Grantley was quickly beside him. He mounted the steps and rang the bell. Even before the coach had pulled away, the front door swung open and the sound of laughter reached out like hands to draw the two men inside the warmth of the hallway.

Candles gleamed in high chandeliers, music rose from the drawing room and the waft of perfume was overwhelming. A pert maid took their outer clothes and a regal butler announced their arrival. Eynon followed Grantley into the crowded room and a glass of porter was put into his hand. At the piano a beautiful young woman was seated, her slim fingers running over the ivory keys. She glanced up and met his eye briefly. His heart moved within him at the darkness of her hair and the tilt of her chin that momentarily put him in mind of Llinos.

Eynon was aware of Grantley at his side accompanied by a lady who eyed Eynon as though he were a prize stud in a stable.

'Handsome,' she said, her head tilted on one side. She held out her hand and, bowing, he took it, noting the fine rings on the ageing fingers.

'Eynon Morton-Edwards, at your service,' he said.

'Ah, a gentleman to boot.' She smiled up at him in what she imagined was a seductive pose but she was old, at least forty years of age, as old as Eynon's mother would have been had she lived.

'Elizabeth,' she said, 'you are to call me Elizabeth, we do not stand on formality here.'

She led him to the chaise longue and sat beside him. He was now behind the pianist and he saw that her upswept hair was coming loose from its ribbons and curling sweetly on the nape of her neck.

'You are interested in little Annabel, I see,' Elizabeth sighed. Eynon felt his colour rise, he was not accustomed to such outspokenness. 'Don't blush, darling!' Elizabeth chided. 'Anyone would think you a virgin still. Well, you shall meet my daughter but remember, she is a respectable young lady. Annabel! We need to talk, darling.'

She gestured to a servant to refill Eynon's glass and moved towards the piano. She spoke to her daughter in low tones and once or twice the girl shook her head. Eynon watched the little scene with interest; it was clear to him that the young lady was as strong-willed as her mother. He smiled to himself; in that way, too, she was very like Llinos.

After a few moments, Annabel left the piano and came to sit beside Eynon. Elizabeth smiled encouragingly.

'Have fun, darlings. You young people are so hot-blooded these days, I'm sure you'll find something exciting to talk about.' She drifted away in a haze of perfume and, in a moment, was the centre of attention at the other side of the room. Eynon ran his finger around his collar.

'You are embarrassed by my mother's outspokenness.' Annabel's voice was soft, understanding, and Eynon turned to her with relief.

'I am, rather,' he said.

'Well, don't worry, she only eats a young man once a month.' She smiled revealing even teeth. He realized that she was very pretty but not at all like Llinos. He sank back against the cushions relaxing a little.

'There, have another drink,' Annabel said, 'enjoy yourself.'

'No,' he shook his head. 'No thank you, I will have to return to my lodgings soon or I'll be locked out.'

'We have plenty of rooms here, don't worry, we won't allow you to sleep on the streets. Are you in love, Mr Morton-Edwards, or is that too personal a question?'

'I am in love.' He smiled. 'And yes, it is personal. Please, you must call me Eynon.'

'Eynon, a strange name, indeed.' Annabel leaned against the cushions and the curve of her breast accidentally touched his arm. Eynon knew he was becoming aroused by her closeness. He sighed as he was handed another drink. 'Perhaps I should be leaving, it's getting late.'

'You don't like me, do you?' Annabel said softly. 'You don't find me attractive?'

He smiled. 'I might be in love but I am human enough to appreciate a beautiful woman when I see one.'

She blushed charmingly. 'Do you really think I'm beautiful? Mother tells me my nose is too large.'

Eynon took a deep drink from his glass. 'Your nose is perfect,' he said. There was a burst of laughter from the other side of the room and Eynon saw that Grantley was enjoying himself hugely. Elizabeth was hanging on his arm, looking up at him adoringly. A servant filled Eynon's glass to the brim and he took a sip of it, worried in case he spilt some on the sweet girl sitting next to him. His head was beginning to feel as though it was not part of him. Quite suddenly his spirits were high and he found the perfume wafting from Annabel's soft skin most seductive.

She looked up at him. 'Have you known many lady friends, Eynon?' she asked. 'I mean intimate friends, of course.'

'I have known several ladies.' He felt the heat of desire hit him, he longed to have a woman right now. He hoped his arousal did not show and yet, somehow, he was not embarrassed. He looked into the glowing red of his drink wondering if some secret ingredient was causing him to lose his inhibitions.

'The ladies I took to my bed were not exactly ladies, of course.' He surprised himself by saying this. 'Not, not like you, Annabel.'

'You are not married then?'

He shook his head. 'No, I'm not married.'

'And your lady, you do not make love to her?'

'No,' Eynon said sadly. 'She belongs to another man.'

She leaned closer to him and her perfume, subtle and fragrant, seemed to wind around him. 'Poor Eynon, so handsome, so wonderful, how could any woman refuse you?'

'You are very sweet,' he said, taking her hand and kissing the palm. 'And very desirable.'

'I am also very lonely, Eynon,' she whispered.

'Lonely, here?' he said in surprise. 'But it seems to me that London is full of life and colour.'

'It is. Mamma protects me, she keeps me away from handsome young men and introduces me only to the old ones who have plenty of money. She wants me to make a good marriage, you see.' She held her glass to the servant who refilled it at once. Annabel took some wine, rolling it around her mouth so that some of the ruby-red liquid clung to her lips. Suddenly Eynon bent forward and kissed her.

When he drew away, she smiled up at him. 'We must entertain each other, don't you think? Give each other comfort.'

'Of course,' Eynon said, excitement rising within him. He accepted a fresh drink from the maid hovering beside him.

'Mother does not like me to drink too much,' Annabel said. 'She believes it makes me silly and childish. Does it, Eynon, make me childish, I mean?'

She leaned against him and looked up into his eyes. 'You really *are* such a handsome man,' she said without waiting for an answer to her question. 'I think I am quite in love with you.'

Eynon drank quickly, flattered and aroused at the same time. 'I'm sure I could easily fall in love with you too, sweet lady.'

Eynon looked around him, his brain felt fuzzy but he was experiencing the most wonderful sense of euphoria. He could see Grantley, his face red, sliding his hand under the skirt of one of the 'ladies' who simply smiled and moved to accommodate him. Across the room, he saw that Elizabeth was clasped in an ardent embrace, the hand of the unknown man firmly grasping her breast. This was a strange place indeed: not quite a whorehouse, not quite the respectable home Eynon had been expecting.

He became aware that Annabel was sinking back against the cushions. Her eyes fluttered as he leaned closer to her.

'Annabel, are you all right?' His voice sounded strange, thick, high.

She lifted her head. 'I have drunk too much

wine. Will you help me to my room, Eynon?'

His need was urgent, he could hardly breathe he was so excited. 'Which way shall we go?'

'Here, through the French doors into the hall.' She leaned heavily on his arm and no-one seemed to notice their departure. Perhaps this was normal behaviour in this household, Eynon thought in confusion, and yet he was going to be alone with Elizabeth's sweet daughter, the one she was supposed to protect. He shook his head, he could not reason any more, he was too swayed by Annabel's nearness.

'Upstairs,' Annabel said, her voice faint. He grasped her around the waist, his thumb brushing the small, jutting breast and helped her up the curved staircase. 'There's my room.'

Eynon looked around him; the room was sumptuous by any standards. Satin quilts and pillowcases covered the large bed. Heavy drapes were drawn against the night and candles gleamed in shining holders.

'Help me over to the bed, please.' Annabel was swaying a little. Eynon's grip tightened as he helped her across what seemed an interminably long stretch of carpet. She sank onto the bed and his eyes fixed on her shapely legs as the hem of her skirt rose above her knees.

'Come on,' she said, 'help me unfasten my gown.'

He sat on the bed and with fumbling fingers undid the tiny buttons. The dress fell around her waist revealing her small, naked breasts and Eynon drew a quick breath. He reached out and touched her gently.

She twisted round to face him, her face flushed. 'Hold me, Eynon,' she said in a small voice. 'I need you so much.'

She rested her head in the hollow of his neck and he felt her flesh against his hands. Groaning, he moved away from her.

'I must go,' he said, his tongue thick, 'before we do something we'll regret.'

She fell back against the bed, her slippers falling from her feet. 'I want you, Eynon, I need you so much. Don't leave me, darling, please don't leave me.'

He slipped her dress from her and peeled down her stockings. Her skin was white as alabaster, smooth and tempting.

'Am I beautiful, Eynon?' she said breathlessly.

'You are very beautiful and you know it.'

'You know what I am, Eynon? I am a virgin in a houseful of harlots,' she said caressing his neck. 'I shall be married to an old man, that is what Mamma has planned and

I will obey her. But first I want to feel a young, strong man possess me. Is that wicked?' She ran her hands over his body, feeling the tension in him with a smile of pleasure.

'You see, you want me, you desire me. Please, Eynon, please . . .'

She pressed her mouth against his. She was soft, submissive, in his arms. Eynon kissed her with passion, the flame of need was too strong for him now. He could hold back no longer.

The first time he made love to her, she cried a little and he held her, crooning soft words of comfort.

'It will be better the next time, it won't hurt so much, you'll see.'

She clung to him, her face buried against his neck and he felt the tingle of protectiveness that he felt for all small creatures. It was not love but now, here in this room, in this strange town, it would suffice.

It was morning, the sun probing fingers of light into the room, light that was diffused by the drapes across the window. Eynon sat up, running his hand through his hair and beside him Annabel stirred, her naked arms touchingly thin and white in the early light. She looked up at him.

'Eynon!' she said softly and the sound was

like a caress. 'We made love last night!' She sat up biting her lip. 'How did it happen?' She took a deep breath. 'No need to answer, I know how it happened; my mamma put something in our drink.' Her head sank onto her breast and her hair swung forward. 'You didn't really want me, it was just that you could not help yourself. You would have loved any woman, even my mother.'

'That's not true.' Eynon was confused, his mouth was dry. Had he been drugged? It seemed more than likely. He became aware of Annabel's distress and put his arm around her. 'You are beautiful and desirable,' he said. 'I wanted you, can't you see that?'

'Make love to me again, just once, then.' She did not look at him but he could see by the pert lift of her breast and the pink of her nipple that she was aroused. It was no hardship to do as she wished. She was pliant but with the beginnings of passion that promised great things once she was a mature woman. It pained him to think of her in the arms of an old man, but if that was her fate he could not interfere. And, in all honesty, he did not want to.

As the light became warmer and the sun rose above the horizon, Annabel led him to the room in which he had been expected to sleep. At the door, she kissed him. 'I love you, Eynon Morton-Edwards, I will never forget you.' Before he could speak, she had turned and hurried back along the corridor.

Inside the bedroom, he closed the door and leaned against it for a moment, his eyes closed. She had been so sweet, his first virgin, and the poor dear girl believed she loved him. He ruffled the bedclothes for the sake of appearance and then moved to the dressing room and threw off his clothes. He washed in cold water from the tall jug and, all the while, his thoughts revolved around the events of the night before.

It was clear that however innocent Annabel might be, her mother Elizabeth was a woman of easy virtue. Eynon did not condemn her for it, a lady alone and unprotected must live by whatever means she could. Still, he could have wished for a better background for her daughter. Not that Annabel meant anything to him, he would return home and forget he ever met her. He knew that he desired her, he knew too that he would never love her; his love had been given to Llinos since the moment he had met her. No other woman would ever measure up to her.

At breakfast William Grantley beamed at Eynon over a huge platter of devilled kidneys and thick slices of ham. 'Did you sleep well? I trust you did, you retired particularly early for a visitor to our fair town.'

'I slept very well, thank you. You?' He lied smoothly but noted the lift of Grantley's eyebrow.

'I slept but little, dear fellow, but my wakefulness was very joyful I assure you!' He laughed out loud and wiped his mouth with a spotless napkin. 'Come along, take your fill from the dishes on the sideboard or ring for the servants to bring you something hot. No point in standing on ceremony, the ladies will still be abed for some time yet.'

He speared a steaming piece of fish onto his plate: his appetite for food, as well as for the ladies, seemed insatiable. 'Now,' he said leaning forward and lowering his voice, 'what did you really do last night? For I happen to know you were not in your room.'

Eynon leaned back in his chair and looked Grantley in the eye. 'I think you are mistaken, sir.'

Grantley clapped his hands together. 'A man of discretion, I like it.' He paused and chewed thoughtfully and after a moment removed a bone from between his teeth.

'But,' he said, 'I believe you spent the night deflowering little Annabel, did you not?'

Eynon was surprised at Grantley's outspokenness. He shifted uncomfortably in his chair, feeling exposed and guilty at the same time.

'Don't worry, dear Morton-Edwards, it was with Elizabeth's blessing, you see. Do you think you would have got away with it if my lady friend did not approve?'

Eynon was growing angry. 'Was last night a ploy to make me marry the girl?'

'No! Not at all!' Grantley said. 'I would not have allowed any such coercion, believe me. Elizabeth has promised Annabel to old Judge Messenger. He is rich and kindly, past his best if you know what I mean. But he needs an heir and will, perhaps, get one on a young, healthy girl like Annabel.'

Eynon wondered if he had been used as a stud, a means of supplying the heir to trick an old man. It occurred to him now that his meeting with Grantley had been more than just a coincidence.

'When is the wedding?' he asked, his voice dry. Grantley chewed another mouthful of fish before replying.

'First thing in the morning, dear chap. By then you will be on your way back home to Swansea. Well out of it.'

Eynon rose to his feet and moved to the window. 'Have I been used, Grantley?' He spoke softly, though anger was raging through him.

'Used? I don't know what you mean. You had a good night with a sweet virgin girl, a gift that any man would give his eye-teeth for. You did not resist her, did you, sir? What you did was without coercion, you can walk away without any responsibilities.' He paused and wiped his moustache carefully. 'I on the other hand, am required to leave a "little something" for my night of pleasure.'

Eynon could see he would get nowhere with this man. Grantley put forward an excellent case. The way he spoke indicated that Eynon had been favoured, not tricked. He was a damn good lawyer and that, after all, had been the reason Eynon had travelled to London.

He stared up at the sky, clouds were gathering, threatening rain. He wished suddenly that he was back home. He wanted to see the river that snaked its way to the sea, he wanted the comfort of the hills folding around him. London seemed an alien place. He returned to the table.

'I hope you act for me as well as you have acted for your lady friend,' he said dryly, and, in the absence of any reply from Grantley, Eynon began to eat his breakfast.

CHAPTER

EIGHT

Llinos stared through the window into the glow of an early summer day. She felt drained of all emotion, it was as though her world had come to an end. She ran her hands along the flat of her stomach: her child was gone, washed away in pain when Joe had been taken from her and put into prison. Tears misted her eyes; she knew she was being weak, women needed to be stoical, to take on life's hardships and deal with them. But how much more could she stand without losing her mind?

She rose abruptly and moved to the window but she saw nothing of the grass outside, or of the bottle kilns rearing from behind the wall. She need not even close her eyes to see Joe, shut away in a dank and dirty cell.

'Oh, God help us!' She covered her face with her hands, despair engulfing her. Joe, her beloved Joe, was used to the vast plains and towering hills of his birthplace. She longed to scream and cry and rail at the heavens; to call on the Great Spirit, in whom Joe believed so fervently, to bring him back to her.

The ringing of the large brass bell on the door echoed through the house. Visitors, she could not cope with visitors. Meggie must send them away. But she did not send them away. Instead Meggie announced the two men, her eyes wide with expectation.

'Mr Eynon Morton-Edwards and Mr Grantley come from London, Mrs Mainwaring.'

'All right, show them in, Meggie.' Llinos rubbed at her eyes with her fingertips and lifted her hand to her hair. She hoped she did not look too dishevelled for her first meeting with the great lawyer.

Eynon kissed her cheek and held her hands in his. 'I hope you're feeling better, Llinos, you've been through the mill, poor love.'

'Don't sympathize,' she said quickly. 'I'll only start crying again. Mr Grantley, how good of you to come all the way to Wales and at such short notice.'

The man bowed over her hand; his eyes were shrewd, they appeared to take in the entire room at a glance as though assessing the wealth and social position of its owner.

'Delighted to make your acquaintance, Mrs Mainwaring, and please, you are not to worry, I shall have your husband freed before another night has passed.'

'Won't you sit down?' Llinos sank into

her chair near the window, wondering at the man's confidence. Did he not realize that many of the stalwarts of the town were bent on keeping Joe in prison?

'Tell me all about it, Mrs Mainwaring.' He spoke in a low voice. 'Every last detail of the way your husband cared for your father. Remember, what you might deem unimportant might be just the key I am searching for to unlock the prison doors.'

'There's not a great deal to tell.' Llinos felt at a loss. 'Joe brought my father home from the wars. He was a hero, he had saved my father's life on more than one occasion, so why would he want him dead? To kill anything, even a spider, was to go against all Joe believes in.'

'Yes, yes, I understand.' Grantley settled back in his chair. 'Go on.'

Llinos sighed. 'Joe always mixed up a potion for my father. He gave it to him to ease the pain. The medicine from the doctor did nothing to help.' Her voice broke. 'I've seen my father crying bitterly. A man who had fought in the wars, who had built up a business, a man with the heart of a lion, crying because the pain was too much to bear. Only Joe had the means to take that pain away and now he's being punished for it.'

'This girl, the maid, the one who let us in?' He waited until Llinos nodded. 'She was the one to accuse your husband I believe? Now, what exactly did she hear?' Mr Grantley appeared relaxed but Llinos could see that his eyes were narrowed, his forehead furrowed.

She chose her words carefully, feeling as though she herself were on trial. 'That my father wanted Joe to help him die.' She rubbed her cheeks with her palms. 'Joe said that he had the means to do it. That was what Meggie heard.'

'Hmn!' Mr Grantley pushed his spectacles back into place. 'What happened then?'

'I was sharp with the girl; I told her she should knock before she entered the room but, as Joe pointed out, she was carrying a tray, she could hardly have knocked in the circumstances. I was anxious and so I was unreasonable, I suppose.'

'You knew your husband's words could be taken the wrong way?'

Llinos nodded. 'Yes, I did. After the maid had gone, I asked Joe outright would he ever consider doing what my father wanted. He said no, it was not in his faith to kill any living thing.'

'His faith, ah, yes, your husband was

brought up by American Indians, isn't that the case?'

'Joe was born out of wedlock to an American Indian and a white man,' Llinos said. 'That throws up all sorts of prejudices for a start. The fact that he used Indian lore to ease my father's pain caused even more problems. Dr Jones was angry because Joe's medicine worked better than his own.'

'I see.' A glimmer of a smile appeared on Mr Grantley's face. 'Mumbo-jumbo, that is what the uninformed would call such practices.'

'Joe was often referred to as a "half-breed",' Llinos said, her voice bitter. 'He's a better man than all of them, a kind and caring man.'

'And rich in his own right, is that correct? Far richer than your father.'

'Well, yes, but does that matter?' Llinos asked.

'It matters a great deal, dear Mrs Mainwaring. It makes any claims that greed was the motive seem somewhat foolish, don't you see?'

'Yes, I see,' Llinos said. 'But then some men are never satisfied with the money they have. They always want more.'

'Quite right but I shall prove that Mr Mainwaring was not that sort of man.'

148

'How will you do that?'

'I have my methods, dear lady. I am not known as one of London's most successful lawyers for nothing!'

Llinos sighed, but this time with relief. She was beginning to like and trust Mr Grantley: he assumed Joe to be innocent and that was a wonderful start.

Eynon had remained silent but now he leaned forward in his chair. 'Mr Grantley is staying with me so if there is anything you want to know or anything you want to say, just send one of the servants over for me.'

Llinos felt her mouth quivering. She had not cried properly for days but now the tears tumbled from her eyes and, embarrassed, she tried to wipe them away.

Eynon put his arm around her shoulders and Mr Grantley took her hands in his. 'I began by telling you not to worry, Mrs Mainwaring, and that is something I shall say to you again now — *do not worry!*' He smiled and dabbed at her cheeks with a huge white handkerchief. 'Your husband will be freed from prison and home again before you know it.'

John Pendennis sat in the snug corner of the Castle Inn and listened as Watt Bevan eulogized about the charms of the sweet

Lily. She was a pretty enough girl but limited in intelligence. Watt could do a lot better for himself, but then he was being led by what he had in his breeches, not by his brain.

John had failed to settle at the Savage Pottery. Even though working in an office was better by far than working at the quarry face. And he had done young Richard a favour too: the boy was happier, better fed and clothed than he had ever been. No, it was not the work or the conditions he objected to, it was the boredom of the daily routine.

He had heard Watt talk once about a chap called Binnie. The man had got out of it, shaken the dust of Swansea, of Britain, off his feet and made a new life for himself in America. That was a possibility that held a growing appeal for John. America was young and new; rich in minerals, with vast uncharted miles of land. A place of opportunity for a young man of intelligence.

'We should go to America, Watt,' he said, interrupting the flow of the other man's words. 'Seek our fortunes. Then, when we are rich, you could come home to your Lily.'

Watt was silent, it was clear the words had jolted him out of his obsession with the little pottery painter. 'You know, you might just have something there,' he said after a moment. 'If Binnie Dundee can do it, so can I.'

'Have you any money saved?' John asked pointedly. 'A passage to America would cost quite a bit.'

'I have a fair bit of money saved,' Watt said proudly. He smiled suddenly. 'After all, what is there to spend it on round here? What about you, how are you fixed?'

'Ah, there's the rub,' John said. 'I have only my few weeks' wages, otherwise I'm a pauper. I could always work my passage, I suppose.'

Watt laughed. 'I doubt it. You look and sound like a gentleman, your life would be hell living in the crew's quarters and you know it.'

'I still have my father's gold cuff links and studs and his gold watch and chain. I could sell those.' John was thinking aloud.

'No need of that,' Watt said. 'I have enough money for the both of us, at least to make a start.'

'I doubt that. In any case, I couldn't take your money!' John was touched but the last thing he wanted was to take advantage of the Welshman's good nature.

'No, listen!' Watt spoke eagerly. 'You

could talk to people, moneyed people, on an equal footing. You could get us a good start, a loan or something to start us up in business.'

'Hey! You're going too fast, what business?'

'Well, what we both know, the pottery business of course. You know the clay to choose and the stone; you know what it is to handle money, to put on a good front, all that sort of thing. I, on the other hand, know the potting business from the ground up, literally.' He smiled. 'My first job was picking up pieces of discarded clay pots and taking them to the bin at the bottom of the yard.'

The idea of going to America was growing in John's mind. He had made the suggestion casually, not expecting much response, but Watt's enthusiasm was inspiring. Another thing, Mrs Mainwaring might well encourage the trip if he suggested taking samples from the Savage Pottery with him. It was clear she was troubled about her husband but she still had enough control over her emotions to run the business in his absence.

'Right then, let's think seriously about this.' He leaned forward, elbows resting on his knees. 'The docks would be a good place to start.' He smiled. 'What do you know about shipping out of Swansea going deep sea?'

Watt shrugged. 'Not much but I can find out quick enough. I'll go down there first thing in the morning.'

'What about Lily?' John asked and Watt smiled. 'I'll marry her before I leave, later she can join me out there, when we are well set-up.'

John doubted the wisdom of Watt's plan. 'You might possibly meet an American lady to fall in love with. Have you thought of that?'

'Not a chance!' Watt said. 'I love Lily more than anything in the world and I want her for my wife.'

'Well, it's your funeral.' John lifted his hand for the landlord to bring another mug of beer. 'Let's have a final drink before we start back to the pottery.' He could not see the self-important Lily wanting the hardships of a voyage to a new country but it was just as well to keep his own counsel on that.

John sank against the wooden seat, his head full of plans. America, the great new country, beckoned to him. Nothing could be as bad as staying in Britain wasting his talents, his education. He would make more of his life than his father had ever done. John Pendennis had no intention of ending up a pauper. He looked across at his workmate. Watt was a good chap, sound and honest, but perhaps lacking in enterprise. Still, John had enough initiative for both of them.

'Come on, Lily, just one little kiss can't hurt anyone, can it?' Watt threw a stone into the river and watched the swirling circles it made as it sank out of sight. He knew he sounded petty; his proposal had not received the wholehearted reception he had anticipated. Indeed, Lily had demurred, saying she was too young to consider marrying anyone just now.

'Why won't you marry me, Lil?' he asked, suddenly humble. 'You know I love you, I'll make you a good husband and, when I come back from America, we'll be very rich.'

'I don't want a husband who is miles away across the sea, Watt.' Lily spoke in a low voice but there was a mutinous expression on her face. 'And as for a "little kiss" not hurting anyone, it's what it leads to is the problem.'

This was a side of Lily he had never seen. She was alarmingly prudish. At first this had thrilled him, he had taken it as a sign of her chastity, but now they were walking out together she could at least show a little warmth. Was she a cold woman, would their marriage be restricted to a quick coupling when Lily chose to do her duty? He had heard of such things many times, working as he did with men in the pottery.

'Why are you looking at me like that?' Lily demanded and Watt leaned forward and pressed his mouth to hers.

'Don't!' she drew away sharply. 'I don't want you to kiss me. Not here in the fields like a hussy.'

Watt was stung to anger. 'Anyone would think you were a high-born lady, not a girl from the orphanage,' he said.

She rounded on him. 'And why was I there, tell me that, Watt Bevan?' She scrambled to her feet. 'It was because my mother didn't have the sense to say no to a man like you who only wanted to satisfy his lust!'

She spun away from him, her skirts flying, and disappeared between the trees. Watt felt the colour burn in his face; she was right, it was lust that was prodding him with pointed barbs, not love. He felt the hardness in his groin and felt that he would go mad if he failed to find release for his feelings.

He thought of Pearl, rounded and willing, bawdy and smelling of sweet grasses. Then he was on his feet, ashamed of the immoral longings he had to bed a married woman who was twice his age. Still, if she should come along now and offer herself he would be too out of control to refuse her. Pearl did not come along and soon Watt began to retrace his steps, heading for the pottery.

Well, damn Pearl, damn Lily and all women. He, Watt Bevan, would go to America, seek his fortune and then the women would want him soon enough.

'So, Judge Cornwall, you will release the prisoner into my keeping?' Grantley concealed a smile: that the judge was confused by the high-sounding legal phrases and the pompous manner of a lawyer from London was all to the good.

'I suppose I have no option, not the way you have put the case.' He paused. 'You believe it to be illegal to keep a rich and educated man in jail without positive proof of his guilt then?'

'I most certainly do.' Grantley paused, enjoying himself hugely. 'Tell me, when did you last have a man who was well-educated and wealthy into the bargain locked up in the castle without even the benefit of a proper trial?'

The judge frowned. 'I can't think of one, sir, not right at this moment.' He smiled suddenly, showing an unexpected flash of humour. 'Nor do I remember a lawyer who talked in riddles and who I felt had tricked me into agreeing with him.'

'Best be on the safe side then.' Grantley winked at the judge. 'So that no slur can taint your good name.'

Judge Cornwall rose to his feet. 'Here,' he held out a sheet of paper, 'take this to the jail and the prisoner will be released to you. But,' his voice held a warning, 'if the man should abscond, it is you who will be held responsible.'

'I accept the responsibility with every confidence in the honesty of Joe Mainwaring,' Grantley said easily. He was not sure at all, but being a lawyer was all about being able to bluff others.

In less than an hour Grantley was seated in the Mainwaring carriage alongside the man accused of murder. He studied Joe covertly, his clothing was crumpled and yet, apart from that, he appeared respectably turned out. His hair, though unfashionably long, was tied back and his high-boned face was clean. The man wore an air of calm which was surprising in the circumstances.

'Have you made up your mind about me?' Joe's voice was cultured and that was a shock. If Grantley had been sitting there with his eyes closed he would have imagined himself to be beside a high-born English gentleman.

'My father was a gentleman.' Joe had an unnerving way of reading his mind. 'I am a bastard,' Joe continued, 'but a very well educated and very privileged bastard.' There was a smile in his voice.

Grantley turned and looked him full in the face. 'You are a strange man, indeed,' he said. 'You have the colour and appearance of a foreigner, the mind of an educated man and you're a mystic to boot; a powerful combination. And to answer your question, I have made up my mind about you. I believe you incapable of killing a man you had grown to love.'

'Even though the man's death might be a merciful release?'

'Even then.' Grantley smiled. 'Is not the taking of life against all you believe in?'

'It is,' Joe said. 'But then the influential men of the town would not believe me when I told them that.'

'We shall change their minds, never fear,' Grantley said. 'For now we must get you home to your wife.'

The night was soft and dark with a plethora of stars gilding the heavens. Llinos was wide awake, lying close to her husband's side. He was home, and her heart was bursting with joy. She could breathe in his scent, touch his silken hair, lay her hand on his chest and feel the rhythm of his heartbeat.

Love washed through her like a tide. Passion had been spent in the frantic joy of their reunion, now what was left was the glow of tenderness he always created in her.

'You can't sleep,' Joe said turning over to face her. 'Neither can I.'

Llinos looked at him in the silver light from the window and saw his beloved face, thinner now, his cheekbones more prominent. 'I don't want to sleep,' she whispered. 'I want to stay awake to drink you in, to assure myself that you are really here with me.'

He slid his arm beneath her and pulled her close to him. His heart beat against hers and her breasts tingled with reawakened desire. He kissed her hair, her eyelids, her mouth, and then his lips moved to her neck.

She was ready when he came to her, his body one with her own. Their rhythm echoed the seas, the grasses, the breezes that rustled the leaves in the trees. Her mind flew from her singing flesh and became elevated to a plane where there were only sensations of joy and love and passion. And, perhaps, a small voice whispered in her head, tonight, on this wonderful night of re-union, another child might be conceived.

In the morning she woke to the sun and turned immediately to look at her husband lying beside her. He touched her hair.

'I'm still here, my little Firebird.' He smiled, his teeth very white against his golden skin. He kissed her once and then rose from the bed and stood in the morning sunshine; tall, majestic, a man possessed of such beauty that Llinos felt breathless at the sight of him.

He disappeared into the dressing room just as there was a knock on the door. Meggie entered with the breakfast tray and Llinos sat up against the pillows.

'A messenger has called from Mr Mor-ton-Edwards to say he will be here with the lawyer man at nine-thirty sharp.' Meggie averted her eyes from the crumpled bed and placed the tray on the table.

'Thank you, Meggie.' Llinos bit back a sigh. The magic of the night was past and the business of the day was about to begin.

CHAPTER

NINE

Now that Joe was home again, Llinos felt she could take charge of her life and remember that she was the owner of the Savage Pottery. The first thing she did on resuming work was to appoint Lily as chief painter, much to the indignation of some of the older women.

'But, Mrs Mainwaring, I've been here ever since the pottery opened.' Pearl was flushed, her meaty arms folded across her breasts. 'Well, except for the time when your dad was missing.'

'You are a very good artist, Pearl.' Llinos smiled. 'But you have responsibilities at home. If one of the children fell sick or if your husband had one of his "turns" you would need time off, wouldn't you?'

'That's true and good you are about it I must say, but all the same . . .' Her voice trailed away. She knew as well as Llinos how many times her husband had been too drunk to get out of his bed and she had been forced to take care of him.

'But, as a mark of respect for your work and your seniority, Pearl, I intend to make you second in command to Watt. If he's

161

busy, or off work, you will be in charge of the painting shed.' The idea of such a post had only just entered Llinos's head. It would be an honorary one; Watt was reliable to a fault, he was never off work. But she was rewarded with a huge smile from Pearl.

'I'd be good at that, Mrs Mainwaring,' Pearl said. 'I was always good at bossing folks around.'

Little did Llinos realize how quickly Pearl would be elevated to the promised position. Later in the evening, as Llinos and Joe, supper finished, were sitting together in the garden enjoying the scents of the flowers and the singing of the birds, Watt, accompanied by the Cornishman John Pendennis, asked to speak to her.

'Bring the visitors out here, Meggie.' It was Joe who gave the order and the maid ducked her head, avoiding his eyes. She felt that she had done him an injustice and was ashamed of herself.

'Sorry to bother you in the evening, Llinos.' Watt twisted his hat in his hand. 'But it would not be a good idea to discuss my plans with the rest of the paint shed looking on.'

Joe looked at Llinos and then gestured for the visitors to take a seat. 'Plans, Watt?' he said quietly.

Watt smiled. 'John and I have decided to go seek our fortunes in America,' he said. 'I will be sorry to leave you, Llinos, we have been together since we were children. We've seen hard times, painful times, but now I feel the need to stretch my wings, to be independent.'

Llinos felt that John Pendennis had more to do with the decision than Watt's wish to be independent.

Joe leaned back in his seat. 'Well, America is a wonderful country, I can attest to that personally. In fact I have had plans for setting up a business there myself.'

'Joe!' Llinos said, suddenly trembling. 'You can't mean to go away?'

'Of course not!' He rested his hand on her arm. 'No, I won't go myself but I have been thinking about appointing someone to oversee the project for me.' He smiled. 'Who better than Watt? He has the necessary enthusiasm and know-how. And the wish to travel. What's more he's loyal so I don't feel I need look further.'

Joe took her hand and Llinos felt his fingers close, warm and secure, around her own. She wanted to hold him, to touch his hair, to kiss his sensuous mouth. The thought of being parted from him again had unnerved her. She squared her shoulders and turned to Watt.

'If my husband intends to back you, you can be sure of success, Watt. You too, John.'

John Pendennis spoke for the first time. 'You have known Watt for a long time, you trust him, but why should you trust me?'

It was Joe who replied. 'I follow my instincts,' he said. 'And my instincts tell me you are an honourable man.' He paused. 'What if I were to fund your trip, pay for you to find lodgings and give you time to search for a site for a new pottery? For your part you will be responsible for exploring the area, I don't want to throw money away on a business which is not viable.'

'So you mean we would look out for competition?' John said. 'Choose a place that is busy and thriving but not one which already supports a pottery.'

Joe smiled. 'I already have a site in mind; somewhere near Albany or West Troy would be a good place to start looking.' He paused to note the reaction of the men before continuing. 'With your charm, John, and Watt's experience in the potting business, I would expect you to do well. But there's no need to rush into anything. If you do decide to work in America, look around you, see what sort of opportunities are open to you. Providing you explore the land I have in mind, that's all I require. You would be free then to do some searching around on your own account; find out what sort of positions might be open to you.' He rose to his feet, indicating that the meeting was over.

'If you decide to work for me all well and good, but if not there will be no hard feelings. As I said, none of us need rush into anything.'

Llinos looked up at him. 'Hang on! I feel as if the ground has been cut from under my feet. You men are making all the decisions. What if I don't agree?'

Watt looked concerned but Joe, knowing her, smiled. Llinos went to Watt and hugged him. 'Of course you must go if you want to but I'm going to miss you so much.' She smiled suddenly. 'Oh, my Lord! Do you know what you've done? You've just made Pearl overseer at the paint shed.'

'You don't mean it?' Watt's eyes gleamed. 'Pearl in charge! She'll be a real dragon to work for! I'm so glad I won't be here to see it.'

'I gave her the post as a sop to her pride,' Llinos said. 'Pearl was angry because I appointed Lily chief painter. Well, it's a promise I will have to honour and take the consequences.'

'We'd better be going, leave you in

peace,' Watt said and John, taking the cue, followed Watt to the door. Once there he held out his hand to Joe and spoke in his soft Cornish voice. 'Thank you for having faith in us, Mr Mainwaring.' He looked at Llinos. 'Thank you too, Mrs Mainwaring. We'd better be going now, leave you in peace.' He smiled. 'In any case, Watt and I have a lot of planning to do.'

Llinos watched as the two men strode across the lawns and towards the drive. Everything was changing, the whole world was changing, and she had no power to halt it by one second. But the most important thing in her life was that Joe was here beside her.

She sighed and rested her head against his shoulder. 'I'm going to miss Watt,' she said. 'Sometimes I wish I could stop time from moving on.'

Joe turned her face up to his. 'He won't be going just yet. In any case, he's growing up into a fine man. He needs to explore the world, to learn what it is he really wants from life.'

'And you in your generosity are giving him that chance.' She pulled his face down and kissed him.

'Come on, wife!' He drew her to her feet. 'You have duties to perform that just can't wait.'

Laughing, Llinos ran ahead of him. She knew that he wanted her and already her blood was on fire.

'Well, Lily, don't just remain there in silence, won't you give me an answer?' They were walking along the river bank of the swiftly flowing Tawe. Grasses waved mysteriously beneath the water and small whirlpools were set up by inquisitive fish rising to the surface. Watt stared into the young girl's face: her beauty was flawless, her eyes large and perfect, her lashes sweeping her cheeks. She was like a goddess, her figure slim and yet shapely, her hands — those talented hands — small and feminine.

'I can't go to America with you, Watt, don't be silly.'

'What is silly about it, tell me?' He was angry, he had expected Lily to be delighted when he suggested they marry as soon as possible and travel abroad as husband and wife. 'You turned me down last time I asked you because you didn't want to be separated from me. Well, come with me, then, that's what I'm saying. It's no longer a risky venture. Joe is funding the trip and I have enough money to pay for your passage, look.' He dipped into his coat pocket and brought out a purse that held his savings. She was not impressed, she turned her face away.

'I don't want to come with you,' she said. 'There now, is that plain enough for you?' She stared at him, two spots of colour burning in her cheeks. Her tone softened. 'Look, I've been given promotion at the pottery, you know that. I can't leave now.'

'But, Lily, you would be in charge of things once we were settled in America. It would be almost as good as owning the pottery, can't you see that?'

She shook her head. 'No, Watt, no!' She sank down on the grass, her gown falling softly around her feet — pale and pink like the petals of a flower. He wanted to hold her and cherish her, to lay her back and pierce her softness. In that brief moment he knew how easy it could be to force her into submission. He picked up a stone and threw it into the water and watched the circles widening outwards towards the bank.

'And you won't wait for me?' He had no pride now, he just wanted Lily to agree to belong to him. He would take any crumbs of comfort she could offer.

'Yes, I'll wait for you, Watt,' she said, but she did not meet his eye and he knew, with a sinking feeling in the pit of his stomach, that she was lying. All at once the prospect of leaving his home, Lily and all that was familiar lost its lustre.

'Well, I won't go if you won't,' he said, and even to himself the words sounded childish and empty.

'Of course you'll go.' Lily's head was bent, her soft hair fell forward and he could see the innocent sweetness of white flesh at the nape of her neck. He knelt and kissed it and she spun away as if he had burnt her.

'Don't take liberties, Watt!' She was angry. He ignored her anger and took her face in his hands and pressed his mouth against hers. She struggled for a moment and then lay as if dead in his arms. There was no warming response, no hint of desire. With a cry of despair he released her.

'You are a cold, frigid woman!' he said, his fury concealing the fact that he was cut to the quick by her attitude.

'I am a good woman,' she said. 'And good women do not enjoy a man's attentions.'

He shook his head in disbelief. Poor Lily, poor misguided girl. Her past experiences had robbed her of all natural joy in being with a man. Reticence in a virgin was all well and good but surely any woman should warm to the man she loved?

'Llinos seems very happy when she's with Joe,' he said, attempting to reason with her. 'She's a lady of good birth and I have seen her look at her husband with a light of love in her eyes that would put the sun to shame.'

Lily's lip curled. 'Any lady who could go to bed with a foreigner is no lady at all, in my view.'

He could scarcely believe she was saying the words that fell spitefully, like darts of rain into the softness of the day. He knew then that Lily was never meant to be his wife. Perhaps one day, when she fell in love, she would change but now there was no moving her, she was all coldness and displeasure.

'And I thought you liked Llinos Mainwaring, respected her,' he said, shaking his head. 'You know something, Lily, I'm sorry for you.' He turned his back. 'Come on, I'll walk you back to your lodgings.' Then, he thought, he must hide away his money somewhere safe.

As he watched Lily walk through the door of the tall house with its blank windows and grimy facade, he felt as though he was watching her walk out of his life.

He turned and strode through the streets towards Wind Street and the Castle Hotel. A drink of beer might restore his lowered spirits. It was just as well he was going away, he thought, otherwise he would be tortured by seeing Lily day after day, desiring her, knowing that he would never have her. Even if she had agreed to marry him, even if she had come to his bed, she would never have given herself to him. Not the inner, secret self that was Lily.

Inside the smoky room of the Castle Hotel, the rise and fall of voices had a soporific effect on Watt. For once there was no-one there he knew and he was relieved, the last thing he wanted was to force a cheerfulness he did not feel.

The beer was rich, brown, strong and somewhat bitter. Its effect on Watt was an almost immediate lightening of his spirits. He realized he had eaten nothing since breakfast. Somehow, it did not seem to matter, nothing seemed to matter.

He drank more than usual and, through his fuddled thoughts, he dimly realized that he was attempting to drown his sorrows in a way he had always despised. It was weak and it was fruitless. All that would be gained was a headache, a sick stomach and in the morning the problem would still be there.

He tried to clear his thoughts: it was time he was getting back to Pottery Row. He rose to his feet and lurched towards the door.

'Hang on there, laddie!' A voice spoke close to his ear. 'You are in no fit state to go out into the night. Come on, there's a decent bed and shelter here. You won't make it home in your state.'

He looked into the face of the serving wench and nodded sagely. 'You are a good friend, Polly.' The words slurred into one as he put his arm around the girl. 'A good friend, indeed.'

She guided Watt out of the room and towards the stairs. They were dark and steep. Watt felt his head swimming. He found himself in a room; the candles were lit and the bed appeared welcoming. He fell across the quilted cover and smelled the clean scent of lavender.

'I'll pay you for the room,' he said, trying to find his pocket.

'No need for that now.' Polly's voice was soft. She was clean and fresh and for once she did not smell of the beer she served. 'The room is empty for tonight and you might as well sleep it off here as tramp the streets.'

Watt heard the door close and took a deep breath. His head was spinning but he felt as if he could conquer the world. He must have dozed because he opened his eyes to see Polly bending over him. She was wearing only a shift from which protruded small, rounded breasts. Her hair swung forward across her face as she bent over him.

'Shall I stay with you tonight?' she said in a whisper. He tried to sit up, attempting to focus his eyes.

'What?'

She slipped onto the bed beside him, her hands busy undoing his clothes. He lay back; it must be a dream, all a dream. Soft hands touched him intimately, he felt hot lips against his skin and he was aroused.

'You are so beautiful,' she whispered, 'so young, so handsome. I could fall in love with you, Watt Bevan.'

He wondered what she wanted with him but he did not wonder long. She sat astride him, her firm white legs encircling his hips and he groaned. It seemed she was going to use him like a stud and somehow the knowledge excited him. She moved above him; her scent was of rose water and summer flowers. She was young and beautiful in the flickering light of the candles. Her hair was soft and golden with a bright ribbon tangled in the curls. He gasped as she drew him to her, he couldn't resist the sweetness that was coursing through him. He was a young man and his hot blood cried out for release.

When it came, his release was like stars exploding in his blood. He gasped and thrashed for a few seconds more, not wishing the sensation to end. She lay beside him and touched his hair.

'Sleep now, go to sleep and rest.'

He turned over, feeling her throw the blankets over him. All he wanted now was sleep and forgetfulness. When he woke the bed beside him was empty. He sat up quickly, realizing he was naked. He slipped out of bed and pulled on his clothes. He wondered if last night had really happened. Had Polly seduced him or was it a dream? It was not a dream; when he pulled on his coat and felt in his pockets he found his money gone. He opened the curtains to search on the floor and moaned as a rainbow of flashing lights caught his eyes. The sunlight brought the sure knowledge that his savings were gone and that he would spend the day suffering for his indulgences of the previous night.

He rested a moment, fighting a feeling of nausea and then, gingerly, he opened the door. The smell of beer from downstairs made him gag but he forced himself to walk into the empty tavern.

'So you are still alive this morning, then?' The landlord was brushing sawdust across the floor. 'I can see you feel rough, what about a drink to ease you into the day?'

'Water, that's all I could drink.' He sank

down into a seat and closed his eyes as the early sunlight slanted in through the windows.

The landlord brought him a mug of water and set it down before him. 'Sleep well?' he asked, resuming his task of attending to the floor.

'That serving girl, Polly, where does she live?' Watt wiped the droplets of water from his lips, the coldness had the effect of clearing his head a little.

'Don't ask me.' The landlord grinned. 'So long as she comes in and does her work that's all I need to know.' Watt swallowed hard.

'You didn't send her up to . . . to . . .' As the words died away, the landlord laughed out loud.

'To service you, that's what you mean, isn't it? Rot my teeth! This is not a knocking shop, my laddie, this is a respectable tavern.'

Watt felt in his pockets, perhaps he had dreamed the whole episode, but there was no money. 'It's gone, all my money is gone, I just don't understand it.'

'Oh, go home, laddie, don't fret your life away. You lost the money or you made a mistake. I'm telling you there are no sluts allowed in my tavern.' Bob patted him on

175

the shoulder. 'So you lost a few shillings. You had a good time, didn't you? A few beers and the sap rising while you slept, what more could a man ask of life?' Still laughing, the man went outside and Watt stared around at the empty room.

On an impulse, he turned and retraced his footsteps up the stairs to the room at the end of the corridor. He pushed it open; the bed was still rumpled, the maid had not been in to clean. He pulled back the quilt and searched the bed but there was nothing, no purse, nothing. But wait, caught on the brass bedpost was a long golden hair, and there, on the wooden floor, lay a bright ribbon.

John Pendennis looked at Watt with a mixture of amusement and contempt: the man had lost his virginity and could not stop boasting about it. Well, who could blame him? It was an event in anyone's life, an event to remember. The fact that he had lost his purse into the bargain was an indication that he had been taken for a fool by some worthless doxy.

'But how can I find where she lives?' Watt was saying. John shifted his position, the sun was warm on the banks of the River Tawe, the river ran fast and free down towards the sea. Soon he would be sailing on the sea, on his way to make a new life in America.

'Forget her,' he said. 'You'll have enough to do when we go away. I've heard that there are more women than men in the new country; you can have your fill of them then.'

He looked consideringly at Watt: the man was strong and healthy enough, intelligent too. He spoke like a gentleman and yet his origins were obscure. John sighed, his own father might be a bankrupt but at least he was from good stock. But then how much would that count for when faced with the task of building up a business from scratch? He would need Watt, need his experience with all aspects of potting. In any case, he was growing to like the man, to feel that Watt had become a trusted friend. John had learned not to give his trust or friendship lightly.

'I would like to see her again,' Watt said, throwing a stone into the river. The ripples spread outwards towards the bank, growing wider before fading into the flow of the water.

'You'd like to experience the joys of lust again, that's what you mean, isn't it?' John said dryly.

'I suppose it's more than that,' Watt said. 'She seemed to really like me and to think me a fine stud.'

'Ah, a very potent combination: flattery and sex.' John moved a little closer to the river and looked into the depths, watching the fish darting in shoals towards an imagined feast as Watt threw another stone.

'You are quite a cynic, aren't you?' Watt observed.

'I suppose I am.' John looked up at the sky: clouds were beginning to gather, soon it would rain. 'Feel like another trip down to the Castle?' he said.

'Aye, why not, you never know, I might just fall lucky again.'

Watt followed as John began to walk downhill. Watt was the taller by an inch or two, though John himself was above average height. They were two fine, upstanding, talented young men, John thought with some satisfaction. They would do well in the new world.

Suddenly he was filled with a sense of hope and something like happiness. John Pendennis was on his way up in the world and, this time, he would see that no-one stopped him.

CHAPTER

TEN

Joe sat in the sunlit drawing room facing Grantley, studying his every move, his every expression. A great deal depended on the man's astuteness and deftness with words.

'So, Mr Mainwaring, is there anything you feel you should talk to me about?' Grantley was relaxed, resting easily against the comfortable chair, but there was an air of alertness about the man, a light of intelligence in his eyes. Joe liked what he saw.

'I believe I have told you everything that was said and done prior to my arrest,' Joe replied. 'But I will go over it again if you wish.'

'No.' Grantley shook his head. 'Though perhaps I could have samples of the medication you administered to Captain Savage?'

'I would have to make some up,' Joe said. 'The good Dr Jones took away all he could find. What do you want it for?' Joe leaned forward.

'I will have the stuff analysed.' Grantley smiled. 'I will also read all I can about the subject of herbal remedies, especially the ones used by you. I like to have as many facts at my fingertips as I can, that way I'm prepared for all eventualities.'

Joe could see the sense of that. 'I can write a list of the roots I used and how I distilled them. The main ingredient I took from poppy seeds before they were ripe. I added some pulped and strained lettuce roots and —'

Grantley held up his hand. 'Write it down. I prefer to ponder over these things rather than try to absorb everything at once.' He pressed his fingertips together. 'These bottles that you used to store the medication, what were they originally used for?'

'Simply potions of various kinds,' Joe said.

'You made sure the bottles were properly washed?'

Joe looked directly at the lawyer. 'I did not always oversee the washing of the bottles if that's what you mean.'

'So that task was left to the maids?'

Joe nodded slowly. 'Yes.'

'That is very interesting. What I need now is to learn precisely what the bottles were used for. Do you understand?'

'I understand perfectly,' Joe said and he did. What Grantley was intimating was that some residue of other substances in the bottles might have corrupted the medication.

Joe did not believe that was true but it was a possibility.

'That might just be our best defence.' Grantley raised his eyebrows. 'You see, you're not the only one who can read minds.' He paused. 'You do so from some kind of instinct; I do so from observation of the human condition.'

'You are very wise,' Joe said. Grantley inclined his head.

'Coming from you I take that as a great compliment.'

Llinos came into the room, her eyes anxious. Both men rose to their feet and Joe smiled at her, his eyes warm. She was his love, his Firebird, his dear wife. He wanted to be with her, his name must be cleared so that they would never be parted again.

'Don't look so worried, Llinos,' he said softly. 'Mr Grantley has everything under control.'

'I have indeed, Mrs Mainwaring. Now, as I am on my feet, I will take my leave of you. I have work to do.'

Llinos rang the bell for the maid to show the lawyer to the door. When they were alone, she moved into Joe's arms. 'Are you sure the lawyer knows what he's doing?'

'I'm sure.' As he kissed her he felt her heart pulsating against his chest. She was

181

like a tiny, frightened bird; more the night-ingale from which she took her name than the firebird he had met and married. She had suffered a great deal in the past months but Joe intended to see the smile return to her eyes and the lightness to her step.

'Trust him, Llinos,' he said gently. 'Grantley is a good man and a clever one. He will make sure that my innocence is proved.'

The maid entered the room, her eyes downcast. 'There's a man here to see Mr Mainwaring,' she said quietly.

'Who is it, Meggie?' Joe asked, releasing Llinos. The maid shook her head, refusing to look up at him. 'I dunno, sir, he's a stranger, a bit foreign if you ask me.'

'Did he give a name?'

'A Mr Marks, sir.'

'Show him in, I'll speak to him in the drawing room.' Joe turned to Llinos. 'It's the man I met in prison. On my release, I paid off his debts. The man didn't deserve to die in a hellhole like Swansea castle.'

He saw her flinch. 'Please, don't worry, everything is going to be all right, I'm sure of it.'

When Marks was shown into the drawing room, Joe hardly recognized the man. He was smartly dressed, his thin hair neatly combed. Joe took his hand and shook it warmly.

'Good to see you, Samuel. Take a seat and tell me what's been happening to you since you got out of prison.'

'Quite a lot, as it happens.' Samuel Marks seated himself and looked at Joe, his eyes damp. 'I thank you from the bottom of my shrivelled little heart for getting me out of that place.' He swallowed hard, his Adam's apple bobbing in his thin neck. 'And I've come here to repay you.'

'There's no need of that,' Joe said quickly. Samuel Marks held up his hand.

'I have no money but I do own land in America. It's wasteland, overgrown with weeds, but there is a great deal of it and I want you to have it.'

'Why didn't you use it to buy your way out of prison?' Joe asked, pouring a brandy and handing the glass to Marks.

'I did, in a way.'

Joe returned his smile. 'Did you?'

Samuel Marks inclined his head. 'If you'd not agreed so readily to get me out of there I was going to offer the land to the jailer as an inducement but I couldn't get hold of the deeds of ownership, not until I was free. I was not going to let my thief of a son get them, oh no! One day that land is going to be worth a lot of money; I feel it, deep in my blood.' He turned his palms upwards. 'But I'm old, I will not be here to see it. Still, you will and your family. So I've spent the days of my freedom sorting the legalities out.'

He took a folded parchment from his inside pocket. 'Here, Joe, it's all signed and sealed and properly copied by a notary. No-one, not even my son, Saul, could dispute your claim upon the land, even if he knew about it.'

Joe took the parchment reluctantly. 'Are you sure about this, Marks? I have money enough, more than I need.'

'The land is yours, you paid for it when you settled my debts.'

'What about you, how will you live?'

'Modestly, I fear.' He smiled. 'I will manage.'

Joe looked carefully at Samuel: in spite of his smart appearance, he was not a well man. There was a grey tinge to his skin and his eyes lacked lustre. The time he had spent in prison had taken its toll on him.

'My needs are few: a roof over my head; a bite to eat; jug of beer now and then and I'm a happy man. You must not worry about me, Joe, I will be all right.'

Joe put the parchment into his pocket. He would consider the matter more fully when he had time to discuss it with his wife. In the meantime it would be lacking in humanity to allow Samuel to sicken and perhaps die alone in some mean boarding house.

'Stay here with us, at least for the time being,' he said. 'We have plenty of rooms, as you can see. The house has been enlarged, we have more bedrooms than we can use.' He smiled down at his wife, knowing she would be kind to the old man. She nodded. 'Please stay, Mr Marks, we'd be happy to have you.'

Joe, seeing the uncertainty in the older man's face, pressed home his point. 'Let us at least offer you that small hospitality until you are better placed.'

Samuel Marks still hesitated. He twisted his thin fingers together and stared around him. Joe could see the longing in his eyes; the longing to be cared for, to be valued, to be with friends.

'You know my beliefs are different to yours,' Marks said. 'The Jewish faith is not the same as the Christian way of worship.'

'That makes no difference,' Joe said. 'Your beliefs are your own and whatever they are, I want you to stay.' He smiled suddenly. 'That's if you can put up with being under the same roof as a man accused of murder.'

Samuel nodded. 'In that case I'll be honoured to accept your hospitality, Joe. I will go to my lodgings, pick up my small bundle of possessions and return.'

He smiled like a pleased child and the smile transformed the thin face: his eyes were alight and his whole demeanour changed. He was a man who was not alone in the world because now he had found a friend.

Eynon looked down at the letter in his hand and swallowed hard. The writing was soft, feminine, just as the writer was. The paper was scented and the fragrance took him back to the house in London, to the bed he had shared with Annabel. He saw again her small white breasts, felt the taste of her nipple in his mouth. But that was all past, a momentary rush of lust satisfied by a young woman he scarcely knew. Reluctantly he unfolded the letter.

My dearest Eynon,
I am writing to you in desperation. My marriage was called off at the last moment because of the sudden illness of the groom who has, since then, passed away. Now I find myself in a shameful dilemma: I am with child by you. I have told no-one, not even my mother.
Please help me.
Annabel

Eynon allowed the paper to fall to the floor, a pulse beating swiftly in his throat. For a moment he felt only sheer panic; it was as though a noose was being tightened around his neck. He swallowed hard, trying to clear his thoughts. Would one night of passion bring about a pregnancy?

He walked to the window and stared out to the front of the house. Below him was the pottery, the kilns appeared to shimmer with heat in the sunlight. Beyond was the twisting River Tawe making its way swiftly to the sea.

'What the hell am I to do?' He thumped on the sill with his fist. The sun was hot through the window. Perhaps a walk in the fresh air would clear his mind.

The maid hurried to fetch his hat and stick, and Eynon strode away from the house, upwards towards the hills that surrounded the town. He was going to be a father, was the prospect so repugnant? No, but he would have wanted his son to be born to Llinos Savage. He would have wanted a child with her darkness of hair, her fine features, her beauty and strength. But Llinos was married now: she was Mrs Mainwaring. She was in love with her husband and she would never love another man the way she loved Joe.

He sank onto a grassy mound and stared outwards to the broad sweep of the bay. It was a clear day, a day of glorious sunshine. He was well and strong; he was young and rich; he had everything he wanted. Wouldn't it be normal to have a wife and child? But then how could he be sure the child was his? Annabel had been a virgin when he had made love to her, there was no doubt in his mind about that, but she had come to his bed so readily. What if later she had gone to the bed of another man just as eagerly?

He could not think straight, he would need to talk the matter over with someone who could see the problem clearly. He returned home by the same route and saw no-one on the way. The town was quiet, folk were at work or else at the market in the heart of Swansea. The hills were soft and velvet, folding around him the dreaming silence of the day.

Once home he sent for Maura. She had been in his service for several years and had been elevated to the position of housekeeper. Since the betrayal of her husband and the death of her child she had become introverted, morose even.

'Maura, come in and sit down.' She had tied her glorious red hair into a bun and put a cap over it. Her gown, even on such a fine summer day, was dark and shapeless. She was a young woman still but she might as well have been an old maid for all she cared about her appearance.

'I would prefer to stand, sir.' She had become so formal, so different to the young, spirited girl she had once been, that Eynon wondered at his judgement in choosing her as the one in whom to confide his problems.

'This is a personal matter, Maura,' he said. 'I want advice from a friend.'

She sat on the very edge of a chair watching without expression as Eynon picked up the letter that still lay where he had dropped it on the floor.

'Read this and tell me what you think, please.' He felt unsure, humble almost. Maura read the few words quickly and handed the letter back to him.

'Sure, and isn't that the oldest trick there is,' she said flatly.

'What? You think she's lying?'

'Definitely. You could be the father if you slept with the girl but then she was promised to another man, about to be married. Sure she's nothing but a whore!'

Her condemnation was harsh but Eynon felt she could be right. She was only voicing his own suspicions.

He sighed and rubbed his hand through his hair. 'What shall I do, Maura?'

'Burn the letter and forget it.' She looked at him shrewdly. 'That's what you want me to say, isn't it?'

'I suppose so.'

'You sure as God is in His heaven don't love this woman or you'd be hotfooting it to fetch her back here. A marriage without love is no marriage as I well know. You asked for my advice, now take it.' She rose to her feet. 'We need more linen, sir, the cupboard is getting low on pillowslips and bolster cases as well as sheets.' Maura was once more the efficient housekeeper.

'See to it then, Maura,' he said sharply. 'It's what I pay you for, isn't it?'

She left the room, her head high; a broken, betrayed woman, old before her time. Binnie Dundee had a lot to answer for, he had ruined the girl's life. Oh, he had done the honourable thing, he had married her, given their child his name, but a fat lot of good that did either of them. In the end Binnie had cleared off, left the country, gone abroad, unable to bear the ties of marriage to a woman he did not love. Was that the sort of future he would want or that Annabel would want come to that?

He poured himself a drink from the tray

on the highly polished sideboard. He would go into the garden, enjoy the sunshine and forget Annabel ever existed. If he wanted a wife, he could have his pick. The matrons of the town were constantly inviting him to soiréees, introducing him to their daughters. No, he did not want another man's cast-off. Slowly he tore the letter into little pieces and threw it through the window, watching the summer breeze take the pieces and scatter them to the four winds.

Binnie Dundee stood at the side of his wife's bed, holding her hand, staring down at her with such love that it threatened to burst from him. She had safely delivered another fine son; that was three in all.

Hortense smiled up at him, her rather plain face beautified by her happiness. 'What shall we call him, honey?' she asked. He touched her hair, it was damp from her exertions. He had watched her labour to bring forth their child, wished that he could take her pain. She was a strong, brave woman; a wife to be proud of.

Unbidden came the thought of Maura, her petulance, her continuous nagging. She was still his legal wife. He pushed the thought away into the recesses of his mind. No-one knew about Maura, no-one would ever know.

'What about Matthew?' he asked.

Hortense repeated the name several times. 'Yes, I like Matthew. He will be everything a man could want to be: upright and good and so handsome that the girls swoon at his feet.'

'Hey, don't go on so otherwise I will be jealous of my own son.'

'Silly boy.' Hortense touched his cheek. 'You know I can't see any other man but you. You dazzle my eyes, you fill my heart with love.'

Binnie felt the tears burn. His wife was rarely sentimental. It was not often that she told him of her love but, now, in the weariness that followed childbirth, she was soft, vulnerable.

'Let me sleep now,' she said, closing her eyes. 'I have worked hard today. Me and Matthew, we both need to rest.'

He kissed her and tucked the sheet around her even though the day was warm and a hot breeze drifted in through the window carrying with it the scent of roses.

'All right, I'll come in later when you feel a little better.'

Outside on the porch Dan McCabe sat with his wife, both of them in their best visiting clothes.

'Another fine boy then, Binnie, my lad,' Dan said. 'You planted the seeds well and I knew my girl would make some man a damn fine wife. You had the pick of the bunch all right. I only wish there were other suitors waiting around to take the two youngest girls off my hands. They'll be old maids if no-one asks for them soon.'

'You were right about Hortense,' Binnie said. 'She is the best wife any man could ask for and I've sired another son on her. What more could a man ask?'

'How is she feeling now?' her mother asked, brushing aside the men's self-congratulations. 'She tired?'

'I expect so!' Binnie said smiling. 'The boy is huge, a ten-pounder or I'm a Dutchman. We've decided to call him Matthew.'

'Ah, a good enough name coming as it does from the holy Bible,' Dan said, nodding his head in satisfaction. 'Goes well with Daniel and Jeremiah.' Dan was puffed with pride that his first-born grandson carried his name. As if on cue the two young children hurled themselves around the corner of the house whooping and calling, their voices sharp on the soft air.

'They're playing at chasing Indians again,' Dan said. 'Boys! Stop that will you!'

Dan's voice boomed out across the large garden and the children stopped their game abruptly.

Danny was three, a tall boy with corn-coloured hair and his brother Jerry was not yet two. He was the other side of the coin to his brother, dark and stocky, more like Binnie himself.

'We was only playing, Grandpa,' Danny protested. 'I was a soldier and Jerry was —'

'I know what you was playing,' Dan said. 'And I ain't havin' it, see? Them Indians belong here more than us, they are not animals to be chased from their homes and I want you to remember that.'

'All right, Grandpa,' Dan said good-naturedly. He found a spider and crouched down to examine it, his game forgotten.

'Where's the danged girl you employed to see to the boys?' Dan asked and Binnie shook his head.

'I don't know, Dan, I'll give her a shout.' Just then a young girl came around the side of the house carrying two mugs of cordial.

'Sorry, Mr Dundee,' she gasped. 'I was getting the boys a drink 'cos they was thirsty and they just ran away from me.'

'If you can't control them, Sandy, I must get someone who can,' Binnie said mildly. 'Now take the two of them indoors and wash their hands before they have their tea. And keep them quiet, their mother's trying to get some rest.'

The thin cry of a newborn baby drifted to where the three were sitting and Mrs McCabe rose immediately to go to her daughter.

Dan looked at Binnie. 'Like to get a beer?' He lumbered to his feet. 'This domesticity is all very well but I sure would like a change from it sometimes.'

The two men walked side by side, at ease with each other. Glancing at Dan, Binnie wondered briefly what the older man would think if he knew about Maura. Ah well, Wales was a long way away, far across the sea. Dan and, more importantly, Hortense would never know that Binnie Dundee was a bigamist.

'You're sure you don't mind Samuel Marks coming to stay, Llinos?' Joe said. She was sitting beside her husband, her hand in his.

Llinos smiled up at him. 'Of course I don't mind. But what on earth are you going to do with a parcel of land in America?'

'We will send Watt and John Pendennis out there to do a survey on it. The two of them want to go to America so this is the perfect opportunity. Let them find out for me what the land is worth and if it's a suitable place for founding a pottery.'

'It's really quite a coincidence, isn't it?' Llinos said softly. 'I mean who would have thought that you would be given land out there when you had already thought of founding a pottery in America?'

'Nothing is ever the coincidence it seems,' Joe said, smoothing her hair from her face. 'These things are all meant, all part of a plan.'

'A part of the Great Spirit's plan, you mean?'

'Mock you may, Llinos.' Joe pulled at her hair. 'One day you will have to agree with me that I am right.'

'Maybe.' Llinos leaned against his shoulder. 'Right now I'm just happy that you are safe here with me.' She sighed. 'I do wish that a date for the trial had been decided, the uncertainty is just awful.'

'Put it out of your mind, Llinos,' Joe said. 'Grantley is handling everything: he is a good man, a capable man, we couldn't ask for a better lawyer.'

'I know.' Llinos twisted around and cupped her husband's face in her hands. His blue eyes looked into hers and she saw the shadow behind them and shivered with apprehension. 'What is it?'

'Nothing, my darling, nothing at all. We are here together now, today. This moment is all we have, all anyone has. The future is never a certainty, not for anyone. Let's make the most of what we have.'

He kissed her mouth and she clung to him. She loved him so much, she could never bear to be without him. He was right, they must make the most of every moment together.

'Please, my darling husband, love me,' she said and, as his hand found her breast, she allowed feelings and sensations to replace the thoughts and fears that had been haunting her.

CHAPTER

ELEVEN

'I have to return to London for a week or two.' Grantley was sitting with Eynon Morton-Edwards in the grounds of his gracious home, beneath the trees that provided a welcome shade from the sun which was high now in the summer sky.

'Look, before you go, can I talk to you in confidence?' Eynon was leaning forward in his chair and from the look of his young face it was clear that something was worrying him.

'A lawyer knows when to keep his mouth shut,' Grantley said. 'What is it?'

'A few days ago I received a letter from Annabel.'

'Elizabeth's daughter? Why on earth is she writing to you, is the girl mad?' Grantley frowned, he had imagined that the night of passion Eynon had enjoyed was a stroke of luck for the young man but now he was not so sure. 'She did marry, did she not?' He saw Eynon shake his head.

'It seems her elderly suitor took sick and died.'

Grantley felt an unsuitable urge to laugh.

'How inconsiderate of him,' he said dryly. 'So what are you supposed to do about it?'

Eynon rose and thrust his hands into his pockets. He was a very handsome man, a little weak around the mouth perhaps, but with fine looks and an elegant build. It was strange he had not been caught in the web of some lady's machinations by now. His next words startled Grantley into giving the matter his full attention.

'She says she is expecting my child.'

'What tosh!' Grantley expressed his thoughts with unaccustomed frankness. 'One night of passion and she's with child; I just don't believe it.'

Eynon shook his head. 'I don't know a great deal about these things.' He smiled ruefully. 'I don't think I want to, either.'

'Then burn the letter,' Grantley said easily. 'While I am in London I will try to find out exactly what is going on.' He frowned; the last thing he wanted was for young Morton-Edwards to think he was party to a scheme to trap him into marriage. 'It could simply be a ploy to get a ring on the girl's finger; I wouldn't put anything past Elizabeth. That woman can smell money a mile off.'

'And yet,' Eynon said, 'I was the one to take Annabel's virginity. Perhaps I owe it to

199

her to meet and talk this over.'

'I would not countenance such a meeting,' Grantley said. 'Can't you see it would be tantamount to admitting guilt? No, dear boy, just leave it to me.' He smiled as he looked at Eynon, his brow furrowed, his hands thrust deep into the pockets of his summer jacket.

'Think of it this way, you might have been the first to sup the flower but how many might there have been since? Once tasted, the honey pot of love is hard to resist.'

The French windows were pushed open and Maura came to stand in respectful silence beside the two men.

Eynon looked up at her. 'Yes, Maura, what is it?'

'I'm sorry to intrude, sir.' Maura glanced uncertainly at Grantley and then her lack-lustre eyes returned to Eynon's face. 'There's a young lady and her mother here to see you. They have no appointment but they won't take no for an answer.'

'What name did the lady give?' It was Grantley who asked the question. Maura did not look at him again.

'It's a Mrs Elizabeth and her daughter Annabel, sir.'

'All right, Maura,' Eynon spoke before Grantley could intervene, 'show the ladies into the drawing room. I will be there in a moment.'

Grantley felt anger build within him. 'This is outrageous!' he said. 'How dare Elizabeth travel here and arrive at your door unannounced; it is most improper.'

'What shall I say to her?' Eynon brushed back his hair in a gesture that was almost feminine. Grantley looked at him closely: he had deflowered the pretty little Annabel without trouble. That was the problem with these artistic types, they never appeared to be very manly.

'Let me do the talking,' Grantley advised. 'You can just deal with the pleasantries but when the subject turns to Annabel's little problem, as it surely will, leave everything to me.'

Grantley followed Eynon into the house and squinted as, suddenly, the corners of the rooms seemed to be filled with shadows after the brightness of the garden. The hall smelled of flowers and beeswax and Grantley thought how wonderful it must be to live at the seaside and not be surrounded by the bustle of the London streets.

'Good day to you, ladies.' Eynon spoke politely enough but Grantley was pleased to see that the young man's tone was guarded. 'Can I offer you refreshment after your long journey?'

'Thank you, something cold, please, it's so damned hot!' Elizabeth's language was most unladylike, Grantley thought. Why did her vulgarity appear acceptable, amusing even, while in London but here, in this gentle corner of Wales, it was so out of place?

'Ah, Grantley, my old friend, I did not realize I would find you here, too.' Elizabeth rose and kissed him on both cheeks. 'Taking a holiday, are you?'

Grantley grunted noncommittally. Soon cooling cordial had been brought and, as Grantley took a seat, he spent a little time scrutinizing Annabel's face and figure. The girl seemed nervous; she was very pale and only sipped at her drink. Now and then she cast anxious glances in Eynon's direction and even Grantley, his heart hardened by the lies of many a man he had defended, felt sorry for her.

'Now, Grantley, this is a private matter,' Elizabeth stared at him, her eyes hooded. 'I am sure you would not like to intrude on what is, after all, none of your business.'

'Dear, dear Elizabeth,' Grantley smiled. 'I am acting as adviser to Mr Morton-Edwards. I was the one to introduce him into your company if you remember. I am acquainted with your daughter's claims and so I shall stay.'

'Well damn you and your lawyer's mind then!' Elizabeth said. She turned in her seat to face Eynon, excluding Grantley from her line of vision.

'So, my little innocent girl is with child by you, sir. What do you intend to do about it?' Elizabeth paused to dab at her cheeks with a scrap of lace. 'Will you make an honest woman of her?'

'Oh Mother, *please!*' Annabel's tone was anguished.

'I would like to know how many lovers there have been since the night I brought Mr Morton-Edwards to your home, Annabel.' Grantley deliberately introduced a note of sternness into his voice.

The girl darted a look at him from soft, damp eyes. 'There has been no-one!' she said. 'No-one but Eynon.'

Grantley, though normally sceptical, was inclined to believe the girl. Still, that was beside the point. Her favours had been given freely on the understanding that she would marry another man. She could not now pretend an innocence and ask for marriage.

Eynon looked towards him for help. Grantley held up his hand. 'Look, Annabel, my dear child, I believe you,' he said. 'I know you are a truthful girl, but Mr Morton-Edwards has met you once only. You surely do not expect him to take for a wife one who gives so freely of herself?'

'Grantley!' Elizabeth rounded on him. 'How dare you put words in another man's mouth? Mr Morton-Edwards can speak for himself, can't he?'

'Now, Elizabeth,' Grantley said, 'you have only landed yourself in trouble through your own doing. The minute you set eyes on Eynon you had him pegged as a rich man. You hoped by pushing your daughter into bed with him that he would be ripe for blackmail, confess it!'

'You liar!' Elizabeth said. 'I wanted my girl to know a young man before, before her marriage to an old goat!'

'A marriage that you arranged,' Grantley said reasonably.

'Stop!' Annabel rose to her feet, her hands over her cheeks. 'Just stop all this!' Tears ran down her cheeks and she wiped them away as a child does with the back of her hand.

'Mamma, I want to go home.'

'No! We are going to have this out. I shall not leave here without some compensation for your troubles.' Elizabeth's face was almost purple with anger.

'Oh, Mamma!' Annabel ran to the door and flung it open. Startled, Grantley watched her departure in silence.

'I'll go after her,' Eynon said and before Grantley could stop him, the boy had left the room, closing the door behind him. Grantley shrugged. 'Well, it seems the matter has been taken out of our hands. We shall have to leave the young people to sort out this mess themselves.'

He poured himself a drink and stared morosely into the garden where he could see Eynon, his hand on the girl's shoulder. He would marry her, that much was clear. Eynon Morton-Edwards would take on the girl out of a sense of duty and Grantley could not help but inwardly applaud the man.

'It seems, Elizabeth,' he said, 'you are about to see your fondest wishes realized.'

Llinos sat staring down at her hands. She was feeling insecure now that Mr Grantley had returned to London, to pursue another case which he was handling in the assizes. Llinos was worried that, somehow, Joe's bail would be revoked and he would be taken away from her again.

She glanced towards him as he sat with

her in the summer house. She heard the wind chimes sweetly singing in the soft breeze and knew that each moment of her life with Joe must be cherished.

The sun was warm on her feet and on an impulse she kicked off her shoes and stepped outside the sun house onto the grass, her feet bare.

Joe came up behind her and untied her ribbons allowing her hair to tumble around her shoulders. 'My little Firebird,' he whispered, 'my darling, my wife. Have I told you that I love you? Apart from which, you smell good enough to eat!' He bit her ear and she slapped him away.

'Blarney! You have a sweet tongue, my boy!' She felt like crying. What was wrong with her? What shadows haunted her now? Joe was here, safe beside her, so why was she so fearful?

Mr Marks appeared around the corner of the house and paused when he saw husband and wife in each other's arms.

'I'm sorry,' he said. 'I'm intruding.' He held a piece of paper in his hand and even from where she was standing, Llinos could see that the old man was trembling.

'Come and sit down, Mr Marks,' she said quickly, disengaging herself from Joe's arms. 'Is anything wrong?'

He sat on one of the garden benches that stretched along the borders of the lawn. 'Look,' he held the letter towards Joe. 'It's from my son, he wants me to go and live with him.' He glanced towards heaven. 'Live with him as if nothing was ever wrong between us?'

'Perhaps he wants to make amends for the past,' Llinos said softly, sitting beside Mr Marks. The old man shook his head.

'If only that was true. No, he wants my land, that's what it is. He has found out about America and thinks he can get his hands on the deeds.' He smiled thinly. 'He doesn't realize he's too late.'

'It's not too late, you know,' Joe said. 'If you and your son do make friends you can have the land to give him as a gift. Why not invite him to visit you here? Find out if he is sorry for what he's done in the past.'

Samuel Marks shook his head. 'You don't know the boy as I do. He would only cause trouble for me, for you too I don't doubt.'

'Just try to speak with him,' Llinos said. 'There were times when I hated my father. I even left home once but I came back and now I'm very glad I did.'

Samuel looked at her wistfully. 'All right, I'll give it one last go. I'll agree to stay with him for a few days.'

'Where does he live?' Llinos asked and the old man shook open the letter.

'By the address here, it looks as if he's moved into a house over at Langland.'

'It's lovely there with the view of the sea,' Llinos said. 'Perhaps a holiday together would do you both good.'

'It's the house Saul's bought with money he stole from me,' Samuel said sadly. 'But people do change sometimes, don't they?'

He looked so small, so sad, that Llinos put her arm around his shoulders. 'Of course they do! People mature, even sons and daughters.' She smiled. 'Once you've made up your mind, let me know and I'll order the coach to take you to Langland.'

'You are very kind.' He looked up at Joe. 'And you are very lucky to have this lovely girl as your wife.'

'I know,' Joe said. 'Don't tell her though or I'll never hear the end of it.'

It was early the following week when Mr Marks took a reluctant leave of Llinos and Joe. He looked back from the coach, his face, framed by the window, appearing old and sad.

'We are doing the right thing, aren't we, Joe?' Llinos slipped her hand through his arm and hugged it to her side. 'We are encouraging Mr Marks to go visit his son and we have never even met Saul Marks. From what we've heard, he sounds a real bad lot.'

'Quarrels can sometimes be mended,' Joe said. 'And, if not, at least Samuel will have tried his best. He'll die when the time comes with an easy conscience.'

'Do you think he's going to die soon, Joe?'

Joe laughed and spun her round to face him. 'Llinos, I am only a man! I do not see everything that is going to happen.'

'Only some things,' Llinos said, refusing to be coaxed into laughter. 'I don't know, I just have a bad feeling about all this. Somehow it's going to rebound on us.'

'Well, for now, let's forget it,' Joe said. 'In any case, I thought you were going to check on the Firebird patterns; you went on about it enough last night when I was trying to get some sleep!'

'Cheek! I did not go on about it.' Llinos punched his arm. He caught her in his arms and kissed her. When she tried to cling he held her away. She looked up at him, her eyes full of tears.

'What's wrong, love?' Joe was all concern. Llinos walked away from him towards the softly scented flower garden. The sweet peas were climbing along the back wall and the lawn was scattered with daisies.

'I wanted our baby so much.' Llinos

heard her voice, small and shaky and hated her weakness. 'When I miscarried, at first I didn't believe it had happened. Even now, sometimes, I put my hand over my stomach, just here.' Her hand fluttered over the front of her dress. 'And I think I can feel movement. Joe, will we ever have a child?'

He took her in his arms, cradled her, and, though he kissed her hair and brushed the tears from her eyes, he did not answer her. She pushed against his broadness and looked up, straining to see his expression.

'Answer me, Joe!'

'The answer is in the lap of the gods, Llinos.' His voice was soft, almost a whisper, and there was a shadow across his face so that she could not see his eyes.

'Go on!' he said suddenly. 'Go see to the pottery, it won't run itself, you know.' He smiled but he seemed distant from her. 'I expect Pearl's causing havoc in the paint shed.'

Sighing, Llinos moved away from him. He was right, the future was not theirs to know. One day she might have children but for now she had Joe and that had to be enough.

'Well, Father, I hope now you understand why I did it.' Saul Marks stood before the imposing fireplace of his house, the house he had cheated and lied for. Samuel studied his son, wondering how the boy could convince himself so thoroughly of the rightness of his actions. He told a garbled story of how events had taken him unawares and the only way to save the business was to have it put in his own name. In order to do so he had forged his father's signature, indicating that the old man was losing his mind. But in his smug self-satisfaction, Saul seemed to have overlooked the harm he had done.

'I was put in prison,' Samuel said gravely. 'I was lucky I did not die there.' He sipped the cordial his son handed him. It tasted bitter.

'I would have got you out once everything was in order,' Saul said. His face was narrow, mean; his eyes close together. Did the boy really believe what he was saying?

'How did you get out, anyway?'

'You know how. Mr Mainwaring paid off the debts.' Debts that were Saul's, but that thought was unspoken.

'And in return what did you give him, Father?' Saul was trying to sound as though he was making a polite enquiry but there was a gleam in his eye that boded ill. Samuel knew, had known within minutes of coming here, that he had been wrong to do so.

There was no path back to harmony with his son. Had there ever been harmony between them? Samuel doubted it.

'He paid my debts because he was a kind honourable man.' Samuel avoided looking at his son: Saul would be merciless in his questioning until he got what he wanted.

'But, Father, you must have given the man something in return, some hidden cache of money, some property.' He paused. 'Or could it have been land you gave him, land that would one day prove valuable?'

Samuel forced a smile. 'Where would I have land from, tell me that, boy? You have access to all my books, all my business records. How could I have anything to offer anyone? You took it all.'

'So this man, this Indian fella, he paid your debts because he liked you, is that it?' Saul's tone was sneering.

'There are kind, honest people about or have you been too busy to notice?' Samuel saw his son's face redden in anger and he knew he must tread warily. He rose to his feet.

'In any case, it's all in the past now we're together again. I'm tired, I think it's time I went to bed.'

Saul moved swiftly. He caught his father

by his collar and shook him. 'Tell me!' He was spitting with anger. 'Tell me what the bribe was or I'll kill you.'

'There was no bribe,' Samuel said desperately. 'Let me go, Saul, this is madness!'

Saul released him. 'You are a foolish old man,' he said bitterly. 'Your sort are only fit for the scrap heap.'

'What do you mean "my sort"?' Samuel said.

'You Jews. You are a blight on society.' There was hate in the boy's eyes. Then Samuel understood: he was being punished for being a Jew, just as he had always been punished by the ignorant and uninformed because of his birthright.

'You are a Jew yourself, Saul.' Samuel was suddenly angry. 'Jewish blood runs in your veins, good Jewish blood.'

'My mother was a Gentile,' Saul said icily. 'And, thank God, I take after her not you! I am ashamed to own you as my father, do you understand that? I want you dead and out of the way so that I need never admit my father was the lowest of the low; so lacking in intelligence that his son was able to deprive him of all he owned.'

Samuel remained silent though the blood was rushing to his head, pounding in his temples. He wanted to strike out and kill that which he had created.

'You are not quite as clever as you thought,' Samuel said. 'I did have land, acres of it. Good land that one day will make the man who owns it a millionaire.'

All at once, Saul was calm, the deadly calm of an animal stalking its prey. 'And where are the deeds of this land?' His voice was ominous.

'They are out of your reach,' Samuel said triumphantly.

'Well then you had better bring them back into my reach,' Saul placed his hands around his father's throat and squeezed. 'Have you signed it all over to that Indian? Tell me!'

Samuel saw that he was in mortal danger. 'No, I did not,' he said flatly, the lie forced out with his breath as Saul released him. 'Would I do any such thing? Me a Jew, give away a piece of prime land? You must be out of your mind.'

Saul was convinced. 'Then you will sign it over to me,' he said. 'Now get to bed and out of my sight. We will arrange things in the morning. Until then I do not want to set eyes on you, understand?'

'Yes, I understand perfectly.' Samuel sat in his room in the brooding silence, staring out into the night sky. He had lit no candles, wanting the cover of darkness. When the last sounds of the house settling for sleep had died away, Samuel drew on his coat. Moving with the stealth he had learned in prison, he opened his door and made his way as silently as a cat down the wide staircase.

He went through the kitchen and, though his bones were old and brittle, he managed to climb out of one of the windows and into the garden. He had no idea of the distance back to Swansea but he was determined to walk every step of the way if need be.

The roads were dark, there was no moon and the only way Samuel could make progress was to feel his way, step by step. He began to feel panic grow within him: soon it would be dawn and with the growing light Saul would come after him and take him by force.

It was then he heard the gentle clip clop of a horse's hooves. He slid into the bushes and crouched there, sweating.

Out of the gloom a rider appeared, a darker shape against the slowly lightening sky. 'Sam!' The voice was familiar, a cultured voice, a kind voice. 'Samuel, don't be afraid, it's Joe, I've come to take you home.'

'Joe!' Samuel stepped out onto the road and took the warm, strong hand that was held out to him. 'How did you know?' Samuel was lifted bodily onto the back of the horse. 'How, in the name of all that is holy, did you know I needed help?'

Without answering Joe turned the animal, and Samuel relaxed in the saddle. He knew he could trust Joe. Joe did not think of him as an outcast, the lowest of the low. Joe was not his son but, at this moment, Samuel loved Joe as though he were bred from his own flesh and blood.

'Where are we going?' he asked, his voice strangely unsteady. Joe turned in the saddle and only the gleam of his eyes was visible against the darkness of his face.

'We're going home.'

'Going home?' Home was the warmth of the house beside the pottery. Home was with people who had been strangers until a short time ago. Home, how welcome the word sounded. Suddenly, Samuel began to weep.

CHAPTER

TWELVE

The exotic Firebird range of pottery took the town of Swansea by storm. So much so that plans were drawn up to expand the business. New kilns were built and more staff employed. Four more throwers were taken on as well as two saggar makers and one talented flower painter, a young man from the Hafod area of the town. Lily, as chief painter, was much admired by her fellow workers. She basked in the admiration of the owners who came from miles away to witness the success of the Savage Pottery, and she knew she had been right not to agree to marry Watt. There were more fish in the sea than ever came out of it, as her friend Polly was fond of saying.

The only cloud on Lily's horizon, as she saw it, was Watt's growing hostility, and in that he was aided and abetted by Mrs Smedley, who had always hated her. It was pure jealousy on the older woman's part: Lily was young, beautiful and talented and, what was more, she now earned more than Mrs Smedley. As for Watt, just because she would not give into his lustful desires he was being horrible to her.

Watt entered the painting room at that moment and began to traverse the length of the shed, bending to examine a pot here and there, commenting on some work that was not up to standard. Her own work, Lily knew, was always up to standard. However, Watt it seemed did not think so.

'This painting is rather off-centre,' he said, taking up a tall jug on which Lily had been painting the absurd bird that was now the trademark of one line of pottery.

'No it is not,' Lily said.

'I'm sorry, Lily, but it is. You see how the tail feathers swoop around to the side and are lost out of view at the back of the jug?'

The very reasonableness of Watt's tone, and the fact that he was patently right, only served to make Lily angry.

'I'll be glad when you leave for America,' she said loudly. Several of the other decorators looked up, happy at a diversion from the dullness of their routine tasks.

'Why?' Watt asked. 'So that your work can become sloppy and inferior without anyone complaining, is that it?'

'My work has never been sloppy or inferior!' Lily said indignantly.

'Well it's going that way.'

'No!' Lily stamped her foot. 'It's just you

picking on me, Watt Bevan.' She put her hands on her slim hips and surveyed the room. 'Just because I'm a good girl, and wouldn't allow him to take liberties with me, Watt is picking on me. It's not fair.'

Llinos was suddenly beside her and Lily stared at her defiantly. 'It's the truth,' she said. 'Watt's a monster, it's not safe for any girl to be alone with him.'

'How I ever thought I wanted to be alone with you, I don't know,' Watt said quietly.

'Lily,' Llinos said, moving away, 'come to the office, I'll speak to you there.'

Sullenly Lily picked up a rag and rubbed the paint from her hands. It was clear that Llinos was going to take Watt's part in all this.

She followed silently, her eyes narrowed against the glare of the sun on the yard and on the whitewashed walls surrounding the pottery.

Indoors the sun was slanting across dusty rows of books. The smell of ink permeated the air but Lily was immune to it; the smell of paint was her constant companion.

'Morning, Mrs Mainwaring.' John Pendennis, seated at one of the desks, scarcely glanced at Lily. Doubtless he thought he was a cut above her.

'Now, Lily, what's all this about?' Llinos

was seated now, looking up, waiting for a reply.

'It's about Watt picking on me.' Lily's voice was sullen. 'He's always doing it, ever since I turned him down.'

'Turned him down?'

'I told him I didn't want to go with him to America.' Lily saw John glance up at her, and there was a smile in his eyes that told her he was pleased about the situation. She turned her head away, refusing to look at him. It was all his fault, she and Watt were all right until John came along and put foolish ideas into Watt's head.

'Well, whatever problems you and Watt have, I would appreciate it if all future discussions about your personal life took place outside working hours,' Llinos said calmly.

'But, Llinos, he's *picking* on me all the time, what am I supposed to do?'

'I'll have a word with him.' Llinos smiled. 'But, in the meantime, Lily, try to make sure that your work is up to standard and then no-one will be able to criticize.'

As Lily returned to the shed she felt anger at the injustice that had been meted out to her. Trust Llinos to take Watt's side, it was always the same, they stuck together these people who had money. Watt forgot that he himself had come from the orphanage; he imagined himself to be one of the toffs.

She smiled then, a secret smile. Watt had been relieved of some of his money, at least. It lay now beneath the night clothes in her drawer. She had not asked Polly to take it into her head to rob Watt. Polly lived with Lily in the lodging house and she had heard her crying one night. Polly had been indignant when she learned about Watt trying to force his attentions on Lily and promised to take revenge on him whenever she had the chance.

'Leave it to me, love,' she had said. 'I was always a good pickpocket. I'll bide my time and watch the bastard and then one day I'll pounce. I'll pay him back for his little games.'

Lily had been somewhat dismayed by the girl's vulgarity but when Polly had brought the purse of money to her she had, after demurring a little for the sake of appearances, agreed to share it.

'Lily, I didn't mean to get you into trouble.' She jumped nervously as she was confronted by Watt himself. She hastily composed herself and looked up at him from under her lashes. Polly had told her not to be a fool, to use men for her own ends. She smiled.

'I'm sorry for the misunderstanding,

Watt,' she said. 'And you're right, the bird was off-centre; you have a better eye than me. I'm sorry, Watt.'

He warmed to her immediately; as Polly had told her, men were fools for a bit of flattery.

'I should have been more discreet about it, though,' he admitted. 'I had no right to show you up in front of everyone. It's me that's sorry.'

'Well, let's forget it,' Lily said. She steeled herself not to flinch as Watt touched her shoulder. She looked up at him, her eyes wide, and, fleetingly, his lips touched hers. She resisted the desire to rub at her lips; to erase the touch of him, the taste of him. For a moment she felt panic: was she unnatural, was she less than womanly? Why did she not like the touch of a man, the caress of lips upon lips? She heard Pearl going on about her exploits and the woman seemed to never have enough of men. But then Pearl was a harlot at heart while she, Lily, was a good girl, a respectable girl.

'Lily,' Watt said, 'you're so beautiful. I don't think you know what you do to a man.' He laughed. 'I think you could ask a king for his crown and he would give it to you for one kind glance from those gorgeous eyes.'

'You're teasing me.' She looked down at her paint-stained hands. 'I'm just an ordinary girl from the orphanage.'

Watt tipped her face up towards him. 'No, Lily, you're not an ordinary girl: you're a talented painter as well as being the most beautiful thing around here.'

'Well, it's kind of you to say all those things to me, Watt, but I'd better get back to work or that Pearl will be gossiping about us again.' She held her head high as she walked across the yard and inside her was the beginning of a glow. It was just as Polly told her: you could use men, manipulate them to your own advantage, if you had the guile. And the looks of course. Feeling as though she was walking on air, Lily swept past Mrs Smedley without giving the woman so much as a glance. She, Lily, had found the power she had and she meant to use it to the full.

Eynon Morton-Edwards and his new bride were the talk of the town. The pair had married in London. Annabel was clearly a wealthy, attractive girl, one of apparently good breeding, but the haste of the marriage ceremony and the seclusion in which the bride kept herself, gave rise to great speculation.

Eynon had been trapped, not so much by Annabel, as by his own guilty conscience. He sat across the room from her now, watching as she stitched with coloured silk, working a pattern of flowers and birds into the cloth stretched over a frame. She glanced up at him, her eyes soft. Annabel was in love with him, she made it clear by every melting look, by the softness of her hands as they touched him. But Eynon could not forget the way she had begged him to make love to her. She had thrown all modesty aside and the thought persisted that perhaps Annabel was following in her mother's footsteps and was a whore at heart.

'Why don't you make love to me, Eynon?' Her softly spoken words shook him from his thoughts. He looked up at her, feeling the heat in his cheeks.

'You are going to have a baby, I don't feel that I should . . .' The child was not the reason and they both knew it.

'You don't love me, do you?' Her voice was little more than a whisper. A curl of hair fell against her neck and Eynon felt an over-whelming sense of pity engulf him.

'It will all come right in time,' he said. 'We hardly know each other, Annabel, we are married strangers. But, one day, everything will be fine, you'll see.'

'You feel I trapped you.'

How could he deny it? He was trapped, married to a woman he would never love. He loved Llinos, his darling, the girl he had wanted since he met her when she was little more than a child.

'You told me you were in love, is that still true?' Annabel was determined to probe into his mind and, suddenly, Eynon was resentful. She had his name, his protection, his company, however unwilling, what more could she expect? He rose to his feet.

'Let's end this discussion right now, shall we?' He moved to the door. 'I'm expecting visitors and I don't want you to say anything that would embarrass me, do you understand?'

She looked him full in the face then. 'I am not my mother. You do not have to tell me how to behave.' Her voice was unexpectedly hard and it was he who looked away.

As if on cue the doorbell chimed and Eynon heard the sound of voices in the hall. Maura pushed open the doors to the drawing room to admit his visitor. Llinos, he saw with a sense of relief, was alone.

Eynon moved forward to take her hands. 'I'm happy you've come. Where's Joe?'

'He sends his apologies.' Llinos looked

across the room and her beautiful eyes rested on Annabel. 'So this is your wife; she's so pretty! Why have you kept her a secret from us, Eynon?'

He sensed the hurt behind her bubbly tone and kicked himself for not speaking to her privately before this.

'It was all rather sudden,' Eynon said and the words sounded weak and lame even to his own ears. 'Llinos, this is Annabel.'

The two women exchanged greetings and Eynon had to hand it to Annabel, she was acting as though nothing was wrong.

'I understand you and Eynon are old friends,' Annabel said graciously. She left her embroidery and took a seat next to Llinos. Eynon compared them, it was impossible not to. Annabel was more heavily built than Llinos, her eyes did not blaze with the same fire. Her hands were not as delicate.

Enough! he told himself. He could never have Llinos: she was married to Joe, she adored Joe.

'I hope you'll be happy here in Swansea,' Llinos was saying. 'It must be rather dull after London.'

'Much quieter,' Annabel agreed. 'But I prefer it here near the sea. The bustle and traffic of the big town was sometimes over-whelming.'

Eynon could see that Llinos was longing to ask questions but they trembled on her lips unspoken. She must be wondering why he had never spoken of Annabel, but how could he talk about her without branding his wife as a loose woman who took a man to her bed at their first meeting? The questions would just have to go unanswered.

'What's Joe up to that he can't come to visit my new bride?' Eynon asked, his tone revealing a false note of jocularity.

'He's gone to London,' Llinos said. 'He needs to talk to Mr Grantley.' A cloud darkened her eyes and Eynon kicked himself for his tactlessness. The threat of imprisonment still hung over Joe. He would remain under a cloud unless Grantley could come up with some evidence to refute the allegations made against him.

'You have no news of the date of the hearing?' Eynon leaned forward and breathed in the perfume that was all Llinos's.

'No.' She looked down at her hands. 'I wish to heaven it was all over. I couldn't bear to be parted from him, not again.'

Annabel moved slightly and Eynon was aware that he had been shutting her out of the closeness between himself and Llinos.

'Anyway, let's not be rude.' Llinos had

obviously picked up on his thoughts. 'We should not be discussing matters your wife knows nothing about. I apologize.'

There was a light tapping on the door and Maura entered the room, a tray on her arm. Eynon concealed a smile: Maura, as house-keeper, had no place acting as a maid but it was clear she was burning with curiosity about the new woman in Eynon's life. She had almost come right out with it and asked him if Annabel was the one who had sent him the letter.

'Maura, how are you?' Llinos smiled at the Irish girl but Maura did not look at her. She placed the tray on the table before an-swering.

'As well as can be expected.' Her tone was sullen, as if, in some strange way, she blamed Llinos for Binnie's defection.

'You have heard nothing of Binnie, then?' Llinos was nothing if not perceptive.

Maura sniffed. 'I never want to hear from that man again. If he was dying of thirst in the gutter, I would not spit on him.'

The silence was sudden and profound. Eynon frantically sought for something to say to cover the moment of embarrassment, but it was Annabel who stepped in with an aplomb he had not believed her capable of.

'We are sorry for your troubles, Maura,'

she said. 'Thank you for the tea and will you please close the door when you go out, I feel there's quite a draught in here.'

Dismissed, Maura left the room and again it was Annabel who broke the silence. 'Poor woman,' she said, 'it must be so sad to be deserted by one's husband.'

She looked meaningfully at Eynon and he faced her squarely.

'You have no need to worry about that, Annabel,' he said. She smiled briefly and sat back in her chair, one hand against her waist.

'You're looking pale as a penny chicken there,' Llinos said and Eynon smiled at the Welshness of her expression. 'Are you feeling all right . . . Mrs Morton-Edwards?' The name trembled on Llinos's lips as though she found it difficult to pronounce.

'Please, call me Annabel and yes, I'm fine. A little back ache is normal for a woman in my condition.' If her words were calculated to shock then she was disappointed. Llinos cast a brief glance at Eynon as if to say she now understood the haste of his marriage. Then she turned again to Annabel and there was a note of sadness in her voice when she spoke.

'I lost my baby, it was a terrible blow.' She took a deep breath. 'But you are going to be fine, I can tell.'

Annabel moved closer to Llinos. 'Oh, you poor dear lady! What a dreadful thing to happen. But you are young and strong and there will be many children, you'll see.'

It was ironic, his wife and the woman he loved comforting each other as if they were old friends. Eynon rose to his feet. 'If you'll excuse me, ladies, this is not talk for a gentleman's ears. I'll leave you to it.'

As he stepped out into the sunshine, Eynon took a deep breath. If he could not have Llinos, and clearly he could not, why not make the best of things as they were? Annabel was young, beautiful and she would bear healthy children for him. What more could a man want?

As he walked around the perimeter of the house towards the stables, he knew with a sinking feeling in his heart that he wanted love; passion he could find anywhere, love was more illusive. Well, he had sown his oats and now he was paying for it. As a gentleman he must take the consequences of his actions and try his best to love Annabel. Somehow he knew it was going to be an impossible task.

'She's very nice.' Llinos was seated beside Joe on the garden swing; the sun was hot on her face. She breathed in the scent of her husband with love and desire and relief that he was home with her again.

'I felt a little sorry for her at first, she seemed so subdued, so apologetic. But then she asserted herself, took charge and told me she was going to have a baby and I understood everything. I understood Eynon's secrecy, the haste of his marriage and most of all Annabel's attitude. Poor girl must feel she's trapped Eynon into marriage. But love can grow, can't it?'

Joe leaned closer and touched her cheek with his fingertips. 'Eynon is in love with you, he will always be in love with you. As he can never have you, it's just as well he's got a wife of his own otherwise I might just be jealous of him.'

'Never!' Llinos smiled up at Joe. 'You know you have me just where you want me.' She was silent for a moment. 'Joe, there will be other babies for us, won't there?'

Joe raised his head to look up at the sky; the line of his jaw was pure, the sun touching his brow and the scimitar of his cheekbones gave golden highlights to his skin.

'It's all in the hands of the gods, my love.' That was all he would say.

Maura sat in the kitchen, a cup of tea held

between both hands. She glanced down through the steam rising from the tea and looked at her hands, really looked at them. They were white, well-kept, but then she did no manual work. As housekeeper she supervised; she did not clean vegetables or scrub floors. Her wedding ring, worn for respectability, gleamed up at her like a mockery. She should be installed in her own home, with a brood of children around her skirts.

'Why so glum, Maura?' The cook was staring down at her, her big arms kneading dough for the bread with ease.

'I don't know, just thinking about things. 'Tis sad for a woman to be alone, don't you think?'

'Suits me fine.' Mrs Benedict was young, tall and strong, a widow newly taken into the household of the Morton-Edwards family. 'I never liked all that . . . that fooling around. No, I'm content with my lot.' She looked down at Maura and there was a frown on her face.

'What is it, what's wrong?' Maura sat up straighter, aware that Mrs Benedict had something important to say as she brushed the flour from her hands and sat down.

'My sister, Mildred, is wife of the landlord of the Castle Inn. She's heard talk.'

Maura suddenly felt a chill shiver along her spine. She knew in her bones that she was not going to like what Cook had to say.

'Sure gossip does not interest me, not at all.' If Maura had hoped to deflect Cook's pronouncement, she was wrong.

'It's about that waster of a husband of yours, Maura. Seems he's been seen in America somewhere.'

'Oh aye,' Maura was sceptical. 'Well, he's dead and gone as far as I'm concerned.' Her tone was hard.

'They say he's got a wife, a brood of little ones and he's well set-up in some pottery business.'

Maura swallowed hard. She might hate Binnie from the bottom of her heart and soul but she burned with anger to think of him taking up with another woman and calling her his wife. It was probably all foolish talk anyway. Why should someone, anyone, find Binnie Dundee in America? And yet the story seemed plausible enough.

'Who are "they"?' she said, staring into her rapidly cooling tea.

Mrs Benedict shrugged. 'I don't know, customers and the like, I suppose. The men who drink down at the inn talk, mind.'

'Well, I don't believe a word of it,' Maura said. 'Binnie would not be such a fool as to take another wife, not when he's still wed to me.'

'There's no accounting for men,' Mrs Benedict said wisely. 'I had a cousin once who married three times and kept all three wives in the same house!'

Maura rose to her feet. 'Such nonsense!' she said, and before the cook could reply, Maura stalked out of the kitchen and up the curving staircase, wanting only to be alone in the sanctuary of her room.

Binnie with a wife and family, well set-up in a pottery business. It all seemed very likely. Binnie had never grown up. In spite of the hardships of his childhood and his youth, he had remained a little boy, coveting all he could not have. She longed to scream and shout and rend her clothes. She knew how penitents of old must have felt when they covered themselves in sackcloth and ashes. She thumped her fist against the solid wood of her door.

'Binnie Dundee,' she ground the name out between clenched teeth, 'if you are alive and living in sin with some whore, I swear I'll find you and ruin you and your so-called family.'

She sank down on the bed, her anger spent. Tears, hot and bitter, rolled down her face. She loved him, in spite of everything, in spite of the bitterness that had grown like a canker within her, she still loved the man who had taken her innocence and turned her from a girl into a woman. She was a foolish woman to get upset. Binnie Dundee was no longer any concern of hers. Why then did she continue to sob and the pain in her heart refuse to go away?

CHAPTER

THIRTEEN

The sun was an orange disc disappearing beneath the horizon. The distant mountains were black against the brightness and Binnie Dundee breathed in the sights and scents of his adopted country with a feeling of affection. America was a good place for a man to mature, to grow and to see his sons grow. The living was good, folded as he was into the bosom of the McCabe family, easy even, a far cry from the days he had spent at the Savage Pottery back home in Wales.

And yet, sometimes, if he was honest, he was homesick for the greenery, the soft misty rain and the freshness of a spring day in Swansea. Homesick for his friends, for Llinos with whom he had grown up, Watt and old Ben, his friends from a different life. Of Maura he rarely thought; she was a mistake, one he must put out of his mind. He knew he could never go home, never. But then he was fulfilled and happy here in Troy, wasn't he? He had a loving wife, fine children and a secure job. What more could a man want?

Hortense came onto the veranda, nursing

the baby. She seated herself beside Binnie on the swing and chuckled as she looked down into the face of her new son.

'He's the image of you!' She smiled, her face softened by love. 'Down to the same tuft of unruly hair sticking up from his crown. He's the spit out of your mouth, Binnie, you could never deny he was yours.'

Binnie leaned towards his wife and kissed her lips gently. 'As if I would want to. I love you, Hortense, and I love the children we have made together. Dan and Jerry and the new babe are the most precious things in my life, after you.'

'I know, honey.' She touched his cheek. 'I bless the day you came into my life. I knew I wanted you even then when I didn't know the first thing about you.'

'Hussy!' Binnie smiled. 'And I took you for an innocent little lady.'

'And so I was!' Hortense protested. 'The trouble was you were so irresistible and I knew my sisters both had their eyes on you, too. I thought I would be the last one you'd look at . . . until . . .' She paused tantalizingly.

'Until what?' Binnie caught her face between his hands. 'Come on, until what?'

'Until you started hanging around me staring down my dress any chance you got!'

Hortense laughed, her teeth fine and strong and white, her skin with a healthy sun-kissed sheen.

'I'm a lucky man.' He bent his head and kissed her mouth. 'I am such a lucky man. I had the pick of the bunch.'

The sound of voices, high and excited, drifted towards them. 'Oh Lord, here come the girls, speak of the devil.'

Hortense shifted the baby on her arm and Binnie sat upright, unwilling to be seen as a milksop canoodling with his wife on the porch, like an old man past his prime.

'Guess what?' Melia sank down on the porch steps, her gown billowing around her ankles.

'I'll tell them,' Josephine said sharply. 'We're having visitors from your part of the world, Binnie. What do you think of that?'

Binnie felt cold. He took a deep breath and composed himself; no-one from Swansea was here, it was impossible. Jo was talking about the British Isles, she must be.

'Oh, who are they?' he said calmly.

Melia hugged her knees. 'Two men have come into town, there's one with the strange name of Pendennis, John Pendennis.'

Binnie's breath escaped with a sigh of relief. 'Sounds like a West Countryman,' he said. 'From Devon or Cornwall. I don't know anyone called John Pendennis.'

'Well now, there's one man from your very town,' Melia said, 'from Swansea. What do you think of that?'

Binnie's mouth was dry. 'Tell me his name and I'll let you know.'

'Well, he's young and handsome by all accounts and knows a thing or two about potting, that's why they've chosen him to come to this neck of the woods.'

There was still very little chance that Binnie would know him; there were lots of men working at both the Savage Pottery and the larger Tawe Pottery.

'What's his name?' Binnie was surprised that he sounded normal; his heart was thumping in his breast and he felt he could not breathe.

'Funny name, Watt Bevan or some such thing.' It was Josephine who answered. 'Not that I would mind being Mrs Bevan if he's as young and presentable as they say.'

It was as though the red of the recent sunset was blinding his vision. From a long way off he heard the excited chatter of the girls. Watt was here, in America, in Troy; his life was in ruins.

'Are you all right, honey?' Hortense was saying. He rubbed his eyes tiredly. 'Yes, I think I was out in the sun too long, that's all.'

Hortense handed the baby to her sister. 'Here, Mel, hold him while I take Binnie inside, he's been working too hard lately.' She leaned over him, her arm around his shoulder and he felt the softness of her breast against his cheek.

'And active at night time, too,' Josephine said, slyly. 'Lucky girl that you are, Hortense.'

'I know. Come on, honey, come inside in the coolness and rest.' It was clear that his wife was concerned and Binnie made an effort to pull himself together. He spread out on the bed in the coolness of the room he shared with Hortense and forced a smile.

'I'm fine, I really am just tired, that's all.' Hortense put her hand on his forehead. He took her fingers in his.

'One thing you can do for me, my love.'

'What is it, Binnie?'

'Ask the girls where these two men are staying. I'd like to get together with them for a bit of a talk.'

'Are you homesick, hon?' Hortense asked and Binnie shook his head.

'No. My home is here, with you and the children. You are the only family I've ever had or ever wanted.'

She left him then and Binnie closed his eyes, trying not to imagine how his wife would feel if she found out the truth. It hurt him even to think about it. He must have slept eventually because when he woke, the sun was rising and it was morning.

Hortense was not beside him. She must have wakened early and gone to see to the baby. He stood at the window and looked out at the land below him. It was his land now; Swansea was a far off place, a place from another life. He could only hope and pray that his past life had not caught up with him.

'It seems strange without Watt to tick us off all the time.' Pearl's voice was loud in the stillness. Lily avoided looking at the woman; she was vulgar and her language coarse. Lily was sitting outside the paint shed a little distance from the other women. It was snack time and to eat in the fresh air, away from the smells of oxide and lead, was something of a treat.

'Missing your sweetheart, are you, Lil?' Pearl bit into a piece of cheese with obvious enjoyment. 'You was walking out with a fine man there but there's plenty more fish in the sea as you'll find out.'

Lily did not reply and Pearl pursued the

subject. 'Mind you, it's all your fault you're not in America right now with a ring on your finger and a fine upstanding man for a husband.'

'Pearl,' Lily said, growing impatient, 'will you shut up about Watt? He's gone away and good riddance to him, I say.'

'Well, you'd better come off your high horse, my lady, otherwise "fish in the sea" or not you'll end up an old maid.'

That would suit her perfectly but Lily did not put her thoughts into words. She never wanted a husband, a man to paw her and do all sorts of disgusting things to her. She knew about such goings on, knew too that some women liked to be pestered in that way, but she was not one of them.

'We'd better get back to work.' She rose and brushed the grass from her skirt. 'We've stayed out here longer than we should already.'

Pearl looked up at her and deliberately popped another piece of cheese into her mouth. She chewed for a while and then looked up at Lily.

'I'm senior hand in the paint shop, remember?'

'And I'm chief painter,' Lily retorted, stung by Pearl's tone of voice.

'Well I'm in charge while Watt is away

and I don't think it's time to start work just yet. For heaven's sake sit down and make the most of the peace. You don't get a medal for working yourself to death, mind.'

'And you get the boot if you sit around gossiping all day!' With that parting shot Lily returned to the dimness of the paint shed. Her colour was high and she was breathing rapidly. Why did she let Pearl get to her that way? Pearl was nothing, she wasn't even a good painter, not half as good as Lily herself was.

She seated herself at the table and picked up her brushes. She cared for her brushes; they were meticulously cleaned after use and never left to stand upright in turpentine the way Pearl left hers. Really she was too good for this place. She wondered what it would be like to paint on the porcelain that was being made at the Tawe Pottery. The production of porcelain had been increased and many of the services were going to grace London tables.

Eynon Morton-Edwards had experimented with a natural mixture of steatite and china clay which seemed to be producing a much more stable body than the rather glassy porcelain first used. And yet, unstable though it was, the glassy porcelain was beautiful: white and so thin you could see your fingers through it. Lily had come by an odd cup with the special ring handle decorated with roses edged with expensive gilding by one of the master painters. It was such an achievement and she wished she had been part of it. Perhaps even now it was not too late. There would be no harm in sounding out one of the workers at the Tawe Pottery about the matter of vacancies for painters.

The afternoon passed slowly and Lily was impatient to go back to her room at the lodging house and wash away the smell of paint. Pearl was not slow to notice when Lily began to clean her brushes and lay them flat on the table to dry.

'Leaving early, Lil?' Pearl asked innocently.

'I've finished my work for today,' Lily replied. 'And I dare say I've painted more pots than you have.'

'I dare say,' Pearl echoed, a smile on her face. 'But then, we can't all be Miss Perfect, can we? Some of us are human: we eat, we fart and we go to bed with a man, things that normal humans do. But then you are not a normal human being, are you?'

Lily turned away, not willing to let Pearl see the angry flush on her cheeks. She left the shed, stepped outside into the cooler air of early evening and walked towards the gate just as Llinos was coming in. Llinos was dressed in a pretty sprigged muslin dress with blue ribbon below the bust and on the hem. She looked cool, pretty and rich. Lily felt envy bite at her.

'Hello, Lily, off home?'

'I've got a bit of a bad head, that's why I'm going earlier than usual,' Lily said, her tone defensive.

Llinos looked concerned. 'I'm sorry to hear you're unwell, I hope you are not coming down with something nasty. Have you had any sickness or pains in your stomach?'

'No, no, it's just the heat in the shed and the effort of concentrating. I'll be all right when I can get out of my working clothes and put on something cool.'

'Everything all right between you and Pearl?' Llinos asked and Lily felt anger burn inside her.

'That woman is so coarse!' she said, the words tumbling out before she could think. She regretted them immediately as Llinos looked at her in surprise.

'She may be a bit strong in her language sometimes but she means no harm. There's not a malicious bone in her body.'

That stung, trust Llinos to take Pearl's

part, but then Llinos was not too choosey about the sort of person she associated with. She was not even particular about who she went to bed with, otherwise she would not be married to that foreigner.

'She's not so kind when she talks about you,' Lily said. 'She's always going on about you and your husband.'

'I'm sure it's in fun.' Llinos was not going to be drawn and Lily felt the blood rush to her head. She was determined now to turn Llinos against Pearl whatever it took.

'It's not!' Lily said. 'Pearl keeps on about the captain and how he was murdered by . . . by Mr Mainwaring. She says there's no smoke without fire.'

'Well she's wrong!' Llinos said. 'If you'll excuse me, Lily, I have to get indoors.' She walked across the yard, her head high and Lily felt a moment of triumph, her barb had struck home. Now, perhaps, Llinos would not be so ready to forgive Pearl everything.

At the lodging house the smells of roasting meat drifted into the hallway and followed Lily up the stairs. She realized she was hungry and smiled at the prospect of supper. There would be an abundance of good food as well as of gossip discreetly displayed as concern for whoever was the subject.

Lily enjoyed her supper time; it was a time when she could listen and learn and pick up pieces of information that were sometimes very valuable. And, of course, she would be with Polly and after supper they would go to sit in the garden until the light faded. They would talk over the day and laugh about the foolishness of the other guests — all men, who simpered, blushed and fussed around the two girls hoping for some sign of approval from them.

And tomorrow, Lily thought as she entered her room and stared out through the big front window, tomorrow, she might just take a walk over to the Tawe Pottery and look for a position worthy of her talents.

'Well, we're actually here in America!' Watt stared around the sunlit room in the pleasant guest house and breathed in the sweet, clean scent of lavender. The room was larger than he was used to but then the houses here seemed to be built of wood and not stone. The sun shone in through the window highlighting the pristine sheets on the two narrow beds. The furniture was sparse but well-polished. They would be very comfortable here, he could see.

The appetizing smell of food drifted up from below stairs. Watt reckoned that he and John had been lucky to get lodgings here at Mrs French's boarding house.

It seemed such a long time ago when he left the shores of England to cross the Atlantic Ocean to America. And Watt had enjoyed every minute of the trip; it appeared to him to be an adventure, a journey into the unknown, one that every young man should make before he settled down.

Watt glanced across the room to where John was stretched out on the other narrow bed, his arms behind his head, his eyes closed. He was taking the whole thing in a most matter-of-fact way; as though he travelled across the world every day of his life.

Watt sat on his own bed and settled back against the pillows. He thought of Lily, of the way her hair curled against her neck and the sweet innocence of her mouth. What a pity that she was frigid and unyielding. But was she? If his approach had been more delicate, would she have responded to him with warmth? The fault could well lie with himself.

'I expect we'll meet some fine ladies here,' John said as though he had picked up on Watt's line of thought. 'It appears there's a shortage of men around here and a plethora of women.'

'You could be right,' Watt said. 'But my

guess is that women here, like back home, will want a ring on their finger rather than a roll in the hay.'

John opened his eyes. 'You have a point.'

'Still, it might be fun to find out.' Watt sat up as the sound of a bell echoed through the house. 'I think supper's ready. Thank goodness for that, I'm starving.'

The two men descended the stairs together, apparently at ease with each other, and yet Watt felt he would never be a real friend to John. Oh, the Cornishman liked him well enough but he was cut from another cloth. John had been born to privilege, to fine food served by servants. Watt, on the other hand, was one of the lower orders, of unknown parentage, taken in by the Savage family and made into a copy of a gentleman. Yet, somehow, his origins must show, must be obvious to someone like John.

'The dining room is over there, judging by the noise,' John said, leading the way across the hall and entering the room full of people without hesitation. Watt would never have that sort of confidence and, gratefully, he followed John.

'Evenin', gentlemen.' Mrs French lifted her hand and gestured for them to come and be seated at the table. 'I hope you like pork cooked with honey?'

Watt sat next to a fellow who was already halfway through his dinner and wondered at the strange customs of the American people. First the food was cut and the knife laid down, and then the food lifted using only the fork. He glanced across to where John was seated next to Mrs French; he was taking a hearty helping of meat and regaling the landlady with some tale or other that was making her laugh. John was very good at communicating with all sorts of people: he would be an invaluable asset to any business.

'You likely to stay here long?' The softly spoken voice of his neighbour caught Watt's attention.

'Yes, I don't know, I suppose I'll stay as long as my plans will allow.' He did not want to appear distant but on the other hand he could hardly tell all and sundry what his business was.

'I'm Leigh Denver, sure like to shake you by the hand.' A brown hand was extended and, somewhat embarrassed, Watt took it.

'Pleased to meet you, my name is —'

'I know your name.' Leigh smiled. 'When strangers come to town, it's something to chew over, before you've time to step off the train everyone knows your name.'

'Is that so?' Watt was amused. The American people were open and friendly to the point of nosiness but somehow he found them easy to like.

'What I don't know,' Leigh continued, 'is what you are doing here.' He smiled disarmingly and helped himself to some sweetcorn. 'Looking for work, are you?'

'No, not as such.' Watt glanced across the table and saw that John was listening. Watt raised his eyebrows in a plea for help and John, adept at conversation, stepped in.

'My partner and I are travelling the world, finding out what we might be missing before we settle down to marriage back home.' He lied glibly. 'I think young men should venture into the world at least for a year or two, don't you?'

Leigh smiled wryly. 'I wouldn't mind half a chance!' He wiped his mouth with the back of his hand. 'I just wish I had the money but my daddy's not rich so I got to work for a living.' There was a touch of envy in his tone and Watt smiled inwardly. If only the American knew the truth, that Watt had no father at all, let alone a rich one.

'Say,' Leigh said, taking a huge slice of the steamed pudding that was being passed around the table, 'I'm going to a shindig later, want to come along?'

'I wouldn't mind. What about you, John?'

John shook his head. 'You go, though, it will be good to meet some more of the local people.' It was clear what his message was: find out what you can without arousing suspicion.

'Right then, that's settled.' Leigh leaned closer. 'Thank the Lord for some young blood. As you can see most of the men here are all past their prime, don't want to go dancing or drinking or womanizing.'

Watt concentrated on his pudding. It was rich and sweet and covered with syrup; it had been a long time since he'd eaten so well. It seemed the Americans believed in eating hearty meals; a practice that he was all in favour of.

Later he walked along the dusty roadway with Leigh and studied the wooden buildings on either side of him. Dried brush drifted along the porches and became caught in doorways. It was hot and yet the air seemed clear; the skies above him were darkening now after the glorious blaze of the dying sun. America was a wonderful place, a place where Watt could put down roots.

'Hey there, Watt Bevan!' The voice struck at him like a bolt from the past. He turned and looked into the face of Binnie Dundee.

'Well I'll be damned!' Watt was clasped in a warm hug and was aware of Leigh looking on in astonishment.

'Lordy, England must be a small place if you knows everyone in it, Mr Dundee.' It was clear from the deferential way Leigh spoke that Binnie was a respected man in the town.

'Where are you going?' Binnie asked and there was a note of anxiety in his voice that puzzled Watt.

'Just to some dance or other with Leigh. Why don't you come along?'

Leigh chuckled. 'I don' think Mrs Dundee would like that, not with a new baby to care for.'

Watt blinked rapidly. 'A new baby?' He thought of Maura at home: an old maid before her time, a woman who had died, inwardly at least, and who lived her life as though it were nothing more than a burden. He remembered too the gossip that claimed Binnie had married again. Could it be true?

'We must get together and talk,' Binnie said quickly. He forced a smile. 'There's so much my American folks don't know about my wild youth and I want to keep it that way, understand?'

Watt frowned and Binnie hugged him again. 'Don't talk about Maura whatever you do,' he whispered the words hoarsely and then drew away. 'Go on, enjoy yourself and tomorrow make time to come over to visit me and my family, anyone will tell you where we live.'

As he watched Binnie walk away Watt was beginning to understand what Binnie had done. He had married again, had children. 'Binnie, you fool!' Watt was not aware he had spoken the words out loud until Leigh caught his arm.

'Mr Dundee's nobody's fool!' Leigh said emphatically. 'He's married into a good potting family and provided Dan McCabe with three fine grandsons. He might have sown his wild oats before he took a wife but he's settled down all fine and dandy now!'

'You're right,' Watt said dryly. 'Binnie Dundee is nobody's fool. Well, let's hope that no ghosts from the past come back to haunt him.'

Leigh looked at him in bewilderment and, abruptly, Watt changed the subject. 'Where's this shindig you talked about? I'm feeling quite dry, I could do with a beer.'

'It's not far now,' Leigh said, his brow clearing, 'and you'll find there's more than beer to quench your thirst.' He laughed and slapped Watt across the shoulder. 'Make up your mind to it, man, you are about to get one hell of a good time!'

He hoped so, but now Watt's mind was on Binnie, on his apparent affluence and the respect he seemed to be held in. He had fallen on his feet, that much was clear, but in doing so he had taken the biggest gamble of his life.

CHAPTER

FOURTEEN

'So the meeting with Mr Grantley went well, did it?' Llinos was seated beside Joe in the dining room. They ate together, as always, and their guest Mr Marks chose to eat in his own suite of rooms. Llinos only picked at her meal; she knew her husband and he was troubled.

'I see no problems at all. Grantley says there will be no case to answer. I expect he's right.'

He met her eyes and Llinos knew he was telling the truth, Joe never lied to her. She changed the subject, hoping to distract him from whatever thoughts were bothering him.

'I don't know what's wrong with Lily.' Llinos dropped her pristine napkin onto the polished surface of the table. 'Her attitude lately is bordering on rude, not to say hostile.'

'Perhaps you should have a word with her,' Joe said. 'It's possible she's just missing Watt; they were walking out together, weren't they?'

'That could be it.' Llinos stared at her

husband across the gleaming silverware and, in the candlelight, he looked like a bronzed idol carved from precious stone. Her heart ached with love for him. He had been through the mill lately. Even now he looked distracted, as though his thoughts were elsewhere.

'What's wrong, Joe?' she asked, leaning forward, stretching to touch his hand. He glanced at her and his eyes were seeing things beyond the room; beyond the thick walls of Pottery House.

'It's my sisters; something is wrong,' he said. 'I think it's time I took a trip up to the Welsh marches to see them. I could see how the estate is running at the same time.' He smiled. 'Financially things seem to be going well, the income improves each year.'

He turned his fingers in hers. 'I would ask you to come away with me, Llinos, but I'll be doing some hard riding.'

She sighed. 'And I would slow you up. I can't leave Swansea now anyway, Joe. I'm needed here. With Watt in America there's no-one to look after the pottery. I would ask Mr Marks to step in but he knows nothing about potting.' She smiled. 'And I can't expect Pearl to handle things, she'd cause mayhem in less than a day.'

She rose from the table and stood behind

him, her arms around his neck, her cheek resting against his glossy hair. 'If you do find there's anything seriously wrong with your sisters, I will come at once, of course.'

He turned, taking her in his arms, and she breathed in the fragrance of him: the scent of his skin, the clean smell of his hair. His hands were pressing into her back; she was so close to him she could feel his heartbeat. She closed her eyes.

'I love you, Joe.'

His mouth lingered on hers, held for a breathless moment and then he moved away.

'I'll get the groom to saddle up at once.' He turned in the doorway and looked back at her. 'I won't be away any longer than I can help. At least I will rest easy knowing Sam Marks is staying in the house and that Eynon is near at hand should you need him.'

'I will be all right,' Llinos insisted. 'I will just miss you, that's all. I hate it when we are apart. Can't you wait until morning at least?'

'No, I don't think I can. The sooner I leave, the sooner I'll be able to return.'

It was less than an hour later when Llinos stood at the gates of Pottery House and watched her husband ride away into the night. She bit her lip, fearing, as she always did, for his safety. She simply wouldn't be able to go on living if anything ever happened to Joe. She looked up at the heavy clouds that gathered over the river and clung to the pottery buildings. It was going to be a moonless night with the promise of rain. Llinos shivered and returned to the warmth of the house.

She felt at a loss as she wandered aimlessly into the empty drawing room. She could take up some embroidery or look at the latest patterns for the pottery, but she was too restless to settle to anything. At last, she climbed the stairs and knocked lightly on the door of Sam Marks's rooms.

She heard his voice telling her to enter and she turned the handle with a feeling of relief that her guest had not retired for the night.

'Llinos, my dear child, you look harassed to death! What is it?'

'Joe has ridden up to his sisters' home and I think it's going to rain. I do hope he rides carefully.'

'Ah, I thought I heard the sound of hooves on the driveway.' Samuel drew a chair nearer to the fire. 'Won't you join me for a little while?'

Llinos sat down, her hands clasped in her

lap. 'Are you lonely here, Mr Marks?' she asked and he shook his head.

'I have always liked my own company, which is not to say that I am averse to the company of a lovely lady now and again. And please, Llinos, don't stand on formality. Call me Samuel, I would like it.'

She nodded. 'I will. Do you miss your son, Samuel?'

'I do not! I want nothing more to do with him.' He leaned back in his chair. 'Tell me, why has Joe ridden off in such haste, is anything wrong?' He was clearly changing the subject.

'He wants to check on his sisters. Joe gets these . . . premonitions some would call them.'

'Joe's talents are many and unusual,' Marks said. 'I would trust that man to rescue me from any sort of crisis that this bad world could throw at me.'

Llinos smiled. 'I feel exactly the same.'

Samuel leaned forward and took her hand. 'But you are unhappy at his departure all the same. You are worried about his safety?'

Llinos nodded, her eyes filling with tears. 'He thinks of everyone except himself,' she said and Samuel patted her hand with his thin fingers.

'Now listen to me. Your husband has fought in the wars. He has survived the most dreadful battles as well as the most inclement of weathers. Joe can take care of himself, believe me.'

She was cheered by Sam Marks's certainty. He was right, Joe was a strong, intelligent, able man. He would sort out his sisters' problems and be home with her in a day or two. In the meantime she had work to do. She would check the books, the stock lists, the products that the Savage Pottery was producing; in short, she would take care of the business her father had founded and which, if God was willing, her children would one day inherit.

'Thank you for talking to me, Samuel.' Llinos rose to her feet. 'You have made me feel much better. Now, I'd better be getting ready for bed. I have to be up bright and early in the morning.'

But once in her room she stood at the window and looked out into the darkened garden, and, though she willed her thoughts to touch Joe as he rode into the night, for once there seemed no answering response.

'You see, Lily, I told you, men are all fools, give them a bit of flattery and they think they are gods!'

'Well, it seemed to work with Watt,' Lily agreed. 'I can't say I wanted him to kiss me, mind, but I managed to pretend I liked it.' She sighed. 'Anyway, he's in America now, I won't have to pretend any more, not for a while at least.' She looked at Polly who was sitting on the edge of her bed, her night-gown wrapped around her none-too-clean feet. 'Do you think I'm cold, Polly?'

'Bloody hell no!' Polly laughed, her head tipped back, her long hair swinging down her back. 'You're no more cold than I am. You're just more careful about who you gives it to. You wait, when the right man comes along, you'll fall for him like a pile of stones.'

Perhaps Polly was right but, somehow, Lily did not think so. She pulled the bed-clothes over her and stared at her friend wondering how many men Polly had slept with. She was not very old, perhaps about seventeen or eighteen, and yet there was a knowingness about her, a worldly-wise atti-tude that fascinated and repelled Lily at the same time.

Had she slept with Watt? She might have, that night she took his money. Somehow the thought was not a pleasing one. Even though Lily did not want him herself, she did not like the thought of Polly having him.

Perhaps, if Watt came back from America a rich man, she would overcome her coldness and marry him. Put up with his pestering in exchange for a ring on her finger and her own roof over her head. She had no intention of slaving in the Savage Pottery for ever more. As for the Tawe Pottery, the snooty-faced man there had turned her down. Told her they had enough painters, good men painters, and did not want a woman anywhere near the place.

'What's it like, Polly?' She asked. Polly stared at her uncomprehending.

'What d'yer mean?'

'Letting a man . . . do things to you? What do they do, exactly? I know they like to kiss and touch but what else?'

'You're a right case, aren't you?' Polly scrambled under the sheets. 'Damn it's getting cold, winter's coming.'

For a long time it appeared she was not going to satisfy Lily's curiosity. Polly lay back against the thin pillow, her arms beneath her head, staring up at the cracked ceiling. At last she spoke.

'Well, it's lovely, it's a lot of fun. Hurts at first mind when he pokes his thing in you but you soon gets used to it.'

Lily was mystified. 'Pokes what thing into you, where?' It sounded rather alarming and Polly had admitted it hurt at first.

'His "thing", you know, that thing between his legs, you daft sod. It feels good, I can tell you.'

Lily was appalled; she had never heard anything so disgusting in all her life. She could not believe that it was a common practice, perhaps it was only people like Polly, the 'lower orders' as the rich called them, who did things like that.

'Llinos and Joe don't do that, though, do they?' she asked. Polly lifted her head and looked at her in disbelief. 'Course they do, you fool! How do you think folks gets babies?'

Lily digested this in silence, trying to imagine anyone treating Llinos in such an undignified way. And babies, that was another mystery. She knew they grew inside the woman, she had seen plenty of swollen stomachs in her time, but the whole sordid procedure was disgusting to her.

'I'll never get married! Well,' she amended quickly, 'I'll never have children at any rate.'

'You might not be able to help it,' Polly said, laughing at her now. 'Sometimes it happens even when you don't want it to.'

'Why haven't you had children then?' Lily said triumphantly, feeling she had scored a point.

'I spits in a toad's mouth every time I plan to go with a man, that seems to help.' Polly did not sound at all sure and Lily knew that she could never bring herself to touch a toad let alone get close enough to spit in its mouth. She would just marry and not allow her husband to do anything but kiss and hold her and even that would be when she felt she could stand it. She knew men liked her. She brought in a good wage, saved most of it and, in addition, Polly had shared with her the money she had stolen from Watt. Oh yes, she would have a great deal to offer a prospective husband without all that sordid stuff. But she would keep that to herself; she did not want Polly to think of her as different, strange even.

'I think I'll go to sleep now,' Lily said but Polly sat up, her cheeks flushed.

'You've got me all riled up now, talking about men.' She began to dress quickly and Lily looked at her in dismay.

'What are you doing?'

'I'm going out. There's this lad, he's new in town, he's working down at the wharf. Dai Jones is his name and I found out today that he's lodging a few doors down from here. He's not really my sort of fella, a bit skinny, but he'll do for tonight.'

'You mean you're going to let him . . . ?'

Lily's words trailed away.

'Yes,' Polly said grinning. 'I'm going to let him poke his thing into me!' She pushed open the window and, before Lily could stop her, swung herself out onto the ledge and was shinning down the clumps of ivy with the dexterity of one well used to the task.

Lily closed her eyes but for a long time sleep would not come. When she did sleep nightmares haunted her: a beast, huge and grotesque, was forcing down on her, hurting her. She tried to scream but her mouth was stopped by a menacing hand.

She sat up sweating, gasping for breath, and to her relief saw that the pale rosiness of dawn was bringing the bedroom to life. The wardrobe had form, the chest in the corner was solid, brushed with early light. She was in bed and she was safe.

Polly's bed was empty, the window still stood open. Before the sun had taken hold on the day, Polly was climbing over the sill, dropping down into the room, her hair tangled, her clothing awry. She flung herself on her bed, arms and legs spread wide so that she resembled a starfish draped with seaweed.

'Hell's teeth, I sold Dai Jones short! He didn't stop; all night he kept on and on. I

266

didn't think he had it in him.'

'You'd better get washed.' Lily tried to keep the distaste from her voice. 'You smell a bit . . . a bit sort of stale.'

Polly puffed out a huge breath. 'I've got to rest, I'm worn out. In any case, I don't have to turn up for work like you at some ungodly hour of the morning. I have other ways of earning a living as well, you know.'

'Then I'll use the water.' Lily washed quickly, wanting to be out of the room, away from Polly's obvious satisfaction with her night's work.

'You'll learn one day that lying on your back being pleasured is much easier than slaving away to make some other person rich!' Polly's parting words followed Lily as she descended the stairs. Perhaps her friend was right, but no amount of money would persuade Lily to allow a man, any man, to do unspeakable things to her. No, she would keep herself for marriage and, even then, she would only give what she must.

The sounds of breakfast — of dishes being placed on the clean wooden table, the chatter of voices — was suddenly reassuring. Not every woman was like Polly; it was she who was strange, not Lily.

She moved into the dining room, a smile of superiority on her face. She was better than Polly, much better, she would demand more of life than Polly ever did and, what's more, with her looks and brains, she would get everything she asked for.

Letitia was dying. Joe knew it, Charlotte knew it and Letitia herself knew it. She reached a thin hand up towards Joe.

'I knew you would come.' Her voice was little more than a whisper. Joe sat beside her and held her hand gently. 'I sent my thoughts out to you and you responded. There truly are more things in heaven and earth than this world dreams of.'

Joe touched her forehead with the back of his hand. Letitia's skin was hot, her eyes overly bright. It was clear she had a fever, a fever that was in its last throes.

'Why didn't I come sooner?' he said and she smiled up at him.

'Because I blocked my mind to you. I didn't want you to come, not until the end. I'm ready, Joe, I want to die and I don't want doctors and such fussing over me. All I want is for you to promise that Charlotte will be all right. She can't live alone, Joe, she's far too timid for that.'

'I know. She shall come home with me,' Joe said, adjusting the covers as if the quilt could protect Letitia, keep the life in his sister's thin frame. Joe thought of Llinos; he had promised to send for her if matters were serious but there was no time. In a way he was glad. Seeing Letitia die would only remind Llinos of the unhappiness of her father's death. She had suffered too many tragedies lately; he did not want to place any more weight on his wife's slim shoulders than was necessary.

'I shall be buried in the family grave,' Letitia said. 'And, Joe, you have a place there too when it's your turn, you know that, don't you?' If Joe had needed proof that Letitia accepted him as her half-brother, this was it. He smiled and touched her sunken cheek.

'Thank you, Letitia.'

'But you won't be buried with the Mainwarings, will you, Joe?' she asked. 'You are your own man, you will go wherever you will, free like the breeze in the trees. But then, you have a long life ahead of you. I have lived mine and am grateful for it.'

She closed her eyes; her lashes were light, almost non-existent. Her breathing was shallow, laboured.

Joe leaned over her. 'You must conserve your strength. Save your breath, don't try to talk any more.'

Letitia's eyes opened and there was a

gleam in them that reminded him of her indomitable courage.

'Save my breath for what, brother, to list my virtues to St Peter at the gate?' She smiled softly. 'It's time. Fetch Charlotte.'

They sat with her for little over an hour, Joe one side of the bed and Charlotte, weeping, at the other. Letitia passed away at dawn light with scarcely a tremor and with the peaceful exhalation of her last breath.

Charlotte began to whisper prayers and Joe bent his head, speaking to the spirits of his ancestors, asking for care to be taken of the soul of this, his sister. The sun climbed higher in the sky, a sharp autumn sun, and Joe rose at last and closed the curtains. He turned to Charlotte and helped her to her feet. 'There are things to be done,' he said. 'And when this is all over, you are coming to Swansea with me.'

Llinos heard the sound of the carriage on the drive and wondered who was coming to visit. Her regular visitor, Eynon, always walked the short distance between the two potteries and, as for other friends, she had few in the town of Swansea.

The maid knocked at the door and without waiting for an answer opened it. 'It's the master, he's back home and he has a lady with him, a rich lady by the look of it, at any rate they've come in a very stately carriage.'

Llinos hurried to the hall in time to see Meggie take the coats and hats. Joe turned and came towards her.

'My love, it's good to be back home with you,' he said softly as he took her in his arms. 'I've brought Charlotte with me, she is alone now.'

'Letitia? Oh, Joe, I'm sorry!' She clung to him and then, behind him, she saw his sister, her head downcast, her shoulders bowed.

'Charlotte, you are welcome in our home, most welcome.' Llinos hugged the older woman, feeling with pity her frailness. 'I'm sorry about Letitia, so sorry. Come, let's go into the drawing room. I'll get the maid to build up the fire in one of the bedrooms, you're shivering.'

Charlotte seemed numbed by her loss. She would have stumbled had Joe and Llinos not been supporting her. 'You poor dear, you must be quite weary with the journey and everything.'

Charlotte was seated near the glowing hearth and leaned back gratefully in her chair. 'I am, weary I mean,' she said at last, her voice low. 'Once my room is ready, perhaps I can go to bed?'

'You can do just what you want,' Llinos said. 'This is your home now, you must treat it as such.'

'You are a kind girl, Llinos.' Charlotte spoke with difficulty, tears blurring her eyes. 'I couldn't bear to stay alone in that big house. Joe, you will see to all the business of selling it, won't you?'

She turned to him for reassurance, holding out her hand. He took it and his look was so tender as he patted Charlotte's hand that Llinos felt a constriction in her throat. It was good to see them together as brother and sister, even if the circumstances were so sad.

Later, with Charlotte safely asleep, soothed by one of Joe's potions, Llinos sat with him and listened as he talked.

'Letitia died peacefully, there was no time to send for you, my love,' he said. 'I arranged the funeral as quickly as I could and then brought Charlotte home. Poor Llinos,' he smiled ruefully, 'I am filling the house with lame ducks, first Sam Marks and now Charlotte, but what else could I do?'

'You did exactly the right thing,' Llinos said, kneeling at his feet and resting her head in his lap. 'You are a good, kind man, Joe, and once again your uncanny instincts proved to be correct. Thank goodness you took heed of them.'

'I owed it to my father's memory to take care of my sisters. I have a very small family now, Llinos. There's you and Charlotte and my birth mother. I have neglected her lately.' He relaxed a little. 'I love her very much but you are the most precious thing in my life, Llinos. You know that.'

'I know, my love.' Llinos brightened. 'Watt will be seeing your mother, remember,' she said. 'He will give her the gifts you sent and she will know you think of her and love her.'

'She knows that without being told,' Joe said. 'Mint needs nothing and no-one. She is secure and happy with her people and when she's old she will become an elder and be cared for by the Mandans. I have no fears for my mother; the way of life is different there in America among the native people.'

'It's very strange,' Llinos said. 'We are supposed to be the civilized ones and yet our old people are prey to loneliness and neglect, sometimes dying in poverty.'

'Let's not get too maudlin,' Joe said. 'In any case, I think it's high time we went to bed.' His eyes gleamed. 'To sleep, my darling wife, so don't look at me like that!'

Laughing, he swept her into his arms and kissed her. 'I'm so glad to be home.' He held her close and she clung to him knowing that she was the luckiest woman in the world.

Charlotte was like a shadow about the house, hardly speaking, until she happened upon Samuel Marks one day. He was sitting in the garden, well wrapped against the autumn chill in a good wool coat with a shawl draped over his shoulders. She had made a point of avoiding him until now, accepting his hand when he had been introduced but unwilling to be drawn into conversation. When Samuel saw Charlotte coming along the path, he doffed his hat.

'Please, dear Miss Mainwaring, forgive me if I don't rise, my old legs are a bit rickety these days. I put it down to the time I spent in prison.'

In spite of herself, Charlotte was intrigued. 'You were in prison? What for?' Immediately she caught herself up. 'I'm sorry, I'm forgetting my manners. It is, after all, your business, Mr Marks.'

'Please sit with me and allow me to tell you all about it. And, please, call me Sam.' They sat for some time until the day dwindled away and the sun sunk below the horizon. But by the time they returned indoors Charlotte Mainwaring and Samuel Marks had formed a friendship that was destined to blossom into something much more.

FIFTEEN

As the autumn days faded into the wettest of Novembers, Llinos began to feel that perhaps the foolish charges of murder had been dropped and Joe was safe at last. Her false sense of security was brief. Her composure was shattered when a letter arrived from Grantley to say he would be in Swansea for a few days towards the end of the week. Why was he coming? Had he heard anything from the judge or the courts? She left the house and walked out into the dank air, unable to concentrate on anything indoors; not even the affairs of the pottery could hold her interest this morning.

The river was swift, running full, swollen by rain down towards the sea. At full height the tidal waters of the Tawe were impressive, washing the banks with greedy strength, swirling thick branches in the eddies as though they were mere twigs. Llinos stood looking down into the river without seeing it. She thought of Joe, meeting Grantley in the sitting room of the Angel Hotel and wondered what was happening. Why the Angel Hotel? Why did

Grantley not come to the house? The questions worried her mind as she searched for an answer that she could not find. She had wanted to go with Joe but he had told her, very gently, that he would go alone. He was a strong, independent man and Llinos understood that he wanted to protect her in the event that Grantley was bringing bad news. So was it bad news?

The rain began to fall more heavily and, shivering, Llinos turned back and walked briskly towards the pottery gates. It was time she pulled herself together, time she took charge of her business and saw that everything was running smoothly. She was allowing herself to fall to pieces, it would never do. It did not help her and it certainly did not help Joe.

The kilns rose high above the walls, shimmering with warmth, the stonework steaming as the rain hit. Inside each of the four kilns would be stacked the freshly made pottery: jugs, bowls and plates set carefully within the saggars. She stood for a moment looking up at the towers and thought of the days when there was only old Ben to see to the fires. Those were the days when she, Watt and Binnie clung together like lost souls. But all was different now. Now she had Joe, didn't she?

She visited each of the sheds in turn, taking her time. In the potting shed, the throwers were up to their elbows in clay, forming the first crude shapes ready for the turners. It was good to see a tall jug emerge from a lump of shapeless clay; just a form without handles, without lips and without finesse, but recognizable in spite of that. She had always loved the pottery, loved everything about it. Now she thought only of Joe.

'Morning, Mrs Mainwaring.' One of the younger throwers dipped his fingers into a bowl of water and pressed them into the neck of a jug he was shaping.

'Good morning, Dai. How is your mam today?'

'Not too good, this weather gets to her chest, see, makes her cough worse so she can hardly breathe.'

'I'm sorry to hear that, perhaps you would like me to give you some medicine for her. I have several bottles laid in the cool pantry.'

Dai looked uncomfortable. 'No thank you, Mrs Mainwaring, my mam won't take nothing funny-like. She don't think kindly to taking the stuff the doctor gives her, let alone . . .' His words trailed away but Llinos knew what he had been about to say. She sighed and moved on, fighting the weak tears that blurred her vision. No-one trusted Joe, not since he had been accused of murdering her father. And how could she blame the townspeople for being cautious? Joe was an outsider, he would always be an outsider wherever he went. Even in America, among the Mandans, Joe did not really have a place because he was of mixed race. But at least there he was not regarded with suspicion.

In the painting shed the smell of lead and oxide hung heavy. The doors had been closed against the damp and a thin light was all that penetrated the windows. A bad light for painting.

Pearl greeted her, smiling widely. 'Morning, missis, we're doing fine in here, no need for anyone to worry about that. Not with Pearl in charge.'

'I'm sure you are looking after things splendidly,' Llinos forced a cheerful note into her voice. 'Still, I expect you'll be glad to see Watt coming back, won't you?'

'Oh, aye,' Pearl said, 'but not too soon, I hope. I'm enjoying myself, I like being in charge.'

Llinos patted Pearl's big shoulder. 'And very good at it you are too.'

Lily was working rapidly on a large bowl, painting a firebird at the deepest part of the centre. The colours were bright, the orange-red feathers springing out from the flat grey background. The black edging around the neck and the head of the bird gave a pleasing sharpness to the painting.

'That's very good, Lily.' Llinos bent closer and when the girl turned and looked up at her, there was no warmth in her look.

'Thank you, Llinos,' she said, her voice devoid of expression.

'What is it, Lily, are you all right?' She was rather pale, Llinos noticed, her cheeks appearing thinner; perhaps she was sick.

'I've just got a bit of a bad stomach, that's all.' Lily sounded defensive and Llinos looked at her in concern.

'Have you been to see the doctor, Lily?'

Lily hung her head. 'No, miss, don't like doctors, they poke you about and such. I'll be all right, don't you bother about me.'

She turned away and continued to work, the angle of her shoulder effectively shutting Llinos out. Llinos felt irritated but what Lily did or felt was none of her business, the girl made that quite obvious.

On her way out, she had a word with Pearl. 'Is Lily all right?' she asked quietly. 'It's just that she seems, well, offhand, as if she's offended by something I've done or said.'

'*Duw*, don't take no notice of her, she's like that with everybody. Thinks she's a cut above the likes of me. Big-headed that girl is and on what I don't know!' Pearl shrugged. 'She's just an orphan living in lodgings, not a well set-up married woman like I am. Sometimes I feel like giving her a good shaking.'

'Do you think she's missing Watt? Could that be it?' Llinos was anxious to find an excuse for Lily's behaviour.

'Bless you no! Lily's the sort who keeps herself to herself. She thinks loving a man is something dirty, poor misguided girl.'

Llinos took a deep breath. 'Well, perhaps no-one has taught her anything different. Coming from the orphanage, I expect her upbringing was strict.'

'Still, most girls got some feelings but not Lil, she shies away from a man, even a nice man like Watt. She's going to lead a troubled life, is that one.'

Llinos left the sheds and looked up at the leaden sky. It was still raining. For a moment she envied Watt, away in the sunny climes of America. But no, she would rather be here in Swansea than anywhere else in the world because Swansea was where Joe was.

Watt stretched his long legs out before

him, sighing with contentment. He was aware of the sunshine hot against the skin of his arms. Already he was beginning to brown, to look like a native of West Troy. Behind him, inside the house, he could hear the loud tones that Mrs French used to direct the coloured maids. It bothered Watt that the landlady spoke to the servants as if they were both deaf and stupid.

John joined him on the porch, a large mug of coffee in his hand. 'Well, what did you get up to last night?' John was smiling but Watt had the feeling he was being patronized.

'Not much,' he said. 'I danced with a sweet little girl and drank quite a bit but other than that, as I said, not much.'

'No roll in the hay?' John asked conversationally and Watt made a face at him.

'No roll in the hay. You were right, as usual. The most I was allowed was an occasional squeeze of the hand and a quick goodnight kiss.'

'I thought you were promised a good time.' John was openly laughing and, after a moment, Watt joined in.

'I found,' he said, 'that by a good time Leigh meant plenty of drinks and the chance to hold a woman in your arms while the music played. No wonder everyone round here is panting to get married.'

He chose not to discuss his meeting with Binnie, that was something he wanted to keep to himself.

'So you didn't learn anything about the area, then?' John asked, picking a fly out of his coffee with the tip of his finger.

'I wouldn't say that.' Watt had learned a great deal, Leigh was a man who enjoyed talking. He talked about Binnie Dundee and his rich father-in-law Dan McCabe and how the pottery business had flourished even more since Binnie had joined the firm. One thing was clear: this was not the place to found another pottery. The land that they had been sent to survey was further inland, close to the river and the hills. He had asked Leigh about it and the man had looked doubtful.

'That's Indian country,' he said. 'They cling to what's their own and who can blame them?'

'But they don't own the deeds to the land?' Watt had asked. He had seen Leigh shrug his big shoulders.

'Don't know nothin' bout no deeds but that land been Indian country since before I was born. They ain't going to give it up without a struggle, see?'

'What are you thinking?' John asked. 'I can almost see the wheels turning in your brain.' Once again he was laughing at Watt.

'I'm going out for a stroll,' Watt said rising to his feet. 'I'll see you later.' He was pleased with himself, he had kept his own counsel. It was good to know more than John for once.

He walked down towards the main street, aware of the sun high above his head. He was meeting Binnie in the hotel on the corner and he wondered how Binnie would explain and excuse himself.

Binnie was there before him, looking tanned and healthy. He was not a tall man but he was thick-set and had become muscular. He looked every inch the prosperous businessman in his light shirt and well-cut breeches.

He led Watt to a quiet corner of the large, airy room and almost immediately a jug of fruit cordial was brought by a rotund, clean-smelling barman.

'Here's what you ordered, Mr Dundee,' the man said. 'My good woman made it up special, just as you like it.'

So Binnie was not a man for hard liquor, that was rather surprising in the circumstances.

'Watt, it's great to see you.' Binnie had not lost the accent of the Welsh people he had grown up with, but now it was smoothed by pleasant overtones.

'It's a surprise seeing you!' Watt said, smiling. 'But you're looking great and happier than I ever saw you in Swansea.'

Binnie leaned forward. 'I am happy, Watt. I'm married to a wonderful woman and I have three fine sons. Business is booming, I'm rich now. What more could a man want?'

'One less wife?' An imp of mischief brought the words to Watt's lips but he regretted them almost immediately. 'I'm sorry, Binnie, that was silly of me.'

'I just want you to keep quiet about all that,' Binnie said soberly. 'I know I've done wrong but I couldn't set my feet in any other direction. I love Hortense in a way I never loved . . . any woman. I don't think I ever loved Maura at all. How is she these days?' He asked the question casually but there was a tension about his shoulders and the set of his jaw that was unmistakable.

'She is still working for Eynon Morton-Edwards,' Watt said. 'And she is still as miserable as ever. Look, Binnie, I don't blame you for what you've done and you can rely on me not to say a word about it to anyone.'

'Not even Llinos?' Binnie asked.

'Definitely not Llinos,' Watt said. 'She really wouldn't understand.'

The two men sat in silence for a time and Watt took the opportunity to look around him. The place was obviously reserved for the more affluent members of society. The walls were pale, the windows large but shaded with blinds. The floor carpet was rich and tasteful and the wide staircase sported an intricately carved banister.

It was so strange coming here to America, a vast country by all accounts, and meeting the one man he had never expected to see again.

'Llinos well?' Binnie asked and it was clear that the subject of his own relationship was closed.

'Yes, she's fine.'

'How many little ones has she got?'

'None.' Watt shook his head. 'Poor Llinos, she lost her baby when —' He broke off; it never did to reveal too much information, information that would explain his real purpose here.

'The old man's dead,' he said. 'Captain Savage passed away after a long illness. It was a kindness to see him go.'

Binnie sighed. 'Everything changes, nothing stays the same.'

'That's just about right.' Watt drank some of the cordial; it was light and refreshing and the coolness lubricated the dryness of his throat. He wondered if Binnie was ever homesick. Even if he was he could never go back to Swansea, never see his old friends. They would ask questions and Maura, well, she would make demands. Binnie was better off staying put.

He took a map out of his pocket, the map that outlined the land Joe owned. 'Look at this,' he said. 'Can you tell me anything about it?'

'Well, it's a pretty big spread of ground some miles west of here. Nothing there, mind, no town, no nothing. Only Indians. Why are you interested in it?'

'I was asked to look at it, that's all,' Watt said. 'Perhaps with a view to developing it.'

'Not much chance of that,' Binnie said. 'The Indians wouldn't like it. Useless land it is, too, barren. Won't grow much there, I can tell you. You're wasting your time.'

Watt folded the map away, disappointed. He had seen the trip to America as a way to grow rich and now it seemed there was little chance of that.

'Well, where would you say was a good place to start a pottery?' Watt decided to take the plunge and tell Binnie at least part of the story. 'What if I wanted to build a pottery of my own for instance. Where would I go?'

'Well, you'd need to be close to water and the land on that map you just showed me is as dry as a bone, scrubland. I would say somewhere near the upper Hudson regions would be my favourite, perhaps Albany or Saratoga.'

Watt sighed. 'Well, it's only a dream. I don't suppose I would ever have enough money to make pots out here.' He looked up at Binnie. 'What do you make in your place?'

Binnie frowned. 'Well, they call it "whiteware". It's good stuff, sturdy and yet some of it is quite fine.' He finished off his drink and rose to his feet, holding out his hand to Watt. 'I gotta go but, if you want a job, you can have one in my place, just say the word.'

Watt shook his head. 'Thanks, Binnie, but I'm just visiting. Joe Mainwaring paid for the trip; he thinks it's time to expand, branch out, something like that.'

'Oh, Lord!' Binnie looked troubled. 'Keep them away from Troy, there's a friend. I don't think my nerves would take another meeting like this.' He pumped Watt's hand. 'I can only thank God that you understand what I've been through and you're willing to keep your mouth shut.'

'You need never fear anything from me.'

He stepped forward and hugged Binnie. He had been his friend since childhood and, meeting him again now, Watt felt he loved him like a brother. 'Have a good life, Binnie.'

He sighed as he sank back into his seat. It was a strange world all right, but at least now Binnie had set his life in order and who was Watt to condemn? He poured the last of the cordial and drank it in one gulp. He was hot and tired and, suddenly, he wanted to go home.

'What did Mr Grantley have to say?' Llinos felt nervous as she faced Joe across the expanse of hallway. She waited impatiently for the maid to take his coat and then linked arms with him. 'Come into the sitting room, tell me everything.'

'There's nothing to be anxious about. He's been digging up some dirt on our Dr Jones.' Joe was frowning. 'It seems there was some scandal about the doctor having concealed a suspicious death some time ago.'

'I don't remember anything about that,' Llinos said thoughtfully. 'Surely the gossips in Swansea would have had a wonderful time regaling each other with such a tale?'

'It was before Jones came to Swansea,

when he lived in Neath. Apparently an elderly widow died leaving him all her savings. The relatives were, understandably, angry and Jones left the area under a cloud.'

Llinos digested this in silence; it reminded her chillingly of Mr Cimla, the man who had come courting her mother. Mr Cimla had charmed Gwen Savage and once he had her confidence, he proceeded to spend her money as if it was from an endless pocket. The pottery had almost gone under in the process. Gwen had paid the ultimate price for her folly, she had died at Cimla's hand though it had never been proven.

'Is Mr Grantley going to bring this up in court?' Llinos asked. She saw Joe frown. 'What is it, love?'

'I asked Grantley to go to the man privately, tell Jones to withdraw all charges against me. I don't want to see the doctor pay twice for the one folly.'

'Sometimes, Joe, you are too charitable. What did Grantley say?'

'That it's far too late for that, the date has been set. I will be required to attend the next sessions.' Llinos clung to him, her face against his shoulder; she was so frightened, she could not bear it if he was sent to prison again.

'It will be all right,' he said. 'I promise

you, Llinos, everything is going to work out fine. The case against me will be dropped, believe me.' He tipped her face up and kissed her. She held him close, loving him, wanting to protect him from pain and worry just as he was attempting to protect her with his reassurances.

'Sounds as if someone is having a good time.' Joe lifted his head to listen. The sound of the piano tinkled through the hallway. He smiled at Llinos.

'Someone plays very well,' he said. 'Let's join them, it will cheer us up to have company.'

As it turned out, it was Samuel who was seated at the piano, his old fingers running nimbly over the keys. Charlotte was sitting close to him, her chin in her hands, her expression rapt.

Sam looked up when they entered the room but continued to play. Charlotte made way for Llinos on the sofa. 'Isn't he wonderful?' she whispered. 'That Beethoven sonata has been my favourite ever since I first heard it.' She looked wistful for a moment. 'Dear Letitia used to play beautifully, you know.'

Llinos took Charlotte's hand and held it tightly. The soft repetitive sounds of the music washed over her and she closed her eyes. That such beauty could be produced by the bent fingers of Samuel's thin hands running across the keys was nothing short of a miracle. The piano had not been played in years.

When the music finished a silence hung over the room, and then Charlotte snatched her hand away from Llinos's and clapped vigorously. 'Bravo, Samuel!' she said, her cheeks flushed. 'Bravo!'

'You're so talented,' Llinos said rising to her feet. 'Will you play us something else?' Sam shook his head and rose from the stool.

'Please excuse me, I'm a little tired to-night, perhaps some other time.' He bowed to Charlotte. 'It is you who bring out the music in me, my dear lady,' he said, his voice thick. 'When I am with you I almost believe once more in God. Now I'm going to bed, if you will all excuse me.'

'Isn't he wonderful!' Charlotte enthused, 'I am so glad we have become friends. Samuel has enriched my life with his knowledge and his talents.'

Llinos met Joe's eyes and smiled. It was good to see his sister so animated. It had been the right decision to bring her to live in Swansea. Here Charlotte had found a new lease of life.

'I think I'll go up, too, if you young ones

don't mind,' Charlotte said. Joe took her arm and led her towards the door.

'How about I bring you a nice hot toddy to see you off to dreamland?' Joe said and Charlotte looked up at him with a wicked twinkle in her eye.

'All right, but if you weren't my brother I'd suspect your motives, young man.' They disappeared into the hall and Llinos could hear Charlotte's voice as she climbed the stairs. Now Llinos was alone worries crowded back into her mind. Joe was going to the next sessions. What would happen then? Her stomach turned over with fear. What if, in spite of everything, he was found guilty? She put her hands to her head as if she could suppress the thoughts whirring around there. She closed her eyes and tried to picture the jail: the filth, the vermin, the darkness. It was too much to bear.

'He will be all right,' she said out loud. 'Joe is innocent, they will not find him guilty.' Even as she spoke she knew she was no longer convinced of the justice of the British courts. Joe had been wronged once. What made her think that he would find justice now?

CHAPTER

SIXTEEN

John Pendennis walked the broad, dusty street towards the edge of town determined to see the McCabe pottery for himself. It had been interesting to spend time talking to Binnie Dundee. The man was strong, well set-up and obviously well respected, but he was just a son-in-law, a man who had gotten lucky with a rich family. Now John needed to speak to the man himself, Daniel McCabe.

The gates stood open and in the yard a group of small boys were picking up bits of clay and throwing them into a large bin. It seemed that the process of making pots did not vary much even on different continents.

He was approached at once by the chargehand, a man in his forties, John guessed, a man whose hair was coated with fine white dust from the china clay. He regarded John from steady, though narrowed, eyes and waited for him to come within talking distance.

'Can I help you, sir?' He took in John's good clothes, the set of his shoulders and the confident manner John knew he drew around himself like a cloak.

'I'm looking for Daniel McCabe,' John said. 'I would like a word with him, perhaps you'll tell him I'm here. John Pendennis is the name.'

'English, is it?' the man said easily. 'Well you won't find Mr McCabe here today. He's at home with his family. I could fetch Mr Dundee for you,' he volunteered. 'He's in charge.'

'No, thank you,' John said. 'Where does Mr McCabe live?'

The man hesitated, torn between politeness to a stranger and the wish to protect his boss from any intrusion.

'You might as well tell me,' John said reasonably. 'I could learn as much from any man in the saloon bar.'

Seeing the sense of this, the man nodded. 'Right, you can find him in Rosemary Street, the big new house on the edge of the town.'

John considered asking if he could look around but decided against it. The chargehand would simply refer him once more to Binnie Dundee.

As he left the site of the pottery, the smell of the stone and clay washed over him bringing a sense of nostalgia and he realized that he was homesick for Cornwall. Well Cornwall was a long way away, far across the sea. In any case, there was nothing for him there, not yet at least. John would return, a successful businessman, and then Treherne could look out.

Anger filled John as he retraced his steps back towards the town. He thought of how Treherne's bailiffs had turned him out into the street when his father was so sick he was unable to stand. Treherne's inhumanity had to be witnessed to be believed. But one day he would be punished for it and John would be on hand to see his downfall.

John acknowledged to himself that he had lost respect for his father, had grown tired of his weaknesses, of his inability to run his affairs. His refusal to allow John to take over had been a constant source of aggravation between them but, still, his father should at least have been allowed to die in his own bed.

Daniel McCabe's house was rambling and yet charming. Flowers of a sort John could not identify grew around the windows and trailed onto the porch roof, bringing a splash of colour to the whitewashed building. Daniel McCabe was, obviously, a rich, successful man.

Through the open door John could see the trappings of success; the fine polished floor was scattered with deep carpets. The furniture was highly polished and fashioned in good hard wood. A brass oil lamp with an ornate shade took pride of place on the table in the hall and an enormous oil painting took pride of place on the far wall.

John knocked as loudly as he could and waited. From inside he could hear sounds of laughter and for a moment he wondered if his timing was inopportune; it seemed the McCabe family were having some sort of celebration.

A maid greeted him, her skin was such a deep, warm brown that her teeth gleamed white as she smiled. Her hair sprung away from her head eluding the grasp of the white cap that seemed to be in danger of falling off at any moment.

'I would like to see Mr McCabe, if it's possible,' John said politely and the maid gestured for him to step into the hall. She disappeared and John was able to have a good look at the room which was much larger than he had imagined. A curved stair-case wound upwards and a cooling breeze drifted in through the large, open windows.

A bluff, red-faced man with a full set of moustache and whiskers came into the hall and stared at John through piercing blue eyes.

'Susie tells me there's an Englishman to

see me. Now how important can your business be, sir, to disturb me on the day when I am celebrating the christening of my third grandson?'

'I'm John Pendennis and I apologize for calling without an appointment,' John said. 'But I will be returning to England in a little over a week so time is short.'

'Sit down, then. I can spare a few minutes I suppose.'

'I'll come straight to the point,' John said. 'I have come to Troy knowing there is a growing potting industry here in the region. I'm looking to set up in business myself and I wondered if the town could support two potteries.'

'I doubt it.' Dan chuckled. 'But there's plenty of land hereabouts and you could surely try, sir, no-one can stop you doing that.' He looked at John closely. 'Mind, you are a well-set-up young man, a gentleman by the way you look and sound. Perhaps I could find a place for you myself.'

'What sort of place?' John was prepared to listen to any suggestion that would advance his prospects of becoming rich.

'I have been thinking of opening another pottery myself, expanding shall we say? Now as I hear it you and your friend have had experience in the potting business.

You've come here already owning a parcel of land over in Indian country. My advice to you is to forget that. It's going to be too damned hard to fight off the folk who are there; the Indians who think the land is rightfully theirs. They don't hold with buying and selling, they think the earth is there for all to share and in my opinion, they got a point.' He shrugged. 'So you might be better off working for me.'

'You are well informed about my affairs,' John said dryly. 'And you seem to own more than a fair share of land yourself.'

'Maybe I do but the land was going begging. I made Troy a town where folks can work and earn a decent wage. As for being informed, I make it my business to be,' Dan said, smiling. John cursed Watt and his loose tongue; he had got drunk with one of the men working for McCabe and must have told him everything.

'Well, you'll know that I have no money of my own,' John said. 'I've been sent out here to reconnoitre the place, to learn the layout of the land that's owned by my boss back home.'

Dan looked at him shrewdly. 'I like your honesty, son.' His tone had warmed, John noticed. 'Think it over, son, and then come to see me here in a day or two. Make it evening time and I'll be sure to be here. We'll talk again then.' He rose to his feet, a big man in every sense of the word. He held out his hand and John took it, aware of the favour in Dan's eyes.

'You are a gentleman, anyone can see that,' Dan said. 'You have looks and brains, you could go far out here. America is the land of opportunity, remember that, son. Now, I must go and see my grandson. The maid will see you out.'

As John retraced his steps along the streets where the more affluent lived towards the lower end of town where boarding houses and stores and bar rooms nestled side by side, he thought over what Dan McCabe had said. Would it be so bad to work here, to put down roots in a new place? Instead of working for Joe Mainwaring he would be working for an American who knew his way around, a man of property and a man well respected by the townsfolk for his integrity.

America might well be a land where any man could become rich, and rich is what John wanted to be. McCabe's offer could not be dismissed out of hand, it was well worth considering, but for now he would keep the offer to himself. Watt was a good honest lad but he was sometimes naive, giving away too much.

'Where have you been?' Watt was sitting outside on the steps of the porch of the boarding house when John returned home. He was looking brown and fit; he was a handsome man and would probably have more than his fair share of women running after him out here in America.

'Just walking about, finding out the lay of the land. That's what we are supposed to be doing, isn't it?'

'I suppose so,' Watt said as John sat down next to him. 'Though I can't see that we'll have any luck round here. Mr McCabe and Binnie got it all sewn up. As for the parcel of land belonging to Joe, I don't think it's worth a light.'

'I suppose we could hire a pair of horses and take a look further up the Hudson,' John suggested. 'We could take some food and camping stuff and at least have a look at the land.'

'Yea, I expect we could but do you think it's a good idea?'

'Why, what are you afraid of?' John smiled knowing the answer only too well.

'I'm afraid of getting an arrow in my back,' Watt said. 'I hear some of these Indians can be a touch unfriendly.'

'You'd be unfriendly too if someone was

trying to take away what belonged to you.' John was suddenly serious. 'I know first hand how that feels and it's not pleasant.'

'Well then?'

'Well then, let's take a look, talk to the Indians, tell them we mean no harm.'

'And I thought I was the daft one!' Watt said. 'You can't talk to shadows; the Indians hide behind the rocks and attack without warning.'

John digested this in silence and then nodded. 'I expect you are right. Still, I think we should at least take a look beyond the boundaries of West Troy. We can hardly go back to Joe Mainwaring and tell him we saw nothing.'

'That's fair enough,' Watt replied. 'Shall we set out tomorrow then, ride a couple of miles up river?'

'Let's leave first thing.' John was thinking of his proposed meeting with Dan McCabe. He would like to learn a bit more about the country before he committed himself to anything. 'We'll need to make an early start, we'll need to ask around for horses and to find ourselves a guide.'

'Suits me,' Watt said leaning back against the wooden post and closing his eyes. 'This sun makes me feel sleepy. I'm sure I could get used to living an idle life out here, just eating Mrs French's food, drinking beer down at the saloon and sleeping.'

'Well, you need money to do that,' John said. 'And you won't get it by sitting around on your backside, that's for sure.'

'You don't have to tell me that.' Watt opened his eyes and there was a hint of anger in them. 'From the time I could walk, almost, I worked at the pottery. I worked long hours too, sometimes not getting enough to eat. We haven't all had the easy life you've had, mind.'

John was silent. Watt was right, his life had been easy up until the time that Treherne had taken it all away from him. But he would rise to the top again, no-one would keep John Pendennis down for long.

The next morning John was up early. He walked the streets trying to find a guide willing to ride with him. He quickly learned that no-one was prepared to take off up country without several days notice. It was clear that the trip would take more than a few days to plan.

Still, unprepared as he was, it was with an unaccustomed sense of eagerness that John made his way, the next evening, to Dan McCabe's gracious house. He had taken extra care with his appearance and knew he looked every inch the gentleman. It seemed that Americans were impressed with a well turned-out, well-spoken Englishman.

Susie smiled a welcome, revealing her strong white teeth. John bowed to her and she looked down in confusion, stumbling as she led the way into the garden at the back of the house. Dan was not alone, a lady sat close by and alongside her were two young, beautiful women, dresses spread out around them like the petals of a flower.

'This is my wife,' Dan said, 'and, Mrs McCabe, this is the English gentleman I was telling you about.'

'Welcome to my humble home,' Mrs McCabe said in a soft voice. 'These are my girls, Josephine and Melia.'

John was aware of how well set-up Binnie Dundee had become by marrying into the McCabe family and he saw now that he was being viewed as a potential suitor for one of the single daughters. He was quite taken by Melia who was bubbly and flirtatious and whose eyes met his with a provocative challenge, but marriage, he wasn't ready for that yet.

Susie brought a tray heavy with china. John resisted the urge to take it from the girl. He felt such an action would be frowned on.

'Have a drink, John. It's all right if we call

you that, isn't it, son?' Dan did not wait for a reply. 'We don't stand on formality here, we all go by Christian names. It's more friendly, I guess.'

Melia was staring at him from under her lashes and John was aware of the perfume that seemed to rise from her skin. She was a lovely girl, slim but with curves in all the right places and she was obviously panting to get a man in her bed.

John made a point of smiling at her and she dimpled charmingly and it was plain that she did not suffer from shyness. 'Where you from in England, John?' she asked moving a little closer to him.

'A place called Cornwall, I don't suppose you've heard of it.'

'Well then you are wrong, John, Cornwall is right down south of the country and the coastline is rocky and sometimes the seas are treacherous.'

John concealed a smile. Melia McCabe had been doing her homework. 'You are quite right, of course. Brains as well as beauty, you are going to make someone an excellent wife.'

He was playing her along, he knew it but she did not. She seemed to radiate the smug self-satisfaction of a job well done and if he had any doubts her triumphant glance towards her sister dispelled them.

Mrs McCabe leaned towards him. 'I know you and my husband want to talk business but I hope you will join us for a meal later?'

'That's very kind of you and yes, I would like that very much.'

'Come on, then,' Dan said, 'these women will gossip to you all day. Let's get out of here or we'll get no business done at all.'

They walked through the long garden at the back of the house and John was grateful for the shade of the trees as the heat that had persisted all day was lasting well into the evening.

'I'm going to make you an offer, a very good offer,' Dan said. 'I want you to open up a new business for me over in Albany. You will be given a salary fitting for a man of responsibility and I'll arrange for a house to be put at your disposal.'

'And in return?' John asked, his thoughts racing.

'In return you will work your balls off just as if the business was your own. If'n when you build it up to a respectable level of profit, I would consider making you a partner.' He changed tack suddenly. 'You like Melia?'

'Yes, I do,' John said. 'She is a very lovely young lady.'

'Rich too,' Dan said laconically. 'That always helps.'

'I suppose so,' John said. 'Indeed I'm surprised that your daughters haven't been snapped up already.'

'No-one good enough round here,' Dan said. 'If any of the locals had any spunk then I'd give my girls away with a good heart but no-one matches up to Dan McCabe's idea of a good man.'

'But you know I've nothing to offer,' John said, not really convinced that he wanted to accept Dan's proposal. On the other hand he was not about to make any hasty decisions.

'You have breeding, son. You have education. As for money, I have more than enough of it. You came from a good family back home?'

'I did that,' John affirmed. 'My father owned a big house and a thriving business until he became too sick to continue with it.' It was as close to the truth as John was prepared to come.

'I'm a good judge of character,' Dan said. 'And in any case, Binnie, my son-in-law, knows a thing or two and he told me you must be a gentleman by the way you act and talk. In any case, I could see that much with my own two eyes.' He smiled. 'You would be on trial, of course, and I would send Binnie out from time to time to see how you're doing. That boy has a good business head on him and he knows the working of the pottery inside out. I trust Binnie with my soul as well as my money.'

'Give me a day or two to think about it,' John said. Dan looked at him carefully and then nodded.

'Cautious, I like that in a man. Come on then, let's go and eat some of Mrs McCabe's apple pie. You ain't tasted nothing till you've tasted my wife's cooking. A real lady is Mrs McCabe.'

The meal was delicious and Mrs McCabe beamed when John accepted a second helping of her apple pie. 'You sure have a fine appetite, John,' she said. 'I like that in a man, shows he's healthy and sound.'

Binnie Dundee was late joining the family meal. He looked across at John and nodded in a somewhat guarded way.

'Watt told you how we grew up together?' Binnie asked. There was a strange look in his eyes and John sensed there was more behind the question than at first appeared.

'No, not really. Watt doesn't talk about the past much at all.' Was that relief he saw in Binnie's face? John smiled. 'I think he's outgrown his childhood, he's more interested now in being a man.'

Binnie winked. 'I know exactly what you mean.'

'Now, boys, careful what you say in front of the ladies,' Dan said easily.

Mrs McCabe rose to her feet. 'Well, you can talk to your heart's content, me and the girls have got work to do.' Obediently, her daughters followed her but not before Melia had cast John one last, lingering glance.

'Get the liquor, Binnie,' Dan said expansively. 'Let the men enjoy a real man's drink.' Binnie left the room to reappear a few minutes later with a jug and three mugs.

'Good stuff this,' Dan said pouring the drinks in generous measures. 'I know because I make it myself. Go on, John, taste it and tell me you've tasted better.'

John took a tentative sip at the drink, it was smooth in his mouth but as he swallowed it seemed as if a fire had been lit in his throat.

'It's good stuff, all right!' He coughed and Binnie laughed at him.

'After a few of these, you'll think you've died and gone to heaven.' Binnie topped up his mug; he was, it seemed, used to the potent drink. That was strange, Watt had claimed that his friend drank only cordial. But then perhaps Binnie had needed to keep his wits about him. Watt clearly knew something about the man, something that was supposed to remain a secret.

The darkness was beginning to close in, shadowing the trees and the rich gardens in a mist. The men had been driven out onto the porch while the ladies saw to clearing away the debris of the meal. John sipped his drink slowly; he did not want to be witless, not now, because there was a great deal riding on his behaviour tonight. Could be his whole future.

Glancing through the open door, he saw Melia watching him and smiled inwardly. She was going to be a pushover. The drink had warmed his blood and he felt like taking Melia to bed and showing her what a real man could do for her.

'I can read you like a book.' Dan's voice interrupted John's thought. 'And I'm here to tell you that my girls are virgins and will remain that way until they marry, isn't that right, Binnie?'

'I'll vouch for the fact that Hortense belonged to no man before me, right enough.' Binnie smiled. 'And since the day we were wed, I've never looked at another woman. Hortense is all I want.'

John could see that Binnie was speaking the truth; his words were not simply a cover to impress his father-in-law.

'You are a lucky man,' he said feelingly. Dan punched his arm and lumbered to his feet.

'Come on, son, you are going to burst if you don't get a woman soon. Ever had a woman, John?'

John coughed in embarrassment; he had snatched a kiss with one of the maids in the days when his father could afford servants but he had never gone to bed with a woman. Now he was ashamed to admit his ignorance. Dumbly, he shook his head.

'Well,' Dan said, 'this is your lucky day, son. I'm going to get you initiated into the ways of women. You'll learn what they like and how to pleasure them. Then, on the day you gets married, you won't act like a damned fool.'

John was suddenly cold sober, events were moving too swiftly for him and he wasn't sure he liked it. Dan led down through the garden and away to the stretch of rocky land beyond. Binnie remained where he was, helping himself to another drink.

In the clearing beyond the trees, there was a small house. It was a pretty house, white-washed with neat curtains at the windows. Dan pushed the door open and called out loudly, his voice echoing through the small rooms.

A girl, no older than Dan's daughters, came into the room. She smiled when she saw them and slid her arm around Dan.

'This is Carla,' Dan said. 'Where are the rest of the girls?' he asked. Carla lifted her eyes towards the ceiling.

'Sleeping the hours away,' she said, her voice throaty and low. 'You're such a strong man that you wear us out.'

'Go wake them lazy women up so's my friend here can have a choice,' Dan said. John looked at him as the girl darted out of the room.

'Is this a house of ill repute?' he asked, his words sounding foolish even to his own ears. Dan sat down on one of the huge chairs. He laughed, his belly shaking over the tightness of his belt.

'If it is, it's my own private one,' he said. 'These are my girls, they keep me happy and I might tell you that no-one else gets a look in, that's the rules. I look after them well enough and they are here just for my pleasure.' He regarded John steadily. 'So now you know the honour I do you letting you have one of them, any one you choose. It's only hospitable for a man to share his goods with a visitor from another land.' Dan walked to the door. 'I'll leave you to it, son, I got things to do.'

When John was alone with the girls, they crowded round him touching his hair, his skin, exclaiming at the breadth of his shoulders and the narrowness of his hips. He suddenly realized that he did not want this: when he took a woman it would not be courtesy of another man, it would be by choice and in his own good time.

'Thank you, ladies,' he said, 'but I've got things to do, too.' He left the house and saw that Dan was waiting outside for him.

'I don't want to offend you, sir,' John said, 'but I'll decline your generous offer and when the time is right, I'll find my own woman.'

'Well the ways of the English are mighty strange,' Dan said. 'But I respect you for being your own man.' He put his arm around John's shoulder. 'Let's go back to the house, I think it's high time we talked business.'

CHAPTER
SEVENTEEN

Llinos felt the chill of the air on her face as she walked in the park with Eynon. His head was bent and his fair hair beneath his hat was ruffled.

'You see, Llinos, I don't love Annabel. I will never love her.' Llinos tried to read Eynon's expression and there was no doubt that he meant what he said. Part of her was sad for him but somewhere, deep inside, she was angry with him.

'Then why did you get involved with her in the first place?' she asked a little acidly. 'It seems you made love to her eagerly enough, she's pregnant!'

'She looked like you.' The words, simply spoken, cut Llinos to the heart. Filled with contrition, she slipped her arm through Eynon's and squeezed hard. She tried to think of something comforting to say but words failed her. Eynon spoke again.

'I suppose my one consolation is that *she* loves *me*.' He straightened his shoulders. 'And I have responsibilities to face, a wife, a child. I shall be a family man in spite of myself.'

The irony in his tone did not escape Llinos. She leaned forward a little to look into his face. 'I want you to be happy, Eynon, you know that. Perhaps you will come to love Annabel. Love can grow out of friendship, can't it?'

'Yes it can.' He met her gaze meaningfully and she was the first to look away.

'How is she feeling, is she well?' Llinos felt a constriction in her throat; she envied Annabel, envied her ability to conceive and carry a child without any problems. Since her miscarriage Llinos had watched her monthly curse with an intensity that was becoming an obsession; hoping, praying, that this time, this month, there would be no flow and instead there would be the beginning of another baby, hers and Joe's baby.

'She is in very good health but then, she's a young strong girl with nothing to do and certainly nothing to worry about,' Eynon said.

'Except the most important thing in her life, the fact that her husband does not love her,' Llinos said, a trifle more sharply than she had intended.

'Love does not come to order,' Eynon said reasonably. 'You know that, Llinos. If it did you and I would have married years ago.'

He was right, of course he was. 'I'm sorry, Eynon,' Llinos said. 'I'm like a bear with a sore head today.' She clutched his arm to her side. 'Joe is to appear at the sessions next Monday and I don't think I can go through the pain and fear of it.'

'Of course you can.' Eynon stopped walking and looked down at her. 'You are the one who kept the pottery going single-handed when your father was away at war, you are the lady who married Joe against all the odds. You have courage, Llinos, you will see this through with your usual dignity.'

'Thank you for your confidence in me.' Llinos smiled tremulously. 'But I wish I was as convinced as you are about my courage.'

Eynon put his arms around her, disregarding the hostile looks of a lady passing with her dog. 'We are all frightened at some time in our lives, it's only human, so don't be too hard on yourself.'

She leaned against him for a moment, loving him but only in the way that one friend loves another. After a moment she moved away from him.

'We'd better be getting back,' she said. 'I'm neglecting my guests.'

Eynon frowned. 'For heaven's sake, Llinos!' His voice was unusually sharp.

'Will you stop all this fear and guilt that's eating away at you, it's not like you.'

'I know.' Her voice held a note of sadness. 'I can't seem to control it. So much has happened these last months, my father dying, Joe being sent to prison, losing the baby, it's beaten me down, Eynon. I can't seem to summon the will power I once had.'

'Well you'd better snap out of it,' Eynon said. 'I love you dearly, Llinos, but I really think you are indulging in too much self-pity.'

His words jarred and Llinos felt as though she had been struck. But was he right? She thought about the past weeks, the way she had moped about the house, only smiling, putting on an act, when Charlotte and Samuel were present.

'Look, Llinos,' Eynon continued, 'you have become thin to the point of gauntness. You are not doing yourself or Joe any favours by acting this way. You are fast becoming drab.'

Llinos took a deep breath, trying to control the anger that suddenly raced through her. She stepped away from Eynon and stared up at him. 'How dare you talk to me like that!'

'Because it's true,' Eynon said. 'Take a good look at yourself, Llinos. I can tell you now, you won't like what you see.'

'To hell with you!' Llinos turned and ran from the park, careless of the fact that her bonnet had slipped off and was bumping against her shoulders. She was heading for the pottery before she realized that the last thing she wanted was company. She turned and made for the river. The waters of the Tawe, when they were calm, always had the ability to soothe her.

The sharpness of autumn was still in the air, the leaves on the trees were turning red and gold. The river reflected the colours, sparkling in the clear sunlight like a myriad of candles. She sank down on the bank and stared into the swiftly moving water. Had she become drab? Was she being unfair to her friends, to Joe? She felt tears, hot against her cheeks and she let them flow; she felt she must cry all the hurt and fear out of her system before she could pull herself together and start acting like the grown woman she was.

'God, this is a strange land.' Watt had dismounted from his horse and was standing on the banks of the huge river staring across the unending landscape. Ahead of them, the guide, half Indian and half white American, drew to a halt and prepared to wait patiently, his horse pawing the dusty ground.

'America is hot and sunny and fascinating,' Watt said. 'But now I've had enough of it. I can't wait to go home.'

'There's not a lot of good news to take back to Joe Mainwaring though, is there?' John was still astride his horse and Watt glanced up at him.

'We can't help that, now can we?'

'Well, no,' John said. Watt watched his face carefully, the man had something to say and Watt wished he would spit it out. He did.

'I'm thinking of staying here. I could work for Dan McCabe,' John said, staring out across the vastness of the landscape. 'What do you think?'

Watt shook his head. 'You'll have to please yourself on that, I can't advise you one way or another.'

John looked fit and well, Watt noticed, his skin was tanned brown already by the sun.

'Do you want to stay?' Watt asked. 'And if you do, are you letting Joe down?' Watt had not taken John to be a man to go back on a deal. His job had been to come out here and find a possible site for a new pottery for Joe and Llinos. Now he had taken Joe's money for the trip, he was thinking of backing out of the deal.

'What is there for me back home?' John asked. 'A job in a second-rate pottery with no prospects to speak of. Why don't you stay too while you have the chance? I'm sure Dan McCabe could find a place for you in his business.'

'No thank you.' Watt's tone was acid. 'I don't renege on deals.'

John smiled mirthlessly. 'You will learn that in this life the spoils come to those who grasp the opportunity, not to those who consider themselves honourable.'

'Maybe, but I've a conscience, I like to sleep at night.' Watt mounted his horse and stared John in the eye. 'And what about young Richard? You brought him from Cornwall and made him think you would be almost a brother to him. How will he feel if you don't come home?'

'Richard will be fine. He's fit in to the work at the pottery, hasn't he? His life is much better now than it was. I've done him a favour. Now I have to think of myself.'

'So you will settle for marriage with the McCabe girl in exchange for a good job, then?'

'Isn't that exactly what your friend Binnie has done?' John asked. Watt shook his head, pleased that he had not disclosed the secret of Binnie's past. It seemed John would not be above using anything to advance his own position.

'Binnie is in love with his wife, that much must be obvious even to you.' Watt was suddenly angry with John, angry at the way he had taken advantage of Joe, had taken his money and used it to his own advantage.

'I'm not letting Joe down, not really,' John said. 'I've written out a report for him. You can take that back to him, at least he will find it literate.' His voice was edged with sarcasm.

'Meaning?' Watt asked.

'Don't be offended but it's clear which one of us has the education. I mean, why do you think Joe sent me along with you?'

Watt felt like punching John's face until the superior expression was wiped away. Instead, he turned his horse in the direction of town, waving to the guide to follow him.

'You must do as you please,' he said coldly. 'But in my opinion, you are nothing but a twisting rat.'

John's derisive laugh followed Watt as he rode away. His blood was up, Watt felt the urge to kill for the first time in his life.

John called after him. 'Go on, run back home where you are safe, where you have to make no decisions, not even about the food you put in your mouth. You are a weakling, it's no wonder Lily gives you the cold shoulder.'

Watt ignored him. He rode his horse faster over the dusty ground, as if by putting a distance between himself and John he could outrun his jibes. But the blood was pounding in his ears and his hands were clenched around the reins until his knuckles gleamed white. And yet there was a sneaking feeling inside him that what John said was right. Perhaps Watt should grasp at any opportunity that presented itself. America was the land where anything was possible; just look at what Binnie had got for himself.

By the time he reached Mrs French's boarding house, he had calmed himself and he was able to smile and ask politely if he might have a bath.

'Don't want to do that too often,' Mrs French said warningly. 'Water can steal your strength.'

'I think you'll find that's a piece of folk-lore that no-one believes in any more,' Watt said but Mrs French wasn't convinced.

'If you're sure, I'll see to it,' she said.

It was good to lie in the tin bath and feel the warmth of the water lapping around him. It gave him time to think things through, to reason everything out. What did he really want out of life?

The choices were clear, to honour his pact with Joe and return home or to stay and work in West Troy. Even as he reasoned it out, Watt knew, without question what he most wanted: it was to be in Swansea with the people he loved. Tomorrow he would make all the arrangements for returning home and to hell with John Pendennis.

'I'll be happy to work for you, sir.' John was seated in the sunny sitting room of the McCabe household holding a glass of fruit cordial in his hand. Dan nodded sagely.

'Smart move, son. What made up your mind for you?'

This was tricky and John knew he must be careful how he replied. It would do no good to say there was no future for him working for Joe Mainwaring and to be seen as an opportunist who swayed this way and that with the breeze.

'I'm impressed by your wonderful country,' John said and he allowed a smile to spread across his face. 'And I'm *very* impressed with your beautiful daughters.' He coughed as if he had let slip something he meant to keep secret. He must in no way allow Dan to know that he had accepted marriage as part of the deal, oh no, he must put on the pretence that he admired the girls and was capable of falling in love with one of them.

'The offer you made me,' he said more seriously, 'it's a very good one. The opportunity for me to start my own pottery from scratch would be a challenge and one I would welcome. I believe it well within my capabilities.'

'So do I or I wouldn't have offered you the job.' Dan smiled. 'I knew I'd win you over one way or another,' he said. 'Tomorrow we'll ride over to Albany, find the best site and stake our claim on it. Then it's all up to you. You can cost the scheme from the building of the kilns to the buying of the fittings. Think you can handle it?'

At this point John felt that honesty was the best policy. 'I will learn, sir. I will learn quickly and very well.'

'That's all I wanted to know. Now, let's call the ladies in. Melia is just bustin' to meet you again, she's talked of nothing else since the first time she set eyes on you.' He rested his big hand on John's shoulder. 'And if you Cornishmen breed the same as the Welsh, I'll be a happy man.'

John was taken aback; he was being compared with Binnie Dundee and being viewed as a stud, a provider of grandchildren for the McCabes. Well, would that be such a difficult task?

John waited until the ladies were seated and then met Melia's eyes, smiling at her with just the right touch of interest and respect. At the same time he was aware of Josephine, young and pretty, her hair dishevelled in the most charming way. His smile included them both and he was amazed at his ability to turn on the charm, to flatter both girls and to coldly consider which one he would prefer to be married to.

Melia was an attractive woman, no doubt about that; she had the poise and charm of those who have known a privileged existence. She was physically attractive, too; a small build, fine features and the look in her eyes hinted at passion. But none of that made any real difference to John as there was something missing: that magnetism that attracts a man to a woman like a bee to a flower was simply not there. Josephine, now, she was different; she concealed her feelings, her eyes remained downcast, she did not provoke him to admire her the way her sister did. Ah, well, it was not a bad situation to be in, he thought perhaps he should just let matters take their course, let fate decide which girl would be his bride. And, if he got bored, there were many girls out there looking for a man, girls who would be willing to be a mistress rather than a wife. Just look at Dan's own little harem.

'John is going to be part of the family now,' Dan's voice jarred him out of his reverie. The big man stood before the fireplace, smiling expansively, thrusting his thumbs into the waist of his breeches as though to ease the strain on his stomach. 'He has agreed to work for the McCabe Pottery and I have great hopes that he will go far.'

Mrs McCabe looked John over carefully, her eyes steady as they met his, and John had the feeling she was not so easily convinced as her husband. Mrs McCabe suspected that his motives were engendered by self-interest more than anything and in that she was right. John knew he would just have to try harder to win her over. For all he knew, she might be the real power in the household.

'I think you should all know something about my background,' he said, but he directed his remark towards Mrs McCabe. 'My father was a very rich businessman in Cornwall and when I was a child I was given every advantage in life. Sadly, my father's death brought his financial problems out into the open and the result was that the Pendennis family lost everything.'

He smiled disarmingly. 'But I am young and strong, and I intend to make my way in the world and what better way to begin than to work for a man as successful as Dan McCabe?'

His words were heartfelt and even Mrs McCabe flashed him a smile of approval. That he admired her husband was obvious and, for the moment, that was enough for her. He was on his way to being accepted as part of a rich, successful family and to John, alone in the world as he was, it was a good feeling.

The sessions were held with a minimum of fuss in the old courtroom. Llinos sat on the scarlet upholstered chair near the back of the chamber, her hands clasped in her lap. Joe stood up before the judge, his head high, his blue eyes clear and direct as they looked straight ahead.

The judge spoke, his voice even, unconcerned. 'Dr Jones has decided to withdraw his complaint against Mr Mainwaring. It seems he lacks evidence to support his claims that Captain Savage was unlawfully killed. Therefore, it is my duty to dismiss this case forthwith.'

The usher indicated that the court should rise but Llinos, unable to believe that Dr Jones had finally accepted defeat and that

Joe was a free man, remained seated. Her legs were trembling, she felt sick with relief. She looked at Joe and he met her eyes, telling her with his unspoken thoughts, that it was over, justice had been done.

It was only when Grantley took her arm and helped her towards the door that Llinos began to cry.

'There, there, dear lady, it's over, your husband is free.' Mr Grantley patted her shoulder awkwardly. 'Nothing more to worry about.'

Joe was allowed out through another door and soon he joined Llinos and Mr Grantley at the front of the courthouse.

'Why did the judge rule that the case fell through?' Joe asked. 'Surely the man had no evidence.'

'The law is strange, a judge might have looked upon the titbits of information that the doctor tacked together as evidence. Still, he saw sense in the end, saw that to go to court would only expose him as a dishonourable man, a man who beguiled an old lady into leaving him her estate. He didn't want to be run out of town so he gave up his foolish vendetta.'

Llinos slipped her arm around Joe's waist and pressed her head against his shoulder. 'Let's go home, please,' she said, aware of the crowd that was staring at the scene as though still expecting some sort of public punishment of the man they saw as a murderer.

She climbed into the coach and Joe climbed in beside her. She leaned against him, wanting to be alone with him so that she could hold him close and convince herself that he was safe.

Mr Grantley sat opposite them and leaned back against the creaking leather seat, sighing in satisfaction. 'That's a good job over and done with,' he said. 'I thought the man would stop making foolish accusations once he was reminded that anyone can make a mistake, even him.'

'I did not make a mistake,' Joe said quietly. 'I gave Lloyd medicine to cure his pain, that was all I did.'

'I know that as you do,' Grantley said. 'But the people of the town chose to think differently. Anyway, you are out of the woods now, it's all settled.'

Llinos closed her eyes, knowing in her heart that the lawyer was wrong. Joe might have escaped prison, even perhaps the hangman, but in the eyes of the townspeople he would always be guilty.

CHAPTER

EIGHTEEN

It was good to step back onto Welsh soil.
Watt stared around him at the soft hills rising
around Swansea and took a deep breath of
the air permeating the docklands that
smelled of tar and salt.

America was a wonderful place, a place of
opportunity, of sunlight, of rich food and
friendship, but for all that it was Swansea
where his heart lay. It was here Lily lived,
where Llinos and Joe lived, where everything was familiar. It was the place of his
birth.

John had been a fool to stay in America
and Watt wondered if Llinos had received
his letter telling her and Joe of his change of
plans. They would both understand, that
was the trouble, they were good, kind
people and John had let them down.

As he trudged up the road heading towards the potteries, Watt looked around
him with fresh eyes. He saw the tall grimy
buildings, the narrow streets, the
fast-flowing river and felt love envelop his
heart. He belonged here and now that he
had made up his mind that he would not live

abroad perhaps Lily would have grown up a little in his absence. It was just possible that she had missed him and realized what he meant to her.

'Watt!' Llinos hurried across the yard, her hair flying, her face wreathed in smiles. He hugged her and she clung to him smelling of paint and clay and the sweet scent of lavender. Then, as Watt kissed her cheek, he knew he was truly home.

'Let me look at you!' Llinos put her small hands on his cheeks and stared up at him. 'You're so brown, so healthy looking.' She hugged him again. 'It's wonderful to have you back, I thought you might stay and settle in America like John, and I would never see you again. Thank goodness you didn't.'

She pulled at his coat sleeve. 'Come into the house, get washed and changed and I'll see you get something to eat. You must be starving!' She laughed with something of the old Llinos in her eyes. 'Then you can tell me all about your wonderful adventure.' She glanced past him and he turned to see Lily standing at the door of the paint shed. She was smiling, she was actually pleased to see him. He hesitated.

'Give me just a minute.' He smiled. 'I want to say hello.'

'I'll tell Joe you are here and we'll wait for you indoors.' Llinos swept away towards the house and, slowly, Watt moved to where Lily was standing.

'You look different,' she said, her eyes taking in the golden tan and the streaks of sunlit hair.

He did not touch her but he was breathless at her beauty; he had forgotten how lovely Lily was. He had forgotten, too, his reservations about her coldness. They were all swept away by the light of welcome in her eyes.

'I'm sure you've grown taller, Watt,' she said. 'You're towering over me.' She looked up at him with unaccustomed coyness. 'And did you meet any beautiful American ladies?'

'I certainly did.' Watt smiled. 'The place where I stayed was full of them!' He was only half-teasing and she seemed to realize it.

'But you didn't . . . like any of them, did you?'

'I liked them well enough,' Watt said, 'and admired their looks, but not half as much as I admire yours, Lily.'

She blushed charmingly and Watt felt his old longing for her return a hundred fold. He smiled down at her.

'I must go in and get washed and changed but could I call on you this evening, Lily? Would you like that?'

She gave him a quick look from under her lashes. 'Of course I would. Come to the lodging house later on,' she said. 'I'll meet you outside the door and we'll have a little stroll down to the river. Is that all right?'

All right? Watt could have thrown his hat into the air for joy. He felt as if he was sailing across the yard towards the doorway of Pottery House and, once inside, he dropped his bag on the floor and took a deep breath of the familiar scents of beeswax and candles. Llinos was at his side in moments.

'The maids have a bath ready for you,' she said. 'I've sprinkled some rose water in it for you.' She smiled. 'So that you'll smell nice for your meeting with Lily.'

Watt tweaked her nose. 'You don't miss much, do you?'

'Not much,' she agreed.

When he entered the dining room, it was to find quite a gathering there. Mr Marks sat next to Joe's sister, Charlotte, who looked flushed and animated. Eynon Morton-Edwards was there too along with a lady who was clinging to his arm in a most possessive way.

Supper was served with quiet efficiency

and Watt scarcely had time to put a mouthful of hot vegetable soup to his mouth when he was inundated with questions.

'Is America as big as they say?' Samuel Marks leaned forward in his chair. 'I hear the land is full of milk and honey, is that right?'

'America is vast, you could travel for weeks and not see another human being. I don't know about milk and honey but everyone out there seems very rich.'

'What about the land?' Joe spoke quietly. 'The parcel I asked you to survey for me.'

'Fine land.' Watt was a little embarrassed. 'Rich land, but not a good place for a pottery, I don't think. It's mostly inhabited by Indians. Anyway, it's not close enough to water.'

'Well that figures.' It was Mr Marks who spoke. 'It was their land before the white man went there.'

Watt sighed. 'I think that's what most folk reckon, the settlers as much as anyone else. But, on the other hand, the Indian people make their own pots, they wouldn't want ours.'

Watt saw Mr Marks grimace at Joe. 'Sorry, looks like I gave you something that's not worth a light.' He shook his head. 'But then, it's early days yet, towns have a habit of spreading ever outwards, look at Swansea.'

'There is a very successful pottery in Troy,' Watt said, 'owned by Dan McCabe. That's who John Pendennis is staying with.'

Llinos nodded. 'I see. Is it very different to our pottery, Watt?'

Watt shrugged. 'They make pots in very much the same way as we do here, no porcelain though, not like you manufacture, Eynon.'

Eynon leaned forward, his fair hair falling over his forehead; he seemed to have matured, Watt thought. He smiled inwardly: in spite of the lady at his side, Eynon Morton-Edwards still had eyes only for Llinos.

'As to the porcelain,' Eynon said, 'I'm giving up my attempt to create the perfect body. I'm selling off the white to some of the Worcester factories.'

Watt looked at him in surprise. Why did Eynon not allow his own painters to finish the job with the porcelain decoration and make a bit of money on it himself? Eynon met his gaze.

'I've allowed one or two of the older workers to have some of the white. A couple have their own muffle kilns and will do a fine job of decorating and make a bit of money for themselves into the bargain.'

'Was it such a failure, then?' Watt asked, feeling it was sad that such a wonderful venture was coming to nothing.

'Most of the good stuff shattered in the kiln. The revised bodies were not so perfect, tougher yes, but the paste was an unpleasing colour. Instead of duck egg, it was turning brownish. We will sell it, no doubt, but I have had it all stamped with the trident mark to set it apart from the better stuff.'

'It all sounds so fascinating,' Charlotte said softly and Llinos turned to her apologetically. 'I'm sorry, we are all rude to talk about business. I'm sure you must be bored with it all.' She gave the men a warning glance, indicating that they should change the subject.

The conversation became general and, after a time, Watt saw Mr Marks turn to Charlotte with obvious relief and fall into a quiet discussion with her. Llinos was talking to Eynon's lady, asking how she was feeling and Joe smiled at Watt and winked. He mouthed the words, 'We'll talk later,' and Watt blinked, thinking of his meeting with Lily.

By the time the steamed pudding was served, Watt was feeling distinctly full. Onboard the ship that had brought him home he had eaten frugally, as did the captain and the entire crew. He tasted enough pudding to be polite and waited impatiently for Llinos to take the ladies into the sitting room where they would probably discuss more frivolous matters like silks and ribbons. Llinos would put up with it but Watt knew she would as soon stay and discuss the process of potting with the men.

When the ladies eventually left the room it was Mr Marks who was the first to speak. 'So you don't think the land is worth much, then?'

'I didn't say that.' Watt hedged. 'It's good land, plenty of it. How did you acquire it, if it's not a rude question?'

'The deeds were willed to me by an explorer friend of my father's. I suppose no-one has thought of inhabiting it in years. Sorry, Joe, it doesn't sound too good.'

'I'll be patient.' Joe was smiling. 'Don't worry, Samuel,' he said to Marks. 'I have a gut feeling that that land is going to be very valuable one day. Maybe not for building a pottery but America is a land of great mineral resources and, as you said, Samuel, it's early days yet.'

It seemed an eternity before Watt was able to excuse himself and leave the house. When he did, he made his way swiftly down to the lodging house where Lily lived. She was there, sitting in the open doorway, her eyes large as they looked up at him.

'I thought you weren't coming,' she said. 'I thought perhaps you remembered you'd fallen in love with some rich American lady.'

'Never.' Watt held out his hand and drew her to her feet. 'Come on, let's walk.' He was aware of eyes watching him though he could see no-one framed in the small paned windows. He shivered and Lily looked up at him.

'A goose walking over your grave?' she asked with a hint of laughter in her voice. He took her hand, expecting her to snatch it away. She seemed to withdraw a little and then she relaxed and let him lead her down towards the river. He knew better now than to take further liberties; she was sweet and virginal, not used to the ways of men. She had been brought up in an orphanage as he had, knowing no mother or father, only the rough justice of the guardians who watched over the children. There the Bible had been used to chastise, the words falling hard, like stones. Lily had been a delicate girl. Was it any wonder she shunned any show of affection?

'Are you glad to be home, Watt?' Her soft voice seemed to reach out to him in the

337

darkness. He could smell the perfume of her and felt his heart swell with happiness.

'I am now,' he said, his voice gruff. They sat on the bank and stared into the water. The moon was growing in strength as the darkness gathered in. The water ran silver towards the sea.

'Tell me all about it, then?' she urged, tugging at his sleeve. He looked down at her, longing to hold her in his arms, but a voice inside his head warned him that he must tread carefully.

He talked of John's preoccupation with the idea of becoming rich. 'He's going to work for Dan McCabe,' Watt said. 'I expect he'll end up married to one of the daughters the way Binnie did.' As soon as the words were spoken, he wished he could snatch them back.

'Binnie?' Lily asked. 'You mean Binnie Dundee? How can he be married again when he's still married to that Irish girl?'

Watt could have kicked himself. He remained silent, not knowing how to retreat from his mistake.

'Come on, Watt,' she coaxed, 'I won't tell anyone, you trust me, don't you?' He sensed the hurt in her voice and turned to her quickly.

'Of course I do. But you mustn't tell

anyone, not even Llinos and certainly not Pearl, she'd have it all over the paint shop before you could finish your words.'

'So who has Binnie married then?' Lily asked in such an innocent voice that Watt made up his mind to tell her everything.

'It's Hortense, Dan McCabe's oldest daughter. Got kiddies, too, three sons. They seem very happy.' He finished lamely.

'Oh, well, live and let live, I suppose,' Lily said. 'It wouldn't do any good to talk about it now, would it?'

He sighed in relief; he had half-expected her to explode with righteous indignation. He leaned closer to her. 'I could have married one of the other girls, if I'd stayed.' He smiled. 'Dan more or less offered both me and John a job and a daughter to go with it.'

'But you weren't tempted, were you, Watt?' Lily's eyes were full of shadows in the moonlight. 'I would hate to think of you being with another woman, sitting holding hands, like we are now. You didn't, did you?'

'Of course not,' Watt said. 'I only thought about you and every other woman faded into insignificance. You are so beautiful, Lily, so talented. Those girls, the McCabe girls, they are spoiled rich girls, waited on by servants. Their father has given them everything they could possibly want.'

Lily nodded thoughtfully. 'So he even buys them a husband. At least I don't need a father to do that for me, do I, Watt?'

He felt his breath catch in his throat; was she really saying what he thought she was, that she would consider him as a husband?

'No need at all, Lily,' he said with difficulty. 'But then no other woman is as lovely as you.'

She rose to her feet then and brushed down her skirt. 'I'd better get back. Will you take me home, Watt? I don't want the old biddy who runs the lodging house branding me as a wicked girl, do I?'

He rose at once and forced himself to smile though his entire being tingled with desire. He wanted to throw Lily down in the grass, to kiss her until she was breathless, to make her want him as he wanted her. She began to walk back towards the road and, sighing in resignation, he followed her.

'Well then, Polly, what do you think of that, then?' Lily sat on the bed, her nightgown tucked around her bare feet. 'What a bit of gossip, eh? Binnie Dundee married to two women at once. You can't believe it, can you?'

Polly's eyes were green like a cat's in the

flickering candlelight. 'Oh, I can believe anything of men, pigs they are, the lot of them. How did he come to tell you, then? I thought you weren't friends with Watt Bevan.'

'Well, I took a leaf out of your book, Polly, and played him along a bit. It was hard going though, I can't bear him to touch me.'

Polly stared at her with half-closed eyes. 'I told you, marry for money, that's the only way.'

Lily chewed her lip, wondering about marriage, about making vows in church knowing that in your heart you did not want the man you were being tied to. Would God strike her dead if she married Watt?

Polly seemed to know what she was thinking. 'I'd aim higher than Watt Bevan if I had your looks, Lily.'

'Who for instance?' Lily shook her head. 'There's no way of meeting any men except for work and there they're all like me, living in lodgings or poky little rooms, earning a pittance from those uppity pottery owners.'

Polly flopped onto her back, her legs stretched out before her, her bare toes pointing to the ceiling. She was cleaner now that Lily had taken her in hand. Polly washed regularly and combed and tied up her thick hair. But she still looked like a street urchin. Lily congratulated herself that *she* herself had something to offer a man, any man; she was good and chaste and a talented painter. The trouble was she did not want a man.

'You still a virgin?' Polly asked and Lily looked at her startled.

'Of course I am!' She felt her colour rising. 'I'm not the sort to allow anyone to take liberties with me.'

'Different to me, then.' Polly laughed. 'They can take anything they like so long as they're paying.'

'Oh, Polly, you shouldn't be like that.' Lily stared at her friend wondering how she could bear to let a man paw her, to put up with all sorts of indignities just for money. 'Why don't you get a job and earn a decent living?'

'Nothing wrong with laying on your back,' Polly said. 'If you don't like the man you close your eyes and think of something else while he gets on with it.'

Lily shuddered delicately. 'I don't think I want to get married, ever.' She closed her eyes, thinking of Watt Bevan and how he loved to put his arms around her and how he tried to steal a kiss whenever he could. It would be worse if she married him.

She snuggled down into the bedclothes and hugged them around her chin. She imagined a life of freedom, earning lots of money, rising ever higher in the pottery, becoming so necessary that she would be paid any wage she asked just to stay on there.

'Well, then, what if you don't marry, what will you do?'

Lily craned her head to look at Polly. 'What do you mean, what will I do? I'll work of course.'

'And what if you lose your job, what if they decide to close the pottery? What if you do stay there? What about when you are too old to work, where will you end up, the workhouse, is it?'

Lily had not thought that far ahead. She closed her eyes, trying to imagine herself without a job, with the pottery closed down; it was impossible. She thought of the savings she had put away, even working for many years to come she would never have enough to keep her in her old age. She sighed, it looked as if she would have to settle for marriage to someone. But then, as Polly said, why not make it a marriage where she would at least have plenty of money?

'I could introduce you to some rich fellas,' Polly said. 'I meet all sorts in my business, doctors, lawyers and such.'

'No thanks.' Lily said quickly. 'No, I'm not ready for that yet, not for a long time.' And, if she was honest, she would not like an introduction from a girl like Polly; any man she associated with would consider her friends cut from the same cloth. No, the way to meet respectable men was to attend the church social evenings which were not so very social as proper and stiff and formal. But at least then she would not be taken for a hussy. And, in the last resort, she could marry Watt.

Meanwhile, she had the titbit of gossip about Binnie Dundee to mull over. The nerve of the man, being married to two women at the same time. She shrugged her way deeper under the bedclothes, feeling weariness creep over her. Her back ached from leaning forward on her stool to capture just the right colour, the finest sweep of her brush. She loved painting, she was never happier than when she was working, but, as Polly had pointed out, she might not be able to work when her eyesight faded and the bone ache set in. It seemed she would have to consider marriage, unless something better came along. She imagined Watt kissing her, undressing her, using her like a breeding animal and, suddenly, sleep seemed a long way away.

CHAPTER

NINETEEN

'So, you ran away from me, Father.' Saul Marks was standing on the doorstep of Pottery House, staring at his father with a mixture of scorn and fury. 'I might have known you'd come back here.' Samuel plucked at the button on his coat in agitation. He had only agreed to talk to his son because it meant sparing the ladies an ugly scene if he refused. He looked into his son's angry face and wondered why he had been cursed with such an unfeeling, grasping, offspring. 'Afraid I'll make a fuss about that parcel of land you handed over without so much as a by your leave, land you should have given to your son, is that it?'

'That's it, exactly,' Samuel said wearily. 'You took enough from me as it is, Saul, more than my money, you took my dignity. It was only by the good graces of Mr Mainwaring that I'm not rotting in prison at this moment.'

'Rubbish!' Saul was almost spitting in his fury. 'I would have got you out, all in good time. I just needed to raise the money, that's all.'

'Money that was mine in the first place,' Samuel said reasonably. 'I never thought you would cheat me, your own father, Saul. How can you live with yourself?'

Saul caught his father by the throat and pushed him against the wall. 'You shouldn't have been such a tightfisted bastard!' Saul's voice was rising and Samuel gasped for air, trying to tell his son to calm down.

'I want that land, Father, and you had better get it back for me or it will be the worse for you!'

'That's enough.' Joe appeared in the hallway, his voice low with contained anger. 'Let him go.'

'And what if I don't?' Saul shook his father hard. Joe moved between them then and Samuel found he was free to breathe again. Joe towered above Saul; his shoulders were set and his fists were bunched.

'Leave my property,' Joe said clearly. 'I don't want to see you near here again, understand?'

'I understand,' Saul said. 'I understand that you have duped a poor old man out of his property.'

'No, you did that,' Joe said. 'You made yourself and left your father to die a debtor. Get out of my yard before I throw you out.'

Saul backed away. 'Oh, I'll go but you

haven't heard the last of me, you can count on that.' He felt like spitting at the half-breed. He turned and strode away, his face clouded with anger.

Lily had been watching the scene from a safe distance, she had heard every word. She had grown to despise Llinos, how could she marry a half-breed, had she no shame? Lily waited for Saul Marks to draw near. When he was level with her, she stepped out into his path.

'I'm sorry,' she said breathlessly, 'I didn't see you coming.' He stared down at her with indifference and she was piqued. He was a very handsome man and rich by all accounts.

'I heard shouting,' she said hurriedly before the man could brush past her. 'That awful foreigner, Joe Mainwaring, was playing the bully again, is that it?'

Saul hesitated and Lily pressed home her advantage. 'He's a strange one, that. I wouldn't trust him further than I could throw him. You know he was accused of murder, don't you?'

'I heard that,' he said. 'But not the details. Perhaps you could fill me in?' She had Saul's interest now. He looked at her more closely and then he smiled and doffed his hat. 'It seems that you and I have a great deal in common,' he said. 'Perhaps we might meet to talk sometime?'

'That would be very nice,' Lily said. 'I sometimes walk near the beach with my friend. Well, she's not really my friend, she lodges in the same house as me but if she comes along, no-one can say bad things about us.'

'Well, then, a proper young lady. It's good to see that someone around here knows how to behave. What if we say six o'clock this evening, will that suit you?'

'Oh, yes!' Lily said, taking in the rich cloth of the man's clothes and the fine gold stud in his shirt.

'Until later then.' She watched until Saul Marks had left the grounds of the pottery and then returned to the paint shed. There were several hours still to work but if she pleaded a headache to Pearl the older woman would let her off so long as she promised to return the favour some time.

Lily's thoughts were flying even as she began painting. She would have to make sure that Polly looked respectable for once. She needed Polly around not so much for a chaperone but to give her courage. Polly was used to the ways of men, knew how to get round them, but Lily felt she already had the key to Saul Marks. She would feed his hate for Joe, pander to his male ego and ingratiate herself so that Saul might come to rely on her. Perhaps he might even fall in love with her. She shuddered at the thought of marriage but she was fast coming to the conclusion that she had no choice. Marriage to a rich man while she was still young enough to attract one was infinitely preferable to working until she dropped. She bent her head, smiling to herself. She would charm Saul Marks, she had the looks and the brains. She would do all she could to please him and her reward would be a comfortable home and a respectable name.

'Poor Samuel, he looked really shaken.' Llinos was sitting up in bed watching Joe undress. He was lithe and slim. His skin was bronzed and when he turned to look at her his eyes were a startling blue.

'That son is a nasty piece of work,' Joe said, slipping into bed beside her. He refused to wear any nightclothes; he was used to sleeping naked and, by now, Llinos was used to the warm touch of his skin against hers. She snuggled into his arms and he cradled her as though she were a precious piece of china.

She traced the line of his jaw with her finger and her happiness was mingled with sadness. 'Joe, will we ever have a baby?' she asked. Above the bed the candles flickered, sending weird shapes across the walls. 'You can see most things, can you see a child for us?'

He sighed softly. 'It will come in good time; we will have a baby.' He kissed her hair. 'But don't wish for it too soon, everything has a time and a season and when we get our heart's desire there is usually a price to pay.'

His words made her shiver. She buried her face in the warmth of his neck and his breath lifted tendrils of her hair. She loved Joe, she could not live without him and if the Good Lord did not see fit to bless their union with a healthy child then she must make the most of what she had, a loving, tender husband.

He made love to her gently that night, as if sensing her sadness and she responded to him with extra passion as though to make up for her foolish, ungrateful mood. He kissed her breasts and then her eyelids and her mouth, and they moved together like the waves of the sea, like the corn waving in the summer breeze. She arched her back and allowed herself to be carried away to the place where there was no conscious thought any more, simply sensations of love and release and joy.

They lay entwined in each other's arms for a long time after their love-making had ceased. She ached with love for him and, even as sleep overcame her, she was murmuring his name.

The evening was dark with the promise of rain threatening to spoil Lily's meeting with Saul Marks. As she and Polly hurried through the misty streets, Lily wondered if he would even bother to turn up. He did and she blushed with pleasure; she had him enamoured of her already.

He eyed her with approval and she knew she looked well in her slim-fitting coat over a deep blue gown. She was well aware that the ribbons of her bonnet framed her face in a most becoming way. It did not occur to her that she was being conceited; she was merely being honest.

Lily introduced Polly, wondering what he thought of her. Polly just nodded a greeting, her head down but her sharp eyes missing nothing. She looked quite respectable for once in a borrowed dress and cloak with her wild hair tucked neatly away.

'Good evening to you, ladies,' Saul said easily. 'May I take you for coffee? It might warm us all up in this chill weather.'

Polly nudged Lily and Lily ignored her,

hoping the girl was not going to make a fool of herself before polite company.

'That is very generous of you, sir,' she said meekly. She fell into step beside him, glancing up at him, trying to imagine him kissing her, making love to her. She shivered, he was very presentable, good-looking even and rich; she was sure she could get used to the idea of intimacy between them given time.

Polly followed good-naturedly. It seemed the prospect of coffee in a warm shop had improved her spirits and she hummed tunelessly to herself.

Saul led the way into the coffee shop and Lily breathed in the rich aroma of ground coffee. The candles were lit early because the day had been overcast and now shadows danced across the floor, throwing weird shapes against the pale walls. Saul beckoned to the waiter and the man led them to a table.

'Please sit, ladies,' Saul said graciously. He ordered the coffee and when it came sat back in his chair.

'Well, this is nice,' he said. 'We can have a conversation in comfort now, can't we?'

Lily remembered then that she was supposed to be talking about Joe Mainwaring. She sipped the coffee, it was unfamiliar, strong, and she tried not to make a face. Polly was not so discreet.

'Ugh!' she said wiping her mouth with the back of her hand. Saul smiled and with his eyes on Lily, advised the ladies to add milk to the drink. Lily used the time to think of something to say about Joe. She leaned forward, suddenly inspired.

'You know Joe was imprisoned because of what he did to Captain Savage?' she said eagerly. Saul frowned. 'It was only because he hired a clever lawyer that he got away with it.'

'He's a murderer,' Polly volunteered. 'He done the poor captain in, that's for sure. I don't know how these rich folks get away with such goings on.'

Lily wished she would shut up. She was ignorant and it showed. Saul did not seem to notice.

'I knew the man was in prison,' Saul said, 'though I confess I didn't know why. I imagined it to be some sort of fraudulent dealings.'

'He gave the captain something,' Polly said, in full flood now. 'Poison stuff that killed him.'

'You are very well informed, young lady,' Saul said looking directly at Polly for the first time. Lily was unnerved; she spoke up, determined to draw Saul's attention back to herself.

'Of course, I knew it all along,' she said, 'working as I do for Llinos Mainwaring. How she could bring herself to marry a man like that I don't know. I think she helped Joe to get rid of her father so that she would have his money.'

'It's all very interesting,' Saul said. 'Do you think you could find out the name of this man, this lawyer from London?'

'I knows it already,' Polly said. 'A Mr Grantley, that's what it is.'

'Ah, I see. Right, then, let us talk about something more pleasant, shall we?' Saul was smiling now, leaning towards Lily, his eyes admiring her fair skin and her large eyes. 'I know you like your work in the pottery, Lily, but how would you like to work for me as well?'

This was not what Lily had been expecting, she blinked rapidly. 'Work for you, doing what?'

'Well, shall we say keeping an eye on things at Pottery House, keeping an eye on my dear old father lest Joe Mainwaring decides to finish him off too.'

'Be a spy, you mean?' Polly broke in, her face flushed, her eyes wide. 'Oh, Lily, what a lovely idea, a spy!'

It sounded easy but what was in it for her? Lily wondered. Saul soon enlightened her.

'In return, I shall wine you and dine you and treat you to all manner of good things,' he said. 'You are a very attractive young woman, I will find it very easy to be in your company as much as I possibly can.'

Lily looked down at her hands as if overcome with shyness. In reality, she was wondering just what Saul had in mind, was he courting her or was he just hoping to use her? She trusted no-one, not working men nor gentlemen.

'That sounds very nice,' she said lamely, deciding that she would play along, see what happened. If Saul was looking to rob her of her virtue then he would have a nasty shock coming.

She forced herself to drink some of the strong coffee but it was not to her liking, not at all. It was vile stuff, tasted like nothing she had ever tasted before or wanted to taste again. She was more than a little relieved when Saul decided it was time to walk the girls back to their lodging house. Outside the door, he took Lily's hand and kissed her fingers.

'Next time we meet I shall have a gift for you.' His glance grazed over Polly who was looking up at him expectantly. 'And a small something for you, too, Polly.'

As he strode away down the street, Polly hugged Lily's arm. 'You're made!' she said. 'He fancies you, you've got him eating out of your little hand, girl.'

Lily did not want him to fancy her. She wanted him to be a proper gentleman caller, respectable and respectful, and she said so.

'Well, give him a chance,' Polly said. 'You have to treat a man like a fish, get him hooked first and then reel him in.'

'I don't know that I trust him,' Lily said. 'Perhaps it would not be wise to be alone with him.'

'Don't talk daft!' Polly said. 'You will have to be alone with him sometimes, if only to get him interested, like.'

'I don't really know what you mean by "get him interested",' Lily said, pushing Polly up the stairs towards the rooms they shared.

'Show him a bit of bosom or a bit of ankle, that sort of thing.' She sighed. 'I don't know, you seem to have a man panting for you without doing a thing. Well if you gives a bit of encouragement, think how far that will get you.'

'Aye, the workhouse with a baby in a shawl,' Lily said sourly. 'No man is going to touch me until I'm married.'

'Well then, if that's how you feel, all right.' Polly looked at her strangely. 'It's nothing to be afraid of mind, it's only natural. You got feelings, haven't you, Lil?'

'When I meet the right man, then and only then will I have feelings,' Lily retorted. Her words were brave but deep inside her she was afraid that she had no feelings, they had been stamped out of her by the atmosphere at the workhouse. There she had been one of many, the despised poor, patronized by people like Llinos Mainwaring, taken in as if she were a stray cat and expected to be grateful. How she hated them all.

'Do you think Mr Marks is the right man?' Polly persisted as she pushed shut the door of the bedroom with her foot. 'He's handsome and rich, he seems to like you.'

'Maybe,' Lily said noncommittally. She shrugged off her clothes and hung her good coat on the hook behind the door. The jug on the table was almost empty and Lily sighed. She would have to traipse downstairs to the pump in the backyard, it was not a prospect she relished. She looked at Polly, the girl was still fully dressed.

'Do us a favour, Poll,' she said, 'fetch some water for me.'

'What for?'

'I want to wash.' Lily sighed. 'Go on, Polly, just as a favour this once.'

'It's cold,' Polly said. 'And dark. I don't want to go back down, I'll catch my death.' She pulled off her coat quickly, followed by her skirt and blouse and Lily shook her head in despair.

She made do with the small amount of water in the jug and pulled on her nightgown. It was no nightgown at all but one of her old and patched shifts; imagine Saul seeing her like this, he would think her lacking in taste. As she climbed into bed, she wondered if she should spend some of her savings on some pretty nightwear. But no, it would be a long time before events moved on in that direction.

'Don't sulk now,' Polly said, taking her silence for moodiness. 'Too much washing isn't good for you, I've told you that before.' She drew the bedclothes up to her chin and stared at Lily with laughter in her eyes.

Lily, disgruntled, turned her back, glad that she did not have to share a bed with the other girl. Sometimes Polly got on her nerves. She closed her eyes disconsolately. Was she destined to be shut up in a small, airless room with only Polly, or someone like her, for company for ever more? The only alternative was marriage and, somehow, she had the feeling that Mr Saul Marks did not have marriage in mind.

It was a long time before Lily fell asleep but when she did, she dreamed of rose petals and lovely silk gowns and churches with bells ringing out. When she woke, she felt renewed. Marriage, she decided, must be her goal. It was, after all, her only way out and though it was tantamount to selling her body, just as Polly did, it would at least be in the respectable role of wife. So when she saw Saul Marks again, she must charm him. She must allow him a glimpse of ankle, just as Polly told her. Or bend forward and let him see the fullness of her bosom. It was not a prospect she relished but, suddenly, Saul's approval had become very important and she would do all she could to get it.

CHAPTER

TWENTY

'I can't say I'm surprised that John Pendennis chose to stay in America.' Llinos was seated close to the fire, her bare feet drawn up beneath her. 'He always seemed a bit aloof, a bit out of place here. What I am surprised about is that we've had no word from him, not even a short note of thanks for the backing you gave him.'

Joe shrugged. 'I didn't buy the man's soul, Llinos. I think there are problems in John's life that have hardened him, made him look out for himself.'

'You are very charitable.' Llinos spoke dryly. 'I'm inclined to believe that he saw the opportunity for a free trip and took it with both hands. Now, from everything Watt tells us, John has thrown in his lot with this American McCabe.'

She glanced across at her husband; his face was in shadow, only the glow from the fire highlighted the red-brown of his skin. She ached with love for him; he was kind, generous and yet he seemed destined to have his kindness thrown in his face.

Charlotte's voice drifted in from the hall,

Llinos sat up and straightened her gown. 'Charlotte,' Llinos said, 'come and sit here near the fire.' Samuel held Charlotte's arm and he led her to a chair and settled her comfortably before smiling and bowing in Llinos's direction.

'You don't mind a bit of company, do you?' he asked diffidently and Llinos smiled warmly at him. She liked the old man; he was gentle and very patient with Charlotte who was afflicted with arthritis. The cold weather made her condition more painful.

'You are most welcome,' she said. 'It's good to see you looking happy together, the company is good for both of you.' She looked meaningfully at Charlotte. 'Do I sense a romance blossoming?'

Charlotte actually blushed. 'Away with you, Llinos!' she said reprovingly. 'Sam and I are friends, good friends. We are too old for anything else, aren't we, Sam?'

'You are the epitome of beauty to me,' Samuel said sincerely. 'I have never been so happy as I am now.'

The old couple sat side by side on the deep, cushioned sofa, smiling at each other like young lovers. Llinos caught Joe's eye and he nodded, willing to join in the good-natured banter.

'Well, if there's a marriage in the offing, I

hope I shall be asked my permission in the usual way. After all, it isn't every day a man gives his sister away.'

'Oh, Joe!' Charlotte's head was lowered but Samuel took her hands in his. 'Charlotte, my dear,' he said, 'I think marriage between us is a wonderful idea. If Joe hadn't spoken, I don't think I would have had the courage to ask you to be my wife.' He held up his hand. 'Now, I know we've only been friends for a short time but for us, at our age, time is short.' He laughed at his own joke.

He slid awkwardly onto one bony knee. 'Charlotte, will you consent to be my wife?' He turned to look at Joe and smiled broadly. 'With your brother's permission, of course.'

'Oh, Sam!' Charlotte clutched his hands. 'I don't know what to say! Yes I do! I would love to be your wife. It's an honour and a privilege I never expected to come my way.'

Llinos looked at Joe, her eyebrows raised. Joe made a face at her. 'Well then, after due consideration of the man and his character,' he paused and Charlotte looked at him anxiously, 'I give my permission and my heartfelt congratulations.'

Joe rang for the maid. 'Meggie, bring me a bottle of the best claret from the cellar,' he said, 'and a tray of glasses. This is a celebration.'

Charlotte held both her small, lined hands to her face. 'Dearie me, a bride at my age, what will people think?' There were tears in her faded blue eyes but happiness radiated from her.

Llinos hugged her. 'They will think that Samuel is a very lucky man.' She kissed Charlotte's warm cheek, breathing in the scent of lavender. Charlotte was small and thin in her arms and a feeling of protectiveness filled her. She held Charlotte away from her. 'You are a wonderful lady, Charlotte, and I am proud you are my sister-in-law.'

The evening took on a festive atmosphere: Samuel played bright tunes on the piano and Charlotte watched him, as adoring as any young lady in love for the first time. And it was the first time for Charlotte, she had never been in the company of men before and even if she had been, she would never have found a man as good, as kind and as understanding as her Samuel.

Later, when Llinos was in bed, cradled in her husband's arm, she prayed that nothing would happen to spoil the calm happiness of her life. Yesterday a letter had arrived from Grantley wishing them well in the future and begging them to call on his services if ever they needed him. Even the sight of the lawyer's name at the foot of the paper was enough to send a wave of fear through her. She was restless that night and it was almost as if she knew that out there, in the darkness of the Swansea streets, someone was planning to do her ill.

'Aye, married to Gwen Savage I was, for a time.' The back room of the Castle Inn was almost empty but a good fire still burned in the huge fireplace and the mugs of beer were delivered to the table at increasingly regular intervals.

Saul Marks looked at the bearded, unkempt man seated opposite him with distaste but he was already aware that this man Cimla could be of use to him.

'How did that come about?' he asked. 'I thought her husband died recently, some say at the hands of the Indian fellow.'

'Nothing would surprise me there.' Cimla supped his drink noisily and wiped his mouth with the back of his hand. Droplets of beer clung like sweat to his tangled beard.

'What do you mean by that?' Saul was growing impatient with the man who was looking pointedly at his empty mug. Saul waved a hand to the landlord and ordered two more beers but left his untouched. He needed a clear head at all times, no-one knew when an enemy would pounce.

He glanced around as though he expected a villain to attack him from behind. Cimla's voice drew his attention once more.

'We all thought Lloyd Savage was dead and gone, killed in the wars with France, but no, he had to turn up like a bad penny brought home by that cursed Indian.'

'So it was out into the streets with you, then?' Saul was interested, it was clear the man would know a great deal about the family having lived in Pottery House. He was a likely candidate to do any dirty work that might be too tedious or too obvious for Saul to do himself.

'Oh, aye, bag and baggage. Gwen died, see, so there was no-one to speak up for me. As for that brat Llinos, she always hated me.'

Saul digested this in silence for a moment. 'What do you know about the Indian?' This was his real concern, that he get rid of Joe Mainwaring. Hate burned inside Saul's breast; the man had taken what was right-fully his, a prime piece of land in America. There had to be some way of getting it back and having his revenge on the man into the bargain. Cimla's answer was disappointing.

'Not a lot, really. I got some of his potions though, stole 'em one night from the pantry at the back of the fool of a doctor's house. I thought that I could use 'em for blackmail or something.' He smiled, his teeth jutting forward as though threatening to fall out of his mouth. 'It backfired on me though, the Indian got off because of lack of evidence.'

Saul mulled this over, wondering if it would benefit him to buy the Indian's potions from the man. They could come in useful.

'How much do you want for them?' he asked casually, but in spite of his careful tone, he saw a crafty look come into the other man's face.

'Don't think I want to sell 'em,' Cimla said. 'I tried one sip out of the bottle and it put me to sleep. Good stuff, see, handy when the bugs bite in the night.'

'Oh, fair enough.' Saul took some change from his pocket and threw it on the table. 'I'll see you round then.' He made to rise but Cimla looked sharply at him.

'Not so hasty! I suppose I would sell the stuff for the right price but, remember, too much of it would kill a body stone dead.'

Saul sank back into his chair. He was hungry for the stuff, excited by Cimla's claims but it did not pay to show the man how hungry.

'On second thoughts, I don't know if it will be any good to me,' Saul said. 'I only wanted to try it on a young lady of my acquaintance, coax her into bed, that sort of thing.'

'Give us a couple of coppers then,' Cimla said. 'I suppose I can always get some more for myself. I reckon the Indian is still making the stuff.' He grinned. 'Want me to fetch it now?'

'Why not? I'll come with you.' The two men left the inn and the landlord, with a sleepy yawn, locked up behind them. Some folks, it seemed, did not have a bed to go to.

It took only a few minutes to arrive at the run-down lodging house that was home to Bert Cimla. Saul wrinkled his nose in distaste at the smell of urine and stale cabbage.

'It's not much but it's all I can afford, thanks to that blasted Llinos and her family.'

Cimla disappeared up the stairs to return shortly with a bottle of liquid. Saul handed him some money and then left the house, glad to be out in the night air. Close to, Bert Cimla smelled like a goat.

In his own lodgings Saul lay on his bed and studied the bottle carefully. It was not labelled. He took out the stopper and sniffed the contents. The pungent scent of flowers and grasses made him gasp. It would be just as well to try it out on someone before he attempted to use it. He smiled to himself in the darkness, he knew exactly who he would try it on.

The next evening he invited Lily to visit his lodging house. She was reticent at first but he managed to convince her that it would all be quite proper with his landlady, not to mention other guests, to chaperone them. She had agreed at last, lured by the promise of a gift. It was clear that the little Lily was an avaricious young lady which to his mind was no bad thing.

'Come along, Lily, I'm drinking myself, don't be a killjoy.' Saul was seated beside her in the comfortable sitting room of his landlady's house. Two older guests were at the other side of the room endlessly knitting and gossiping and, after a brief appraisal of the couple, had ignored them.

It was no hardship entertaining the young woman who seemed to have taken such a liking to him. It was clear she admired him by the way her face lit up when she saw him. Of course she was far beneath him socially but still, to all intents and purposes, she was a prime candidate for his little experiment. She had no family, no ties, no-one who would ask questions if anything unforeseen happened to her. Indeed, in some ways, he hoped it would, then he would know he could accomplish his task of ridding himself of his father and laying the blame at Joe Mainwaring's door.

'There is no alcohol in it, I promise you,' he said. 'The landlady made it herself and she's against strong liquor.'

Lily took a tentative sip and smiled. 'It's nice, it tastes of oranges and petals and something I can't quite make out.'

Saul took a deep draught of his own cordial, it was the same as Lily's except for one important ingredient, the potion Cimla had given him. He watched Lily carefully as she seemed to relax from her usual tight reserve. She smiled more and a becoming blush coloured her normally pale face.

When she had emptied her glass he refilled it, watching her carefully all the time. Slowly, she sank back in her chair and her eyelids began to droop. Saul rose to his feet and took her arm and guided her from the room. In the hall he paused, she was becoming heavier in his arms, it was time he got her home. Out in the street he thanked his lucky stars that her lodging house was only a short distance away.

The house was dark and silently, Saul half-carried her up the stairs. He knew which was her room, he had seen her in the window often enough when he called on her. Unerringly, he took her to the bedroom expecting to find the irrepressible Polly in residence but the room was empty and silent.

Saul lowered Lily onto the bed and bent to adjust her skirts around her legs. Then he paused; why waste such a very good opportunity? She wanted him, she had made that plain enough more than once and chances like this one, to be alone with a young woman, were rare indeed.

He sank onto the bed beside her and slowly began to undress her.

'*Duw*, what's happened to you, girl?' Polly's voice startled Lily into wakefulness. She sat up in bed and gasped when she saw that she was naked. Her thighs were bruised and it was as if a fire was burning low down in her belly.

'Don't tell me, you got bedded at last, 'bout time too!' Polly flopped on the bed and snuggled down under the blankets even though the dawn light was already warming the room into life.

'What do you mean?' Lily said in a small voice. She strained to look down at her breasts; there were marks near her nipples.

She fell back in bed pulling the blanket over her as though by hiding herself she could pretend nothing had happened.

'Who was it?' Polly giggled. 'And was he any good?'

Lily swallowed hard, trying to clear her muddled thoughts. Saul, she had been with him in his lodging house. They had drunk a little and she had felt lightheaded almost at once. She remembered him leading her from the room but after that everything was a blur.

'I've been taken advantage of,' she said uncertainly. 'Saul Marks must have got me drunk and had his way with me.' She was too shocked to cry. Polly put her arm around her.

'There, there, don't fret, love, you lost your innocence and no harm done 'cos you didn't feel it hurt, being drunk, did you?'

'I was saving myself though.' Lily felt outrage run through her like a fire, what she had deemed her finest asset, her innocence, had been taken from her. She pushed Polly aside and slid out of the bed, tipping the water from the jug into the bowl and began to wash.

'I'll tell everyone what the monster has done to me, he can't get away with it!' she said angrily.

'Hey now, hang on there.' Polly was sitting up in bed, her eyes wide. 'You can't go accusing anyone, especially not a man like Saul Marks. He won't take no nonsense, not him.'

Lily began to shiver and Polly drew Lily back into the warmth of the blankets. 'No, sir, think about it. He'll just say you were drunk, that you wanted it, that's what they all say, that's what started me on the caper.'

Lily felt worse. Polly thought she was just the same sort of loose woman that she was. She put her hand over her mouth to prevent herself from screaming and Polly sighed and brushed back her hair.

'There, you calm down now. I'll slip downstairs and sneak some milk for you, that will make you feel better.'

When she was alone Lily stared down at herself, unable to believe what had happened. But it was true, she had lost her innocence and there was nothing she could do about it. She said as much to Polly when the girl returned with a mug brimming with milk. Polly looked at her for a long moment.

'Now I don't know about that,' she said, rubbing her cheek. She frowned in concentration, biting her lip with the effort to think.

'What about his family, 'as he got any folks?'

'Well yes,' Lily said. 'His father lives with Llinos. He's very old and I don't think he gets on with Saul.'

'Well there's more than one way to skin a cat. He must like you a lot, don't you think? He's always giving you presents. So why don't you play your cards right and butter him up? Men are fools for a bit of flattery.' She hunched her knees and rested her chin on them.

'I'd say go to his folks if you'd done it with some young lad or something but Saul Marks is a rich man, a catch, you reel him in, love, that way he'll pay all right.' She laughed. 'For the rest of his life if I know you.'

'What do you mean?' Lily felt an ache begin to spread through her body and up to her head. She felt sick and ill and knew that nothing could induce her to go in to work today. She would be missed but that was just too bad, she had to think of herself right now.

'Well, string him along, give him what he wants and then when he's really hooked on you, get him to take you up the aisle. Say you're having his kid, anything. The least he'll do is give you money to keep you quiet. You like money, don't you?'

How could she ever explain to Polly that she wanted only to be respectable? She had worn her chastity like a cloak of protection and now it had been torn away from her. But marriage to Saul, how would that work out?

Lily thought about it, it was the only possible solution. She did not love Saul but then she could not love any man. So why not heal some of the hurt by making the relationship a proper, respectable one?

'Perhaps you're right.' She sipped the milk and placed the mug on the table, lying back dizzily against the pillows. 'Poll, will you do something for me?' Her voice was faint, she needed to sleep again, to remove herself from the painful thoughts that were plaguing her. 'Will you go to the pottery and tell someone that I've been taken bad, I can't come in to work today?'

'Sod them!' Polly said. 'They can go stew. You never take time off, let them come and find out what's wrong, see if they care as much about you as you do about your precious job.'

She was probably right. In any case Lily was too weary to think any more. She felt the warmth of the darkness flood over her and it was so welcome that she surrendered herself to it.

'Don't know where Lily is. Sorry, Watt.'

Pearl was not the least concerned about Lily, any fool could see that and Watt was no fool. He sighed and went back to the gate, staring along the row, hoping to see the small familiar figure coming towards him. Lily never missed work. He could not remember any time when she had not turned up at the usual time.

It had started to rain. He pulled up his collar wondering if he should go down to where she lived and make enquiries about her.

'Watt!' Llinos's voice drew his attention. 'Watt, can I see you a moment?' She was waving to him and with a reluctant smile he went towards her. Work called, Lily would have to wait.

It was evening before Watt could make his way to the boarding house where Lily lived. He knocked on the open door, smelling the roasting meat without feeling hungry. He had not eaten all day, he had been too worried.

'Come in, son.' The landlady called to him, her hands covered in flour. 'What can I do for you?'

'I'm looking for Lily.' It was warm in the kitchen with the fire roaring invitingly up the chimney.

'Aye, she's in bed, took sick in the night,

poor girl,' the landlady said. 'Polly's with her so you can go up if you like but only for a minute mind, and leave the door open. I don't allow no hanky-panky here.'

He took the stairs two at a time, his heart thumping. He knocked on the door and it was Polly who opened it. She looked up at him in surprise.

'Oh so someone has come from that pottery to see if Lil is dead or alive, 'bout time too.'

He looked towards the bed and was relieved to see that Lily, apart from being a little pale, did not appear too bad.

'How are you feeling?' He edged gingerly into the room. Lily turned her face away and Watt felt at once that his visit was unwelcome.

'She's bad, got a sick stomach.' It was Polly who answered. 'Girls get bad pains in their bellies sometimes, mind.'

'Lily?' He said and she lifted her hand without turning to face him.

'Just leave me be, Watt, I'll probably feel better tomorrow.'

With that he had to be content. Polly ushered him towards the door and shut it firmly in his face. He stared at the wood panels for a moment and then, with a sigh of resignation, made his way down the stairs and out into the street.

He thrust his hands into his pockets and stared around him, feeling restless and not knowing where to go: back home to the pottery or down to the Castle Inn for a drink and a chat with some of the men.

The Castle won. Watt walked swiftly now, wanting to be out of the stinging rain and cold. The fire in the large front room of the inn offered warmth and comfort. Gratefully, Watt sat down in the one available seat and ordered a mug of beer. He glanced round and saw that two men were huddled in the corner, talking quietly together. His gaze lingered on them because they seemed improbable mates. The older man sported a heavy grey beard and a greasy hat pulled down over his eyes. The other one he recognized from his visit to the pottery some time ago; it was Saul Marks, Samuel's son.

He leaned towards them slightly, trying to hear their conversation. He could only pick up snatches of it, most of it was unintelligible to him.

'Worked fine.' The words drifted to him. '. . . any more?' He turned as though to look towards the door, expecting the appearance of a friend.

'Aye, could be.' The older man spoke in a sibilant whisper but his words were clear.

'Risky though, I'd need some more help —
if you get my meaning.'

A few more words were spoken and then
Saul Marks rose to his feet and left the inn.
He was smiling in an unpleasant way as
though satisfied with his night's work.

Watt slid over towards the old man. 'Was
that Saul Marks you were with then?' he
asked and the man turned his face away.

'Sod off!' he said. It was then that Watt
recognized him, not by his appearance, that
was greatly changed, it was his voice that
gave him away.

'Bert Cimla!' he said. 'So you've turned
up again, have you? Well let me tell you
something, you keep away from the pottery
or it will be worse for you.'

The man turned sullenly to look at him.
'Why?' he said, his bloodshot eyes full of
venom. 'What are you going to do about it?'

Watt grasped his greasy collar. 'I'll thrash
you till you scream as you used to make me
scream.' He ground the words between his
teeth.

Bert Cimla started back in his chair.
'Landlord!' he shouted. 'This drunk is at-
tacking me.'

The landlord came over to the table and
stared down suspiciously at Watt who was
still holding Cimla by the collar.

'What's wrong, Watt, gone mad have you? Better go home, boy, and sleep it off, too much beer don't do anyone any good.' The landlord spoke calmly and Watt gave Bert Cimla one last shake that rattled his teeth. 'I'm going, but this is a warning to you, Cimla, keep away from Llinos and keep away from me.'

He strode out into the street, his mind racing. What did Bert Cimla have to do with Saul Marks? Whatever it was, Watt did not trust either of them. He thrust his hands into his pockets, he must warn Llinos to be on her guard because, whatever the two men were plotting, it did not augur well for anyone.

The wedding was a private affair with just family and close friends in attendance. Charlotte looked beautiful in a cream dress and a jacket edged with fur and a matching hat. Llinos thought how touching it was that Charlotte had embraced Samuel's faith, she must love him very much indeed.

Llinos looked up at Joe and he put his arm around her. 'Don't they look happy?' she said softly. 'I think they are going to be almost as happy as we are.'

He kissed the tip of her nose. 'No-one could be that happy,' he said, smiling. 'I have the most beautiful, most accomplished, most wonderful wife in all the world.'

Llinos leaned her head on his shoulder. 'Flattery will get you everywhere, my dear Joe.'

A small reception was held in the dining room at Tawe House and Eynon's generosity knew no bounds. The table was loaded with food: roast duck, game pies with crusty brown pastry coverings, as well as huge dishes of freshly baked bread. For those guests whose preference was for fish, whole salmon with the heads left on graced silver salvers.

Eynon's wife was the gracious hostess and in spite of her condition, which was obvious to everyone now, she looked well and happy. Llinos greeted her politely.

'Are you keeping as well as you look?' she asked, aching with envy for the girl who carried her badge of fertility so proudly.

'I am extremely well, thank you.' Annabel's reply was reserved; she regarded Llinos as a rival for Eynon's affections and it showed in the cool arch of her brow and the downward turn of her lips.

Llinos sighed. 'Please don't keep your distance. You have nothing to fear from me, you must see that.'

The girl shook her head. 'I only see that

my husband can't keep his eyes off you,' she said. 'I have tried to put it all out of my mind but every time I see you, the wound is opened again. I wish only that you would keep away from here and leave me and my husband to get on with our lives.'

'But, Annabel, we are here at your invitation. I could hardly stay away from the wedding, could I?'

Annabel regarded her steadily. 'No, I concede that much, but perhaps in future you could refrain from tête-à-têtes with Eynon, that would make me feel much easier in my mind.'

At that moment Eynon joined them. He leaned forward and kissed Llinos's cheek and in an involuntary movement she pulled away. He stood back, his eyebrows raised.

'What's this, Llinos, have I done anything to offend you?' He looked from Llinos to his wife and understanding dawned in his pale eyes. 'Please, take no notice of Annie, women in her condition have strange feelings, or so I am led to believe.' He bowed stiffly and turned away.

'You see what you do to him, to us!' Annabel's voice was almost a cry and after a moment she left Llinos and walked slowly towards Eynon. Llinos saw her put a placating hand on his arm. He looked down at her, his face white, his anger clear in the darkening of his eyes.

'Anything wrong?' Joe was at her side, his hand sliding protectively around her waist. She looked up at him, swallowing the lump in her throat.

'It seems I can't do anything right.' She spoke in a low voice. 'I can't please my old friend, I can only upset his wife! I envy her, Joe, she's big with her baby and here am I unable to give you the baby that we both want. I'm a failure, Joe. Why can't I accomplish what other women do so easily?'

'Don't let it eat away at you, Llinos,' Joe said softly. 'That way lies madness.' He drew her close. 'Cheer up, little Firebird, I think we might well try to work the miracle tonight because I can hardly keep my hands off you.'

But for once Llinos was not mollified by Joe's words. She walked away from him and stood looking out of the window. The leafless branches of the trees poked dry fingers into the mist. The trees were barren just as she was barren. In the spring they would put forth buds and grow new leaves, but would she ever have her heart's desire? She was beginning to doubt it.

Saul looked at Lily's upturned face and

saw that she was vulnerable. It seemed from her words that she would do anything to marry him. In turn, she could be very useful to him so he decided to play her along a little.

'My dear Lily, I admit I was carried away with love for you the other night but you were eager for it too, my dear.'

'Was I?' The words were uncertain and he pressed home his advantage. 'Of course, do you think me a bounder who would take the woman I love by force?'

'Well, no, it's just that I've never, never, well you know.'

He took her in his arms and held her close, his lips against her hair. 'I do know that you are a nice girl, not a hussy like some.' He held her away from him.

'Look, Lily, let's consider ourselves betrothed, shall we? I'd be honoured if you would wear the ring that was my mother's, as a token of my love and devotion.'

He saw that Lily was pleased. He had no ring from his mother, she had left none or, if she had, his father had disposed of it. Tomorrow he would go and see the goldsmith, ask him to make up some sort of ring in gold, nothing too expensive. He bent and kissed her mouth; she smelled sweet and clean and her hair was soft to the touch. His hand strayed to her breast but she pushed him away.

'No, Saul, there will be no more of that until we are married.' She sounded prissy and momentarily he was angered.

'All right, let's have a little drink together, here in my lodging house. What do you say?'

Lily turned lovely eyes to look at him. 'No thank you! I've had enough strong drink to last me for the rest of my life.'

'All right,' he said in resignation. 'I'll be good and wait.' He saw her smile and knew he had played the right card. Suddenly, he found himself remembering her sweetness, the tiny breasts, the slender thighs. Lily was a lovely girl and a good artist by all accounts. It was true she had no background but what did that matter? She earned a good living and perhaps, just perhaps, she would make a very good wife. At least she was a Gentile like his mother, that was enough to recommend her.

'Come along then, my shy little mouse,' he said. 'I'd better take you home to your solitary bed.'

As they left his lodging house and walked along the quiet roadway, Saul was already planning exactly what Lily must do for him before he would even consider marrying her.

CHAPTER

TWENTY-ONE

'Why can't you love me as you love her?' Annabel's voice was querulous but then she was large with child now and women had these strange moods, or so Eynon had been assured by his mother-in-law. Elizabeth had taken up residence in Swansea now, bringing with her from London a coach full of bags and baggage. Eynon wondered if he would ever get rid of her.

'Did you hear me, why can't you love me?'

Eynon sighed; it was a great pity that Annabel was not as amenable as Llinos. It was not that Llinos lacked fire, Joe's pet name for her was apt indeed, it was just that she had a sunny nature, she was calm and serene even in the face of difficulties.

'There, you see, you are thinking of her now!' Annabel turned her face away from Eynon and he cursed himself for hurting her.

'How do you know what I'm thinking, Annabel?' he asked. 'I was thinking of you, my dear girl.'

'Oh no, your whole face lights up when

you think of Llinos or when you speak of her. And when you see her I think you are going to fall down at her feet and worship her!'

His wife spoke with some justification and Eynon knew it. He leaned forward and patted her hand. 'I am doing my best, can't you see that, Annabel?'

'Well then, your best is simply not good enough. Am I not as pretty as Llinos? I am younger than she is and at least I am able to bear my husband children, something she seems singularly unable to do.'

Eynon's patience snapped. He rose to his feet and stood facing her, his face flushed with anger.

'Will you stop nagging at me, woman! I did the right thing by you, I married you, gave you my name.' He paced to and fro before the fireplace. 'I have given my name to the child you carry, a child that might not even be mine. I am a fool, I accept that. You might well have slept with a hundred men for all I know. Now shut up or leave my house, do you understand, Annabel, do you understand?'

Annabel burst into tears, loud sobs racked her but, for once, Eynon was impervious to her mood. He slammed out of the house and strode towards the pottery. He had enough to think about there, heaven knows. The last of the white porcelain had been sold and now the pottery had reverted to making only earthenware. The goods were still selling in large quantities but the money Eynon had spent on experiments had drained his resources. He was only just managing to make ends meet. Even the inheritance from his mother was gradually being dissipated. Now he had a wife to think of and all that entailed.

It was cold outside and Eynon started to walk along the river bank staring morosely into the swiftly flowing waters. He faced the fact that he was unhappy, discontented with his lot. He could never have Llinos, that much was clear, but he had been far better off as a single man. In the days before he married, he could come and go as he pleased. Now he was plagued by his wife's jealous reaction to all he did. He was wrong if he left her alone for too long and he was wrong if he suggested she take part in the social life of Swansea. Nothing, he felt, was going to satisfy her.

The lights of the Castle Inn gleamed into the darkness like a beacon and Eynon made his way towards the open doorway. The sound of cheerful voices greeted him as he entered the large firelit room. He had come a long way since the days when he had been afraid of his shadow, a target for every bully in the streets of the town. He had filled out now, his shoulders were broad, his legs strong. He would never make a pugilist but his manner, his air of authority, was enough to deter anyone from taking liberties.

'Evening, sir.' The landlord came to the table and dabbed at it with a cloth, soaking up only a fraction of the beer that lay in pools in the indentations of the wood. 'What can I get you?'

'Some porter, landlord.' Eynon smiled impulsively. 'And some respite from a nagging wife.'

'Aye, sir, that's why most of my customers come in here and sit! I'll be with you in a moment, sir.'

With the glass of gleaming porter before him, Eynon looked around the room. He did not expect to see anyone he knew, as he did not usually mix with the sort of company that frequented the Castle Inn. It was strange he had never made friends with anyone in the town. Indeed, the only true friends he had were Martin, Llinos and, by association, Joe. He was a loner, a man who needed no-one. But he did, he needed Llinos to love him and hold him and tell him he was the finest man in all the world.

Over the years his love for Llinos had not diminished, it had grown stronger. He had been with her through her troubles and joys for so long that she had become a part of him.

Restlessly, he drank his porter and, throwing some coins on the table, left the warmth of the fireplace for the chill outside. He retraced his steps and found himself heading towards Potters Row. He wondered if Llinos would mind him calling at such a late hour but he was willing to take the risk.

He was greeted with the warmth he had come to expect from her. He entered the drawing room and witnessed the cosy scene with a feeling of envy. Llinos was seated beside Joe, her hand in his, and opposite, like two benign pets, sat Charlotte and her new husband.

'We were just going to have some mulled wine and cake,' Llinos said. 'Will you join us, Eynon?'

He was accepted into the circle at once and here he felt loved for himself, not for what he could do or give. He wondered if he should mention that Bert Cimla was back in Swansea. It would be a good idea to put Llinos on her guard against the man but, then, it would be equally good to allow her a peaceful night with her relatives. In the end he decided to hold his tongue until a better moment.

The hours passed towards midnight, the logs shifted in the fireplace and still the conversation was animated, the atmosphere full of warmth and comfort and camaraderie.

Eynon looked up at the sudden disturbance in the hall and Llinos rose to her feet, her face pale, her hand to her heart. He knew at once what she feared, that the yeomanry had come for Joe again. But it was his mother-in-law who bustled into the room, her rouged cheeks flushed, her mouth set in a grim line.

'Oh, come in, Mrs . . .' Llinos's voice died away as Elizabeth came to a halt before Eynon.

'Sir, you should be ashamed of yourself,' she stormed. 'Sitting here enjoying yourself and your wife alone at home worried out of her wits!' Elizabeth spoke like a harridan, her cultured tones overlaid with the coarseness of a woman of the streets.

'You do realize that she is in a very delicate condition, don't you?' Elizabeth continued. 'Do you want your wife to fall sick and lose the child? Is that what you want?'

Eynon rose swiftly and took Elizabeth's arm. 'Will you excuse my mother-in-law's rudeness, Llinos?' He propelled Elizabeth towards the door, anger building within him. 'I shall see you tomorrow some time — to apologize.'

He almost dragged Elizabeth the small distance to the big house and, once inside, he turned on her, his heart hammering with anger he could hardly contain.

'How dare you!' he said. 'How dare you burst into the home of my friends and make a spectacle of yourself and me?'

Elizabeth drew back as if fearing a blow. 'I was worried about my daughter; it's only natural, isn't it?'

'You think you can run my life, do you?' he demanded. 'Well I'm here to tell you that I will not stand for it. Do you hear me? Any more scenes from you or your daughter and you can pack your bags and get out of my house, both of you.'

'You can't do that,' Elizabeth tried to bluster. 'You are legally married to my daughter, she is having your child.'

'Is she indeed?' Eynon said. 'Would any judge in the land agree with you, I wonder? If I told everyone the circumstances of my meeting with your daughter I think I would gain a divorce with very little trouble.'

'You wouldn't!'

'I would and I will if you and your shrew

of a daughter do not stop interfering in my life,' Eynon said.

The maid was hovering anxiously beside him in the hall, waiting to take his coat and hat. 'Bring me some wine,' Eynon said and the girl bobbed a curtsey, her eyes downcast. 'And bring it to my room.'

Eynon favoured Elizabeth with a last, withering look and left her standing openmouthed, her cheeks red, her breathing uneven. Suddenly she looked what she was, a raddled whore and, in that moment, Eynon almost relented.

'You despicable man!' she said in a low, venomous tone. He shook his head and climbed the remaining stairs to the privacy of his own room.

'I felt so sorry for Eynon.' Llinos was frowning, her hands clasped together in her lap. 'I don't know how he could bear to live in the same house as that awful woman.'

'Does he have much choice?' Charlotte's soft voice asked. 'Even I can see that such a woman would be the bane of any man's life.'

Joe looked at Samuel and smiled. 'We men have to put up with a great deal from our wives, don't you agree, Sam?'

'Indeed, I do. We are hard done by, taken

advantage of by the little feminine tricks women learn in the cradle.'

Charlotte threw a cushion at her husband. 'Then be quiet, wretch, know your place.'

Samuel shrugged. 'You see?'

Charlotte rose to her feet. 'Come, Sam, I think it's time we went to our beds and left these young people to themselves.'

He rose at once and took his wife's hand. His thin face was alight with love and Llinos swallowed a lump in her throat.

'Good night to you both,' she said. 'See you at breakfast.'

Samuel paused in the doorway. 'Llinos, Joe, there's something I think you should know.' He shrugged again. 'It might be of little importance but it seems my son is still in Swansea.' He took a deep breath. 'He is living in a lodging house and is keeping some very strange company. Just be on your guard, both of you.' He hung his head. 'Saul is a wicked, ruthless man, I fear he will stop at nothing. He is driven by greed, it rules him.'

Charlotte slipped her hand through Sam's arm. 'There, my love, don't think of him now. Come to bed and sleep, my brother will take care of everything.' She smiled at Joe, her eyes full. 'I bless the day you came into our lives, Joe,' she said softly. 'I have never been so happy in all my life. Is that selfish of me when I know that poor, dear Letitia isn't here to share my happiness?'

As Samuel led his wife from the room, Llinos moved closer to Joe. 'You see how you are loved and needed?' she whispered. 'And no-one loves and needs you more than I do. Hold me, Joe, because I have one of those awful feelings that something is about to go very wrong.'

'You want me to put this stuff in your father's food?' Lily looked at the bottle curiously. The liquid inside clung thickly to the sides of the glass. 'What is it?'

'Medication,' Saul said flatly. 'My father refuses to take it and, without it, he is not well, not well at all.'

Lily smiled. 'But, Saul, I work in the paint shed. How am I supposed to get into the house, the kitchen is always full of people?'

Saul smiled down at her, his finger under her chin, tipping her face up to his. 'My clever little wife-to-be will find a way.' He kissed her lightly and her lips were cool, childlike beneath his. After a moment, Lily drew away. She looked up artfully at Saul and slipped the bottle into the small velvet bag hanging from her waist.

'Are we going into town to have my ring fitted today, Saul?' she asked. He shook his head and she bit her lip in sudden impatience. 'When will we get it, then?' She knew her words had carried an edge to them and she knew too, it was not wise to anger a man, especially a man like Saul. 'I want everyone to know that I belong to such a wonderful man,' she added hastily.

Saul moved to the edge of the river and stared into the depths. Lily moved beside him and slipped her arm through his. 'You know Watt Bevan still pursues me, don't you? He would give anything to have me for his wife.'

Instead of rousing jealousy in Saul as she had intended, she saw that he was angry. He turned to her, his face dark and gripped her arm. 'Are you betrothed to me or not?' he demanded.

'I am, my love, as soon as you put a ring on my finger.' She had taken just about enough of him. She dragged her arm away and flounced back onto the road, making for the busy streets of the town. She had expected Saul to run after her, that is exactly the way Watt would have behaved, but he did no such thing.

She was committed to her walk, if she

turned back she would lose the ground she had gained. Saul must not think that he had her just where he wanted her. It did not do to allow any man too much power. Anger flowed through her; she felt so powerless, at the mercy of a man who did not even keep his word about their betrothal.

The town was busy with market shoppers. Sides of beef hung from market stalls, the meat dark and dried. Lily stared at the stall, repulsed by the gruesome sight of the butcher hacking a leg of lamb.

She turned to leave the market when, across the street, she caught sight of Maura Dundee. The woman held her head aloft and sailed through the crowds as though she was a great lady not a servant. She had always been a snob, no-one would ever think from her manner that she was a deserted wife.

'Day to you, Maura,' Lily said staring in scorn at the ring the woman wore on her finger. She had the badge of marriage, respectability and yet she was as dried up as an old maid.

Maura looked down at Lily without recognition. Her eyes were aloof, she did not smile. 'Do I know you?'

It was a deliberate insult. Maura knew her, of course she did, anyone with any connection with the potteries knew Lily, the talented painter.

Suddenly the desire to hurt and wound rose up like a sickness and Lily jostled Maura's arm, almost upsetting the basket of eggs and ham.

'What do you think you are doing, girl?' Maura's voice was hard. 'Run away and play like the child you are.'

'Not such a child that I don't know what your husband is up to,' Lily said spitefully. 'Gone off to America, as far away from you as possible and married again, with three fine sons.' She looked up pleased at the startled expression on the older woman's face. 'Oh, didn't you know? Well everyone else does, a laughing stock all over Swansea, you are.' With that last parting shot, Lily turned away and lost herself in the crowds.

Serve the old cow right, looking down her nose at decent respectable folk. Who did she think she was? All the same, Lily felt a sudden sense of disquiet; she had promised Watt she would say nothing about Binnie Dundee and his new life across the sea. Well, Watt was nothing to her now, she had bigger fish to fry. If she had to sell herself into marriage it might as well be with a rich, well set-up young man like Saul Marks.

Lily suddenly knew she must see Saul,

must make up for her bad temper of earlier. Best to bide her time though, give the old man a drop of the medicine so that Saul would be pleased with her. But it was not so easy to accomplish that, Lily scarcely went into Pottery House.

She made her way at a brisk pace back along the streets towards the spot where the tall stacks of the kilns reared upwards above the houses. The smells, the sounds, the feel of the pottery were all so familiar to her, all she had ever thought she wanted. Now something better beckoned, a good life of leisure with a man who could afford the finer things in life. And once the old man, his father, was dead, who knew what riches Saul would inherit?

On an impulse Lily took the bottle and stared at the contents thoughtfully. Did Saul want his father dead? Then, dismissing the thought as impossible, she returned the bottle to her bag.

It was a triumphant Lily who met Saul in his rooms that evening. She was a little worried about being alone with him but she did not want the old busybodies who inhabited the lounge to hear their conversation.

'I've done it,' she said. 'I've managed to bribe Meggie, the maid. She's promised to put the medicine in your father's food and drink for a small reward, of course.'

'What reward?' Saul asked suspiciously.

'Nothing that costs any money, don't worry, I'm too clever for that.' Lily was already aware that money was a very important commodity to her husband-to-be. 'I've promised to give Meggie a chance to go out with Watt Bevan. That way I'll kill two birds with one stone.' Lily slipped her arm around Saul's waist and he drew her close at once, his hand pressing against her breast. She felt uncomfortable but did not want to offend him by drawing away. 'I will have to go out with the two of them, it's the only way to get Watt to agree. He's daft on me of course, but at least Meggie will have a chance to get him to notice her.'

'Fat chance!' Saul said passionately. 'He won't see anything, not with you around. Your beauty would outshine any other woman. Look, I've got a surprise for my best girl.'

Lily looked up at him, her face flushed. 'The ring, Saul, you've got the ring!' Lily watched breathless as Saul took a small pouch from his pocket. He tipped it up and a sparkling gold band lay in the square palm of his hand. He took her fingers, slipped the ring on and it fitted perfectly.

'How beautiful!' Lily stared at the shining

gold band, entranced. 'It's perfect, it's the best gift I've ever had.'

Saul moved away from her and opened a bottle of ruby red wine. 'Now we must celebrate our betrothal in style,' he said.

She took the glass, feeling more than a little apprehensive. She sipped it and the warmth spread like a glow through her veins. She had never tasted wine so rich. Saul took her towards the bed and sat her down.

'Come along, drink up, be happy, we are going to be married just as soon as I can arrange it.'

To please him she drank deeply and felt the wine hit the pit of her stomach like a blow. It was really quite a nice sensation, she realized. Saul refilled her glass and she giggled like a child.

'I can't believe it, Saul, I'm going to be Mrs Marks. Won't all the girls envy me?' She leaned forward in an uncharacteristic mood of happiness and kissed his cheek.

'I'm glad to see you so happy.' Saul tipped her glass towards her lips and, obediently, she drank the wine. The world seemed a light place, the candlelight shimmered on the gold on her finger and her head and heart felt light as feathers. Why had she worried so much about marrying?

Just look how good and kind Saul was being to her, giving her a wonderful time, buying her expensive gifts, she was so lucky. How envious Polly would be when she told her the news.

Saul took the glass from her hand and pressed her back against the bed. 'Talking about rewards,' he said, 'what about my reward?'

An edge of doubt penetrated the rosy haze in Lily's mind. 'I love you so much, Lily, and I want you desperately. It's only natural, isn't it?'

She tried to think clearly. Polly said that it was natural, she even enjoyed it. And Lily had allowed Saul to lie with her once even though she could not remember it. Strange, the wine was not affecting her at all in the same way as it had on that occasion. Although her mind was hazy now, she knew exactly what she was doing.

Saul was undressing her, she felt her clothes being pulled away from her and tossed aside. The cold of the night air touched her breasts and she looked down to see her nipples harden, pale pink against her white skin. She knew she was no longer able to stop him. If she protested now he would never forgive her. She hoped that he would at least blow the candles out. He did and the darkness enveloped her.

Then he was beside her, touching her, kissing her. She tried to respond, tried to like what he was doing but she cried out in pain when he thrust against her, hurting her. He took her cries for ones of pleasure and redoubled his efforts. He moaned and laboured and every convulsive movement pained her. It was just as bad as she had thought it was going to be. There was no passion, no feeling, just disgust. She bit her lip, hating every moment, until at last he fell on top of her, breathing hard, his hairy chest pressed disgustingly against her soft breasts.

'My little Lily, my love,' he said. 'Do you know what? I think I've actually gone and fallen in love with you!' He sounded surprised as though he had never put a gold ring on her finger and said she was his girl. She tried to clear her head but the wine was too strong. Now that the ordeal was over Lily wanted only to sleep. She curled her legs up to her stomach and allowed the darkness to overwhelm her.

Eynon paced about the room, hearing the cries of his wife in the bedroom above with a feeling of dread. He had come home to find his wife had gone into labour, prematurely, or at least that was what she had told him.

Dark doubts assailed him. Had she been pregnant even when he had first lain with her? But no, that was impossible, she had been a virgin, he could swear to it. But could he? Women had a way of being able to fool a man.

His friend Martin had been called and now the cleric entered the room, his face grave. 'She's bad, Eynon, very bad. I think you will have to brace yourself for the worst.'

'Oh, God!' Eynon sank down into a chair, his hands over his eyes as though he could shut out everything around him.

'I'll ring for someone to bring you a drink,' Martin said gently. 'Buck up, my old friend, this is part of the great plan, you know. Life, birth, death, it is all so natural and we just have to accept it. I'll just slip back upstairs, see if there's anything I can do.'

It was Maura who brought the tray of drinks. Eynon looked up to see that her eyes were swollen with weeping. What on earth was the matter with the woman? She could not be crying for Annabel as she scarcely knew her. He sat up straighter: something had happened, something that was outside this household. The thought brought with it almost a sense of relief; that someone else's

403

life was as stormy as his own.

'What's wrong, Maura?' he asked. She looked at him dully.

'Sure, an' you've enough to put up with as it is without worrying about me.' For once her voice was soft, sympathetic, and the silly weak tears started in Eynon's eyes.

'You are very upset, Maura, please tell me what's wrong, perhaps I can help. Come here and sit down and talk to me.'

Maura sank into a chair as though her legs had become too weak to hold her. Her mouth trembled and all at once she looked like the young woman she really was.

'My husband is married to an American woman, he has three sons by her. It isn't the first time I've heard such gossip and I hate him for hurting me all over again!'

Eynon was taken by surprise. 'It's possible, of course, but if it is true, I've heard nothing of it. Gossip can be cruel, try not to let it upset you so, Maura, until you know for sure what the truth is.'

Maura pressed her hands together until her knuckles gleamed white. 'I must find out about Binnie or I'll go mad,' she said.

Eynon could see she was confused and hurt. 'Look, why not speak to Watt Bevan?' he suggested. 'Watt has been out to America, he might just have heard something.'

Maura nodded slowly. 'That's a good idea, I will speak to him.' She rose to her feet. 'Thank you for listening to my troubles when you've got enough of your own. Can I get you something else?' She was speaking now like the girl she used to be, not the frozen iceberg she had become since her husband left her.

Eynon smiled at her. 'No, no thank you, Maura.'

'Can I just say how sorry I am, about your wife.' Maura winced as another scream rent the air. 'She's having a bad time of it to be sure.'

Elizabeth came flying into the room almost knocking Maura off her feet. 'Come quick, Eynon, the baby is born.' Her glance was anguished, two spots of colour burned in her cheeks. 'As for my poor girl, I think . . .' Her voice trailed away and she rushed from the room, her skirts flying.

Eynon was loath to go into the bedroom. His mouth was dry, his breathing rapid. He knew it was cowardly of him but he did not want to see Annabel suffering. He took a deep breath and opened the door; the room smelled of blood, and a feeling of nausea swept over him.

'Here's your baby, a girl,' the midwife handed him the child and Eynon looked into the tiny crumpled face with something like trepidation. He saw the tiny nose, the closed eyes and the waving fists and experienced an immediate feeling of tenderness for the tiny scrap of life in his arms.

The baby blinked and stared upward for a moment and Eynon looked into pale grey eyes and saw the fall of pale hair and knew that she was his own.

'She's small but strong. She'll live,' the midwife said. She leaned closer. 'As to your wife, it's all in the hands of the gods.'

Eynon handed the baby back to her. 'Take good care of my daughter.' His voice was thick with emotion. He moved to the bed and sat beside his wife, taking her pale hand in his.

'You did well, my love,' he said quietly. 'You've given me a wonderful daughter.'

A small smile parted her lips but only briefly. 'I'm sorry, Eynon.' Her voice was a thin whisper. 'I'm sorry for everything.' She sighed. 'Take good care of our child and be kind to Mamma.' She closed her eyes as though too weary to keep them open and with a long drawn out sigh her life ebbed away.

Martin began to pray and Elizabeth to cry. Eynon stared at them both and then at the pale, still face of his wife. He was in a state of numbness, he could not accept what was happening. Annabel had given him the greatest gift any woman could give her husband and now she was dead. In that moment he hated himself for never having loved her.

Elizabeth's sobs became a wail of grief. She fell across the bed and tried to clasp her daughter in her arms. Eynon felt moved to his bones. Whatever she was, however badly she had behaved, Elizabeth was a mother who had lost her child. Eynon knew then that he would keep Elizabeth in comfort for the rest of her life, however much it cost him. He hung his head and tears rolled down his cheeks as, slowly, he left the room.

CHAPTER

TWENTY-TWO

Llinos was in the drawing room with Charlotte, both women staring silently into the warmth of the fire. Joe was upstairs with Samuel who was feeling poorly and had gone to bed early.

'I'm worried, Llinos,' Charlotte said at last. 'Sam is not himself, he hasn't been right for over a week now. Do you think we should call out the doctor?'

Llinos dragged her thoughts back to the present; she had been thinking about Eynon and about the sudden and tragic death of his wife. She knew he was beset by feelings of guilt and yet his pride in his daughter was wonderful to see. She had spent as much time with him as possible over the past days. So much so, she thought, that she was neglecting her own family.

'I'm sorry, Charlotte, I've been preoccupied with Eynon. Perhaps I should have sent for the doctor sooner, but I'm sure it's just a chill,' she said comfortingly. 'It's the time of the year for colds and fevers.' She shivered as a gust of fierce rain hit the windows as though to add emphasis to her words.

'No,' Charlotte said, 'it's not just a chill, it's something more serious. I don't like the colour of his skin and he is in constant pain so that he scarcely eats anything.'

'We'll have the doctor tomorrow,' Llinos said decisively. But it would not be Dr Jones. With the thought came a wave of fear that was purely selfish. If anything happened to Samuel, Joe would be blamed, it was inevitable. There had been so much hostility shown to Joe since the death of her father and the attitude of the townspeople seemed to be getting worse. Only yesterday someone had thrown a stone at the horse Joe was riding, almost causing an accident. But nothing was going to happen to Samuel, she was becoming hysterical.

She looked up as Joe entered the room. His expression was grave and her spirits plummeted. 'What is it?' she asked, careful not to show her fear.

'I think Sam needs a doctor,' Joe said. 'He's not too poorly at present but neither is he showing any signs of improvement.'

Charlotte put her hands to her face. 'Oh, dear, I knew he wasn't well.' She rose shakily to her feet. 'I must go to him.'

When Charlotte had left the room, Joe came to sit on the deep sofa, slipping his arm around his wife's shoulder. 'I can't make it out, it's almost as though Sam is being poisoned.'

'How could that be possible?' Llinos asked, fear constricting her throat. Joe shook his head.

'I don't know. His symptoms are those of an overdose of the medicine I used to make up for Lloyd.'

'You have none of that here now,' Llinos protested. 'It was all taken away when my father died.'

Joe took her hand and raised it to his lips. He did not speak and she stared at him anxiously, trying to read his expression. The silence seemed to drag on, punctuated only by the shifting of logs in the fire.

'Where did the medication land up, that's what I want to know,' Joe said at last. 'In the wrong hands, it's lethal. But then, who would want to harm Sam? Could I be the target?'

'Samuel's son hates him,' Llinos said flatly. 'And Saul Marks is capable of anything.' She frowned thoughtfully. 'How would your medicine get into the food or drink though, who could be doing it? It has to be someone in this house.'

Joe nodded. 'I agree. The medicine, if added in large amounts to food or drink, could prove deadly. But if that's been the case, why aren't we all sick?'

Llinos rose to her feet and paced across the room, her hands clasped together. She trusted Cook with her life. The woman was too lacking in guile to do anything like adding medicine to the food. In any case, Cook knew she would be the first one to be suspected. Llinos paced back across the room. One of the maids then, Meggie perhaps. She had never liked Joe. But why, what could the girl hope to gain?

Joe answered her thoughts. 'Yes, I must be the real target. If there was another suspicious death in this household who would be held responsible?'

Llinos slipped her arms around his waist. She closed her eyes feeling the beat of his heart against her own. She would protect Joe with her life. Might she have to do just that?

She sat back on her heels. 'In the morning I'll have all the servants assembled in the hall so that I can speak to them. You could take the opportunity to search the kitchen for anything suspicious.'

Joe's face relaxed as he smiled down at his wife. 'You are such a little Firebird, aren't you? Spitting fire, breathing fire, defending what is your own with every nerve in your body. I love you, Llinos, do you know that?'

411

He kissed her and she felt joyful and fearful at the same time. But Joe would not be taken away from her a second time, she was determined on it.

'Come on,' he said, 'let's go to bed, there's nothing we can do tonight.'

They climbed the stairs hand in hand and Llinos paused outside Charlotte's bedroom. A small voice called for her to enter and when she opened the door, it was to see the elderly couple lying in each other's arms. Llinos forced a smile.

'I'm sorry to intrude but I just wanted to know how you were feeling, Sam.'

'Not so bad, you ladies worry too much.'

On an impulse, Llinos took the glass of milk from the side of the bed where Sam was lying and sniffed at it. 'I think this is a little sour,' she said. 'I'll change it for you.'

Sam shook his head. 'No need, really, Llinos, don't trouble yourself.'

'No trouble.' Llinos left the room. Joe was waiting outside on the landing and she handed him the glass with a meaningful nod and then retraced her steps down the stairs.

In the kitchen the maids were clearing up the last of the cooking pots. The fire burned low in the grate and the candle flames hissed in the pools of wax at the bottom of the holders. Llinos ignored the strange look that Meggie gave her and walked into the coldness of the pantry.

'Do you need anything, Mrs Mainwaring?' Meggie was at her side as Llinos took up a small jug. 'I just felt like a drink of milk, Meggie. Would you bring me a glass?'

'Don't drink that milk!' Meggie said and took the jug away from Llinos. 'It's been there too long, the flies will have got into it.'

She took up a large pitcher and poured a foaming glass of milk, handing it carefully to Llinos. 'There, that's nice and fresh, do you a whole lot of good, miss.'

'Thank you, Meggie.' Llinos returned to the landing where Joe was still standing. She lifted the glass of milk and followed Joe into the bedroom, closing the door securely behind her.

'We must compare the taste of the two glasses of milk,' Llinos sank onto the bed. Joe nodded.

'I can do that myself by simply tasting the milk.' He took and sniffed one of the glasses and then took a small sip of the milk. 'This has been tampered with, no doubt about it.'

'Oh my God!' Llinos said. 'Then Meggie is involved in whatever is going on. She practically pushed me aside so that I wouldn't touch the jug of milk on the shelf.'

Joe was busy tying a ribbon around the

413

suspect glass of milk. 'No-one else could tell the difference,' he said. 'That's the benefit and the danger of the medicine. Take Sam his drink and let's go to bed, we'll sort this out in the morning.'

Later, as Llinos lay in the circle of her husband's arms, she knew she would not get much sleep that night. Thoughts were rushing around her head like roaches caught in a trap. Someone was out to harm Joe through Sam and it did not take a great deal of imagination to guess who was behind it. That son of his was wicked, evil, but how on earth had he managed to involve one of the servants? She sighed heavily and closed her eyes wishing only for morning to come so that she could do something positive.

The sun was warm on his face as John sat on the porch of the McCabe house. Beside him Josephine was swinging her dainty feet to and fro, her dress fluttering in the breeze. He wondered briefly where her sister was. Melia usually kept a close eye on him, thinking him her property, and it was beginning to irritate John. He glanced at the girl beside him, she was not as pretty as Melia nor as vivacious but she was practical, down to earth and more importantly she shared John's sense of humour. She was a good listener and did not simper the way her sister did.

'What are your ambitions, John?' Josephine asked quietly. He heard the swing creak as she turned to look at him.

'I suppose I want to make my fortune,' he said. 'And then go home to Cornwall to have my revenge on the man who ruined my father.'

'That's an honest answer,' Josephine said dryly. 'I half expected you to say that you wanted to marry my sister and settle down and have a brood of young uns the way Binnie did.'

'That sounds enticing enough,' John said. 'But I'm not sure I know my mind, perhaps I don't know what I want.' He took Josephine's hand in his. 'I think your sister has got the wrong idea about me.'

'Oh, dear.' Josephine's voice held a smile. 'That's going to dampen my dear sister's ardour, isn't it?'

John laughed with her, she too had been aware that Melia had been panting after John from the moment she saw him.

'It's sure strange how a man never wants that which comes too easy.' Josephine's voice was soft. 'I think I should learn a lesson from that when it's my turn to look for a husband.'

John took a deep breath and leaned across to take Josephine's elfin face in his hands.

'I've got a feeling you don't have to look very far.'

Josephine rose abruptly. 'Look, honey,' her voice was sharp, 'we girls are not cookies on a plate to be picked up, examined and thrown aside. In any case, what makes you think you are such a great catch? Goodnight to you, John.'

John stared up at the star-studded sky. The air was balmy, the breeze soft. He smiled to himself. Josephine was not going to be a pushover and that made the chase so much more interesting.

'Evening, John.' The figure of Binnie Dundee loomed up out of the darkness. 'Dan in?'

'He's down on the estate, somewhere.' Both men smiled, knowing what that meant.

'I don't know how the old goat keeps going,' Binnie said. 'I hope I've got half his energy when I'm that age.' He sank down beside John and leaned back, his feet stretched out before him.

'How are the plans for opening up in Albany going?' Binnie asked.

'Slowly,' John replied. 'I think I'm being kept here as girl fodder at the moment.' He smiled into the darkness. 'It's a hard life choosing between two lovely girls, don't you think?'

Binnie laughed out loud. 'Lucky bastard!'

'But are you happy with Hortense?' John asked, curious to know if the other man had settled for a convenient marriage in return for a life time's security.

Binnie leaned forward, his elbows on his knees. 'I love the girl so much that it drives me to distraction to think of losing her.' He spoke with deadly seriousness.

'Why should you lose her, she's not sick, is she?' John asked.

Binnie shook his head. 'No, she's not sick, Hortense is never sick. She's a strong, healthy American girl.'

'Well then?'

'I have secrets, John, just as everyone else does, things from my past that I would prefer to remain there.'

'I suppose most men have,' John said. 'But no-one expects a man to be pure as the driven snow when he marries, do they?'

Binnie looked up and, for a moment, it seemed he would speak. Then he dropped his head. 'No, I suppose not.'

'Oh there you are, John.' Melia's voice startled the two men. 'I've been looking for you, hon.'

She sat beside John, resting a proprietary hand on his arm. 'Evenin', Binnie, looking for Daddy are you?'

'Aye, I was but it was nothing important, it can wait. I'll just sit here for a while, see if he comes back.'

'Oh, I see.' Melia sounded disappointed and John smiled to himself: he had been given a reprieve, he would not have to be alone with Melia, suffering her cloying attentions, at least for a while.

'Hortense brought the boys over today,' Melia said. 'The baby is a sweet thing, so good and cheerful. I can't wait to have babies of my own.'

John raised his eyebrows and saw Binnie hiding a smile. 'Well, Melia, you have your pick of all the lads in town,' Binnie said. 'Any one of them would give his eye-teeth to have you for a wife.'

Melia preened, touching her soft curls. 'Your lips have tasted the honey pot, Binnie, but I know you keep your sweet talkin' for my big sister.' She rested her hand on John's arm in the proprietary way that used to amuse him but now only irritated him.

'He's an old happily married man, isn't he, John?'

'Seems like it,' John said. 'Perhaps he got

the pick of the bunch, lucky man.'

Melia withdrew her hand, pouting, and John laughed, taking her hand and kissing the palm. 'Just teasing, little girl, just teasing.'

'Oh, you!'

'Hey!' Dan McCabe loomed up out of the darkness, smelling strongly of drink. 'This a reception committee or something?' He slumped into the rocking chair and stretched his legs out before him.

'Go and get your daddy something to drink, honey, and don't show your mother.' He waved his hand and Melia rose reluctantly, flouncing from the porch, her skirts flying.

'Well then, John, my boy, are you going to speak out for my girl or not?' Dan sounded a trifle impatient.

John took a deep breath. 'I do want to speak out but perhaps what I say isn't going to be what you expected.'

'Don't talk in riddles, boy!' Dan said. 'Come on, spit it out before my girl comes back. Don't do to let the wimmin folk know everything that's going on.'

John leaned forward. 'I was drawn to Melia at first, she's by far the prettier of the two girls.' He sighed. 'But I've spent a lot of time with Josephine and I think I'm falling in love with her.'

'Well then,' Dan said, 'for heaven's sake put us all out of our misery and ask for her.' He chuckled. 'Knowing her, she might refuse you though.'

John took a deep breath. 'That's what I'm afraid of.'

As Melia returned, Dan rose to his feet and took the pitcher from her. 'I'm off to bed, I'll leave you young uns to sort yourselves out.'

'Daddy's drunk,' Melia said. 'And he stinks of the sheds. He's been with those girls again. I don't understand Ma, I wouldn't have my husband cheatin' on me that way.'

'I'm going home.' Binnie rose and stretched his arms towards the sky. 'I'm happy with my lot, don't want any other woman, but then men are not all the same, are they?'

He rested a hand on John's shoulder. 'Good luck, mate.' He strolled easily down the porch steps and out onto the open ground. It was only a short walk to his house and John watched him with a feeling of envy.

'John.' Melia's voice was soft. 'John, what did Binnie mean telling you good luck?' He shrugged and she continued relentlessly. 'I know you got a fancy for me, why don't you ask Daddy for me?'

John turned to her and took her hands in his. 'Melia, I like you a lot,' he said. 'You are pretty, good-natured, a wife any man would be proud of.'

'But not you,' she spoke flatly. 'I thought you were falling for me, John, that's the impression you gave us all.'

'I think you are charming,' John said quickly. 'And I don't want to hurt your feelings but I just don't love you enough to marry you.' He decided that honesty was the best policy, not realizing that sometimes honesty needs to be tempered with tact.

'To tell you the truth, I think I've fallen in love with Josephine.' He avoided her eyes looking out into the darkness. He felt her stiffen.

'You low-down rat!' Her voice was low, venomous. 'You led me up the garden path all this time, partnering me at the dancing, treating me like your girl and all the time you wanted Jo.' She rose to her feet and stared down at him, her face hard.

'If ever I can serve you ill, John Pendennis, I will.' She walked away, her shoulders set, her hands clasped to her sides crushing the soft cotton of her dress. John sighed heavily. What was he letting himself in for? Perhaps he should just go on home, live his life without complications. But he knew he would do no such thing. The lure of a good life, a pottery of his own to run and prospects of marrying a wife who would one day inherit quite a fortune, was too potent to ignore.

'I can't do it any more.' Lily was sitting beside Saul in the dimly lit sitting room of his boarding house. 'There's been such a rumpus up at the house what with Mr Mainwaring searching the pantries and cupboards and Mrs Mainwaring summoning the servants to question them.'

'But they didn't find anything, did they?' Saul said reasonably. 'In any case, no-one would tie any of it to you, would they? You work in the pottery, not the house.'

'It's not that simple. Meggie would blab rather than take the blame.'

'I repeat, nothing was found so Meggie won't be questioned any more. You worry too much, Lily, my lovely little bride-to-be, do you know that?'

'Oh, Saul.' She rested her head on his shoulder, her thoughts were confused, her nerve endings on edge. She knew that any moment he would want to take her up to his room. How she hated it, the sweating, the straining, the pain of his body connecting with hers. She shuddered as his hand slid over her shoulder to brush her breast.

'Come on, Lily.' He bent to whisper in her ear. 'You are irresistible and I want you.' He took her hand and she glanced around her as though looking for a means of escape. 'Come on, none of the old biddies will notice us,' he said, misinterpreting her reluctance. 'Anyway, I've a little gift for you in my room, something to show how much I appreciate you.'

She suppressed a sigh as she went with him up the stairs. How she wished Saul's landlady was as vigilant about visitors as her own was.

In his room, he took her to the bed and pushed her backwards, his hands on her buttons impatient. She took a deep breath; this was going to be a quick affair, she was learning the signs now.

She moaned but Saul took it as a sign of her pleasure and thrashed above her, his face red with exertion. She closed her eyes and thought of other things, it was something she was adept at doing now. It was over quickly and, with a sigh of relief, she pulled her skirts into place. She knew that in the morning her pale skin would be bruised and she would ache all over. She sat up and

Saul sat beside her. He was holding a box towards her, a smile on his face.

She opened it and inside, nestling on a velvet cushion, was a small gilt pin fashioned into the shape of a bouquet with colored stones. 'Thank you, Saul,' she said, quietly trying to fight back the tears. He seemed to think he could buy her with cheap trinkets and, in that moment, her sense of resentment was almost overwhelming.

'So you will go on helping me, won't you?' he coaxed. She looked into his face, studying his expression carefully.

'Are you trying to kill your father, Saul?' There it was said, her growing suspicions spoken out loud.

He laughed. 'All you need to concern yourself with is the money we will have to start our married life. Come on, it's time you went home.'

He walked her to the end of the street where she lodged and then, without a word or a kiss, disappeared into the darkness.

'You're out late, Lily.' Watt's voice startled her and she paused for a moment, wondering what to say. But then why should she worry about Watt Bevan? His opinion of her was worth nothing to her. Since Saul had come into her life, she had avoided Watt like the plague, unwilling to put up with his questions. Now, though she looked round hopefully, there seemed no means of escape.

He took her arm and drew her towards the lights from the windows. 'I see you've been enjoying yourself, Lily. You could at least have stopped to tidy your hair.' His voice was hard.

'Mind your own business,' Lily said. 'What I do is no concern of yours.'

'You've let him have his way with you then?' His voice was thick. 'What has Saul Marks got that I haven't?' He laughed shortly. 'I suppose the answer to that is easy enough, it's money, isn't it? I never thought you were the sort to sell yourself, Lily. Nothing but a common street whore that's what you are.'

'I'm not!' Lily protested. 'I love Saul and he loves me. See, I'm wearing his ring, we are going to be married.'

'And pigs might fly,' Watt said. 'Lily, stop and think, you are being fooled by this man, he will use you and throw you away, is that what you want?'

'Go away and leave me alone!' Lily pushed him aside and let herself into the lodging house. Quietly, she climbed the stairs to her room and sank down on the bed, the tears falling hot and fast.

'What's wrong with you, Lil?' Polly slid into the room with the strange cat-like silence that was characteristic of her.

'Watt Bevan!' Lily said. 'He says that Saul is just using me. He's not, I know he's not, he loves me.'

Polly sank down on the bed. 'Bedding you, that's all men are interested in,' she said. 'You're a fool if you believe in love. Haven't I told you often enough that you must use your looks while you got them? Look, just don't believe all you hear and only half wot you see, right?'

'Don't you start on me, Polly, I've had enough. Saul loves me, he's going to marry me. I shall be Mrs Saul Marks and then I can cock a snook at all of you.'

Polly's mouth fell open. She slid to the edge of the bed to peer more closely into Lily's face.

'You don't mean that, do you?' she asked. Lily looked at her and on an impulse, took Polly into her arms. 'No, not you, Poll, you are the only one who ever cared about me, apart from Saul that is.'

'So when you're married, you'll ask me to your posh house and we'll have parties and all sorts?'

Lily slipped into bed and closed her eyes.

'Of course I will, Poll,' she said, but she knew she would never invite Polly to visit. Hers would be a respectable household and once she had a wedding ring on her finger, she would call the tune. There would be no more silliness, no more being mauled to slake Saul's lust. She would be a good wife in every other way, but not that one.

First, a small voice inside her head told her, she would have to do what Saul wanted and continue, somehow, to add the contents of the strange bottle to Samuel Marks's food and drink. She was not sure just how she would manage it but she must try for the sake of her future. She closed her eyes and allowed the darkness to draw her into a dreamless sleep.

CHAPTER

TWENTY-THREE

'Look, Maura, what can I say?' Watt was struggling to keep his friend's secret but in the face of Maura's persistence it was proving difficult.

'You can tell me the truth. Please, Watt, just put me out of my misery, will you?' She looked at him, her long red hair tangled on her shoulders, her eyes bright with weeping. She had seemed like an old woman to Watt but now he realized she was not so much older than he was.

'What good would it do you to know?' he prevaricated desperately. 'Could you go to America and confront him, even if you could find him?'

'No.' Maura looked down at her hands. 'It's just that I can't bear the not-knowing. The gossip, the tittle-tattle, the thought of other people knowing something about my husband that I don't, is driving me mad. If I know the truth I can face it, come to terms with it. What I can't face is the uncertainty, the hope that one day Binnie will come back to me.'

Pity tugged at Watt's heart. He could see

the lines of strain in her face, he could not fail to hear the entreaty in her voice. 'Look, sit down,' he said at last. 'Let's talk quietly.'

Maura looked around the kitchen of Pottery House, aware of Cook watching her every move and Meggie hovering ever nearer the corner where she was talking to Watt.

He caught her glance. 'I know, it's not very private. Would you like to come up to my room?' He spoke tentatively, not wanting her to get the wrong impression.

'All right.' She sounded relieved. 'If you're sure Llinos won't mind.'

Watt led her up the back stairs and opened the door of his room wide. It was a large room with a deep window in which was placed a table and two chairs. 'Please sit down, Maura. Can I get you something to drink?'

'No, thank you. Just talk to me, Watt, please talk to me.' She clasped her hands together in her lap: small, well-shaped hands with well-kept fingernails. Her position as housekeeper demanded good administration rather than hard physical work.

He thought of his promise to Binnie, thought of the new wife and three children Binnie now had, and sighed heavily. He would have to tell the truth, he was not clever enough to lie and to keep lying, not in the face of Maura's despair.

'It's true,' he said at last. 'Binnie is married.'

'How could he do such a thing?' Maura's voice was soft. 'How could he break all the vows he made to me?'

'Look, Maura, he's happy, his wife adores him, his children think he's a wonderful hero. Please don't do anything that would upset the little family, it wouldn't do any good, not to anyone.'

Maura hung her head and her thick red hair fell over her face hiding her expression. She was silent for a long time and Watt waited for her reaction to his words. He was not prepared for the pain in her eyes when she at last looked up at him.

'I loved him so much, Watt.' She sighed heavily. 'But perhaps it's time to give up waiting for him. I know that if I chased him I would be hurting innocent people, some other woman would suffer as I've suffered. But all I feel now is hate and the desire for revenge.'

'Don't destroy yourself, Maura,' Watt said. 'Hate and revenge are destructive feelings and nothing would ever bring him back here.'

'But, for all that, I'm shackled to Binnie

Dundee for the rest of my life. I will never be free of him. Not until I die.'

'Don't talk like that, Maura,' Watt said gently. 'You are still a young, lovely woman.'

'But I'm not a loved woman and to be loved is what every woman wants.' Maura rose to her feet. 'Thank you for being truthful, Watt, thank you for being kind. I won't keep you any longer.'

'Let me walk you home,' Watt said, rising to his feet. Maura waved him away. She paused in the doorway and looked back at him for a long moment in silence and then she disappeared and he heard her light footsteps running down the stairs.

Later, when Watt joined Llinos and her family for supper, he felt unable to eat. He was unhappy, restless. He knew that he had hurt Maura even though it was at her own prompting. Love was not a simple emotion, it brought with it pain and tears as much as laughter and happiness. Take his feelings for Lily, he would have given her the earth if she would only belong to him. But she had shunned him and, after all her protestations about being a good girl, she was in Saul Marks's bed. Life was such a mess.

'You look pale. You're not going down with a sickness like Samuel, are you, Watt?'

Llinos's voice interrupted his thoughts.

He met Llinos's eyes. She could read him well, she knew he was hiding something. And yet he could hardly tell her the truth, at least not all of it. He sat up straighter in his chair and forced a smile

'Disappointed in love, that's all,' he said lightly. 'I think my best girl has fallen in love with another man.'

'Lily, you mean?' Llinos asked and there was an edge to her voice that he did not quite understand. 'She's going out with Samuel's son, isn't she?'

Watt wondered how she knew that but then there was not much Llinos did not know. He shrugged. 'That's about it.' He looked at Sam, he could hardly say anything about the man's son. 'My loss, his gain,' he said. He put down the pristine napkin and rose to his feet. 'Please, if you will all excuse me, I think I'll go for a walk, clear my head a little.'

'Of course,' Llinos said. 'And have an early night, Watt, you'll feel better for a good night's sleep.'

Watt left the house and stood in the driveway breathing in the cold evening air. He looked up at the stars, they were brilliant against the darkness, appearing so close to earth that he felt he could reach up and touch them. He shivered, he had better start walking before he caught his death. He thrust his hands into his pockets and strode out along Potters Row.

It was quiet in the house. Charlotte and Samuel had gone to bed and Watt was still out. Llinos and Joe were sitting alone beside the dying fire in the drawing room. Joe was holding a glass of wine in his hand, turning it round and round so that it caught the light.

'Perhaps we were mistaken,' Llinos said. 'Samuel seems much better now, doesn't he?'

'Well, Llinos, when you spoke to the servants it was as good as a warning to them. Whoever was doing this is biding his time. I expect it will all start again as soon as everything quietens down.'

Llinos thought of her meeting with the servants: without exception they all denied any knowledge of the medicine. Cook had been particularly vociferous.

'See, Mrs Mainwaring, I am careful in the food I prepare. All the kitchen maid does is see to the vegetables.'

Llinos sighed and Joe looked up at her. 'We must be on our guard, Llinos,' he said. 'Make sure that no-one comes into the kitchens who has no right to be there. No friends taking tea, no gentlemen callers, no-one.'

'That's rather a tall order, Joe,' Llinos said. 'We can't make prisoners of the staff, can we?'

'No, but if we make rules they will know we are watching events carefully. It might just deter anyone from taking risks.'

'I can't help wondering if Sam's son is behind all this,' Llinos said. 'We know he's seeing Lily, there's a connection there that I don't like and don't trust.'

'If Lily is involved, she would need an accomplice, someone inside the house. Who would be the most likely person?'

'Meggie.' Llinos spoke without hesitation. Joe nodded his agreement and put down his glass. 'There's your answer. What we don't know is where the medication is coming from. It was taken from here by Dr Jones. In the morning I'll ride to town and see him. Perhaps the medicine was stolen from him, that might be one reason why there was no case to answer when I went to court.'

He took her hands in his, drawing her close, his cheek resting against her hair.

'Don't worry, little Firebird, we will get to the bottom of this and when we do, someone is going to suffer for what they have done to Samuel and to us.'

In the darkness of the kitchen two women sat huddled over the embers of the huge fire. Lily was frightened; if she was caught inside the house, everyone would know that she was up to no good. She looked at Meggie, trying to see her expression in the gloom and failing. Outside, Saul was waiting; he would be getting impatient, expecting her to have everything settled by now.

'Are you going to do it or not?' Lily whispered. Meggie slowly shook her head, her eyes downcast.

'I'm afraid I'll get caught,' she said. 'We've already been questioned by Llinos Mainwaring and I don't want to end up in jail, mind.'

Lily felt anger burn inside her. Meggie was a coward, a weakling. Well weaklings were easy to bully.

'You'll end up in jail if you don't do as I say.' Her sibilant whisper held such venom that Meggie looked up at her in confusion.

'What do you mean?' she asked, her voice rising.

Lily caught her arm and squeezed it tightly. 'Shut up, you fool!' she hissed. 'Now, I'll explain this to you so that you understand. That stuff you've added to the food is poison. If you don't continue to add it to the old man's food, I'll be sending little notes around telling everyone what you've done.'

'But you've done it too, Lily,' Meggie said. She began to cry, her lips trembling, her eyes brimming. 'I didn't know it was poison, you said —'

'Never mind what I said.' Lily shook the maid. 'I've never been in the house until to-night and I could easily explain that away by saying, you sent for me and asked me for help. All the medicine was put in the food and drink when I was working in the pottery. So who do you think would get the blame?'

'But then why would I want to poison anyone?' Meggie asked rubbing her face with her apron.

'Who knows and what's more who cares? It was you who pointed the finger at Joe when the captain died, so folk will think you were only covering your own trail then as you are now.'

Meggie put her hand to her mouth as Lily held the bottle out towards her. 'Take it, or it will be the worse for you,' she said. 'I'm going now; you make sure you do as you're told, do you understand?'

Meggie nodded, staring down at the bottle which gleamed in a sudden shower of sparks from the fireplace.

Lily let herself out through the back door and looked around carefully before hurrying across the open lawn towards the road. Saul was waiting for her, his hands thrust deep into his pockets. 'Well?' he asked.

'She's going to do it,' Lily said and smiled as Saul took her in his arms and held her close, his cheek against her hair.

'That's my clever girl,' he said. 'Now come on, I've got to get you back to your lodging house before anyone realizes you're missing. Can't have folk talking about my bride-to-be, can we?'

Neither of them saw Watt Bevan standing under the shadow of the trees or realized that he watched until they were out of sight. Both were congratulating themselves on a good night's work. Lily felt pleasure at what she'd done and Saul was thinking that perhaps he and Lily had more in common than he first realized.

It was the screaming that woke Llinos. She leapt out of bed and saw that Joe was already dressing. It was still dark.

'My God!' Llinos said. 'What on earth is happening?'

Joe lit a candle, watching as the flame flickered into life. 'I don't know but I intend to find out. Stay here, Llinos, until I see what the noise is all about.'

She heard running footsteps, calling voices, and sat on the bed in a fever of impatience. Then she got to her feet, knowing she could not wait any longer, she must find out what was wrong.

The noise was coming from the direction of the kitchens. Llinos ran along the passage and came to an abrupt halt as she saw Cook and the maids standing in a circle staring downward. Joe was kneeling on the floor bending over an inert figure.

Llinos pushed her way through and stopped in her tracks. 'Meggie!' she gasped. The girl was stretched out on the cold flags, her arms flung outwards as if to ward off an attacker. Joe felt her temple, trying to find the throb of life in her veins.

'It's no good, sir, she's dead as a door-nail,' Cook wailed. 'Cold as the grave she was when I found her.'

Llinos bent over the maid's still figure. 'What is it, Joe, what's wrong with her?'

He looked up at her, his face grave. 'She's been poisoned,' he said, holding up his hand. Llinos felt her mouth go dry with fear as she saw the small glass bottle, the candlelight reflecting on it. She recognized it, of course, everyone in the kitchen recognized it. It was a bottle of Joe's medication.

'I don't know, Constable,' Joe said again. 'I don't know where the girl got it from. The last I saw of any of the bottles was when Dr Jones took them away. Why don't you go and question him?'

The constable plucked at his moustache and frowned, his heavy eyebrows drawn together as he tried to concentrate on the problem before him.

'But you could have made more, sir?' he said at last.

'I could have, but I didn't,' Joe said. 'There was no need.'

Llinos stared out through the windows, not seeing the lawn and the stark branches of the trees. It was a nightmare, a repeat of what had happened when her father died. Meggie had been taken to the infirmary although it was clear she was beyond help. Behind her, silent and white-faced, Charlotte and Sam were seated side by side, clutching each other for support. Outside in the row, people were grouped together, staring up at the house, mumbling among themselves, no doubt accusing Joe of yet another murder.

'Why would anyone want to harm Meggie?' she said in a low voice. 'Perhaps she took the medicine herself.'

The constable continued to question Joe as though he had not heard her.

'You are the only one who knows the ingredients of this stuff, aren't you?'

'Yes, I've never denied that,' Joe said. 'But I told you, I had no reason to make any more, there was no-one sick in the house.'

'That's not what the kitchen staff have been saying.' The constable sounded triumphant. 'I understand the old man . . . er, Mr Marks, was taken poorly a few days ago, wasn't he?'

'Yes, he was,' Joe said. The silence became oppressive and Llinos put her hands over her eyes. This could not be happening, not again.

The door opened and Watt entered the room. He was flushed as though he had been running. 'I've got to talk to you,' he said. 'I saw two people here last night, creeping about the back of the house.' He stared at the constable. 'I think you should be questioning Saul Marks and Lily, not Joe and Llinos.'

The constable sighed heavily. 'Why, sir?' he asked.

Llinos looked at Watt and her heart fluttered with hope. He caught her eye and she could see that he was white and trembling with the effort of betraying the girl he loved.

'I saw Lily from the paint shop and Saul Marks, Sam's son. They had no right to be around here and Lily should not have been inside the house.'

'I might have known it.' It was Samuel who spoke. 'It's that son of mine up to his evil tricks again.'

The constable looked from Joe to Samuel and back again. 'You've had trouble with this son of yours before, sir?' he said.

Samuel sighed. 'Oh, yes.'

'Well, perhaps I'd better talk to them. Can you get hold of any of them?' He addressed his remark to Watt.

'I'll fetch her, she should be on her way in to work by now, perhaps I will meet her on the way,' he said heavily. After he had gone, no-one moved. It was as though they were frozen into a sense of disbelief. A young woman was dead, but why?

The constable began talking quietly to Samuel, questioning him about Saul. It seemed like an eternity before Watt returned with Lily beside him. 'What's happening?' she asked. 'I can't get a word out of Watt. Is Meggie sick or something?'

'Why should you ask that?' The constable said slowly.

Lily looked at him pityingly. 'I saw her being carried out of here, we all did.'

The man nodded. 'This young man,' he pointed to Watt, 'says he saw you outside, late last night.' He paused. 'With a man.'

Lily flushed and lowered her head. 'I know it was wrong but, see, we're in love.' She held out her hand and the ring sparkled in the early morning sunshine. 'We weren't doing any harm, mind, just courting, that's all.'

'Sir?' The constable looked at Watt. 'What did you see, exactly.'

'I saw her coming out of the back door. I saw her being met by Saul Marks. I saw them kissing.'

'And then?'

'And then, they walked away down the road. He was taking her home I suppose.'

'Doesn't sound very dangerous to me, just meeting up and kissing,' the constable said reasonably. He turned his attention back to Lily. 'You work in the paint shop?'

'Yes, sir,' she said softly.

'Then why were you in the house?'

Lily was startled, her eyes grew large and she swallowed hard. 'I came in to see Meggie,' she said at last. 'We were friends, you know, and she's been upset lately. I was worried about her.'

'Upset? About what?'

'I don't know, she wouldn't say.' Lily licked her lips.

'So you came to see her at that late hour?' The constable asked.

'Well, I was going to meet Saul and I saw the candlelight in the kitchen window. I guessed it was Meggie, she was always the last one up, so I went in.'

'What did you see?'

'Nothing, sir. Meggie was sitting by the table holding a little bottle in her hand. She said it was medicine Mr Mainwaring had given her to make her better.'

'You liar!' Watt spat out the words. Lily looked at him briefly.

'I'm sorry, Watt, but I can't help it if I like Saul better than I like you. Don't be bitter, please, it won't help you or anyone else.'

Watt looked at the constable. 'She's lying and maybe, just maybe, I can prove it.' He moved to the door and paused, glancing back at Lily.

'I never really knew you, did I?' he said sadly. 'I worshipped a dream, an image. Well, Lily, you have told your last lie and I think I know just how to get you to tell the truth.'

He left the room and Llinos watched him go, knowing that all her hopes were pinned on him. If Watt failed, Joe would be accused of murder and this time not even the clever tongue of the lawyer Grantley would save him.

CHAPTER

TWENTY-FOUR

Bert Cimla stared at the shelf where he had left the remainder of the stolen bottles of medication; only one contained any of the liquid and that was only half full. 'Damn and blast!' He held up his hand to throw the bottle against the wall and then thought better of it. He was desperate for money, he had not eaten for two days, his belly was growling in protest even now. Perhaps he could refill the bottle with something, but what?

He searched around the rooms of his mean lodgings but it did not take him long to realize that he had nothing that would serve his purpose. He looked through his window and saw that his landlady was outside at the gate berating the baker for some shortcoming or other. Quickly he made his way down the dark passage towards the kitchen and, not noticing the smell of old cabbage and boiling washing, began opening cupboards. He kept glancing over his shoulder, afraid of discovery. Mrs Beadle had a sharp tongue on her and he usually kept well clear of her, particularly when he owed rent as he did now.

Under the shelf in the scullery, he saw a container full of white powder; it was probably used for cleaning the floors or something. He picked it up. Perhaps he could get away with mixing it with a little milk or water, it was worth a try. He scooped a handful of the powder into the palm of his hand and beat a hasty retreat back to his room.

The water from the bowl on his table was murky; he had not used it to wash and it had been standing there for some days. Still, he could not risk another trip downstairs. He mixed a little of the powder, making a milky paste of it. It was difficult getting it into the bottle and on inspection, the mixture looked a little thick. Perhaps Saul Marks would not even notice.

Cimla sank onto the sagging chair near the window and smiled in satisfaction. Idly he shook the bottle, mixing the powder more thoroughly. It did not look too suspicious. He smiled, feeling he could look forward to his meeting with Saul Marks in the anticipation of receiving enough money to keep him for at least a week.

Llinos waited, white-faced, for the young doctor to make his pronouncement on the cause of Meggie's death. Dr Walsh was new

446

to the district, tall, young and eager to acquire a healthy medical practice. Beside him stood the constable, his sharp eyes missing nothing.

Llinos glanced at Joe; he was standing before the fire, his hands thrust into his pockets, staring out through the window into the distance. Samuel and Charlotte were seated side by side, Charlotte clutching nervously at her husband's sleeve.

'It looks as if the young lady took her own life,' the doctor said. 'The bottle was found with her, I understand?' He smiled at the constable who nodded knowingly; he had probably discussed the matter with the doctor before entering the house. The constable was well dressed, because of his position and reputation. Llinos could only hope he was reasonable and would accept the doctor's findings without question.

'I talked to Dr Jones,' the doctor continued, 'and he agreed that the medication had been stolen from his house at some time. Goodness knows how it came to be in the possession of this young girl. That is something we will never know.'

Llinos breathed a sigh of relief. She glanced up at Joe but he seemed preoccupied and for once did not meet her eyes.

'There was the smell of alcoholic drink on

the young lady as well as traces of the medication around her mouth. Poor girl was probably harbouring some feelings of unrequited love; such things are common in girls of her age and class.'

'Well then.' The constable opened the door. 'I can go and make my report on the matter.' He seemed anxious to be on his way. 'Thank you for clearing the matter up for us, Doctor.'

The doctor inclined his head graciously. 'I was trained by very able doctors myself,' he said. 'One of my tutors took a special interest in poisons and, fortunately, passed his knowledge on to me. The medication would probably not be lethal in itself but by the smell and the edging of powder on the rim I can only assume that other poisons were introduced into the medication. With the addition of alcohol . . .' He shrugged. 'Death was inevitable.' He looked at Joe. 'I shall send you my bill in due course and if there is any other way in which I can help, please do not hesitate to send for me again.'

Llinos sighed hugely and rose to her feet. 'Thank heavens no-one is accusing you, my love.' She looked up as Joe came to her side. 'But what on earth would make Meggie take her own life? Perhaps I should have seen that she was distressed, I might have been able to help her.'

'No-one is to blame, at least no-one in this household,' Joe said. 'But I intend to find out as much as I can about her death. I must before anyone else takes the medication.' His mouth was set in a grim line, the blue of his eyes dark with anger.

'I know who is behind this,' Samuel spoke abruptly. 'It's my son. I spoke to Watt and then to Maura Dundee, both of them saw Saul here on that night. I don't know what he's up to but I do know he wants me out of the way and you too, Joe.'

'But why should he want to harm you? Surely he was only courting with Lily, wasn't he?' Charlotte asked, slipping her arm through Sam's as if in support.

'There was more to it than that. He thinks I have undisclosed assets, assets that he would inherit.' Samuel looked at Joe. 'He also wants that parcel of land. You think so too, I know you do.'

Joe nodded. 'You're right, Sam.' He rubbed his cheek with his forefinger. 'I've thought long and hard about this and I think the plan was that Meggie put more medication in your food, Sam. Obviously she couldn't bring herself to do it. She must have been so frightened that she took her own life.'

Llinos bit her lip. She wanted to catch hold of Lily and force the girl to tell the truth. She saw Joe smile for the first time.

'Remember, little Firebird, there is more than one way to snare a fox.'

Samuel rose to his feet. 'I think I'll go out for a walk, I feel I need some fresh air.' He looked down at his wife. 'And before you say anything, yes, I will wrap up warmly, I promise.'

Joe followed Samuel into the hallway and Llinos heard him talking quietly. 'You're not going to confront your son, are you?'

'No no,' Samuel said quickly, too quickly. 'I simply need to blow the cobwebs away, that's all.' He raised his voice. 'I have to get away from my nagging wife sometimes, you see.'

Charlotte did not smile. She stared down at her hands and a tear slid down her lined cheek. 'He's going to do something silly, I know he is.'

'I know,' Llinos said. 'I think Joe will follow him, just in case.' She was right. When Llinos looked into the hall it was to see Joe pulling on his overcoat.

'Be careful, my love, I don't want you in any more trouble.' She crossed the space between them and clung to him, pressing her cheek against his heart, loving him, wanting to protect him. But she knew that nothing she said would change his mind. 'Just be careful, that's all, my darling.'

Watt and Maura stared at each other across the polished floorboards of her sitting room at the top of the house. 'It was good of you to back me up about seeing Lily and Marks together,' he said.

She looked different somehow; her hair had been cut and soft curls, red and gold in the pale sunlight, framed her face.

'I just told the truth,' she said. 'I did see them together.' She smiled ruefully and a dimple appeared in her chin.

'What is it?'

'The other servants,' Maura said, not looking at him, 'they think you and me, well that we were up to no good out there in the darkness. Now, inviting you to my room has confirmed it, at least in their eyes.'

Watt blinked suddenly. Maura and him, did the servants really believe that? She was older than he was and married.

'Sure, 'tis sorry I am,' she said. 'However much I denied it they were all convinced that I've got tired of being an old maid in all but name and have taken myself a lover.' She glanced up shyly. 'I would be a lucky woman if only half of it was true.'

Watt smiled at her; she was so vulnerable, so alone. He made up his mind. 'Tell you what we'll do,' he said. 'We will give them something to talk about. Please, Maura, would you come out with me to town on your day off? We can drink coffee and let the whole town see us together. What do you think?'

'You don't have to do that,' Maura said. 'We don't have to pander to silly gossips.'

'We don't have to, but wouldn't it be fun?'

'Well, yes, I'd like that, but coffee shops cost money.' Maura plucked at the edge of her woollen jacket.

'I am not a poor man, Maura, Llinos pays me well.' He stared at her. 'In any case, I would like to go out with you.' He realized he meant it. Maura was a woman who at least did not deceive and torture a man. Lately she had ceased talking about Binnie, had stopped planning to go to America and have her revenge. She seemed more interested now in making a life of her own.

'All right.' She smiled brightly and her face was transformed. 'Sure 'tis going to be the talk of the place, mind.'

'Good!' Watt rose to his feet. 'All right then, when is your day off?' He smiled down at her and there seemed to be an imp of mischief in her eyes.

'Today, why do you think I'm in my rooms and not working?'

'Oh, I see. Right then, get your outdoor clothes on, we're going to town.'

Joe followed at a safe distance; always keeping Sam in his sight. Samuel did not seem to be aware that he was being watched. He walked along the river bank staring down into the waters as though he could read something there. After a while, he turned towards the town. Joe smiled, Sam was no fool, he would not go directly to his son's house.

At the bottom of Wind Street, Sam suddenly lifted his hand and climbed into a cab. The horse was jerked into motion and the wheels of the cab rattled past where Joe was standing. It did not matter, Joe had recognized a figure in the distance, making his way towards the Castle Inn. It was Saul Marks. Even if Sam did look for him, he was heading in quite the wrong direction.

Joe watched Marks disappear inside the inn and then followed him. Joe seated himself in a corner behind a large man and his group of equally large friends. He could see by bending his head forward but it was very unlikely he would be seen.

Marks took a purse out of his pocket and handed it to a roughly dressed man. In return he accepted a loosely tied package and slipped it into his pocket. He did not speak a word, he rose swiftly to his feet and left the inn. After a moment Joe rose and moved to the bench which Marks had just vacated.

'Buy you a mug of beer?' Joe asked, studying the man's rough exterior: the long beard, the grisly grey hair poking out of a battered hat. He was familiar and yet Joe could not place him.

The man looked at him sourly. 'Why, what do you want?'

'Just some company,' Joe said. 'Not many folk around here like me very much.'

The man stared at him, taking in his appearance. Foreigner, Indian. Husband to that brat Llinos.

'Married to her up at the pottery, aren't you?'

'Joe Mainwaring.' Joe did not hold out his hand but gave his order to the landlord who was avoiding the scowling faces of some of the other customers.

'Serving murderers now, is it?' a voice mumbled. Joe shrugged and smiled disarmingly. 'You see what I mean? No-one wants to drink with me.'

'Then why should I?' The man looked round. 'Should I drink with him, Ben?' He addressed the old man in the corner.

'A pair well met if you ask me,' the old man said sourly. 'You know I've got no time for you, Bert Cimla.'

Joe realized who the man was: Bert Cimla, at best a thief and a liar and at worst a murderer. Gwen Savage had died at the man's hand and he had gotten away with it.

'Ah shut your gob!' Cimla said. He looked at Joe again. 'Go on, then, I'll have a drink with you so long as you don't expect one back. I've got no money.'

The landlord brought the beer and took the coins Joe handed him. 'Look, you'd better not stay here long,' he said quietly. 'Folks are riled up about that young girl who died at your place, that Meggie. Poor dab didn't hardly have a chance to live.'

Cimla looked shifty-eyed and Joe leaned forward. 'Poisoned herself,' he said. 'Took medicine by the bottlefull instead of a small dose. Know anything about it?'

'Shove off!' Cimla said. 'Hell's teeth, I wouldn't set foot within a mile of the pottery, not after the way I was treated by the Savage family.'

'Oh yes,' Joe spoke affably, 'I heard you murdered Gwen Savage.'

Cimla's face flushed to the roots of his tangled hair. 'That's a lie,' he said. 'The silly cow fell, she was always falling. Looked after her, I did, and that brat of a girl of hers. Fat lot of thanks I got for it.'

He made to rise to his feet but Joe caught him by the greasy lapels of his coat. 'Oh, no, not so fast. What deal were you doing with Saul Marks?'

Cimla looked round but no-one was inclined to help, though most watched the proceedings with interest.

'Don't know what you mean,' Cimla blustered. 'I talk to anybody, me, that's why I'm talking to you.'

Joe shook him. 'I want to know what you were selling to Marks. Don't deny it, I saw him handing you some money.'

'It was just a parcel of fish.' Cimla's voice had become a whine. 'So I do a bit of poaching, that's not going to hurt anyone is it?'

Joe shoved him back in his chair. 'Pretty small fish. You wouldn't know the truth if it hit you in the face.'

'Landlord!' Cimla said. 'Are you going to let this . . . this foreigner treat your customers this way? I'm a regular, mind, I shouldn't have to be pushed around by the likes of him.'

'Aye,' old Ben called from the corner. 'We haven't much time for the likes of Bert Cimla but he is one of us, so take a walk, righto?'

The landlord was at Joe's side. 'Things are going to get ugly, you'd best go while the going's good.'

Joe rose to his feet and stared around the assorted customers. Without exception they looked away, avoiding his direct stare.

'I'm going, I'll get no more out of this piece of rubbish,' he said. As he made for the door, a beer mug was thrown, it caught him on the back of his head. Joe turned in a swift movement.

'Anyone who wants to take me on, man to man, stand up now.' No-one moved. Joe shook his head and left the inn, anger flowing through his veins like wine. He walked towards home, trying to concentrate his thoughts on the exchange between Cimla and Marks. There could not possibly be any medication left, not unless someone else had made it up. Suddenly he was icy cold. He would have to check everything that was cooked, everything to be eaten or drunk. Otherwise, there would be another death in Pottery Row.

Over the next few days Maura went out

with Watt as often as they could both manage it. He was a handsome man, younger than she was, but so kind, so gentle. It was a balm to her damaged pride to be seen with him. She did not love him, she would always love Binnie, however much of a rat he had turned out to be. She still felt a savage anger when she thought of her husband with another woman but then, she reasoned, he had never been a real husband, not to her.

She smiled as she thought of Watt; she enjoyed his company, loved his sense of humour. He was thoughtful and kind and he seemed to enjoy being with her. She was feeling better than she had done in years, released somehow from the chains of gloom that had hung round her for so long. She sang old, familiar Irish songs as she went about her work and even Eynon noticed the change in her.

'What's come over you, Maura?' Eynon seemed to have aged since the death of his wife. He spent a great deal of time with his child and the only other companion he had was Father Martin.

His mother-in-law was still living in the house but she seemed to have changed too. She was quieter, her clothes were more suitable to a woman her age. She no longer rouged her cheeks and it was obvious that she loved her granddaughter dearly.

'I've just found a friend, that's all,' she said as she counted the linen napkins and placed them in the sideboard drawer. She looked at Eynon. 'I know I've lost Binnie for ever and I've accepted it at last. I'm not going to waste any more time fretting for him. I mean to get on with my own life from now on.'

'About time, too,' Eynon said. 'You are a good-looking woman, Maura, and I have seen you blossom lately into an even more attractive woman. I understand exactly how you feel about Binnie. I'm in the same position. I'll never possess the woman I love.'

Maura realized he was talking about Llinos. A wash of pity engulfed her. Eynon was so lost now, so alone. It was a great pity he could not forget Llinos and meet someone else more worthy of him.

Maura's resentment towards Llinos had tempered with the years, although she would never see why everyone else thought the woman so special. Eynon's next words startled her from her thoughts.

'I am thinking of selling the pottery,' he said. 'I have lost my enthusiasm for it.' He smiled. 'I never was very keen on it anyway.' He must have seen the consternation in her eyes because he hastened to reassure her. 'Don't worry, I'll be keeping on this house and even if I do move out, you and the rest of the staff will come with me.'

She swallowed hard. 'Thank you, sir.' She finished her task and left the room, her thoughts in a whirl. At least now she had someone to talk things over with. She had Watt and even if he was only offering friendship, she would grasp it with both hands. She glanced out of the window at the gathering darkness. Soon she would be meeting him; they would talk and laugh and she would forget, if only for a time, that she was a woman deserted and humiliated by her husband. She could be a person again, a woman again.

'I tell you he's on to something,' Cimla said in the whining voice that grated on Saul's ears. 'The man saw me give you the parcel and take money for it.'

'So what did you tell him?' Saul forced himself to appear calm. There was no telling what the man would do if he sensed any feeling of panic.

'Said it was fish,' Cimla said. 'Can't I come in? It's damn cold standing here on the step.'

'No you can't come in, we shouldn't be

seen together any more, at least not for a time. In any case, I've got visitors.'

'Oh aye, that bit of skirt you're sleeping with, is it?'

Saul resisted the urge to thump the man's slack mouth. 'That bit of skirt happens to be my intended,' he said.

'Well then, more fool you.' Cimla turned away. 'All right, I'll keep out of your way but make sure nothing comes back to me. I'm not taking the blame for no murder.'

Saul slammed the door with necessary force and turned back into the warmth of the house. Upstairs Lily was sitting on the bed wearing only her shift. The ring on her finger gleamed brightly in the light from the candle as she turned her hand to look at it.

'You've got to marry me now, haven't you, Saul?' she asked in her little-girl voice. 'Us telling folks we were courting that night.'

'Lily, there's no "have to" about it. I want to marry you, you know that.' He sat beside her, his arm around her shoulder, his hand searching for her breast. He felt her shift a little and smiled to himself. He was getting to know little Lily, she was not a passionate woman. She allowed him to take her whenever he wanted and that was fine by him; he did not relish having a woman who made demands on him between the sheets. To the contrary, Lily's apathy excited him. Her docile acceptance of what he did pleased him. It wasn't right that a woman should enjoy it, only whores liked bedding a man, whores like that Polly. He would not touch her even if she paid him, not now he had his Lily where he wanted her.

'Pity that girl died,' he said, unbuttoning the bodice of Lily's shift. 'Bit inconvenient all round. You must have frightened her too much.' He laughed cruelly. 'It seems you have become as ruthless as me.' He pushed her back on the bed. 'Let me have you, Lily. I want you very much tonight, can't you feel it?'

He pushed himself against her and she sighed. 'All right then, you know I can never say no to you.' She closed her eyes as he removed her shift and, taking his fill, he stared down at her pale body. She was small-breasted but her hips were well rounded and her legs were beautiful. He ran his hand over the flat white belly and saw her shiver. He smiled, knowing it was not passion that drove her. That was all to the good.

'Don't worry, darling,' he said. 'I'll enjoy this enough for the both of us.'

Later they sat and talked, seated beside the fire. 'What shall we do now, Saul?' Lily asked. It was gratifying the way she deferred to him in all things. His lust sated, the medicine bottles tucked away in the drawer, Saul felt the world belonged to him.

'I've got an even greater motive for doing away with the old man than I thought,' he said, knowing that Lily would share the avarice that he felt when he told her his news. 'The old bastard has other land, land he has never spoken about, land enough to buy me just what I want.'

Lily's eyes gleamed greedily in the firelight. 'Tell me!' she begged, clasping her hands together like a child about to have a treat.

'I'm planning to buy myself a pottery.' He was triumphant. He saw her look up at him with adoration in her eyes.

'You are going to buy the Savage place?' she asked, leaning towards him. He fondled her hair, feeling an affection for her that he had never felt for anyone in his life. She was like the other half of him, as bad and as cunning as he was.

'No, not the Savage Pottery,' he said. 'The big one, the Tawe Pottery. When I get going, I'll make it so successful that the Mainwarings, if there are any of them left in Swansea, will have to go under.'

'Saul, you're so clever!' Lily kissed him in

an uncharacteristic mood of affection and Saul laughed down at her.

'You're so pretty, so tempting that I think I must take you to bed again, my little love.' Lily sighed but acquiesced, slipping onto the bed and waiting for him, her eyes closed. Saul smiled. They were going to make a great team he and Lily, between them they would one day own the whole of Swansea.

CHAPTER

TWENTY-FIVE

'I thought you were in love with Melia. We all thought you were in love with her, even Melia herself.' Josephine was not looking at John. She stared out across the porch, apparently studying the stars with great interest.

'I know that's the impression I gave,' John said. 'I suppose I was just flirting with her, being nice. I didn't realize I would fall in love with any of you girls. Marriage was the furthest thing from my mind when I came out here.'

'Was?' Josephine still did not look at him. He sensed that she was tense, her shoulders were stiff, her knuckles gleaming white in the light from the lamp on the wall. He felt more daring and moved closer to her, trying to take her hand in his. She resisted him and he knew he would have to eat more humble pie if he was to get anywhere with her.

'Look, I'm a young man, I'm not used to women,' he said. 'As you yourself said, it's like showing a child cookies in a jar. You just don't know which one you would prefer.'

She looked at him then, her eyes large.

'Until you have tried them?'

'No, of course not!' John protested. 'I have never even kissed Melia, I promise you.' He shifted uncomfortably, wondering what Jo's sister had been saying. 'My intentions towards you are honourable, Josephine, please believe me.'

'I believe you.' Her voice held the chill of a woman displeased. 'That does not mean to say I want to marry you. No, if you want to become a McCabe so badly, honey, then forget me, I'm simply not interested.'

Her words were a shock; John had not expected to be rebuffed so soundly and it was a feeling he did not much like. He felt angry and humiliated but he managed to keep his voice even when he replied.

'Thank you for being so honest, Jo.' He sighed. 'I'll soon be out of your way.'

She did not look at him. 'Going home?'

'You know I'm not going home. I'm going to Albany to sort out the new business for your father. I need to find a decent site for the pottery and then, I suppose, we shall start to build.' He paused. 'So you see, Jo, marriage is not a necessity. I will make a career for myself here with or without a McCabe as a wife.'

'I'm sure you'll be back here from time to time.' Josephine spoke as though she had not heard him. 'You'll have plenty of opportunity to pursue my sister then.'

'You're wrong,' he said flatly. 'I have already told Melia I'm in love with you. If I can't have you then I won't marry anyone.'

She pulled her shawl around her shoulders. 'That would be a shame.' She turned to face him and looked him up and down as though he were an animal she intended to purchase. 'You are a fine setup man. Good shape, good legs, strong arms and shoulders. Perhaps a bit immature, but there you are, life has been easy for you so far, hasn't it?'

He caught her arms, gripping them so tightly that she winced. 'You think so?' His voice was hard. 'Perhaps you should climb down from your high horse and learn a little of poverty and humiliation and what it does to a man before you judge me so readily.' He released her and cleared the steps of the porch in one bound, striding out into the darkness, his mind seething, his eyes filling with silly tears. Were they tears of anger, of self-pity, he wondered, or of genuine distress that Josephine had refused him? He was not quite sure. All he knew was that he was hurting and it was not a pleasant feeling.

'What's upset him?' Binnie came to stand beside Josephine on the porch. From within the house he could hear the sounds of laughter, the laughter of his children, and a warmth filled him. He was grateful that he had come here to America, had met Hortense and married her. It was true that he was sometimes filled with guilt and regret about his past but then no-one had a perfect life with no regrets to mar it.

'I'm afraid I did,' Josephine replied. 'He asked me to marry him and I turned him down.'

'Oh?' Binnie tried to see her expression in the light from the porch lantern but her face was in shadow. 'I thought you admired John.'

'Oh, I do.' Josephine turned to look at him. 'I more than admire him, honey, but he can't think that every woman he meets is just waiting to fall into his arms.' She bent her white neck archly. 'What comes easily no man values, haven't you learned that yet?'

Binnie thought about it. Perhaps that was what had been wrong with his marriage. Maura had wanted him so badly, wanted to be his wife more than anything, and he had been a reluctant bridegroom.

'Yes, I suppose I have,' he said. He had

never really believed he would win Hortense. He had approached her in trepidation, fearing her scorn, even her laughter. Now that they were married, he loved her more than ever, valued her highly. 'On the other hand perhaps I've just grown up, Jo, and realize what real love is at last.'

'At last?' Josephine said. 'Have you had many lovers then, Binnie?'

'Of course not.' He laughed. 'Well, perhaps one or two. A man has to sow his wild oats, mind.'

'And a woman needs to remain good and virginal. Do you think that's fair?'

'I think that's just the way it is.' Binnie touched her shoulder. 'Jo, just don't turn John away because of pride, you could be giving up your one chance of real love, real happiness.'

Josephine turned away from him. 'Go in to your wife and family and leave me to sort out my own life, brother-in-law.'

He left her on the porch and returned to the warmth and light of the McCabe household. He was a lucky man and his luck would last just so long as no-one from his past caught up with him.

It was almost a week later when Binnie helped Dan and John prepare for their journey to Albany. Four carts with drivers had been mustered and loaded early that morning with foodstuffs and drink, the drink carefully disguised in the form of a water cask. Dan was like a child about to embark on a treat. Binnie watched him, wondering at the older man's zest for life. But then Dan was a straightforward sort of man, if he had any complexities of character he hid them well behind a bluff exterior. Dan took all life had to offer with both hands and Binnie envied him his tranquil mind.

He smiled as he saw Josephine walk up to John and touch him on the arm. When he turned, she reached up and kissed his cheek. He spoke and then smiled and Binnie knew that one day, perhaps very soon, John would have his wish and marry into the McCabe family.

As the carts rumbled away, he thrust his hands into his pockets. He was in charge now, the responsibility for the pottery and the well-being of the McCabe family was in his hands. He felt pride run through him; the boy who had grown up with nothing now had everything he could wish for. Everything that was except a quiet conscience. Well, he would have to live with his guilt. What man ever lived who had nothing to hide? He turned away from the dust ball rising from the trail and went into the house.

'It's wonderful to be together again, Eynon. It was a good idea for us to go out for tea.' Llinos looked across the table of the elegant coffee shop and smiled at her friend. Eynon was looking older, his pale hair held streaks of grey. He was still a young man but he seemed to have the weight of the world on his shoulders since the death of his wife.

'It's pure selfishness on my part,' Eynon said, with a flash of his old humour. 'I wanted some company and you were there.' He sobered. 'You are always there when I need you, Llinos.'

'How's the baby?' Llinos quickly changed the subject.

'Jayne is just fine,' Eynon said. 'Elizabeth and the nurse spoil her of course, but she remains good-natured, hardly ever crying and never cross in the way babies are supposed to be. Jayne is the joy of my life.' His pride was evident in the timbre of his voice.

He held out his hand to cover hers. 'I know you long for a child, Llinos, but it will happen. One day, when the time is right, you will be a mother and a damn good one at that.'

She sighed. She was beyond hope in that

direction. As her monthly curse continued with monotonous regularity, she gave up expecting anything else. Perhaps she was destined never to be a mother. But she was not here to feel sorry for herself, she was with Eynon in the hope of bringing him out of his shell a little.

'Now, my dear friend, tell me what's on your mind because something is.' She smiled. 'You didn't bring me here just to make small talk.'

'No,' he said. 'The truth is, I'm thinking of selling the pottery. Indeed, I've already had an offer for it, a very good offer.'

Llinos stared at him openmouthed. It was unthinkable that Eynon should give up the pottery. Her sense of loss was almost like a blow.

'Oh, Eynon, no,' she spoke in a low voice, reaching out to touch his hand. 'I can't bear to think of some other man living next door, running the Tawe Pottery. It just doesn't seem right.'

'I've had enough of it,' Eynon said. 'My dream of the perfect porcelain body proved to be just that, a dream. I've wasted enough time and money on it as it is.'

'But your goods are selling well enough,' Llinos protested. 'In fact you have the biggest share of the market. You're even beginning to export pottery to other countries. You can't give it all up.'

'Yes, I can.'

'Who is going to buy it?' Llinos asked at last.

'A consortium of Swansea businessmen. The pottery needs a body of men to run it, it's just too much for me, I admit it.'

Llinos bit her lip. Who were these men and what would the sale of the Tawe Pottery mean for her own, smaller business? Would it be swallowed up in the name of progress?

'Look, Llinos,' Eynon spoke softly, his tone begging her to understand, 'I have my daughter to think of. I need to conserve the small capital I have left. I can't afford to speculate, not now I'm a father. Jayne is all I have and I intend to devote myself to her. Please, my dear, don't make this more difficult than it already is.'

'I'm sorry.' Llinos forced a smile. 'You must do what you feel best. I'm just being selfish wanting you to stay, wanting everything to remain the same. All I hope is that someone as honest and decent as you buys the Tawe Pottery.'

'Everything will run along as smoothly as ever, I'm sure,' Eynon said. 'There are good people working in the sheds: managers, potters and painters. The only difference will be that I no longer have the responsibility of the place.'

Llinos picked up her gloves. 'I'd better be getting back,' she said slowly. She covered his hand with her own. 'I'll miss you, Eynon, I will really miss you.'

He stood beside her and helped her on with her coat. 'I'm probably not even going to leave the area, Llinos, and, even if I do, I won't be moving to the back of beyond. We will still be able to visit each other.'

Out in the street Llinos took a deep breath, wondering at the way life was for-ever changing. She was still young, she should welcome change, not fear it like an old woman.

A voice rang out, shattering the silence: a crude, harsh, all too familiar voice bringing a feeling of dread with it. It was the voice of Bert Cimla.

'There she goes, see her, bold as brass, wife of a murdering foreigner!' He was standing beside her then and she stared into the bearded face half hidden by the greasy cap, feeling sick.

Eynon put his arm around her. 'Clear off.' He pushed Cimla's shoulder. 'Get away from here before I take my riding crop to you.'

People turned to stare, Llinos was frozen

to the spot, unable to think, only to feel. The old hatreds rose up within her: this was the man who had killed her mother. How dare he stand there accusing her of murder?

'She walks the streets as though she owns the place,' Cimla shouted. 'Strange how yet another one has died up in that house, a poor innocent girl who did no harm to anyone. Cursed, they are, the Savage family should be wiped out, none of them are any good.'

A crowd began to gather and Llinos edged closer to Eynon. She saw faces all around her, hostile faces and she knew that many of the townspeople agreed with Bert Cimla; the prejudice against Joe had hardened since Meggie's death.

'Come on, let's go home.' Eynon caught her arm and began to lead her away. A clod of earth flew through the air, striking Llinos on her shoulder. The blow did not hurt but the act frightened her. How could she be hated so much by the people of the town where she had been born?

'Run out of town they should be, the lot of them!' Cimla called after her. 'That Indian fella is a murderer and this woman is his whore! What decent lady would marry his kind? Just answer me that, Llinos Savage!'

Eynon turned around, his face red with anger. 'Shut your mouth, you scum! I'll have you arrested and thrown in jail for your insolence. I know who you are, Bert Cimla. Gwen Savage died at your hand and we all know it.' He raised his riding crop. 'Now get out of my sight before I give you the hiding you deserve.'

He hurried Llinos away down the street and she clung to his arm for support. She was trembling but with anger more than fear. She had longed to lash out at Bert Cimla, to tear at his grimy face, to slap him until he closed his evil mouth.

'Forget it,' Eynon said firmly. 'The man is obviously demented, no-one will take the least bit of notice of him.'

But they would, Llinos knew it all too well. Joe had been branded a murderer once and it was all too easy to lash the townsfolk into a frenzy of hate against him. Suddenly she felt defeated. Perhaps she and Joe should follow Eynon's example, sell up the pottery and move where no-one knew or cared about them. But no, that would be giving in to the gossips, allowing folk to believe the worst. In spite of her brave thoughts Llinos felt tears run cold, like ice, along her cheeks and she was too weary even to brush them away.

John rode his animal alongside the McCabe caravan and watched as Dan pulled up beside him. 'Great country this, eh, John?'

'It is.' John breathed in the fresh, scented air, felt the sunshine on his face and smiled. 'I don't think I could live at home in the cold and rain ever again.'

'You asked my girl to marry you and she turned you down then?' Dan chuckled. 'Women don't know their own mind half the time.'

'Oh, Jo does,' John said wryly. 'She knows mine too, that's why she wanted to put me in my place.' He glanced at Dan. 'But I'll win her over yet you'll see.'

'I know you will, son, you're made of the right stuff.' Dan stood in the saddle and pointed up ahead. 'There, boy, you can just see the faint haze on the horizon. That'll be a herd of buffalo. We must be nearly there.'

John felt a twinge of excitement. Albany, even the name had the power to enchant him. One day he would make his fortune in Albany. He would build the biggest and best pottery in the whole of America. And when he did, when he was rich enough, he would go home to Cornwall just for long enough to destroy Treherne and all he stood for. He sighed in contentment. For now he was happy to live his young life, to explore new worlds. One day, he vowed, he would be as powerful a force in the land as Dan McCabe. He smiled; beside him would be the woman he loved.

CHAPTER

TWENTY-SIX

'We just have to get rid of the old man and soon!' Saul was pacing around the room, his hands gesticulating wildly as if to add emphasis to his words. 'If I am to be the major shareholder in the Tawe Pottery I have to make a show of money and I can't do that until I get my hands on the old man's property.' He sank into a chair and rubbed his eyes. 'I've racked my brains, Lily, and I still don't have the answer.'

Lily watched him, admiring his strength, his single-mindedness. If she could ever consider herself in love then Saul was the man. As to the physical side of it, she could put up with that. Saul, and the prospect of a bright future with him, was worth it.

She looked out of the window of the house they had rented. The garden was small but the street was clean and broad; the house, she thought with satisfaction, was situated in one of the better areas of the town. Polly had been most impressed when she saw it.

Lily glanced quickly at Saul. He did not approve of Polly and said so in no uncertain terms. Still, Lily felt she had some rights since most of the money for the rent had come from her savings. Saul was keeping all he had to buy out the pottery.

'You'll think of something soon, Saul,' she said comfortingly. 'Would you like me to get you something to drink?' Without waiting for a reply, she rushed on. 'You know, we really should get a maid, she would be a chaperone, too, at least until we're married. After all, as owner of a pottery you can't afford a scandal, don't you agree?'

'Not now, Lily!' Saul said. 'And yes, I would like a drink.' He stared at her and his face softened. 'Well, on second thoughts, perhaps you're right, you are looking a bit tired, managing this place on your own. Get Polly to come in, at least we know her, but make it plain it's only a temporary arrangement.'

'That's a very good idea.' She spoke meekly, smiling to herself at the ease with which she had manipulated him. 'I'll go to see her in the morning.'

'In the meantime, woman,' Saul smiled, 'bring me a drink and then we'll get ourselves off to bed. I might think more clearly when I've had a rest.'

'Right, love, whatever you say. All I want

is to please you, my dear.'

As she brought him the drink, he caught her hand. 'You are a fine woman, Lily. I'm not one for sweet words but I do appreciate you.'

'I know.' She knelt beside him and he ruffled her hair. She closed her eyes, imagining all the money they would have when his father was out of the way. It would be a good life, better than anything she would have had with Watt Bevan. She snuggled up to Saul; he was her future, her destiny. Saul would take care of her always.

Polly called her all sorts of a fool. 'He's using you, Lil,' she said. 'I know he's a good-looking man, rich and ambitious but is he worth dumping your good job and your lovely room here for? We was doing all right as we were.'

'Oh, come on, Pol,' Lily coaxed. 'I love Saul, you know that. Come and live with us. Please, Poll, I need the company, Saul is out a lot and that big house scares me sometimes.'

'All right then, I'll do it, for you.' Polly hugged her. 'But don't forget, you still wants him to marry you, you can't put up with things as they are for long or he might go off the idea.'

'Once he settles this business matter,

we'll get wed. Now come on, pack up your things and let's tell the landlady you're leaving.' Lily smiled. 'That will cheer her up no end.'

'I'm not telling her nothing!' Polly said. 'I owe her four weeks rent.'

Lily laughed. 'Come on, slip out while she's in the kitchen, let her stew, the old crow!' Giggling, the two girls left the lodging house and Lily looked back at the window of her room. The curtains billowed in the breeze and, for a moment, she wondered if she was doing the right thing. Then Polly was taking her arm. 'Come on, slowcoach! Let's get away from here before anyone sees us.'

Saul was late returning home that night. As soon as Lily heard the door slam, she gestured to Polly to go up to bed. 'He'll want to talk,' she said. 'I do hope he's not in a bad mood.'

Polly slipped silently from the room. She was as agile as a cat and twice as cunning, but she was the only friend Lily had and Lily loved her.

'I'm fed up with all this waiting.' Saul threw his coat onto the back of the chair and sat down. 'Get me a drink, Lily, I'm parched with talking. I've been trying to persuade the other men in the consortium to wait a bit for me to get the money to-gether.'

She brought him a drink at once. 'Why not just ask him for it?'

'He wouldn't see me. Oh no, he's been taken in by Llinos Mainwaring and that husband of hers. He's living in the lap of luxury, pretending he's a young man again with a new bride. He's nothing but an old fool and I hate him.'

'He is a fool not to care about you, Saul, you are the most wonderful man in the world and you deserve better. Don't worry, you'll think of something, I know you will.'

'Come here.' He took Lily in his arms. '*You* think up a plan. I know you're a bright girl and you're familiar with the way things work up at the Savage household so what do you think we should do?' He kissed her neck and Lily shivered. What would she do if anything happened to him? She realized now how much she had come to depend on Saul; her life would be empty without him.

'I don't know what to say, Saul, but I don't want you taking any risks, do you hear me? I'd die if I lost you, you know that, don't you?'

'I know.' He smiled at her and she thought again how handsome he was.

'Well, what can we do then?' His tone was

suddenly belligerent, the drink was having an effect. Lily bit her lip. 'I'll think of something, don't worry.'

Lily sank down into a chair and chewed her fingernail thoughtfully. 'I know!' she said excitedly, 'I've got an idea!'

'Go on, I'm listening,' Saul said, downing his drink and handing her the empty glass. She refilled it quickly.

'Look, what if we rile up the townsfolk, get them really mad, turn them against Joe and Llinos? I could make up a story about them, say I only left because they were up to all sorts of evil magic and such. I could say that's why Captain Savage died and that stupid maid, too!'

'I don't know, who would believe you?'

'Most people. You know how superstitious they are around here. Everyone is suspicious of the Indian as it is, it won't take much to convince them. I'm sure Polly and I could make a good job of it. I hate that foreigner and I've no time for Llinos either. I would be the first one to throw a stone, believe me.'

'Go on.' Saul was interested, his drink was forgotten as he looked at her, waiting for her to speak.

Lily was alert now, her mind clear. 'Folk think I befriended Meggie so they won't be surprised if I'm angry and suspicious about her death. I think I could cause enough fuss to make people believe I saw Joe give Meggie the poison because she saw too much of the goings on in the house.'

'Might work.' Saul rubbed his finger along his jawbone. 'We could get Bert Cimla involved, he hates the entire family. From what I hear he was having a go at Llinos, making a spectacle of her in the street. A right rabble-rouser, is that one.'

Saul looked at her with growing enthusiasm. 'While they are quelling the mob, I can slip in the back way and get rid of the old man.'

Lily was worried but she was afraid to show it. She had imagined the mob setting fire to the house, burning all the occupants. She did not fancy the idea of Saul actually doing the deed himself. Still, she had better humour him. For once she took the lead. She looked into Saul's face and slid her hands gently along his cheeks.

'I think we should celebrate. Come on, Saul, it's time we went to bed.'

Llinos lay in the crook of Joe's arm, her body tingling with happiness. Whenever he made love to her she felt renewed, as though she were a young girl again instead of an old married woman. Well, not all that old, she was still in her twenties, young enough yet to have many years of marriage and lots of children. Hope rose within her, she would be a mother yet, she just knew it.

She turned to rest on her elbow and looked down into Joe's face. She thought he was asleep but he felt her scrutiny and his eyes opened.

'Why are you staring at me like that?' He smiled, his teeth very white against the sheen of his skin. 'Are you wondering what sort of bargain you've got?'

Llinos bent and kissed him, her hair swinging over his face. He held her cheeks between his fingers. 'Are you?'

She lifted her head. 'I know what sort of bargain I've got, Joe. I've got a man I love and respect and desire.' She sighed. 'I love you, Joe.'

'Then why so sombre, is something worrying you?'

'I don't know. I'm just uneasy. I was upset by that scene in the street with Bert Cimla. Good thing Eynon was with me because the reaction of the townsfolk worried me, too. Why are they so hostile to us, Joe?'

'They don't understand me or my race,' Joe said softly. 'So they are suspicious, frightened by the unknown.'

'But how could they believe you would kill anyone?' She fell back against the pillow, her hair spreading around her. 'Meggie's death has angered the people of the town and their anger is directed towards us. It frightens me.'

'Don't be afraid, Firebird,' Joe said, caressing her cheek. 'Go to sleep, everything will seem better in the morning.'

It was a long time before Llinos fell asleep. In spite of Joe's reassurance she felt in her bones that life and destiny were hurtling towards her like stampeding horses and there did not seem to be anything she could do about it.

CHAPTER

TWENTY-SEVEN

'So you see, Llinos, I feel it best to sell up, especially now that the offer has been increased.' Eynon had asked Llinos to come for supper with him. He had made it clear he wanted to speak to her alone and so, tactfully, Joe had decided not to come along.

Llinos was aware of Eynon looking at her across the dining table; the candles glowed on the polished wood and the silver sparkled as though it were encrusted with diamonds. Llinos felt sad at the prospect of losing Eynon as a neighbour; he had been more than that, of course, he had always been her good friend.

'I'll miss you,' she said softly. 'You know how I've always loved being with you.'

Eynon sighed. 'But, alas, you never loved me. Well, now it's time to move on. I've had enough of the pottery, it never was really my ambition to remain in control of it.'

He paused and turned his glass round in his fingers so that the wine glinted like rubies in the candlelight.

'The only reservation I have about selling the pottery is that Samuel's son is part of the consortium making the offer for it. I had no idea he was wealthy enough to put in any sort of stake in the place.' He sighed. 'Apart from that, I just don't like the man. I'm not sure even now that the sale will take place. Trusting Saul Marks is a bit like building a house on shifting sand.'

'Well, just be careful, make sure the paperwork is all in order,' Llinos said. 'Just because you don't like the man you mustn't let that stop you. If you really want to sell up, then do it.'

Eynon reached across the table and touched Llinos's hand. 'Anyway, enough of business, this is really my opportunity to say goodbye to you, properly.'

'I know.' Llinos left her chair and moved quickly around the table to put her arms around her dear friend. 'It's not really goodbye, though, is it? You won't be moving far away, will you?' She felt a tremor of something she could not quite put a name to. Eynon had been part of her life for a very long time, an important part of her life, and she would be lost without him.

He hugged her and dropped a light kiss on her hair. 'If ever you need me, I'll come running, my dear Llinos.' His voice was muffled. 'Now, I'd better take you home.'

She looked up at him and smiled. 'Yes, I

think you'd better otherwise I might just start blubbing!'

As Llinos walked, arm in arm with Eynon, across the ground between the potteries, she heard sounds of voices from the row. She lifted her head, trying to see in the darkness.

'Strange, there's quite a gathering outside your gate,' Eynon said. 'I can see that fool Cimla there, he's shouting the odds about something.' He led her inside the gate and paused at the door.

'I won't come in, Llinos, say farewell to Joe for me.' He disappeared into the darkness and Llinos stood for a few minutes, staring up at the sky, wondering where Eynon would go. She watched the moon slide from between the clouds and then, in the silence, she heard Bert Cimla's voice as clearly as though he were standing next to her.

'It's about time we all took action,' he was shouting. 'Listen now, the foreigner is a murderer, he practices the evil arts. You only have to ask Lily here; the girl is so frightened that she's left her job rather than stay near that man and his whore of a wife for a day longer. Soon you will all lose your jobs; you will be thrown out without a penny's pay; they're already planning to sell

490

the place to my friend Saul Marks. Ask around if you don't believe me. Now are you going to do something about it? Are you men or cowards?'

Llinos spun round on her heel and walked back through the gates into the row. 'Don't listen to this man!' she called. 'He's a fool and a drunkard. We are not selling up at all, he's talking about the Tawe Pottery. As usual Bert Cimla has got his facts wrong. Now get away from here before I take my father's musket to you!'

'Liar!' a voice called. But slowly the men began to disperse. Bert Cimla looked back over his shoulder.

'We'll be back,' he said and spat at the ground before walking away.

Trembling now, Llinos made her way back to the house. Bert Cimla was a fool and the workers were worse than fools for listening to him. None of them seemed to remember that Cimla had been a cruel, grasping man. He had killed Llinos's mother and, though it was never proved, he had left the town under a cloud. Now the pottery workers were listening to his nonsense, allowing Cimla to turn them against the very people who paid their wages.

'Harlot!' Cimla shouted as a parting shot, and trembling, Llinos went into the house and closed the door, bolting it securely behind her. As she stood in the hall, she clasped her hands together and, suddenly, she was more frightened than she had ever been in her life.

It was barely light when Llinos woke to a sound that became louder until it reached a crescendo. At first she could not pinpoint the noise, it was animal-like, inhuman, but it was human. Joe was standing at the window, magnificent in the dawn light, his naked body gleaming, his hair hanging darkly against his spine.

'What is it?' she asked, clutching the bed-clothes around her. 'What's happening, Joe?'

'There's a crowd outside,' Joe said. 'I don't know —' He ceased talking abruptly as a crashing of glass echoed through the house.

Llinos slipped quickly out of bed and pulled on her clothes. Her worse fears were being realized: the mob was outside her doors baying for blood, Joe's blood.

Joe was dressed before her and he left the room, taking the stairs in quick bounds. Llinos followed as quickly as she could, her heart in her mouth. She looked down into the hallway and saw the servants gathered there, staring wide-eyed in fright as Joe approached them.

She hurried down the few remaining stairs. 'Go back to your work,' Llinos said as calmly as she could. Another stone crashed through the window and, as though galvanized into action, Cook turned and ran along the passage towards the back of the house followed by the maids.

Joe opened the front door and a clod of earth hit his chest. Behind him Watt was hurrying down the stairs into the hallway. 'What's going on here?' he cried as he reached the front door.

'Get back, Watt,' Joe said.

'No,' Watt said. 'You can't tackle that lot alone!'

Joe himself stood on the step and looked around him at the baying crowd. The breeze lifted his hair and the sun slanted across his cheeks so that he looked more foreign and more wonderful than Llinos had ever seen him.

'Watt!' Llinos spoke urgently, drawing Watt back into the shadows of the hall. 'Try to get over the wall to Eynon's place. Tell him to fetch some men.'

'I can't leave you alone,' Watt said desperately.

'Go, please, it's our only chance.' Llinos

pushed him towards the drawing room. 'Get out of the window, climb over the wall there, no-one will see you then.'

Watt hesitated for a moment longer and then climbed out into the garden. Llinos returned to the hall just as a scream rent the air. Charlotte was hurrying down the stairs, her frail body tense, her eyes wide.

'Joe, help me!' she cried. 'Saul is here, he's climbed through our bedroom window. There's another man with him, they're trying to hurt Sam!'

Joe turned as though uncertain and Llinos took the opportunity to slam the door and bolt it. 'You're needed in here, go help Sam,' she said.

She held Charlotte in her arms and tried to calm her. Events were happening so swiftly it was difficult to think clearly. 'My father's musket,' Llinos said, 'I must fetch it.'

She heard the sound of retching from upstairs and Charlotte gave Llinos an agonized glance. 'Please God, help him. Don't let them kill Sam.'

Llinos stood uncertainly, wondering if she should rush upstairs to help Joe or fetch her father's gun.

Then it was too late to do anything. The door was hammered and abruptly, with a splintering of wood, it crashed inwards.

'There she is!' A voice cried, Bert Cimla's voice. 'The murdering Indian's woman. Let's get her.'

Llinos pushed Charlotte behind her and stood facing the angry mob. The hallway was suddenly full of men wielding pick handles, tree branches, pitchforks, anything that would serve as a weapon.

'Oh, God help us!' Charlotte cried.

'Where is he?' Cimla snarled. 'Where is the Indian?'

Lily pushed her way forward, her face was white, her features contorted with anger. 'You're not so uppity now, are you, madam?' she said.

'Get out of my house.' Llinos spoke in a hard, cold voice. Lily flinched and hesitated and then Bert Cimla pushed her out of the way.

'Tell us where the Indian is.' His face was ugly. He caught Llinos roughly by the arm and shook her. 'Tell me, or it will be the worse for you!' She stared at him defiantly and he twisted her arm behind her back. Llinos could not help herself, she cried out with pain. Bert Cimla, his eyes narrowed, spittle coming from between his thick lips, shook her again.

There were more cries from upstairs and a door was banged violently. Bert gestured for some of the men to go up to the bedroom. 'We'll do for him,' he said. 'The Indian is a dead man.'

'No!' Llinos said desperately. 'Joe has done nothing wrong, leave him alone.'

'We'll leave him alone when we've finished with him.' Cimla was smiling unpleasantly. 'Now we'll deal with you, madam,' he said maliciously. It was Charlotte who spoke up, her voice quivering with fear.

'You'd better get out of here,' she said. 'Watt Bevan's gone for help. There'll be men here soon, men with guns. Look out there if you don't believe me, Watt's just climbed over the wall.'

Cimla stared through the drawing room at the open window leading out to the garden. 'Bastard!' he said venomously.

'I'll have to move fast, then.' He looked triumphantly at Llinos. 'I'm going to take you out and hang you from the nearest tree, it's only what you deserve, you bitch!'

'Joe!' Llinos gasped for breath; fear was crushing her, fear for Joe more than for herself. She was hustled outside into the dawning sunlight, blinking the tears away, her heart hammering.

'Joe! Where are you?' She tried to twist away but Bert Cimla held her fast as he rummaged in his baggy pockets and brought out a rope with a noose already tied at one end of it. He had come prepared.

'Hey, mun, don't go too far, now.' It was one of the potters who made the protest. 'I don't mind punishing the Indian but Mrs Mainwaring is a lady, mind.'

'Rubbish!' It was Lily who spoke from the edge of the crowd. 'She was in the plan to murder her father, wanted his money, didn't she? And poor Meggie, she must have found something out because she's dead too, killed by the Indian's medicine. How many others are going to die before you do something? Are you men or mice?'

Llinos felt her hands being twisted behind her back. She was dragged towards a stout oak tree and the rope was thrown over the nearest branch. Behind her she could hear Charlotte screaming for help.

'Someone get a horse from the stable,' Bert Cimla shouted. 'Let's do this job properly.' As Bert Cimla slipped the noose around her throat, she felt the roughness of the rope against her skin. He looked at her, his eyes dark with malice.

'I'm going to have my revenge at last,' he said in a low voice. 'It's taken me a long time but I shall see you hang.' She was hoisted onto a horse and the creature whinnied with fear.

Suddenly a voice called out from the back of the crowd. 'Bert Cimla is mad!' Celia-end-house pushed her way forward. 'Have you all forgotten that it was he who murdered Gwen Savage? Killed her stone dead in her own house. Are you going to let him murder the captain's daughter as well?'

'The old woman is right. We'll all feel the cut of the rope ourselves if we don't stop this.' One of the workmen turned away. 'I want nothing to do with no hanging.'

The voices of the men rose in dissent, men quarrelled with each other and a fist fight broke out at the edge of the crowd. In the confusion Bert Cimla slapped the horse hard on the rump. The animal reared in fright, threatening to throw Llinos. She managed to hang on, her knees gripping the horse's flanks. Bert lashed out again, the terrified horse bolted and there was nothing Llinos could do.

She felt a sharp jolt as the noose at her throat tightened. The blood rushed to her head, darkness was closing in on her. She tried to drag air into her tortured lungs. She was going to die. Her legs kicked uselessly in the air and then everything went dark.

'The mob are up at Llinos's house, you'll have to come at once!' Watt had woken

Eynon Morton-Edwards, roused him from his bed. 'They are out of control, the only thing they'll understand is the sound of a musket.'

'I'll get up there straight away.' Eynon dressed hurriedly, his shirt collar awry. 'You get some of my men together and follow me, right?'

Watt nodded and as Eynon took his musket from the cupboard he sighed with relief. Llinos would be safe now. He rushed into the huge yard where the workers were standing in groups, wondering what the noise was all about. Watt waved his hands at them.

'Mr Morton-Edwards wants you all up at Pottery Row,' he called. 'There's trouble and he's gone ahead to sort it out.'

Some of the men murmured between themselves, reluctant to take any part in what did not concern them. 'Go on, move!' Watt called.

Maura came out of the house. 'The boss is in danger,' she called to the men. 'Are you just going to stand there and let Mr Morton-Edwards face a mob alone? Are you cowards, the lot of you? Are you still taking your mother's milk like little babies? Do you want me, a woman, to lead the way?'

Shamed, the men began to move towards

the row and Maura caught Watt's arm. 'I'm coming with you,' she said.

'You'd better stay here, Maura,' he said. 'I don't want anything to happen to you.'

She smiled, her face alight. 'And *I* don't want anything to happen to *you*.' He embraced her swiftly and then, hand in hand, they followed the workers towards Pottery Row.

There were flashes of light against her eyes and Llinos became aware that she was lying on the ground. She tried to move, she was gasping, dragging the sweet air into her heaving lungs. She looked up to see Joe standing protectively over her, his face a mask of anger. In his hand was a knife, his clothes were torn away from the golden skin of his chest. His teeth and eyes gleamed. He looked every inch an Indian warrior.

'You treat me like a savage and I will act like a savage.' He thrust the knife towards Bert Cimla, cutting a slash in the man's cheek. 'Come on, you were so brave when it came to killing a woman. What will you do with me, you scum of the earth?'

The crowd fell back, staring at Joe as if unable to believe their eyes. Llinos edged herself against the tree, trying to recover her breath. Her throat burned like fire, her wrists were bleeding from the bite of the rope, but she was alive.

'Murderer!' It was Lily who screamed the word. 'Kill him, don't let him get away with it!'

Joe balanced silently from foot to foot, protecting Llinos, daring any man to come near. Saul Marks came towards him brandishing a thick branch. 'Get him! He's just tried to kill my father!' he called. No-one moved. 'I'll kill you myself then.' Saul's voice carried little conviction.

'Stop this!' The voice sounded loud in the silence. 'Listen to me, all of you.' Samuel was stumbling forward, clinging to Charlotte's arm for support. 'Saul Marks is lying to you!' It was an effort for Samuel to speak, he was trembling visibly. 'It was he who tried to kill me, my own son.'

Saul gave a bellow of rage and lifted his arm threateningly, the thick branch poised to strike.

A musket shot blasted out silencing the sudden roar from the crowd. Saul staggered and then fell to the ground and lay still. Lily began to scream like a banshee, falling on her knees beside her lover.

Llinos struggled to sit up, she rubbed her eyes, trying to wipe the mists away. Eynon, musket in hand, stood facing the mob.

Behind him was a crowd of his men armed with sticks.

'Get out of here,' Eynon said. 'Every man jack of you. You are a murdering, gullible band of no-good villains. If I see you around here again, I'll shoot on sight.'

Bert Cimla began to whine. 'This is none of my doing, it was him.' He pointed to Saul's still body. 'He made me do it, said he'd pay me well. I didn't want to hurt anyone.'

'Save it for the judge,' Eynon said and nodded to his men. 'Take him away, we'll deal with him later. You, Watt, fetch the constable, tell him what's happened here and why I was forced to shoot a man. As for the rest of you, go home if you don't want to see the inside of a courthouse.'

Eynon knelt beside Llinos. 'Are you hurt?' He glanced over his shoulder at Joe. 'That's a stupid question. I can see your husband frightened the lot of them and I'm not surprised; the way he looks at the moment he'd frighten anyone!'

The crowds began to disperse and Llinos drew deep gulps of precious air. 'We're all right,' she said, her voice little more than a croak. 'We're all going to be all right now.'

Eynon took her hand and kissed the back of it. 'I don't think I'll be leaving here after all, do you?' He stepped back and Llinos saw him go over to Saul's inert body and cover it with his coat. Samuel was weeping for his son and Charlotte was comforting him.

'He tried to kill you, Sam,' she said softly. 'Saul lived violently and he died violently, it was his fate.' She smiled tremulously at her brother. 'It seems some of your teachings have rubbed off on me, Joe. Go on now, take your wife inside, the danger is over.'

Llinos held out her arms to Joe. He lifted her and she clung to him, her face in the warmth of his neck. Tears trembled on her lashes as Joe carried her indoors and up the stairs to their bedroom. He kicked the door shut and looked down into her eyes.

'You look like a heathen, Joe,' she said softly. 'With your hair tangled and your body naked. Have I told you that I love you? If it weren't for you . . .'

He smiled, his eyes as blue as she had ever seen them. 'Now, how could I let the mother of my son die?' He spoke against her mouth and, as she kissed him, Llinos felt a warmth flow through her. He knew, Joe knew as he knew everything, that at last she was going to have his child.

'How do you know it's going to be a boy?' she said. He set her gently on the bed and lay beside her, his arms around her.

'I knew from the moment he was conceived. He will be strong and brave and handsome and clever like his mother.' He sighed softly, his breath sweet against her cheek.

She closed her eyes then, hearing sounds from downstairs, familiar sounds, voices talking, the voices of loved ones and friends. Outside the birds were singing, the sun was shining, it was a new day, a new beginning, and she was here with Joe. She was safe in his arms. She pressed her face against his heart, listening to its beat, and within her womb beat the heart of the son who would one day be a great man just like his father.